Kevin Michael Phillips

HUNTER HIGH

"Of all the thousands of thoughts, words, and images that cascade through my mind each day, only a few truly hang on at the precipice of my consciousness and refuse to tumble down into the great Niagara of the Forgotten.

It is the gathering, the adhesion, the assembly of these stubborn few that forms my memories, directs my thinking, and guides my destiny.

My precious memories I polish and treasure, but what will I do with the memories of my worst experiences – the recollections that haunt me – when they stubbornly hang on and refuse to tumble down?

I must choose whether I will consider them 'offal' to be cast out and consigned to oblivion, or 'awful' by which to see the hand of God directing me to the greatest light by way of the deepest darkness – in my world, in my life, and in my own heart."

excerpt from "Still In the Eye of the Storm"
Chapter 5

1

DANIELLE BENNETTON
Psychologist

Daddy paid extra for the teak wood frame.

And then he insisted on eighteen karat, gold leaf lettering – so proud was he of his little girl, graduating university with her master's degree in psychology.

But now that desktop nameplate just seems to sit there beside my computer – mocking me.

The degree, the title, the nameplate – and his pride – only add a burden of guilt and shame to my underlying sense of inadequacy. It wasn't really *me* that he was proud of, after all, it was the academic achievement.

He still trusted the judgement of the whole educational system, but I no longer could. I couldn't even trust my own.

"Accredited Psychologist" – who do I think I am, anyway, to unravel and decipher human behaviour and events? In the eyes of the world I became this internationally acclaimed analyst of the Hunter High School siege – this celebrity psychologist. But when I'm alone, there in my office, just me and that nameplate, the doubts reign supreme and all the old questions echo once more in my mind.

I pick again at the mental scab of my guilt and let the accusations bleed into my conscience. If only, what if, what should I have done instead? The terrible and tormenting Triplets of Regret – Should Have, Could Have and Would Have. Should I not have known? Could I not have predicted? How would I defuse the crisis if only I had it to do all over again? How many lives might I have saved?

Perhaps my only true qualifications are that I just happened to be there, and I just happened to survive.

As a kid I had no ambition to be a psychologist. No special gifts of observation or discernment. No ambition at all, really. Former classmates now looking through their old high school yearbooks would be hard-pressed to link my face or name to any exceptional talents, accomplishments or, indeed, even participation. I *endured* high school, grateful for my cloak of anonymity.

The average student, the middle of the bell curve – that was me. Some might have even said that mediocrity was my home. But I never felt "at home" in high school at all. I was uncomfortable even in my own "comfort zone". Years ago I thought I was the only one. Perhaps we all did. Now I know better.

I was the youngest of three, with my two older brothers always looking out for me. They led the way, their suggestions and experience sparing me from having to break any new ground of my own.

I wore their reputation and achievements like so many hand-me-down clothes. "I didn't know you were David Bennetton's sister." "Do you share Keith's musical talents?" "If you're a Bennetton, you must be great in the pool." Some people seek the limelight, I preferred their shadows.

I was always considered a "tomboy". But that label, like most labels, is much more convenient than it is true. "Insecure" would have been much more accurate. I was only a tomboy because I followed my brothers. If I had two older sisters, I would have been described as feminine. I just followed. I was a follower.

My brothers tried tying reins onto their bicycles, I tied reins onto my tricycle. They were cowboys, I was a cowgirl. When they played army commandos in the pool, I was the sentry they killed. They got plastic archery sets for Christmas, and I was their target.

But we all learnt from experience and, after my thirteen stitches and a broken arm, Daddy warned them to stop abusing me or he'd break their necks.

When the boys finally got their air rifles, I became a shooting partner. When they graduated to using .22s on our rural property, I learnt about ballistics and was fascinated – perhaps because it was all so scientific and predictable. Precise muzzle velocity, a trajectory you can track, a tin can target whose wounds you can examine in your hand. You can diagnose the pathology of human tissue damage – suture, operate, and amputate as necessary – but who can know the true depth of psychological damage?

Challenging to quantify, difficult to treat, perhaps impossible to ever truly heal.

We do the best we can with the hand that we're dealt. But how much does that hand shape our destiny? What if I had been the oldest, or one of three girls? Would my world have been entirely different, perhaps? What about my destiny? What about Hunter High? I guess I'll never know.

Me, I responded to the hand that I was dealt by becoming Daddy's Little Girl, and The Peacemaker between two troublemaking boys and my father's heart condition. I'd lay awake at night, The Nurse, listening to Daddy snoring from his bedroom across the hall. I confidently assumed that no one could snore through a heart attack – I don't know where I picked that up – but I'd set my alarm repeatedly through the night and stuff it under my pillow to muffle the sound. When it woke me, I'd sit up and listen – still snoring, still alive. Then I'd reset the alarm while everyone else in the family slept soundly.

With no ambition to speak of, I graduated from high school, got a job in the local credit union, lived at home, and saved my money. I wanted to travel the world and meet people. I loved to listen to them. Perhaps because when they were talking, I didn't have to. Perhaps because Daddy always said that he could figure out any problem just by talking it over with me.

So I travelled, and I listened, and I discovered that people everywhere love an open ear.

I started thinking about becoming a counsellor, but neither of my brothers had gone into counselling, and the maze of counselling responsibilities seemed too daunting for me to venture into on my own. One brother was a bank manager, and the other a teacher.

I loved to travel, so I became a high school geography teacher. How's that for a career decision? For how many of us is destiny determined by the flip of a coin, a chance meeting, a flighty decision, family factors, or simply fear of the unknown?

Often it takes a crisis, a death, or a confrontation with mortality, before we ever really consider the responsibilities and consequences of our decisions.

It's funny, how I didn't consider classroom teaching to be as daunting a responsibility as I had counselling. Sad, how I didn't even reflect on my own discomfort and lack of performance as a high school student before "qualifying" as a staff member myself.

High school teachers must be trained and qualified in their chosen subject areas, yet their skills at inspiring and supporting their students usually go unquestioned, unassessed, unchallenged, and undeveloped.

I might have been an unexceptional teacher with only mediocre classroom skills, but I *did* listen to the kids, and that made me an exceptional adult. Students would hang around after class, ask for me at the door of the teachers' staff lounge, and keep in touch after graduating. Daddy's Little Girl, The Peacemaker, The Nurse.

I taught not only geography but also social sciences. Social sciences led me to sociology, psychology, and back to my interest in counselling. I extended my studies online, attended tutorials and seminars at the university, and became an accredited school counsellor.

Like all graduates before me, I studied for years to "qualify" for a job I had never even performed. And then I even had the audacity to function in that aspect of my job description that included career counselling – if you can believe it – and I "guided" each poor, unsuspecting student seeking advice in my office to make as ill-informed a career decision as had I.

I began my work as a high school counsellor on rotation between three Newcastle schools. Hunter High was one of the three.

I listened to the students, reconciled, and pacified. I monitored their emotional pulse, their psychological vital signs. Or so I thought.

After the siege at Hunter High, I was the obvious choice to counsel with the students. Then the Department of Education asked me to sit in on the Coroner's Inquest and compile a report on the causes and aftermath of the siege, which formed the basis of the State Inquiry and, ultimately, the Australian Royal Commission into Teenage Stress and Mounting School Violence.

I eventually developed that study into my master's thesis in psychology entitled *"The Sociological and Psychological Context and Factors as Background and Precipitators of the Hunter High School Siege"*.

That thesis was then published and, when it became an international best-seller in the academic world, I became a celebrity psychologist.

But it was all very clinical and antiseptic. The "system" sheds no tears, makes no apologies, and suffers no regrets. The New South Wales Police, Department of Education, and Ministry of Justice all did their due diligence. Reports were filed, recommendations made, guidelines put into place.

The police commander on the scene – who didn't dare to enter the school himself that day, yet criticised the tactics employed by those who did – ended up writing a best-selling book, sold the movie rights for half a million dollars, retired from the police force, and now lectures and consults with police around the world.

Case closed, reports filed, movie made. But there's just one problem. The *whole* story was never really told.

Each witness was only able to report *their version* of *their experience* of the siege – which was only a small part of the overall events of the day. And then every word in every report was written – every decision from every court and committee was made – by people who weren't even there. Not in the classrooms and corridors of Hunter High. Not that day. Not on Black Friday.

Most were government employees constrained by confidentiality, physically and chronologically distanced from the events, and each contributing as only a small part of a much larger analytical team.

I was the only one who personally survived the siege and was then given unrestricted access to all evidence from all sources – police reports, eyewitness statements, taped interviews, video footage, text messages, mobile phone call recordings, transcripts of all police radio communications, forensic evidence, courtroom testimony, and inquest deliberations.

But it took me three years to truly appreciate that fact.

Slow cooking. Crock potting. Accolades, master's degree, television talk shows, magazine interviews, and a gnawing in my stomach.

Then suddenly the glaringly obvious, that I hadn't even considered, finally dawned on me. Not only was I the *most qualified* person on earth to tell the whole story – I was also the person on earth who *most needed to hear it*.

I was so busy, after the siege, playing the peacemaker and the nurse to all the traumatised survivors that I postponed and then neglected counselling care for myself – putting it off while I worked on inquests, and committees, and wrote my master's thesis.

Catharsis, that's what I need. Release and relief. Deep purging and thorough cleansing.

I need to relive that day in hindsight. I have thirsted for the time to identify, and mourn, and bury the dead. Not file numbers, or forensic photos, or snippets of testimony – but the events of the siege appreciated as a story and recounted as a story, as an episode set within the context of people's larger life stories, a memorial to a collision of lives that lasted less than an hour.

It happened in a flash, but we thought it would never end.

It's a story about an intersection of lives and deaths, mistakes and misunderstandings that were prohibitively expensive, and yet which continue even today in the hallowed halls of our educational institutions.

Critics may try to ban this book from our classrooms and censor its tale of terror and violence – but such a ban, I fear, would ultimately create more victims than ever fell that day at Hunter High.

Some from the educational and judicial systems have voiced their fears that such a book would only inspire other confused, angry, and unstable young students to copycat the original crimes. But I believe just the opposite – that evil, like all deadly viruses, thrives and breeds best in the dark and can only ever be destroyed if first identified, labelled, and exposed for what it is.

It's taken three stressful years, but I've finally come to realise that I can never learn from a truth that is swept under the rug, and that each of us is ultimately responsible for our own response to evil.

Yesterday, when I told my publisher that I was going to write this book, she was very supportive and immediately launched into advice about format, rewrite schedules, and deadlines.

I listened politely for twenty minutes, but after I got off the phone with her I booked a cabin by the beach for four weeks, turned off my mobile phone, and sent an email advising her that I would write this story only once – for me. There will be no rewrites. Nor will there be any teak wood nameplate to mock me here in this cabin – I left it back on my desk at home.

Out of touch with everyone for four weeks here in this cabin by the beach yet, hopefully, more in touch with myself and the truth than I have ever been. Just me, my laptop, and the twelve hours of edited audio and video recordings that were used as evidence for the inquests.

What you are about to read is my retelling of the events, three years after they happened, as best I can communicate them. And that's no simple task, because simultaneous events were experienced by different people in different locations. Therefore, I must warn you in advance that one minute of real time can seem like five or ten when recounted from eight people's points of view – it being impossible to ever *truly* capture or communicate life in any word, or image, or medium.

I also warn you that if you choose to read on you will be sharing in my catharsis – and my experience of evil. Police reports and coroners' inquests are not intended nor equipped to address evil.

My publisher began to advise me on the literary devices employed in the best-selling fictional novels about evil. But the existence and power of true evil is not fiction, certainly no source of entertainment.

It is not taught in our schools, nor recognised in our counselling – yet I walked with evil as it stalked the halls and hearts of Hunter High on that Black Friday, and then I wasted three years trying to explain and analyse it away.

Wasted lives, and wasted years.

But, now that I am *finally* committed to conveying the truth about what I witnessed in the corridors and classrooms during the Hunter High School siege, I am determined not to pander either to the strategies of publishers or the appetites of readers – even if that means I am never published and I end up holding the only copy of the whole story ever printed.

2

Sydney, New South Wales, Australia.

Sydney Harbour, Bridge, and Opera House – iconic symbols all – luring millions of visitors to Australia each year from around the world, worth billions in tourist dollars.

Million-dollar views from multimillion-dollar properties.

Image, façade, spin, fantasy, fairy tale, legend – and Sydney is inhabited by some of the wealthiest and most powerful myth-makers in Australia, determined to keep the dream alive.

But the dream becomes a nightmare when the average wage earners – the consumers, the members of the home audience – embrace the fantasy, and end up believing their own propaganda. Mortgaged for life to some of the most over-inflated real estate in the world when, in truth, much of Sydney is very old, run-down, oven-hot in summer, chronically traffic-congested, poorly serviced by public transport, nowhere near the waterfront, and pockmarked by low-income Housing Commission estates – while many of Sydney's inhabitants suffer an all-pervasive level of striving, stress, and frustration just below the surface of their lives which goes largely unnamed and unaddressed.

A constant craving, a restlessness, a lack of peace.

And the fairy tale sucks not only the lifeblood of Sydney's residents, but also the resources of its neighbours – like Newcastle, the largest coal-exporting port in the world (a two-hour drive north of Sydney), and Wollongong, the biggest steel city in Australia (eighty minutes to the south).

It was cities like Wollongong and Newcastle that built the industrial spine of Australian wealth – employing immigrants with no other options, and horrendously underpaying them to toil in coal mines and steel works that ravaged their health and jeopardised their very lives.

And so, anger, resentment, and revenge brewed just below the surface of these blue-collar towns. The fathers and grandfathers carried industrial-size chips on their shoulders and passed them down to their sons and daughters as an inheritance – charging the next generation to never again let the wealthy and powerful take advantage of them.

Newcastle is door to the beautiful Hunter Valley, wine-growing and horse-breeding country to rival any in the world. But the vineyard, the thoroughbred, and the ocean frontage property are typically only afforded by the entrepreneurs who harness the labour, the money, and the dreams of the blue-collared masses.

Hunter High School was located on the outskirts of Newcastle, and surrounded by the Hunter Valley. Its students were mainly middle and lower class – the "next generation" that had ignored the warnings of their forefathers as antiquated and no longer relevant in a new age of human rights and labour laws.

But slavery takes many forms, and they were already addicted to the media, and brainwashed by advertising, to work all their lives for toys, trinkets, and a lifestyle worth far less than the lifeblood, debt, and stress demanded for their attainment.

It was Sunday night, the eighth of October, and Newcastle, Australia was shifting gears in preparation for another week. In fact, most workers and students were not just shifting but actually *grinding* their gears, and their teeth, at the thought of another Monday morning. Lunches were being prepared and refrigerated, clothes ironed, and homework completed at the last possible moment – often between commercials.

If only the weekend was a little longer. If only the vacation could go on forever. If only we didn't have to grow up. Monday morning blues – like the mini-depression faced by moviegoers the world over whenever the house lights come back up, the cinema has to be cleared, rubbish swept from the floor, and reality faced once again.

Just another Sunday night for most people – but not for Leon Spitzer and his Dregs. Tonight was the launching pad for their master plan.

Most people's coping mechanism and escape plan is an ill-defined and fragile optimism, fuelled by the weekly purchase of lottery tickets. Leon opted instead for a self-confident pessimism, and a willingness to pay any price in order to win a losing game. Leon had called a meeting of the Dregs to finalise details.

3

Leon Spitzer certainly had a flair for the dramatic, there was no doubt about that.

The vast majority of suicide notes are still handwritten affairs – even in an age of word processors. But a handwritten note would not suffice for Leon Spitzer.

In fact, his was not to be a suicide *note* at all but, rather, a carefully choreographed suicide *production* designed to shock and intended for a global audience.

Leon had done his research on the internet with all due diligence – like any other high school project – and concluded, quite rightly, that reaching a truly global viewing audience would require an Ultra High Definition, digital, broadcast-quality video camera. He had the top model GoPro Hero delivered to his home and charged to his father's platinum credit card. Next month the proof – the evidence – would scream out at his father from his very own credit card statement.

Undeniable, embarrassing, shameful.

Leon would make his own father an accomplice! The Great Anton Spitzer, an unwitting dupe, a pawn in the destruction of his own reputation. Sublime revenge – Leon could almost taste it.

The video camera now rested in Leon's hand – a black cube, a technological marvel similar in size and weight to a box of wooden matches (maybe two) yet capable of recording at professional, international broadcast standard for over sixty minutes on a thirty-two gigabyte, micro SD card the size of a postage stamp.

To the camera Leon had affixed a pair of Immortal Mics, one on each side. Each microphone was embedded within a moulded plastic replica of the human ear and designed to be attached to either side of a helmet or head strap in order to replicate human "3-D binaural immersive" hearing. The protype mikes had been hailed by action sport enthusiasts around the globe as the ultimate audio enhancement of the GoPro's already breathtaking digital images.

Leon made certain the GoPro was steady on its tripod, and that the reflection of his head and shoulders was centred in the lens, as he turned on the camera and smiled.

He was very photogenic, young Leon. Black shoulder-length hair with just the slightest of chemically induced golden highlights, and a seventeen-year-old face that required daily shaving even at his early age. He habitually flaunted a three-day growth of beard – just like the movie stars and models – and he always dressed in black.

His smirk, his grooming, and his attire were carefully orchestrated to project an air of neglect and apathy. Most people were fooled. But behind his cynical eyes worked the brain of a young genius – darkened by years of loneliness.

"Good evening, ladies and gentlemen," he began, friendly and confident like a TV host – only smirking.

Leon Spitzer was a natural born leader. Money, looks, brains, charisma, vision – he had it all going for him. He even had a following, a gang, disciples.

All this potential at seventeen years of age, yet totally devoid of hope. His only vision was revenge, his only vehicle was Hunter High School. A big fish in a small pond, yet setting out to make a very big splash – a tidal wave, in fact – whose ripples would be felt around the world.

"Or should I say 'Good evening, officers? Detectives? Inspectors?'

You police will be the first to view this video.

Followed by our next of kin – initially as proof of our involvement (they won't believe it when they're first told), perhaps also for purposes of identification – but ultimately in order to gain their cooperation with the investigation."

Leon had a far-off look in his eye, like a wild prophet gazing into the future. No longer smirking, he was now chillingly confident. His tone of voice a toxic and almost intoxicating blend of prophecy, promise, threat, and showmanship.

"Then some resourceful media hounds will be offered a peek 'off the record'– perhaps as a bribe for the future, or a repayment for some past favour done for the police. They will undoubtedly plan to broadcast it. Perhaps they could film the reaction of the victims' parents – just think of the ratings. But then the leak will be leaked. Court orders will be issued, injunctions served. 'Classified evidence …. jeopardising an investigation'. And the footage will be pulled minutes before airing.

The police will first analyse, and then re-enact the course of events. Pathologists will time and measure, based on video footage. Lawyers will pour over the transcripts. Coroners will take notes in the courtroom, and make recommendations based on what they have seen.

Scandalised by the video indictment, the New South Wales State Government and Department of Education will follow up their own inquests with legislation, new policies, more funding, and anger management training for teachers and students.

Snippets of the video will inevitably make their way onto YouTube. The set of DVDs will become sought-after, precious, priceless – simply because they are forbidden. Eventually the video might even be broadcast with appropriate viewer discretion warnings. Several books will be written, documentary and dramatised films will be made."

Then Leon reverted to his very best Tweety Bird imitation, "And to tink it aww stawted wight hewe in my humboo widdle twee house wit a few of my vewwwy cwosest fwends …."

Leon stepped slowly back from the camera to ensure a dramatic unveiling of his lair. As he grew smaller, the interior of the magnificent tree house filled the frame – lit eerily by hundreds of candles.

Gathered around a heavy, medieval-looking table in the background, behind Leon, silent and unmoving, sat his four headless Dregs.

All detail obscured by flickering candlelight and sinister shadows, the four Dregs *appeared* to be dressed in long, black, hooded robes – the hoods devoid of faces, and even heads. Caves of empty blackness just sitting upon their shoulders. The effect, again, was chilling.

"But please forgive my rudeness for not introducing my colleagues earlier. We are the Dregs, the scum, the offal, the slag, the entrails of society – or so you treated us. We were alienated, each of us, in our own way and through no fault of our own. So we came together – sharing our loneliness – a lonely hearts club, an anti-society, a family of orphans.

Oh, we might have worked our way back in, I suppose, but as Groucho Marx once said 'I don't want to belong to any club that would have *me* as a member'.

We are the Dregs. We are about to pour out the cup of our wrath, and you are about to drink it – right down to the last drops, the bitter dregs.

Perhaps a brief intro from each of our team members might now be appropriate?"

"Okay with you if I begin?" he asked his Dregs.

The four empty hoods nodded silently in approval, and Leon again approached the camera.

Only this time he kneeled, leaned into the lens as he adjusted the camera tenderly downward with both hands, sat on his haunches, and lowered his voice.

"My father, The Great Anton Spitzer, a legend in his own mind, is at the cutting edge of computer technology – usually communicating with his own son by email. Recognised worldwide as a success – yet, at home, a miserable failure as a husband and a father.

He only ever had two reasons to take me on a business trip: either because he really needed me to entertain the kids of a business prospect, or because my mother really needed me to stay with her.

Anton Spitzer paid his wife to leave – *bribed* her to abandon her only child. But two weeks later she came back. It took her *two weeks* to decide that I was priceless! She came back and told my father he could keep his money, that she would just have to struggle along on my two-million-dollar trust fund.

He made my mother a counter-offer that she couldn't refuse, and when she did, he vowed that he would hound her to an early grave.

It's not that he didn't want to lose *me*, you understand, he just didn't want to lose. Just like in business – after a certain level of financial success it was no longer about the money, it was the winning, the power, the control. He just wanted to beat someone else to the discovery, the patent, or the bid, so he could watch *them* lose.

So, one night, with the Spitzer legal team snapping at her heels, my mother took an overdose of sleeping pills to escape beyond the borders of my father's global empire. I'll never know if she just wanted to escape for the night or forever, whether it was an accidental overdose or a selfish suicide – she had always told me that she couldn't live without me."

He paused for a while, apparently lost in his own painful memories, before resuming his address to the camera.

"You might not have *heard* of Anton Spitzer, but his hand has shaped your life, because his fingerprints are on every computer in the world – hardware and software, components, programs, and patents.

These are the days of digital processing, instant access, and exponential networking – but nothing of real value is passed down from generation to generation. These are days of techno-isolation and phobic insulation, when office cubicles have become the slave galleys of the twenty-first century.

I was brought up on Xbox, PlayStation, Google, Facebook, and YouTube. The only well-developed muscles in my body were in my fingers.

Entertainment, consumerism, mass media, and global marketing.

Australian teenagers wearing American baseball hats backwards – we don't know the American cities, we don't support the teams, and we don't need the visors to protect us from the sun, because we never go outside. We're too busy in the dark, all alone, talking to our disembodied friends on Facebook. Virtual friends. Cyber pseudo-relationships."

His voice trailed off into a menacing whisper as he peered deeply into the lens. "But *I'm* not alone here in the dark, am I? Those four seated there behind me, backing me up, are my blood brothers."

The five Dregs had assembled in Leon's tree house, but it could easily have been a movie set – *Walt Disney's Swiss Family Robinson* to be precise, albeit a two-thirds, scaled-down version constructed when Leon was only twelve, perched nine metres off the ground on a platform anchored between two huge trees and only accessible by rope ladder. Due to its compressed scale, anyone entering the tree house looked, and felt, strangely larger than life – sometimes even disoriented and dizzy.

The tragic irony was that the Swiss Family Robinson story was all about a close-knit family who survived by the work of their own hands. In contrast, Leon's tree house was designed by architects, built by carpenters, and never once even visited by Leon's ever-absent business mogul of a Dad.

At the multimillionaire's insistence, no nails had been used in its construction, only hand-carved wooden pegs. And all because Leon's father had never even read the book. He had instinctively assumed that Pacific Island castaways would have had no access to nails but, according to the story, the Robinsons had salvaged tons of building tools and material from their shipwrecked vessel.

Leon, however, *had* read the book, and his silence on the matter had cost his father an additional seventeen thousand dollars and provided Leon a source of great amusement whenever he recounted the tale.

And even now, three years later, having viewed the video countless times since its first police screening, I can never help but feel voyeuristic whenever I watch that clandestine, candlelit meeting.

I remind myself, each time, that Leon intentionally shot it for public viewing, with the camera in full view of the other participants, but I am still distressed by Leon's evil intent that his father would hear his son's bitter indictments against him when the video was played back at later inquests. Still haunted by that guilt, that sense of complicity, that never-ending nightmare, that was also part of Leon's plan for all his victims. An integral part.

"And now let me introduce you to my Dregs …."

4

Her name was Wendy Stankowski, and that wasn't her fault. Lots of Stankowskis had emigrated to Australia from Poland after the Second World War.

She was a solid girl, some would say "big-boned", and that wasn't her fault either.

She experienced a real growth spurt in the year or two before kindergarten – "grew like a weed" – and thus evolved her nickname around the house. A nickname meant to stay around the house. An expression of love. A term of endearment. Her pet name. "Weed".

But names, it seemed, would wield an awesome and terrible force in Wendy's life.

"Stankowski" – a name, a handle, a tool at home – would soon be sawn-off, whittled, and sanded into a weapon at school.

"Stinkowski". "Stinkhouse". "Stink", "Stank", "Stunk" – Wendy was taunted and haunted in every tense, and in every sense.

By Year Three, Wendy and her friend Vesna D'Ambrosi were inseparable, a name-taunted sorority of two. The victimised girls *always* sat beside each other in class, they shared lunches, and secrets, and sleepovers. Then, one day, Wendy even shared her pet name – after all, Vesna was like part of the family, and the pet name was another of the shared secrets that so bonded them together.

But, in Year Four, Sharon Tilden moved to the school and stole Wendy's desk, and her best friend, in the same day. It was only shortly after, that Sharon Tilden launched the "Stinkweed" campaign – broken promise, stolen secret, violated friendship. The name stuck like a poison-tipped dart, and Wendy felt betrayed by both friends and family – if only they hadn't come up with her nickname in the first place.

And there she was, Stinkweed, locked outside the safety of her home to bear the embarrassment and humiliation all alone. Abandoned, surrounded, and hounded.

A leper at the mercy of a merciless pack.

Shunned at school, Wendy then began isolating herself in her bedroom at home. She grew sullen and distant with her parents, and never really enjoyed another laugh or conversation with her father throughout all of Years Five and Six.

She immersed herself in Dolly magazines and the like – image and celebrity gospels for prepubescent girls. Her walls filled with posters of famous, beautiful, and airbrushed teen idols.

Then came another growth spurt – this time horizontally. The kilos piled on mercilessly, and her breasts developed too large and too early.

The posters came down in her room. She might not be able to silence the mocking at school, but she didn't have to put up with it in her own home.

The nightmare that was primary school for Wendy Stankowski seemed to be highlighted by a two-pronged graduation present. During the last few months before the summer break, she was simultaneously struck by the ravages of acne, and the sudden death of her father early one morning. Wendy's mother, Joyce, responded promptly to both crises – but they each still left their scars.

Wendy's cheeks were red and angry by the time her mother figured out the right combination of skin care and low dose antibiotics. Wendy's father was blue and lifeless on the bathroom floor by the time the paramedics arrived, her mother's face still covered with his shaving cream from thirteen valiant minutes of administering CPR.

The school bus, with many of her classmates on board, drove past Wendy's front door just as the body bag containing her father was being loaded into the morgue van. Wendy would later comment to relatives that there was something unrecognisable in all their faces. Perhaps it was compassion.

Perhaps not. Perhaps their puzzled expressions were no more inspired by compassion, than their words of torment were inspired by hatred. They were just a roaming pack, seeking a leader. A lost flock, lacking a shepherd, and looking for direction. Disappointed by parents, who had been disappointed by their parents before them. One generation lost after another.

I used to think that adolescence was just naturally a time of testing and rebellion. But not any more. Now I wonder if it's not a time when the hordes of youth are simply hungering after leadership, like compass needles searching for true north. Where leadership, identity, purpose, and direction are provided, there seems to be a natural – and relatively painless – growth into adulthood.

What if much of the teenage "rebellion" in the Westernised world is simply anger against the elders who have let them down, against the preceding generation who have been negligent in seeking their own direction and passing it on?

Isolation. Insulation. Alienation – one person from another, one generation after another. Intrinsic, inherent, endemic to the twenty-first century.

Society declining, accelerating, reeling, careening, spiralling out of control.

And amidst this lack of identity and direction rises an all-consuming need to create "others", *outsiders* whom we can distinguish from ourselves on the *inside*, "them" whom we can distinguish from "us".

Someone, anyone, whom I can condemn as worse off than me.

Someone, anyone, over whom I can exercise power and thereby lessen my own feelings of powerlessness.

Consumerism at its worst: my satisfaction fuelled by dehumanising others. My identity solidified, and my feelings soothed, by robbing others of their identity and disregarding their feelings.

The false identity of belonging, the abusive power of exclusion, the simultaneous creation and destruction of the misfit.

Later, when Wendy received the condolence card signed by the thirty tormentors in her class, it seemed only surreal – not insincere, or hypocritical, or even ironic.

For overnight, it also seemed, all her anger and blame had shifted focus from God and Class 6C to Wendy herself for squandering her father's last two years.

Her self-pity sharpened to guilt and self-loathing.

Rejection, loneliness, isolation, anger, regret, self-loathing – and her descent was now complete.

"Settled on the bottom of the ocean of despair – just like a whale," she wrote in her diary. She gave up, and felt ironically relieved in her hopelessness. Relieved of all expectations.

The black clothes that she wore to her father's funeral seemed oddly comforting – a graphic expression of her morbid soul.

When her father died – she died.

Weed never answered to the name of "Wendy" again.

She never returned to primary school.

She never again faced her tormentors, as a pack, on their turf, in a primary classroom.

She dyed her hair black, she wore heavy black eye makeup, black nail polish and lipstick. Her black fishnet stockings were never without holes. The only splashes of colour in her Gothic attire were purply-red army-style boots, and random tufts of hair in dyed-to-shock shades of fluorescent red, green, orange, or purple. Her acne scars now went unnoticed as people stared instead at the rings and studs piercing her eyebrow, nose, and lip.

And Wendy's isolation was painfully highlighted by a growing chasm of misunderstanding between her and her mother – the seemingly unshakeable competence of Joyce Stankowski illustrated perfectly by her assisting the morgue attendants to load her husband's body into their van while her daughter stood by, blubbering uncontrollably.

But it was only her mother's *aura* of competence that caused Wendy to shrink away – the recently widowed Joyce Stankowski had actually never felt more helpless, and she struggled to hold herself together only for her daughter's sake.

Then Joyce silently went along with Wendy's Gothic phase, because she was afraid of losing her only child through confrontation. And thus a yawning chasm, a bottomless pit, a deadly crevasse of non-communication, gaped open between them.

Wendy's primary school tormentors dispersed to several different high schools, and were then divided again amongst different homerooms. So that if and when any of them *did* cross paths with Weed at Hunter High, not only had the roles and wardrobes changed, but also the odds.

For now Wendy had, herself, become one of the odds, the misfits. She wore the uniform of a self-sentenced outcast. She now *expected* rejection. She invited it. She welcomed it. She dressed for it. She wore it like a cloak.

Year Seven, at twelve or thirteen years of age, might seem quite young to become a full-on Goth in black, but the furnace of childhood affliction seems to accelerate character development – becoming either hard and brittle, or supple and adaptable, at an early age.

Weed was somehow brittle without any bitterness. In fact, with her still-soft heart, "fragile" might be a better word.

Her redemption came in her fourth year of high school, in her eleventh year away from the protective love of her parents, in Year Ten, and in the form of the Dregs – a fellowship of outcasts whose very acceptance guaranteed rejection.

Weed had finally found her place in a pack of her own.

5

His name was Latska. Last name, family name, history, heritage, pride, identity – all "Latska".

The responsibilities of his family's honour lay heavily upon his shoulders and deeply, visibly etched upon his brow. He looked older than his sixteen years. On his good days, he never smiled. On his bad days, he scowled.

His straight black hair was never long, but always thick – as though a barber had simply put a bowl upon his head and trimmed off everything that stuck out. His haircut and dress seemed twenty years out of style. He was a diligent student, and his shirt pocket always contained three pens.

He was of Slavic descent. His forefathers had all lived, and worked, and fought, and died, in their one ancestral valley in Eastern Europe. A valley whose possession was long disputed between Serbia, Bosnia, and Croatia, each claim and counter-claim underlined in blood – all borders, flags, and faiths ultimately meaningless in the face of centuries-old hatred, religious wars, and genocide in the name of God.

The boy and his family were Latska, and that would never change. Latska pride, independence, defiance, and stubbornness – all were passed on from father to son. Guns and ammunition were always stored in their cellars along with the crops of summer. There was never a season without bloodshed, or a wedding without sentries, and no occupying force ever remained in their valley for more than four years. Ever.

And it was towards the end of his four years of high school hostilities, that the young Latska joined up with the Dregs.

His first name was Slavé, originally spelt with an accent over the e and meant to be pronounced "slav-ay". But such punctuation marks are difficult or impossible to find on most computer fonts and keyboards, so the accent was dropped on his Australian immigration papers.

It seemed like such a small thing, just a grain of sand, only a minor aggravation or irritation.

But irritations unresolved can grow and fester – sometimes producing pearls, it's true – but usually the pus, inflammation, and infection of bitterness, feuds, and wars.

Slavé protested the misspelling loudly in his broken English, but he was only eleven years old at the time of immigration, and his mother was still in shock over the death of her husband.

Slavé's father, his hero, had been killed one night, behind the barn, in an argument over three chickens – dying, honourably, between the bodies of his two assailants.

Immediately after the funeral, Slavé, his mother Lilliana, and younger sister Katiyanka were hustled off to the Australian embassy to apply for refugee status. They had no choice, really. Slavé had an aunt in Sydney, and his uncles in the valley knew that the relatives of the chicken assailants would be back for Slavé.

There would be no appeasing them, for it was now a matter of honour, and only a matter of time.

Slavé was whisked away, leaving his father, his laughter, and his youth behind him in the ancestral valley of no return. He was now the man of the house and – as the only living male Latska in Australia – ultimately responsible for the two women in his home.

The responsibilities of his eleven-year-old Australian classmates, however, usually included only homework and earning pocket money, while their experience of violence was limited to its on-screen portrayal.

For a young man surrounded by strangers in a strange land and all speaking too quickly, Slave's English was not bad, really. It's just that his accent was strong and he sometimes took a while to find the right word. It was much easier for him to listen, than it was for him to speak.

The difficulty in learning any new language is threefold: the speed with which natives speak, the almost imperceptible gaps between their words, and the importance of context. Foreign language tutoring CD's are always so clear, and slow, and repetitive – life is not. Yet another example of the ideal of education being far removed from everyday experience and application. Educational Theory is just that.

But Slave's Australian peers had no appreciation of his life context, in fact, no empathy at all. From their point of view, Slave simply seemed sour and grumpy. A sour and grumpy outsider who just had to loosen up. What he needed was some fun, even if it was paid for at his own expense.

So his Year Five classmates quickly educated him on the English pronunciation and meaning of the word "slave".

At eleven years old in Australia, it was all about fun and entertainment – music clips, smart phones, giant cinema screens, and video games.

Modern technology, psychology, sociology, advertising, and education had all conspired against centuries of slow progression. Changes were rapid and radical. Children and teenagers now boasted shorter attention spans, quicker texting and Xbox reflexes, less exercise, more obesity, and a much stronger sense of entitlement, than had their forefathers of only a few short years before.

Self-denial was considered absurd – if ever considered at all. Truth, wisdom, responsibility, and age-old standards were relegated to the darkened wings, while the spotlight shone brightly on optimism and positive thinking at centre stage. Ethics were forced to bow before individual freedoms, while the shifting sands of relativism seemed able to support almost any belief, philosophy, practice, or trend – anything other than an absolute, that is. Never an absolute.

Even multiplication tables, spelling, and grammar were all sacrificed on the altar of the twenty-first century god of "Sincerity". Pointing out spelling mistakes to a primary student was now considered to be a constraint on creative self-expression, and the memorisation of multiplication tables was typically deemed pointless in an age of calculators.

The result was not so much a dramatic drop, as it was a gradual and apathetic slide, in the standards of literacy and numeracy – with high school students, working part-time as cashiers, often only able to provide the correct change if it was displayed before them on a computer screen, and the skill rarely even exercised in these days of EFTPOS.

With the coinciding breakdown of the nuclear family, the teachers' age-old classroom mandate of "the three Rs" (reading, 'riting, and 'rithmetic) had now been replaced by the Reduce, Reuse, Recycle mantra – and their teaching commission now stretched, strained, diverted, and splintered to include laying down even the most basic foundations of focus, discipline, responsibility, and respect, with those two or three or four or five students in each class whose home lives were in total chaos.

Students now found themselves adrift in a society where the most vocal minority, the best organised, and the most adept at media manipulation, wielded the greatest political power. The theory being that if the squeaky wheel got the oil, then surely the politician got the vote.

So the Australian federal and state politicians (with their three or four-year terms of office, respectively) bullied the public servants with decades of experience running the Department of Education who, in turn, threatened the career-minded principals, who pressured the already overworked classroom teachers.

The result was the dreaded "New Year's Memo" that greeted every primary and secondary school teacher at the end of each January. The Memo lay in the dark like a serpent, coiled and waiting, in thousands of pigeonholes in hundreds of staff rooms (or in teachers' email in-boxes) across the state. All teachers, upon returning from their six weeks of combined Christmas and summer break, were responsible for the immediate digestion and implementation of the Memo's latest educational agenda.

Novice teachers considered them pedagogical developments.

Experienced teachers recognised them for the political tides and currents that they were.

The Memo would range from fifteen to seventy-five pages and could encompass a vast array of topics – nutrition and parental custody, for example, with teachers expected to assess their students' breakfast habits and shoulder full legal responsibility for releasing their pupils to the correct guardian on the correct day. In other words, total accountability for all factors outside classroom hours that might conceivably affect their students while at school.

And the list of these factors grew yearly as politicians continually sought to counter every possible criticism from the public, to avoid all responsibility and blame, to quash any electoral or public service career repercussion.

Some principals followed up the Memo's implementation to the letter. Many just asked their teachers to wait until they got home before throwing them out.

And the result? The bleak report card, across the state and around Australia, was that the dwindling number of experienced, committed, and passionate teachers who hadn't yet quit found themselves under increasing pressure year by year. Frustration and disillusionment ran high, with new graduate teachers often feeling unqualified, unsupported, and overwhelmed – fifty per cent of them quitting within the first five years.

And into this educational arena walked Slave Latska, gladiator.

Slave was a fighter, like his father. And like his father before him, he fought back. Beyond all logic and in the face of overwhelming odds, he fought back. He was no one's slave, and he would never bend the knee or bow the head. No matter how long the fight or how slight the offence, he would fight on. He was Latska, and it was all about honour. His father had, after all, died over three chickens.

Slave arrived in Australia midway through Year Five – and by then classroom and schoolyard cliques were set firmly in place.

Slave would often feel dizzy by the afternoon bell from trying to keep up with the English, yet still he insisted on honouring his commitment to his afternoon job.

He worked at a local gym. He found the routine of his menial tasks there a refreshing escape from the daily mental stretching of the classroom, and he was rarely even required to converse with the gym members. Then, after work at seven o'clock, he was free to train on the equipment himself.

During the day, he was mocked and pushed – largely because of his refusal to smile or laugh upon demand. In the evening, he would build up his strength, and plot his revenge.

Towards the end of Year Six, his mother Lilliana was offered a job in the horse-training industry around Newcastle. She possessed an exceptional eye for equine potential and was respected, even by the men in her homeland valley, as a gifted breeder and trainer.

Her hope was to move out of Sydney and provide Slave with a fresh start in Year Seven at a Newcastle high school.

In Year Five he had been consistently bullied, in Year Six repeatedly suspended for beating up all his assailants from Year Five. He was Latska, after all.

His mother offered him not only a fresh start, but a new name – or, at least, a new spelling. Legally changing his name to "Slavay" would, hopefully, end all the taunts relating to slaves and slavery.

Stubborn, like his father, he refused. Instead, he found himself a new gym in Newcastle.

He would need it.

6

Initially, in Sydney, Slave was hounded by the pack as a muscle-building exercise for them.

Stunned by his father's death, Australian culture shock, and the English language, he was easy prey for even the novice bullies – their first taste of blood, so to speak.

However, by the time he began high school in Newcastle, eighteen months later, only the tougher leaders would dare to challenge him.

Slave's obvious strength and developed physique were immediately respected by the Newcastle locals. His Slavic features and foreign accent were attractive to many of the girls and, therefore, envied by many of the boys.

But he just refused to fit in. He displayed no school spirit whatsoever, and declined all invitations to participate in any team sports – whether intramural or extramural.

Even just a willingness to smile or laugh would have gone a long way towards knocking down walls and building bridges, but he would have none of it. Slave's independence and resistance seemed to somehow mock the students' culture, and upset the established pecking order.

The top jocks and bullies of Hunter High launched their initial challenges and assaults against him. But every one was either squashed immediately, or avenged subsequently.

The principal of Hunter High School was Earl Kennedy, a good man who managed to retain the heart of a teacher, and a father, even after being promoted away from the students he loved.

Mr. Kennedy had fallen victim to the Department of Education's propensity for "promotion to the lowest level of incompetence". As the teacher at Hunter High most respected by peers and students alike, he was promoted to principal. But his gift was not administration, it was teaching. It had always *been* teaching, and hundreds of former students had graduated Hunter High rarely able to recall curriculum content, yet never able to forget the name of Earl Kennedy, nor his inspirational influence upon their lives – nor his tie clip.

Old-fashioned, out of style, and bearing his chunky initials, the clip was given to him by his three beloved daughters, and purchased with six weeks of their combined allowances when they were only little. Twenty years later, and Earl still wore it. Every day. His ties wore out, and their replacements widened or narrowed with the fashion, but the tie clip remained unchanged. On the sports field, Earl even dangled his whistle from the tie clip as a joke.

Earl knew within his first week as principal that he would climb the educational career ladder no higher. He had reached his lowest level of administrative incompetence.

He always mourned his promotion away from the hands-on opportunities of the classroom, yet never did he regret his decision nor doubt that it was the wisest move financially, eight years off early retirement as he was when offered the promotion.

Earl was not only a great teacher, but also a perceptive student, and he had quickly come to learn that the Department of Education respected position and title, not talent or skill. Hunter High was a diploma factory, an educational assembly line. Excellence in teaching was not rewarded, nor was negligence penalised. Their goal was efficiency, not effectiveness; to foster knowledge and intelligence, not wisdom; to groom employees, not entrepreneurs.

Teachers, from preschool right through to university, were all employees, every one, and their mandate was to mould cooperative students who would, in time and in turn, become profitable employees themselves – twenty-first century office fodder, programmed to feed the system created by visionaries outside the system.

Education for the masses had only begun in the 1800s, and only then because of the need for factory fodder at the dawn of the Industrial Revolution. Literacy increased the earning potential of a factory employee, simple as that. Educating the masses was no more a humanitarian crusade, than had slavery before it been a celebration of cruelty – both were merely economic expediencies.

Schools were factories of the mind, and administrators were paid more than teachers just as factory managers who kept the machinery running smoothly had always been paid more than assembly line workers.

Economic leverage and true wealth were never developed nor enjoyed by the teachers or the future employees that they trained, but only ever by wealthy family dynasties or individuals who thought and worked outside both the education and the employee paradigms.

But even from his admin office at the centre of his new bureaucratic universe, Earl Kennedy always made sure that he stayed tapped into the

Hunter High grapevine. He knew what was going on in the classrooms and on the school grounds, and he offered the victimised Slave every support, both personally and in the authority of his office as principal.

Slave, however, refused to identify his attackers as a matter of honour, and assured the principal that he would ask for help if he ever needed it. Without Slave's cooperation, Kennedy could only threaten his suspected assailants. He called the ringleading jocks and bullies into his office one by one, then he addressed the bullying issue at a general assembly one day when Latska was off sick.

As principal, he did all that he could within his power, but Earl still had a gnawing feeling in his gut that he could have somehow done more to reach Slave, if only he had daily access to him in the classroom.

Passionate teachers are always haunted by the feeling that they could have done more to *really* help their students – if only there were more time, fewer pupils, and less schoolwork.

Yet this gnawing feeling about Latska was different somehow. Earl even discussed, with his wife, a sense of foreboding – that a series of sinister forces and events was unfolding and unstoppable at Hunter High – but he asked her not to mention anything to their daughters.

7

Slave always washed his hands and face before heading off to his after-school job at the gym.

He wanted to look fresh for his boss, he needed to wake himself up after six mentally exhausting hours, and he liked to symbolically cleanse himself from the peer pressure and stress of the day.

It was towards the end of his fourth year of high school oppression that Slave Latska closed his eyes and splashed his face for the last time. He reached for a paper towel and made contact instead with a rubber mask. Slave opened his eyes to find himself surrounded by the absurdly smiling rubber faces of Mickey Mouse, Donald Duck, Goofy, and Bugs Bunny.

Latska didn't yell and the student representatives didn't say a word. They simply overpowered him, hustled him into a toilet stall, and forced him to his knees.

It is impossible for five strapping young men to jostle each other inside the confines of a toilet cubicle without everyone involved getting bruised. And they certainly did. But the very constraints of the cubicle also limited the force and flight paths of swinging fists and kicking feet, and no full-force blows were struck.

As his head was pushed towards the toilet bowl, Slave would have seen the toilet brush on the floor and realised that the cartoon characters had cleaned and flushed the toilet in preparation. Not spotless, to be sure, certainly not sanitary, but Slave would have quickly realised that the intent of his attackers was humiliation and not harm.

The heart of the young Latska, forced to his knees, would have immediately registered defeat, dishonour, and then, instinctively, revenge. Slave's last attempt at resistance was redirected towards the rubber faces. If he could just unmask *one* attacker, just recognise *one* assailant, then he could track him down and beat out of him the names of the other three.

But the cartoon characters expected as much. They winded Slave with a punch to the stomach and forced his head into the toilet. Slave tensed his neck muscles against the dunking, the back of his head hitting the upraised seat and his temple bruising against the porcelain rim. Only his thick black hair was actually submerged. He finally screamed in rage – not a word, just a deep guttural protest. But his cry was muted by the flushing water that blasted his eyes, his ears, and his mouth.

As he coughed, and spluttered, and spat, his attackers made good their escape. Slave cleared his eyes and pounded the cubicle door that they had slammed behind them.

Goofy had been assigned the task of tying the stall door shut with a skipping rope from the school gym. This, undoubtedly, saved the attackers' lives because, out in the open, enflamed by rage, and in pursuit of four fleeing individuals with flight rather than ambush on their minds, the odds would have been in Slave's favour.

Slave was incensed. He screamed Slavic curses as he stretched the limits of both door and skipping rope. A minute later he emerged, fists and teeth clenched, lip bleeding, assailants long gone.

"Try to calm down there, son, or you'll blow a gasket."

Slave almost ran into Luke, the school's thirty-two-year-old janitor and maintenance man.

Luke was a Maori, a towering and muscular Polynesian giant, native of New Zealand, member of a fiercely proud nation that was never truly defeated in any war but, ultimately, had their land stolen in British courtrooms.

Luke's face, arms, and hands bore the traditional black tattoo markings of the Maori warriors – self-inflicted scars of ink, meant to strike fear into the hearts of their enemies.

"I am not your son," growled Slave – spitting out first blood, then words.

"Not my son, maybe, but by the way I've seen you treated around here, I reckon you'd definitely qualify as my brutha."

Slave spat repeatedly into the sink, splashed his face and hair with water, rinsed his mouth, and blew his nose on a rough paper towel.

"Did you get a good look at them?" demanded Latska when he was almost finished.

"Didn't see anyone at all, I just heard you cursing."

Luke kept handing him paper towels as needed.

"I will get them."

"You will never beat them at their own game," said the janitor, well respected for his words of wisdom by those few students who chose to listen to the man behind the tattooed face – who chose to appreciate the depth and resonance of each word. "The deck is stacked against you, the game is fixed."

"I am playing no game," Slave spoke softly as he picked up his backpack and headed off to the gym, still shaking from the adrenaline cocktail of fear and anger.

But the assault in the toilets was only one of *four* catalytic events in Slave's life, the combination of which would send shock waves around the world.

The second event occurred just six days later, when Slave's mother announced her engagement to a local horse breeder with whom she had been working for twelve months.

Slave knew him quite well. He was a good man who had, quite happily, offered to legally adopt her two children. Slave rejected the offer immediately – he would only ever call one man his father, and only ever be known by one surname.

But Slave was happy for his mother and overjoyed for himself because, now relieved of his burden of responsibility over the household, he was free to pursue vengeance with unfettered and passionate abandon. Immediately.

A man's word, promise, and honour were so intrinsically linked in Slave's mind, that the very offer of marriage to his mother, and adoption of his sister, guaranteed their fulfilment.

The third catalyst was the schoolwide publication of Latska's dishonour in the toilet. Colourful little stickers of Mickey Mouse and Donald Duck began appearing on his locker, his desks, and even his books. Word had obviously spread behind his back, although no one dared say anything to his face.

The final assault, the ultimate humiliation, occurred the next month. No single person ever admitted to being a participant or even a witness. But photos began circulating between mobile phones and via the internet. Photos of Slave naked, tied to the school flagpole, surrounded by a dozen Mickey Mouse-masked assailants, his clothes hoisted up the pole and flapping in the breeze overhead. The photos were taken from far enough away to include the flagpole from top to bottom, and were not graphic. But the nakedness was obvious, and the humiliation complete.

Once again, it was Luke the school janitor who found Slave alone, assaulted, abandoned, and restrained. Luke later told Earl Kennedy that he took the shirt off his own back and covered Slave, while he cut the ropes and retrieved the clothes. Luke said nothing but "Brutha" two or three times. Once he was dressed, Slave said nothing but "thank you", shook Luke's hand, and walked off.

Earl was shocked when he heard the janitor's report, but he went absolutely ballistic when he got word of the photos. He called an immediate assembly – ranting and raving at the students. Drops of his flying spit were backlit by the stage lights in the school auditorium. Red in the face, he yelled until he was hoarse, then became almost speechless in his anger. Some students later swore that he was crying.

He continued, almost in a whisper, "Tyrants are empowered and tyranny is fuelled, not by the evil of one or even a few, but by the abandoned responsibilities of a sea of silent individuals.

Fifty thousand German guards exterminated more than six million Jews during the Second World War, while the whole world slept."

Kennedy then made all students remain standing in silence for twenty-five minutes after his assembly address. Every five minutes throughout that time, he repeated this phrase: "The only thing necessary for the triumph of evil, is for good men to say and do nothing."

After the assembly, Earl Kennedy sent notes and emails home to parents. He notified the Department of Education, called in the police, and somehow enforced a blackout on the media. He carried out random spot checks on mobile phones, USB flashdrives, school computers, and student laptops. Every student knew that possession or transmission of any photos relating to the flagpole incident would result in dire consequences – and all images vanished from the school without a trace.

After the assault at the flagpole, Slave never again returned to Hunter High – as a student. He abandoned his career plans to be a quantity surveyor, and began working full-time in the gym.

But the very day that Slave quit the school, he joined the Dregs.

Leon had been trying to enlist him for months – obviously alienated outsider that he was. But Slave was a loner, and, as the only male Latska in Australia, he had fought off all attackers on his own.

That is, until the end of the fourth year, when he realised that a faceless, masked mob was too much even for a Latska to handle alone. With no other choice before him but team vengeance, Slave joined the Dregs as an "external student" – an off-campus affiliate, so to speak.

8

Drew MacDonald shrugged his shoulders – a lot.

As a boy, Drew's father nicknamed him "Shrug", and his friends called him "MacDunno" – don't know, don't care, dunno.

Drew's parents worried about his apparent apathy, but all the relatives assured them how lucky they were to have such an easy-going child.

Drew was a mediocre student with no athletic skills to speak of, no hobbies, no drive, no ambition, no interests. That is, until Year Five when his classroom teacher, Miss Howard, introduced a study unit on mythology.

When interviewed by police after the siege, Miss Howard could specifically recollect neither Drew nor the unit. Only recently graduated from teachers' college at the time, she recalled only being intimidated and exhausted by the diversity of needs to be met among her first twenty-eight students.

Overwhelmed by the pressures of her profession, the novice teacher failed to realise the enormity of her influence – and she would never remember the unit that Drew would never forget.

To Miss Howard it was only a unit. But to Drew it was so much more. It was a door. A corridor from Drew's mediocre, shoulder-shrugging, and apathetic world.

Not so much a door into another world, as just a door out of this one. Not an alternative, just an escape – like running into a cave and being embraced by the darkness, with nowhere to go but further into its depths.

In his new world of mythology, castles, dungeons, dragons, wizards, rings, keys, swords, and mystical princess warriors, no hope was offered to Drew, really. Just an ever-deepening hunger to be elsewhere, otherwise – even other-worldly.

A gnawing hunger, a delicious pang, a constant craving, an intoxicating desire to have been born in another time and place. Another world, another dimension perhaps.

Supernatural powers, immortality, an appointment with destiny. Mystical quests, and heroic battles.

Anything was better than Newcastle, Hunter High School, and working his life away at some job that he hated.

Over time, Drew's wardrobe, like his mind, evolved into blackness. His books, his movies, and his Xbox games all reinforced the same theme – quest for power, escape, victory.

His earbuds were addictively inserted in his ongoing attempt to blot out the call of the mundane world with heavy metal and death metal music. The earbuds were not exactly biological appendages requiring surgery for their removal, not exactly, but they certainly required negotiation and threat by both parent and teacher.

By Year Nine, all of Drew's classmates habitually called him "Druid" as per his request, enamoured as he was by all things Celtic, pagan, and mystical.

He researched religious sacrificial offerings through the ages and regularly brought to school the bodies of small animals that he had dissected – birds, lizards, frogs, once even a cat that he said he had found dead.

And I remember him telling me one time, as his career counsellor, that the only profession he had ever seriously considered was to be an undertaker.

Drew's mother, Alison, later recounted how Drew had found one of his father's police forensic magazines in his early teens. Ronnie had always diligently kept them hidden from the children because of their graphic content, but somehow Drew found an issue on suicide which included the coroners' colour photographs – gruesome images that seemed to simultaneously haunt and seduce the boy.

One man had secured a long chain around a tree, sat behind the wheel of his car with the other end of the chain bolted around his neck, and driven off. Another man had welded himself into a chair in front of a shotgun whose trigger was rigged with a timing device. A scuba diver had padlocked himself to an underwater concrete block so that when his air ran out, there was no possibility of escape.

It was almost as though all the victims had been lured into a plot to destroy themselves, and make impossible any last minute change of heart.

Drew became an avid reader of the police magazines until his mother saw a darkening of the boy's mind, and demanded that Ronnie have them mailed to the police station and never brought home again.

Ronnie, on his part, had only agreed to pass on the magazines to Drew because they provided some area of shared interest, and afforded an all-too-rare opportunity to converse with his son.

For a while Ronnie told himself that maybe the young man was even leaning towards a career in law enforcement or forensic science. But you can only lie to yourself for so long and, when the magazines were banned from the house by Alison, Ronnie was relieved.

9

Drew eventually became known throughout Hunter High as a serious user and dealer of illicit drugs.

His contacts were good, the quality of his product was high, and his service was reliable. Drew had finally found something that he was good at – but success at what price?

All the interviews, research, and consultation undertaken in response to the siege at Hunter High, the repeated findings of the inquests, the corroborating testimony and data from teenagers, parents, teachers, doctors, psychiatrists, psychiatric hospitals, emergency wards, and the police, all national and international evidence and experience – all of it referred back repeatedly to the dark power, the toxic cocktail, of magic, mythology, the occult, drugs, and death metal music.

And yet the media would never report our findings.

Unlike the exposés of asbestos and tobacco poisoning in which the public was sceptical and slow to embrace the truths uncovered by the media, the very opposite seemed true when it came to the spiritual realm. It almost seemed as if the media, the scientific community, and the educational system had all conspired together to dismiss what a growing sector of the public had come to suspect, and even experience, long ago.

Drug-fuelled images and psychotic hallucinations often coincided exactly with mythological and occult writings and illustrations.

Heavy and death metal lyrics were laced with Satanic references celebrating, inspiring, and exhorting anger, chaos, anarchy, violence, and death.

The downward spiral of teenage isolation, alienation and, ultimately, antisocial behaviour reported by heartbroken parents was often the result of their teenagers being tormented by paranoid, psychotic, and paranormal memories and nightmares long after their drug abuse had ended.

Doctors – not just psychiatrists, but even general practitioners, family doctors – regularly witnessed teenagers' personalities and characters totally and irreparably damaged from drug intake, often from "harmless" drugs like marijuana, and sometimes even from just one-time use.

Seasoned police officers, hardened to violence, sometimes had to transfer out of drug squads because of the darkness they encountered.

The Australian Royal Commission into Teenage Stress and Mounting School Violence watched live internet testimony from a police detective in Detroit who was attacked by a machete-wielding teenager crazed by ice (crystal methamphetamine hydrochloride, or "crystal meth") and on the rampage in a shopping mall.

The officer wept as he described having to shoot the boy to pieces, with fifteen hollow-point bullets at point-blank range, in order to stop him. The detective emphasised that the teenager's strength and rage were superhuman, far beyond any drug-induced explanation, and more demonic than psychotic. Haunted by the experience, the detective was forced to retire after twenty-seven years of service and, like a little child, could no longer sleep without a nightlight.

And, again, the officer's testimony was never even reported in the Australian media.

It was only after all the inquests had concluded, that I was finally free to consider, and able to research, the connection between drugs and the occult over the centuries and around the world.

In one civilisation after another, the medicine man, witch doctor, wizard, sorcerer, shaman or priest relies on drugs as the key to his power, healing, vision, blessing, or curse. Medicines, drugs, poisons, narcotics, hallucinogens, and intoxicants are all referred to time and again by authors researching *"magic"*.

Many scholars and scientists therefore rush to explain and dismiss all resultant "extraordinary" and "hallucinogenic" experiences as nothing more than chemical counterfeits of the supernatural.

But what if drugs are, in fact, a doorway – or, at the very least, a window – leading into supernatural and spiritual realms?

Demonic images, experiences, reports, and illustrations are remarkably similar around the globe and across the centuries – and simply cannot be attributed to drugs, because the majority of them originate from drug-free cultures and witnesses.

Psychologists often trace them back to the "collective unconscious" and "archetypal images" shared by the Everyman – I know, I studied Carl Jung in university, too. And, at that time, I dared not be the only student in the lecture hall to raise my hand and ask the obvious questions. But I'll ask them now.

Universal images of evil, originating where and based on what? Nightmares inspired and inherited how, exactly? What possible scientific explanation for identical, recurring images and nightmares experienced and recorded around the globe and across the centuries – even documented in completely isolated tribes and communities?

Should such ingrained fears and forebodings be dismissed simply because the source and object of the fear has not, as yet, been brought to light? Because it challenges and contradicts our scientific paradigm? Because it strikes fear into our hearts?

The doctors and scientists who fought against surgical infection and pioneered sterile operating room procedure were ridiculed by their peers at the time for suggesting that tiny "germs" and "bacteria", invisible to the naked eye, were to blame – that is, until their patient mortality rates started dropping.

Most of us in the modern Western world pride ourselves on our scepticism of the supernatural, yet the accomplices, witnesses, and victims of evil remain undeterred in their fear of the demonic – and not just as a force, but as a being. Satan, the Evil One, the Lord of Darkness – actively plotting to destroy mankind, while strategically masking his very existence.

Regaining sanity, waking from the nightmare, or recovering from the effects of the drug, usually leaves the victim (or participant) of evil *more* convinced, not less. For some, evil even becomes intoxicating with its promises of power, escape, or satisfaction. False promises, lies, baits, hooks, chains – traps for the unwary.

I spoke with a professor of theology from a Sydney university early on in my research, and he warned me that throughout history Satan has always been referred to as a liar, a thief, and a murderer – the father of all lies, and the master of deception.

What if the age of magic has not passed at all, but only become more subtle and sophisticated? What if the greatest trick of the evil master of illusion was to convince the audience of the twenty-first century that they are too sophisticated and scientifically advanced for such primitive folklore, and that the Evil One is just a fable?

Is it a telling commentary that one of the earliest, prototype designs of the film projector in the 1600s was called "lanterne magique"?

"Movement" itself, in film, is actually an optical illusion. A series of images, flashing at a rate of approximately twenty-four per second, creates the illusion of movement in the human brain. "Movies" are actually just a series of still images, changing rapidly. Watching a film out of sync with its soundtrack quickly exposes the illusion, and destroys the power of the fantasy.

Enhance that optical illusion with an editing process that accelerates time, compresses space, and constantly shifts point of view – and the result is a medium to taunt and tempt viewers to escape into an orchestrated world of illusion without boredom.

And then drive home that fantasy with the seamless, digital special effects of the twenty-first century where the earth, the clock, the calendar, and the laws of physics, are no longer boundaries.

The result? Lanterne magique.

The once humble and primitive projector – now morphed into cable and satellite television, and beamed to billions of homes around the globe. High definition, surround sound, dozens of channels, thousands of cable choices, live streaming, ever-growing screens that take up the whole wall and suck in every member of the family. Distraction, media addiction, and advertising that breeds discontent with the mundane world and everyday relationships – twenty-four frames per second, twenty-four hours a day.

Digital deception. Illusion, sleight of hand, manipulation. A constant craving, a restlessness, a lack of peace.

Drew MacDonald was blinded by lanterne magique.

Fearing and fleeing the mundane, the responsible, and the uphill climb, careening instead down a slippery slope – his descent fuelled by the media, ignited by the internet, and accelerated by fantasy, the occult, and drugs.

10

Drew's descent into darkness was mirrored by his parents' silence, denial, refusal to confront, and sense of helplessness. Drew was a quiet boy who maintained class attendance and avoided failing any subjects. Although a couple of Hunter High students were usually exposed each year for drug dealing, Drew was never one of them. No one would *dare* report him – for though Drew MacDonald was never respected, he was always feared.

The tall, thin, and deceptively quiet teenager with the flaming red hair never threatened physically or verbally. He was always soft-spoken, but looking into his dark blue (and often red-rimmed) eyes was like peering into a cave or a deep, dark well. And his response to being crossed, mocked, or challenged, was to stare, long and hard, at the offender.

Local legend had it that he killed the dogs of two different students who crossed him. Neither student would ever confirm, nor would either discuss, the rumour that both dogs had been found dissected.

And so, with Druid's activities outside the house never reported back to them, Drew's parents were free to deny his descent into darkness, even though his father was a police officer and should have known better, should have recognised the signs. But his father was busy – too busy, as are all twenty-first century parents – busy providing for his son, by protecting "the community".

Ironic, that. For, in truth, "the community" faced its gravest danger from his very own son who was fading to black, right before his father's eyes.

Drew MacDonald by birth, Druid by choice, Dreg by enlistment. Drew's initial recruitment began eighteen months before the siege, when Leon Spitzer set him up as a drug dealer. Previously Drew had used a bit and sold a bit, but the quality and availability of his drugs were never reliable.

Leon simply took him aside and asked Drew if he'd like to upgrade all aspects of his drug involvement overnight: quality, supply, and profit margin. The young MacDonald was thrilled at the offer, so Leon made one phone call and Drew became established, sought-after, profitable, grateful (and indebted) beyond his wildest dreams – all at once, and out of all proportion to his lack of ambition and diligence.

But a business partner to Leon Spitzer, Drew was not. Not even a business associate, really. For Leon had learnt many things from his father Anton. He learnt that great wealth, power, and influence belong not to he who works the hardest, but the smartest.

The winner is always the visionary, whether a Hitler or a Gandhi, who can mobilise a great many people – little people with little dreams, and little nightmares. Fulfil their dreams, resolve their nightmares (or even just convince them that you will) and you can leverage their support and investment to realise your own grand – or apocalyptic – vision.

Networking. Anton Spitzer did it when he shook the hand of Bill Gates, Leon when he recruited the Dregs.

Leon had all the money and the networking skills necessary to access or distribute drugs himself, without limit, had he wanted. But he was never known to have consumed either drugs or alcohol – perhaps he felt the loss of control was too high a price. He introduced Drew to the right man in Newcastle, and nothing more. For Leon Spitzer wanted no partners, only pawns. Thus recruited and ever grateful – baited – it was then a simple matter for Leon to tug Drew's line, and set the hook.

When Leon invited Drew to his tree house headquarters it was like walking onto a movie set. It *was* a movie set, actually, and since all of Drew's inspiration in life came from the media (and nothing, sadly, from his own imagination) the lanky MacDonald was irresistibly drawn into Leon's fantastic world of youth, good looks, unlimited funding, drug world contacts, secret society, and clandestine candlelight meetings.

And there sat Leon Spitzer in his tree house fortress, like some prince of darkness, offering Druid the hand of brotherhood, a ring to seal the oath of secrecy, and a cloak of blackness.

The "cloak" was actually a riding coat – the iconic brown Australian stockman's full-length oilskin raincoat made by Driza-Bone.

The style worn by the Dregs, and supplied as a gift by the young Spitzer heir, was mid-calf length and waterproof like the original version, only black. The ring, also a gift to each member, was silver with spilling chalices engraved all around. The rings were custom-made to Leon's specifications, and symbolised the bitter dregs about to be poured out upon the world.

Offering Druid such a membership, to such a brotherhood, in such a tree house, was the equivalent of offering a six-year-old boy a complete little cowboy's outfit with cowboy hat, shirt, leather chaps, boots, spurs, and a holstered set of six-shooters.

And Leon knew it.

Leon actually *remembered* it. He had been given just such an outfit for Christmas when he himself was six – and a live pinto pony to go with it. That was the year Anton Spitzer was away wrapping up a big business deal in Singapore.

11

All the Dregs wore black. Black clothes, black raincoats, black Doc Marten boots.

For Leon, Weed, and Druid, black was already habitual.

Slave readily agreed – brought up as he was amidst war and army uniforms and never concerned much for style, he didn't care what he wore.

Although school uniforms were mandatory in most Australian primary and secondary schools from the first to the final bells of the day, the Dregs were free to wear their black riding coats to and from school in the cooler weather, and often wore black-hooded sweatshirts under them, sometimes even black T-shirts underneath, and peeking out of, their school uniforms' white shirts.

They were also free to go black on uniform-free "mufti" days – usually on a Friday, or the last day of term, and often organised for the purpose of raising money, each student making a one or two-dollar gold coin contribution to the appointed charity for the privilege.

But since black clothing could not be the Dregs' trademark – their recognised sign of membership – during normal school hours, it had to be, instead, the silver chalice ring.

The Hunter High athletes' gang (the "Jocks") and the gang of school bullies (the "Thugs") might well mock the Dregs behind their backs and ostracise the likes of Weed, but no one dared lay a hand on any one of them, because all who wore the ring were sheltered under the covering of Leon Spitzer, and everyone knew that Leon would secure revenge at any price.

Though tall and fit, Leon was not physically intimidating. He was, instead, financially "secure" (untouchable – invulnerable, even) in much the same way that billionaires surround themselves with teams of lawyers and burly bodyguards, discreetly intimidating in the same way that necktie-wearing heads of state have recourse to their own Special Forces with blackened faces.

Leon's insistence on attending the very public Hunter High School, located in a mostly-blue-collar suburb of Newcastle, was a premeditated act of psychological torture directed at The Great Anton Spitzer.

Stress, frustration, irritation, annoyance, worry, disappointment, embarrassment, humiliation – a litany of woes inflicted upon his father. All fuelled and fanned simply by Leon's refusal to attend a private secondary school – of his own choosing and anywhere in the world – *anywhere* other than Hunter High.

Leon's only concession to his father's high school advice was in agreeing to martial arts training. Leon conceded only because it suited his particular style, his chosen persona, his handcrafted image – and because he knew he would probably need it at Hunter High.

Anton suggested karate or kung fu, but Leon began researching the internet and decided instead on Krav Maga, the official defensive tactics system developed for the Israeli military and security services by the Israelis themselves. Rather than specialising in striking like karate or locking and throwing like judo, Krav Maga incorporated the best core elements from many different martial art disciplines and offered pragmatic, efficient, self-defence training and a high level of proficiency in a relatively short time.

Leon was a Spitzer, and Spitzers loved a return on investment. Krav Maga seemed to offer more bang for its buck, more quickly, and without all the bowing and formality associated with most other martial arts. Krav Maga was developed in one of the world's most dangerous regions, tested and improved under real-life conditions, in modern times, and against modern weapons.

Karate, for example, does not teach its students how to break an assailant's trigger finger while disarming him of his handgun. Krav Maga does.

The only problem was that Newcastle, at that time, had no Krav Maga instructors sufficiently qualified for Anton Spitzer's liking, so he had to pay for an expert instructor from Sydney to drive to Newcastle three times a week – six hours of paid teaching, twelve hours of paid driving.

Such was the price for living in Newcastle, but it was worth it.

Moving there had been purely a business decision – commercial property was far cheaper there than in the glitzier cities of Australia, and one Newcastle shipping company agreed to drastically undercut the ports of Sydney and Melbourne both in cost and in loading time. Anton Spitzer just *could not* refuse the deal, so blissful was he at the thought of saving money each step of the way between his Asian factories and his Newcastle warehouse.

But when it came to his only beloved son, no cost was spared. For Anton Spitzer truly did love his son, in his own way and in his own love language – money. But this was a disastrous miscommunication, because his son's love language was time – time set aside, downtime, quiet time together, father-and-son time valued and prioritised – and Anton never had any to spare, nor set aside any to invest in him.

Leon was left to negotiate the Krav Maga details on his own, just as he had been left to negotiate and navigate the rest of his life.

The Sydney instructor set the price, and Leon paid him double, just because he knew it would pain his father to be gouged.

It didn't *actually* hurt Anton, of course, because he could afford it and because he was ignorant of the betrayal – so, in the end, the overpayment was just another teenage cry of anger and pain that went unnoticed, unheard, and unheeded.

Thus The Great Anton Spitzer brought Krav Maga to Newcastle. And, in return, Leon Spitzer was trained in the deadly Israeli martial art – trained against attack in all positions, against single and multiple opponents, against a variety of weapons, using everyday objects as weapons and shields, in everyday locations both indoors and out – in order to prepare him for street self-defence, in the case of attack whether expected or surprised.

And thus Leon was ready, physically and financially, to defend himself on all fronts.

When accosted at Hunter High on two different occasions, he broke one student's nose and both the arms of another.

Threatened by Earl Kennedy with expulsion in the event of any further demonstrations of Krav Maga, Leon was then forced to hire off-campus thugs to beat up any subsequent challengers.

He was not touched again.

When a classmate accidentally locked bumpers with Leon in the parking lot and refused to apologise, Leon later set fire to the student's car.

No one actually saw Leon do it, of course, and the car was worth only a few hundred dollars – but when its young owner was alerted by friends and came running, there sat Leon in his intimidating black Jeep, watching the vehicle burning, and then offering his classmate the business card of the Spitzer family's law firm should he need any advice.

An intellectually, physically, and financially formidable foe who outclassed all his peers, Leon was an angry young man aching for a fight. But no one dared.

And when you wore the silver-chaliced ring on your finger, all that protection was extended unto you. For Leon, untouchable Leon, was stalking the halls, headhunting, mustering, enlisting.

Eventually, each of the four alienated and isolated Dreg recruits was caught up in his net of vengeance, irresistibly inducted into Leon's plot, protection, apocalyptic vision, and control – inducted not just with ring of silver, clothes of black, and oath of secrecy, but also with the signing of a covenant contract in blood:

"We, the Dregs of Hunter High School,
are not at home in this world,
not content to fit in with this high school
or with the social order that created it.
Our classmates rejected us,
our teachers failed us.
Treated unjustly and judged unfairly
for too long, it is now our turn.
We are committed only to each other –
blood-bonded brothers and sister by choice.
We move as one body, we think with one mind.
We are bitter with good reason,
and this high school will be made to drink
from the cup of our wrath
right down to the bitter dregs.
We swear loyalty only to each other
and sign below in our own blood."

12

Young Aron Wade was old beyond his years.

Nothing about home or family had ever been warm, or soft, or trustworthy, for him.

Where there should have been a father, there was only a void and a hunger. No memories, no photographs.

Aron's two older brothers bore a few memories and a few scars from "the old man" – but they never spoke of either.

Aron told me once in my office that he could not picture his mother, Beryl – was not able to recall a single memory of her – without either a cigarette or a drink of alcohol in her hand, and at least one eye on the ever-blaring television, or her head buried in one of her weekly celebrity gossip magazines. Talk shows, soap operas, reality TV, crossword puzzles, horoscopes, and lottery tickets – that was Beryl.

And then he laughed – a scoffing, self-sufficient, survivor's laugh. He had a lovely smile, Aron did, but I always wondered where he got it, or how he ever managed to maintain it.

Aron was drawn to my office because of the subdued lamp lighting that I intentionally provided the students as an alternative to the constant glare of the classroom fluorescents. Aron's mother had never owned any lamps that he could remember, their home always lit by bare, overhead bulbs – no lamps, no light shades, no carpeting. Nothing warm, nothing cosy, nothing pretty, nothing soft – never even a hug.

During Aron's first visits to my office he would say nothing, just sit in the corner by the dimmest lamp and close his eyes. He would often leave when any other students dropped in – he later told me that he just wanted to rest his eyes and ears, no glaring lights, no blaring TV.

The Department of Community Services was like a part of Aron's family – an *integral* part when Beryl had no money for food, or tried another detox program, or was back in hospital, or went off with another man for a few weeks. Sometimes the three boys were put into foster homes, but usually short-term crisis care facilities.

When the experience was a good one, they hated returning to their mother. When it was bad, it was usually so bad that even Beryl looked good – it seemed the boys could never win.

Aron's brothers were seven and nine years older than him, and, as the years went on, it became more difficult for Community Services to keep them in touch, and almost impossible to keep them together.

It seemed, to the older boys, that the best way for them to show their affection when they *were* together was to prepare their little brother for the cruel realities of life by toughening him up, by teaching him how to defend himself, and by reinforcing the message that he must never show any pain, weakness, or mercy – that payback was the order of the day. "Trust no one, you're all alone" – the mantra they hammered into his hardened heart and head.

Aron was always small for his age – he sometimes wondered if it was because of malnutrition, but he was pretty sure it wasn't because his two brothers were tall, and they had never been fed any better than him.

Aron was just the runt of the litter and his brothers never referred to him as anything else, but they warned the little Runt that if he didn't bash everyone else who ever called him names, then they would beat *him* up.

When Aron was about ten, Vernon Linder moved in with Beryl Wade and brought with him a certain level of predictability – some semblance of *family*, albeit dysfunctional. Behind his back, Aron always referred to him as "Vermin" because the combination of his dark eyes, pointy nose, and pencil-thin moustache created a rat-like or ferrety appearance.

Vernon was a sullen and sour man, except when he was drunk – then he became violent.

He never drank during the week, so, in glaring contrast to all the other boys at school, Aron came to dread the weekends.

Aron's nineteen-year-old brother was living somewhere in Melbourne when Vernon moved in, and his seventeen-year-old brother fled the violent household as soon as he could, five months before his eighteenth birthday.

So, at ten years of age, Aron was left behind, all alone – abandoned at home – to continue his apprenticeship in toughening-up and never showing pain or weakness.

Because Vernon Linder had himself been abused as a child and only beat Aron when intoxicated, his lawyers would have pleaded diminished accountability and alcohol addiction.

But the domestic crimes were never *heard* in any court because Vernon, abused though he'd been, was still calculating enough to leave Aron with minimal signs of bruising.

Aron was sharp as a tack but his academic performance, on paper, had always been inconsistent – and it only worsened under Vernon's hand.

For now, under the care of his new stepfather, Aron was often absent on Mondays and Tuesdays. Sometimes he couldn't even walk until Wednesday. And, when he *was* at school, he would use lunch and recess time to hone his fighting skills on someone his own size.

By the end of Year Six, size was no longer an issue one way or the other, because every one of the senior boys was bigger than Aron and he would take on all comers. He had learnt how to take a punch, endure the pain, and persevere until the inevitable victorious conclusion.

By the time he entered Hunter High and Year Seven, he was known as "Wade" by one and all. "Aron" just seemed too studious, and he had a hard-earned reputation as a pugilist to maintain. All of the students and most of the teachers complied with his request, although the crankier, more rigid, staff members refused to refer to him by his (preferred) surname.

By Year Nine, Vernon's health was declining and he couldn't throw a punch as well as he used to. Beryl's boy was much quicker and harder to hit and, now that he was older, Wade would often choose to stay out all night rather than having to face Vernon.

Wade came home early one Sunday morning, tired and expecting Vernon to be in a near-comatose condition as usual, but his de facto stepfather was still up, and cranky, and waiting.

Vernon carried three times the weight of the boy, but Wade was sick of it all, and well-trained, and payback was the order of the day. Wade beat, and bashed, and thrashed his former abuser all around the house, while Beryl shrieked hysterically and begged her son to stop, like she had never begged Vernon to stop beating *him*.

Unlike his stepfather, Wade was not concerned with bruising, and he sent Vernon to bed for a week.

Six weeks later, Vernon staggered home on a Saturday night with three of his drinking buddies to back him up in his revenge attack. Wade was badly beaten, and might well have been killed, had he not been able to outrun the four drunkards.

When Leon saw Wade's battered face the next week at school, he extended to him the hand of Dreg membership. Wade accepted, and slept soundly in Leon's tree house every weekend from then on.

Inside that tree house, and within the circle of the Dregs, Wade experienced two things he had never known before – belonging and commitment. He gladly signed in blood.

He also found a third something – a sister. His brothers were tough and his mother hardened, but Weed was fragile and vulnerable. Her quiet and timidity, her scars and piercings, birthed in Wade and drew from him a longing to protect her from hurt, like he himself had never been protected.

He spoke quietly with her, and listened.

When he called her "sister" it seemed only natural, and when he called her "Weed" it truly was a term of endearment, a pet name within the family of the Dregs. There was no sting in it, no "Stink" in it.

He sat with her in class – seven periods a week, when their schedules coincided. No words were needed then, it was enough just being together, for no one else had sought to sit with her for six years.

He joked about "Weed and Wade" – it sounded right, kind of poetic, they made a good team. It took weeks, but her downcast gaze was slowly raised and she started making eye contact with him.

They shared a secret – her headphones were just a prop. Druid had downloaded all his favourite death metal songs for her, but all that noise in her ears just made her nauseous. However, by wearing the *silenced* headphones, not only was she able to avoid socialising with classmates, she could even listen in on conversations they thought she couldn't hear.

And now, with Wade, she had come full circle – from eavesdropping on enemies, to sharing secrets with a friend.

13

So there you have it – the five Dregs.

And although it is important to appreciate a bit of the background and life context of the perpetrators of the siege, I think it also imperative at this point to acknowledge that no human could ever fully understand *all* the nuances and shadings of character, personality, experience, relationships, and events that came together on Black Friday, the thirteenth of October – just as each of us never seems to fully understand even our own selves, or why we did or continue to do the wrong things that we do, or can ever truly predict how we would have reacted in another's situation or, indeed, even how we will react tomorrow in our own.

It has taken me a number of years to begin to appreciate that we are, all of us, more alike than we care to think and yet – simultaneously and paradoxically – more unique, special, and precious than we ever dared to dream.

We need only consider the uniform of the Dregs, and how something intended to illustrate uniformity was actually perceived so differently among the five.

For Leon, recruiting someone into the uniform meant power and control, identity, and influence. And, ultimately, you didn't wear the uniform unless you had sworn the oath and signed the blood covenant.

For Slave, the uniform meant that he was part of something bigger than himself, a team to back him up in his fight for honour and revenge.

Druid, wearing a black uniform and swearing a blood oath, was living a dream come true, the realisation of a fantasy life. For him, wearing the uniform was a chance to knock down the constricting walls of reality, although exactly where those walls stood in his mind was always a bit blurry.

For Weed, black clothes had always been a symbol of death and mourning, guilt and regret—with her anger aimed only at herself. Compared to the others, there was almost an innocence or naivety about joining the Dregs and wearing their uniform – a lack of malice, an absence of revenge. For her there was only relief, almost a muted sense of celebration or joy that she now had friends with whom to share her loneliness. Weed, having known what it was to be alienated, would now do almost anything to support her friends, would pay almost any price to keep from losing them.

For Wade, the black uniform was official, representing a form of authority – a secret police force perhaps, an undercover officer. His motivation seemed to be deliverance more than revenge, *now* being the time to enforce a justice for Weed that had always been denied to him.

Although no one dared to harass Weed openly now that she wore the covenant ring, there were still smirks and whispers behind her back. Weed chose to ignore them, while Wade made mental notes. Weed's classmates, who had for so long judged and condemned her, were now themselves under surveillance and they didn't even know it.

The bitter Dregs. That's who they were and that's how they came to be gathered in Leon Spitzer's tree house on that Sunday night, the eighth of October, assembled and introduced to a potentially global audience on video.

Leon, having welcomed viewers to his tree house lair, now stepped offscreen and behind the camera as he released it from its tripod and walked it, handheld, towards his team so they could each introduce themselves in close-up.

As the aperture adjusted to the flickering candlelight and shadows around the medieval table, the four hooded and headless robes now became distinguishable as black Driza-Bone raincoats – each Dreg face hidden within the cave of its own black hoodie and only exposed, in turn, as each hood was dropped in self-introduction.

Weed managed to look straight into the lens. "My name is Weed. I used to feel like a whale, all alone on the bottom of an ocean of despair. But I no longer feel like an animal, I feel like me, only camouflaged, able to take on the colours and patterns of my surroundings – blending in. I always wanted to just blend in. Now I'm a Dreg, and where they go, I'll follow."

Weed smiled. Leon must have given her some acknowledgement or encouragement from behind the camera, perhaps the thumbs up, before panning to Wade – sitting beside Weed as usual.

"My name is Wade, and I can't *wade* till Friday. Only five more sleeps to go." He smiled as he finished, then laughed, but there was menace in it – anticipation, threat, and the promise of payback.

Slave sat upright, his posture formal, his pronunciation slow and deliberate for this official record. "My name is Slave Latska. S-L-A-V-E, L-A-T-S-K-A. My father was Roman Latska.

My mother Lilliana and my little sister Katiyanka will soon change their name from Latska – but before they do, I will first restore honour to it."

The camera panned finally to Druid, his blue eyes wide, red-rimmed, and glazed with excitement like a little kid on Christmas Eve, his whole body shaking to the staccato beat of his foot tapping under the table. "I always knew I would find a way out of this world someday – but Drew MacDonald always held me back. Well, now Drew MacDonald is as good as dead.

I thought I would have to journey to that other world alone – but then I met Leon. He is king of the Dregs, I am his druid, and this coming Friday the thirteenth – Black Friday – marks our ascendancy to power."

The introductions, dramatically and effectively brief, were over. Ominously strewn across the medieval table before them were half a dozen Hunter High School yearbooks, scissors, and glue. The Dregs had gathered to finalise their "blacklist", their wallet-sized wanted posters, for Friday's siege – now less than five days away.

14

Ronald Malcolm MacDonald may have been born in the toughest section of Glasgow, Scotland, in a neighbourhood where brawling was considered the second most popular spectator sport after soccer, but Ronald himself was not tough.

He was tall and thin, with flaming red hair, and huge feet. Worse still, he was a nerd long before the term became popular and he grew up enthralled by all things technological, electronic and, eventually, computerised. And, to make matters even worse, always being referred to as "little Ronnie" by his parents only added to his torment at the hands of the Glasgow bullies.

Even Ronnie's bookish schoolteacher of a father was once beaten up by a neighbour whilst complaining to him about the victimisation of little Ronnie by his peers.

When the MacDonalds sought police intervention in Ronnie's life of persecution they got it – but not as expected. During his multiple visits to the local police station, Ronnie struck up a friendship with the desk sergeant that led to an invitation into the police radio room, and eventually an apprenticeship as a communications technician.

Over time, the complete police upgrade to computer, internet, and digital technology fell under Ronnie's expert supervision and his reputation grew nationally. Ronnie was then sent to London to study that city's massive grid of urban CCTV cameras in order to replicate it in Scotland.

It was cheaper, in the long run, for the Scottish Police Authority to employ Ronnie as an officer rather than as a contracted technician, so they pinned a badge on him – explaining it as the only way to allow him unrestricted security access to confidential police intelligence.

He took the badge, changed his name back to the more official "Ronald", never carried a gun himself, and seldom even ventured into the field. Ironic, therefore, that his font of nerdy knowledge eventually overflowed to include weapons and ballistics.

He was a technical adviser, a resource, even an armourer of sorts. But a true police officer he was not. He never actually touched the criminal, the victim, the evil, or the pain – information without experience, communication without relationship, ballistics without violence.

While attending an international police conference in Germany, one conversation led to another, one contact led to another, one thing led to another, and he was ultimately offered a job as Technical Consultant/ Inspector with the New South Wales (State) Police in Australia. (There are no local or municipal police in Australia – only state and federal.)

His longing to flee the cold, damp, and often-depressing climate of Scotland was whetted by the subtropical photos of Australia that he downloaded from the internet. But he was always concerned about raising his three young sons in larger, more violent, cities like Glasgow or Sydney, so a compromise was reached and the New South Wales Police offered to have MacDonald based in Newcastle if he agreed to regular travelling. The offer was too good to refuse.

Unfortunately, Ronald MacDonald the police officer from Scotland landed in Australia the same year that Ronald McDonald the hamburger clown from America made his biggest-ever Australian promotional tour.

So the six-foot-three-inch MacDonald, with fiery red hair and huge feet, was met on day one of his arrival at Sydney's Mascot airport by the mocking Australian humour of his new police colleagues.

It took Inspector Ronald MacDonald only three days to revert back to "Ronnie".

It took his Australian colleagues much longer before agreeing to drop the "Ronald MacDonald", but they finally compromised and thereafter resorted to his toned-down, Aussie-issued nickname of "Big Mac".

15

Some fathers are *never* really any good with their children. Others think infants too fragile, or find changing nappies too repulsive, but are fantastic with toddlers.

Ronnie MacDonald was a great dad from the time his wife was first pregnant, right through until his two older boys started high school. And then something happened.

They no longer sought, nor were satisfied with, their father as a playmate – their growing independence at least partially fuelled by their dwindling paternal respect and hero worship. Familiarity often breeds contempt, and they'd lived under Ronnie's roof for over twelve years.

His jokes were now boring, they could outrun him, their friends knew better, and Ronnie grew quickly old-fashioned. Conversations were infrequent, sentences shorter, and vocabularies more limited.

One evening, Ronnie's wife Alison found him parked in his work van in the driveway – "just sitting and thinking," he explained. "Here I am, a communications expert, with no interpersonal relationship skills whatsoever – I got on great with my parents, but never with childhood friends, or now my own kids. To watch them grow up is to watch them grow away."

"You're just tired from work. You've always had great communication skills with me, Ronnie," Alison consoled him.

"Maybe it's just a generational thing then," Ronnie said optimistically, "and I can only communicate with people who are middle-aged."

But Alison hated being called middle-aged, and didn't speak to him for the rest of the night.

16

The earliest video footage from Black Friday was recorded at 7:11 a.m. with the lens focused on a bedroom ceiling.

The bare bulb is off, the room grey.

The camera rolls over on the bed, checks the radio alarm clock, then rises and walks across the room to a mirror, atop a chest of drawers. Aron Wade's reflection appears in the mirror, dressed in full black Dreg uniform, including riding coat.

It is a miserable spring morning and the rain is pelting down outside, hammering against the tin roof overhead.

In the centre of Aron's forehead is affixed a GoPro video camera, identical to the one used in Leon's tree house, now attached to a head strap that also supports the Immortal Mics in place, just above his own ears – the idea being that whatever a Dreg sees and hears, so too will a global audience, recorded in high-definition video with 3-D sound.

Wade checks his reflection in the mirror and confirms that the red recording light on the GoPro is blinking, before walking down the hallway to the kitchen where Vernon and Beryl are seated and having their breakfast of toast, coffee, and cigarettes. Their chrome and vinyl-cushioned kitchen chairs are mismatched, decades old, and purchased from the Salvation Army shop.

Vernon is dressed for work in his grey factory uniform, Beryl is undressed in her pink tracksuit pyjamas and pink fluffy slippers, this week's pile of celebrity gossip magazines within arm's reach.

Vernon snarls up at Wade, "What the hell science fiction movie did you walk out of, little retard?"

"Movie? Haven't made it yet, Vernon – shooting starts today." Wade's voice is crystal clear, like an offscreen narrator.

"Is that a video camera on your head? Where'd you get that? It's not stolen is it?"

Beryl seems suddenly awakened by Vernon's suspicion.

"No, it's not stolen, but I do have a confession to make …."

"Here it comes, nothing but trouble," Vernon flicked his head towards Wade with contempt, while glaring at Beryl.

"You know that .22 calibre rifle you've got hidden out in the back shed?"

"What!?" Vernon's secret exposed, like a raw nerve.

"Well, I'm afraid I've wrecked it." Wade's camera looks down at the pocket of his black riding coat while he pulls out the weapon. With amputated butt, stock, and barrel, it is now just over thirty centimetres (twelve inches) long.

"You sawed it off? GIVE IT HERE!" bellowed Vernon, as he jumped to his feet.

Wade stepped back as he pointed the barrel at his abuser. Beryl shrieked. She started low, and began increasing in volume.

"Shut up, Mum."

Wade stepped back even further, slowly waving the gun from one target to the other. Beryl fell silent as she covered her own mouth with her hand.

"YOU GIVE IT HERE, BOY!" Vernon was livid now, towering above Wade and holding out his right hand.

Wade shot the hand, right through the palm.

"You usually punch me with the right one, don't you, Vermin? You are vermin, aren't you? I've been calling you that for years. Cuz if that's not your name, I've brought the wrong gun – .22s are meant for shooting vermin."

Vernon just stared in shock at the bullet hole.

"Or is it the left?"

The rifle cracked again, the bullet passing through Vernon's left hand and into the femoral artery of his thigh.

The second spent shell ejected from the chamber, sailed through the air, and rolled across the kitchen floor. Vernon groaned and flopped back down into his vinyl seat. His bleeding hands squeezed his spurting thigh.

The rain hammered on the roof, almost deafening. No neighbours would even hear the shots.

Beryl's toast started burning.

The Immortal Mics were able to clearly record Vernon's voice, even amidst all the rooftop hammering. In only a few seconds, his tone ranged from contempt to anger, shock, pain, and then a pitiful kind of moaning or whining.

The little .22 calibre rimfire is often mocked and rejected by "serious" shooters who prefer more powerful, larger calibre, centrefire bullets, and dismiss the .22 as a target, "varmint" or vermin gun – but that's only because they've never been shot by one.

Hydrostatic shock. Deflection and deformation as the little bullet passes through human tissue, bodily fluids, and bone. Pain. Blood loss. The long-term risk of infection as the bullet drags into the wound with it hair, clothing fibres, and debris – all of these dangers are contained within its forty grains of lead.

Blasting from Wade's barrel at fourteen hundred kilometres an hour, the .22s shattered Vernon's body and spirit in seconds. "Please put it down. I'm sorry, I'm sorry."

Vernon was pale and sweating. Beryl was white, all blood drained from her face. Her toast was burning.

"No, *I'm* sorry, Vermin," Wade corrected him, "I think you should kick me." Wade shot him in the right foot, near the ankle. Vernon screamed and almost fell off his seat.

"You can't very well shoot a man in the toes when he wears steel-capped boots, now can you? Kick me! KICK ME LIKE YOU USED TO!"

Wade shot him in the left foot.

Vernon doubled over in his chair, crying.

"You'll be dead in sixty seconds, Vermin. Any last words?"

"I'll leave this house and never come back," Vernon gasped in desperate negotiation. "You'll never see me again."

"Not good enough, Vermin, I want you to leave *the planet.*"

Wade came closer and squatted down to Vernon's level.

"Do you know what hurt me the most, Vermin? Your mouth – 'stupid, idiot, retard, loser, runt, midget, dwarf, reject, no-hoper, pathetic'…."

"I'm SORRY."

Wade stood back up. "Open your mouth!"

Vernon was still doubled over in his chair – in fear, in pain, and nursing his wounds – in a kind of sitting fetal position. He now tried to protect his mouth by burrowing it into his blood-soaked thigh. "Please don't shoot me in the mouth!" came his muffled plea, sounding just like a little boy.

Wade stepped forward and patted his de facto stepfather on the back of the head.

"I won't shoot you in the mouth, Vernon. The problem really wasn't your dirty little mouth, or your hands, or your feet – it was your evil little mind, wasn't it, Vernon?"

Wade shot him in the back of the head, three times, at point-blank range.

It was a semi-automatic rifle, reloading a fresh bullet from the spring-fed magazine and into the chamber even while the previous spent cartridge was being ejected. It could fire as quickly as the trigger was pulled, Wade discharging those last three rounds in less than two seconds.

Vernon Linder died in the fetal position, in his lime green vinyl kitchen chair, with much of his blood in a pool around his feet. As per his request, he was not shot in the mouth, the bullets instead entering the base of his skull and exiting his throat.

The smoke detector screamed. Wade shot it twice and killed it.

The rain still pelted on the roof. The kitchen would have smelt of burnt toast and gunpowder.

Beryl sat there before her son in frozen fear, white and catatonic, her hands still over her mouth.

"You're my mother, you were supposed to protect me. Why didn't you protect me from that man?"

"He was too strong, I was afraid that he'd hurt me."

"Why didn't you just take me and run away?"

"I didn't want to be alone."

The rain pelted, the toast burned.

"Neither did I," said Wade.

Wade's hand reached up to the camera, and he fumbled to switch it off. "Neither did I," he repeated.

Seven hours later, when the police received no response to their phone calls, knocking, and enquiries, they forced entry into the Wade residence and found the de facto couple both dead at the kitchen table. Vernon's face on his thighs, Beryl's head buried in her glossy magazines.

The police recovered fifteen empty shell casings scattered across the kitchen floor. Wade had shot his mother six times, in and around the heart, pulling the trigger until the magazine was empty.

17

Gary Dixon always wanted to be a soldier.

No one in his family could ever remember a time when he hadn't seemed destined for the military – not Gary himself, none of his four younger siblings, not even his mother who treasured memories of his youngest actions and words that he himself had long forgotten. And so soldiering was assumed to be written in his stars, or his genes, or both.

But who can say how greatly Gary's "destiny" was influenced by the death of his father – a policeman shot and killed while defending the victims of an armed robbery, murdered only three days after the birth of his fifth child.

Gary was not yet nine years old, his hand on his father's coffin, when he dedicated himself to supporting his mother, and shepherding his two younger brothers and two younger sisters.

Gary was always big and strong for his age – almost as though God knew of the premature and disproportionate burdens of responsibility he would have to bear – and all his teachers loved him. He was always the dependable teacher's aid, and the respected student representative.

Young Dixon ensured that his siblings were never too rough or too mean with each other, yet everyone in the neighbourhood and the school playground knew that to pick on any one of the Dixons was to fight the five – led always into battle by the eldest.

The Dixons were invincible and, as such, always found themselves welcome in the inner circle of the leaders, winners, and champions of their peers. But, instead, Gary encouraged his siblings to associate with the common folk in the schoolyard and the neighbourhood – those unwelcomed in the winners' circles.

Gary was always an upholder of the peace and an enforcer of the law and, because his mother remarried when he was sixteen, his way was clear to join the Australian Army as soon as he turned seventeen. His duties as son and brother were fulfilled at home, and now there was a whole country out there – a whole planet – to protect.

Like his father before him, Gary Dixon started balding early. And, like his father, he refused to be intimidated by the receding hairline, refused to submit to nature's timetable – so he took charge, and shaved off all his hair. Like father, like son.

And it suited him, his bald head only enhancing Gary's physique, posture, attitude, demeanour, and uniform to complete the picture of an action man and army hero.

Dixon thrived and excelled in the army, not so much in rank and promotion as in reputation and respect. Sergeant was the perfect role for him, as mediator between officers and enlisted men – and that was fine with Gary, for his only burning ambition in life was membership in the elite Australian SAS.

Sergeant Dixon had to attempt the gruelling twenty-one day Special Air Services selection course four times before he was finally accepted, but then served for twenty-two years as an elite commando, decorated three times for exceptional bravery under fire while fighting in seven different countries, across four continents.

At forty-two years of age, he rejected the army's strong nudging towards a desk job and volunteered instead for two years of service with the United Nations Peacekeeping Forces.

Dixon hated it.

Bogged, bound, and gagged by politics, he was not only powerless to prevent or avenge injustice – he was actually forced to stand by and document it, time and time again, ultimately witnessing thousands of innocents slaughtered by rebel guerrillas.

At forty-four, he quit the army and returned to settle in his home town of Newcastle. But "settle" was the last thing that he could do – bored, restless, antsy, and chafing at the bit after only a few weeks into civilian life.

And then the phone rang.

A friend, of a cousin, of an old army mate, had recommended him to Newcastle Police Superintendent Rod Stanwych, and now Rod was on the line talking about Dixon's SAS experience, outstanding reputation, and the proposed training of police tactical squads in a new commando technique.

Gary showed up an hour early for their lunch appointment, and offered to pay.

18

In the 1960s, police around the world began developing their own "in-house" paramilitary units in response to hijackings, terrorism, rising urban violence, and the increasing use of automatic and military weapons by criminals better armed than the police themselves.

The popular U.S. television series "S.W.A.T." misled many viewers from around the world into thinking that this was an American initiative begun first in Los Angeles and, consequently, such police teams were referred to as "Special Weapons and Tactics" squads for many years after, in much the same way that people refer to all colas as Coke. But, in truth, the initiative was global and the labels varied, with the prototype team arguably launched in Shanghai in 1926.

As with many things in life, initial inspiration and inventiveness, over the years, diminished, declined, and deteriorated into the status quo, and police tactical squads came to habitually assume a siege mentality – containment, control, risk minimisation, intelligence-gathering, and negotiation.

The mindset of police commanders became "minimise the risk of lives lost" and, throughout the 1970s and '80s, hostage negotiators were glorified in many a feature film.

But the siege mindset of the police proved itself totally ineffective against the slaughter and suicide mentality of the irrational and the fanatic and, by the 1990s, more and more concern was being voiced at international police conferences about hostages being shot by the dozens and bleeding to death while tactical squads established a perimeter and observed from a distance – often for more than an hour.

Media coverage, automatic weapons, global terrorism, and cheap, home-made explosives concocted with ingredients like fertiliser, diesel fuel, hydrogen peroxide, and acetone, made much of the old siege mentality and tactics obsolete, and even embarrassing, in the twenty-first century.

But the thinking of the old guard always changes much more slowly than does technology, and what I have found to be true in psychology – the importance of constantly evaluating how we think and reason, rather than becoming bogged by emotion and sentimentality – is true across the board in life, including warfare and law enforcement.

The dawning of the nightmare that was the American Civil War, from 1861 to 1865, was largely the result of employing outdated fighting strategy in the face of modernised weapons. Infantrymen – thousands of them, shoulder to shoulder – were maimed and murdered while advancing across open country and into the sights of newly developed and highly accurate rifle-bored muskets with quick-loading percussion caps, and the latest artillery.

But the nightmare was only fully and finally realised fifty years later in the trench warfare and suicidal machine gun charges of the First World War.

Twenty-five years after that, Hitler, himself a veteran of the trenches, stunned the world with his lightning-fast blitzkrieg – mechanised and mobilised armoured warfare that swallowed Poland almost overnight and simply bypassed France's entrenched, fortified, and impregnable Maginot Line.

But, then, that modern industrialised war machine itself only triumphed for twenty years and, by the 1960s, even the American B-52s could not rout Vietnamese peasants in their jungles and tunnels.

Lone skyjackers blew up airliners in the 1970s, Afghan tribal fighters with shoulder-launched missiles brought the mighty Russia to its knees in the 1980s, and three commercial airliners crashing into New York's Twin Towers and the Pentagon in 2001 embroiled high-tech American forces in a fight against the Taliban, and their improvised explosive devices, in Iraq and Afghanistan.

History. Seasons. Winds and tides. Subjective truth.

Amidst their ongoing wars against terrorism, America and Israel forget that they were both condemned by their British oppressors at the time for using "terrorist" tactics in their own struggles for independence.

One man's terrorist is another man's freedom fighter and, time and time again, young idealistic rebels ruthlessly squash all opposition once they inhabit the palace.

Warfare, weaponry, tactics, and the politics of killing – all of them morph, evolve, change their names, and undergo plastic surgery as they enter the twenty-first century.

In many ways, a global, materialistic, consumer society can no longer afford national and international conflict – it's bad for business. And world wars, it would seem, have now been replaced by "limited actions", boutique terrorism, independent arms dealers, international conglomerates, and trade treaties.

There seem to be no more black-and-white conflicts, such as the Allies versus the Axis in the Second World War.

The colours on classroom maps and globes have become faded and watered down – blurred and running into each other, often bleeding into each other – as the world turns grey before our eyes.

Perhaps the last remaining Great Cause will be religious fundamentalism, but even that must bear the pressure and pass the test of the next generation – a global youth market seeking comfort and pleasure, consumers all. Indoctrinated, brainwashed, sold – each and every one, one *me* at a time.

But such great and contentious topics never reared their ugly little heads at the lunchtime conversation between New South Wales Police Superintendent Rod Stanwych and retired Australian Defence Force Sergeant Gary Dixon.

For they were just soldiers wearing two different uniforms, and society would always need men and women in uniform willing to uphold law and order, take out the garbage, maintain the illusion of a modern civilisation growing ever more humane, not ask the difficult questions, or necessarily feel the need to make public the truth about police infighting, political corruption, dirty little skirmishes, unpublished body counts, and shallow unmarked graves.

Brothers-in-arms, they simply shook hands and discussed the need to update police tactics.

Immediate Action, Rapid Deployment: the term had been coined and the strategy developed in America, in the light of tactical squad sieges gone horribly wrong – mainly workplace, high school, and university shootings.

Each IARD officer was trained and authorised to act as a one-man tactical response unit in the event of a mass shooting. Whoever arrived first on the scene was to proceed immediately, and with extreme caution, towards the source of the gunfire. The officer was under orders not to evacuate the building, administer first aid to the wounded, or wait for reinforcements – his was a seek-and-destroy mission, pure and simple.

If the shooter could be captured alive – well and good – but the "Immediate Action" order was backed by a shoot-to-kill mandate. No charges would be laid and no criticism levelled against the officer's use of deadly force, nor would any excuses be offered to the public.

But such a policy was as much political as it was strategic, and could only be successfully implemented at a time when the majority of voters were demanding a tougher police response to violent crime.

In America, for example, at the scene of one shopping mall shooting, where an estranged husband killed his cashier wife and then went on to shoot seven bystanders, the media hushed up the fact that two civilian shoppers then shot the husband dead with their own handguns, thereby saving many. The liberal newspapers knew that the story would only fuel the conservative gun lobby's long-argued case for self-defence.

Politics, timing, presentation, media coverage, electoral response – a complex and sensitive cycle – and the lunchtime meeting with Sergeant Dixon, though apparently informal, actually represented a quite extraordinary alignment of five individuals.

The State's conservative Premier, Minister of Justice, and Police Commissioner had long been in agreement about the need to bolster police presence and toughen police response.

Then the much-publicised recent feuding among rival motorcycle gangs in Sydney had hit a nerve with the public when a fourteen-year-old boy was shot in the head and killed as he stepped out of his parents' apartment – and happened to witness a bikie murder in the hallway.

The New South Wales Police Commissioner was a good friend of Newcastle Police Superintendent Rod Stanwych, and Rod readily agreed to act as political scapegoat by "suggesting" and implementing the Immediate Action, Rapid Deployment training scheme.

If Gary Dixon took on the assignment, he would personally train six general-duty police officers per week in a five-day crash course of commando tactics and techniques.

Once that training was completed statewide, the SAS Sergeant could then develop team skills among those graduate police commandos so that, in effect, tactical squads would be available any time and any place in the state to respond immediately when needed.

Dixon agreed before dessert was served.

19

I once read that the Eskimo language has over forty words to describe all the different types of snow.

I don't know how many kinds of rain there are but, on Black Friday, Newcastle's downpour was set in for the day, torrential, unrelenting, cold, and miserable. It was the kind of storm that made you glad to be inside and, if you *had* to step outside, you ran for cover. When the wind gusted, the rain blew almost horizontally so that umbrellas were useless.

If weather expressed emotion, then Newcastle surely wept that day.

John Lennon once said that life is what happens to you when you're making other plans. The weather was the first of many unexpected "happenings" to challenge Leon's "other plans" for the day. The rain *actually* made little difference to anything, but Leon was still very disappointed with himself for never even having considered it – he thought he had considered everything.

The Dregs had discussed, plotted, planned, timed, and sketched out their day to the minute, with Leon always suggesting, leading, guiding, endorsing, criticising, and vetoing, as called for by his original vision.

Druid, true to form, had originally proposed Halloween, the thirty-first of October, as the date of the attack. And while Druid argued all the magical and mystical reasons for the anointing of that particular date, Leon considered the audience appeal and marketing potential to more than three hundred million North American viewers, for whom Halloween was a much bigger deal than it was for Australians.

But they soon remembered, to their grave disappointment, that the senior students of Year Twelve, in preparation for their final, gruelling, High School Certificate exams, were class-free from mid-October.

Although the Australian academic year follows the calendar year with graduations each December, the last day that the whole student body of Hunter High would be present and attending a seniors' farewell assembly was Friday the thirteenth of October. And, so, as the Dregs set the date for their assault to coincide with the final assembly, Druid still grumbled that even Friday the thirteenth was a poor second to Halloween.

The Dregs had drawn up a "blacklist" of forty students and staff members who they planned to cull from the crowd of 710 students, thirty-four teachers, four admin, and two maintenance workers.

The printer's annual deadline for delivering the Hunter High student yearbooks was always mid-September. That way, if printing problems or delivery hassles created even a fortnight's delay, there was still another two-week safety margin before the final assembly.

The Hunter High yearbooks were delivered right on schedule, four weeks before the siege, giving the Dregs plenty of time to each create their own illustrated, cut-and-paste copy of their blacklist – forty names and faces to memorise and find quickly in the crowd. And this was *literally* cut and paste – with scissors and glue – not a computerised, electronic editing. In every aspect, this was going to be very much a hands-on operation, not sterile and electronic, and hands were going to get dirty.

On the morning of the siege, Leon was home alone with his Filipino housekeeper, Yvonna. Anton Spitzer was away in Melbourne, and not due back until nine o'clock that night. Sometime shortly before 11:00, Yvonna watched Leon drive away in his menacing black Jeep – "The Beast" – and disappear into the jaws of Newcastle's rain squall, death metal music blaring from his speakers.

She took no special notice of the fact that Leon was wearing his Dreg (and not his school) uniform. She noticed nothing exceptional at all about his attitude or his behaviour – only, perhaps, that he seemed more animated than usual. She had attributed it, at the time, to Friday relief – another week over.

Slave's mother was at work and his little sister at primary school when Leon would have been picked him up around 11:15. Slave always worked afternoons and evenings at the gym, and had his days free. Therefore, Slave's mother thought his schedule unchanged on that Friday. She did not know that Slave had quit his job and worked his last shift the night before.

Two of Wade's young truant neighbours later testified to seeing him entering Leon's vehicle around 11:25. They thought nothing of the black clothes nor the late hour, Wade's school attendance having always been patchy. They saw no sawn-off .22 or any traces of blood, heard no squealing tyres, and observed no signs of a hasty departure from a murder scene.

Yet, ironically, both witnesses could recall every detail of Leon's four-door Jeep Wrangler Rubicon soft top, with its matte black military paint job, oversized Mud-Terrain tyres, boosted suspension, and black-tinted windows. Mounted across the roof was a two-tiered LED lightbar, and in front of the radiator a pair of blinding LED spotlights – their red-rimmed and honeycombed lenses bulging out of the grille just above the "BEAST" number plate. People saw what Leon wanted them to see, and remembered what Leon wanted them to remember.

Weed's mother, Joyce, always had to head off early for work at the bank, leaving Weed to lock up the house and catch her school bus. Joyce was surprised, that Friday, at her daughter's black attire because the school usually announced uniform-free days in the weekly newsletter. As they kissed good-bye at the front door, Weed gave her mum a clinging hug and began crying. This surprised Joyce Stankowski, because there had really been no tears since Weed's black-clad school friends had welcomed her into their little club.

"Are you okay, Weed?"

"I just wish Daddy were still here, that's all, I never said good-bye to him."

"I miss him, too. I hate to leave you alone like this."

"I'm not alone, I have my friends."

"I'll see you tonight."

Weed sobbed. Unable to answer, she just nodded her head.

It was in the next three hours that Weed wrote her mother a seven-page letter.

At 11:30, Leon's Jeep pulled up at Wendy's house. Wade stepped out of the back seat and into the rain to hold open the rear car door for his sister. She was still crying.

Druid told his parents that he was off to catch the school bus at 8:20. He was dressed in black as usual, always changing into the detested school uniform only upon his arrival so as to avoid wearing it for one minute more than he had to – 8:50 a.m. to 3:10 p.m. precisely, and no longer.

His family could later report no unusual communication with him – there was, as usual, no communication at all. Since the only alternative seemed to be high-volume arguments, maintaining silence had become the family objective. Truth be told, his parents had already given up on Drew, and wanted only to learn from their mistakes with him in order to do better with his two younger brothers.

Druid had told Leon that he preferred to walk to school rather than be picked up by The Beast, so filled with excitement and anticipation was he. Hunter High was a twenty-minute walk away – Druid took three hours. It was somewhere en route that he ingested a triple dose of crystal methamphetamine hydrochloride, always referred to as "thrice the ice" when he sold it to his customers.

Two blocks away from the high school – at the corner of Loftus and Alcorn – Leon pulled over, slipped on his Dregcam head unit, and pressed the record button. He looked around at his three passengers before continuing on into the storm.

At 11:43, surveillance cameras in the Hunter High School parking lot recorded the Jeep pulling up in front of the flagpole and alongside the waiting Druid. Ironically, the cameras had been installed as a direct result of Slave's flagpole assault, and he had not been back to the school since – only returning now, for revenge.

They were all late for classes, obviously, and out of uniform. There *was* no mufti day. Leon had briefed and rehearsed them so well that there was no need for recapping anything during the drive in, or now at the parking lot.

Slave turned off the deafening death metal music and they all disembarked quickly into the tempest, each of them again appearing headless within their hoodie caves of blackness. Leon opened the tailgate and unzipped the rear vinyl flap of his Jeep to personally distribute five vital pieces of equipment to each of his four team members.

The Dregs had always planned to gather tightly around their leader in a semi-circle as they prepared for the assault, so that no prying eyes in the parking lot would be any the wiser. What hadn't been planned or rehearsed was the pouring rain.

Ironically, they each had to first take off their black raincoat in the downpour in order to don their equipment, so they now had the added incentive of huddling beneath the vinyl flap to keep dry. They all got soaked anyway, but the torrential downpour motivated them to move faster, kept them clustered together in a tight knot, obscured their actions from surveillance cameras, and ensured the parking lot was devoid of witnesses.

When reviewed later, the CCTV footage confirmed to investigators that even *had* someone been watching security monitors at the time, no alarm would have been raised by the five student terrorists gearing up.

Leon handed each Dreg an identical Ruger 10/22 semi-automatic rifle with shoulder strap. The strap was slung over the neck and shoulder and the rifle hung straight down, its muzzle dangling around knee-length. The straps were, ironically, guitar straps – wider and more comfortable around the neck and shoulder than were actual rifle straps.

The black overcoats were then quickly slipped back on, effectively concealing the weapons. Each rifle held a twenty-five-shot magazine, slightly curved like a banana. Leon had decided to follow the thinking and mandate of the U.S. Secret Service: all of their agents trained with and carried identical handguns loaded with identical ammunition, so that picking up and firing a fallen colleague's weapon would present no surprises – the weight, feel, handling, and performance all identical.

Each Dreg was then handed a black canvas army surplus pouch which they slung over the other shoulder and outside of their coats. Each pouch contained nine extra, loaded magazines. The four Dregs were now armed with one thousand rounds of ammunition – forty magazines in total – which they could easily load and fire off in less than three minutes. Easily. And there were only 750 people in the high school building.

The ammunition was all .22 calibre Long Rifle hollow point which could be fired at three or more shots per second, "as fast as you can pull the trigger". The semi-automatic rifles were fast, light, and dependable (affording pinpoint accuracy at up to forty or fifty metres) – while their bullets assured maximum damage upon impact (the hollow points more easily distorted, mushroomed, deflected, or shattered into multiple fragments than a standard solid core).

Being such a light bullet, so easily warped and deflected by bone and sudden changes of medium (air, tissue, bodily fluids, muscle, and bone), the .22 was renowned for its bizarre trajectories through the human body. For example, a person shot in the wrist could easily end up with an exit wound in the shoulder, or a bullet deflected internally from the collarbone could emerge near the groin. The .22 calibre bullet was also notorious for leaving tiny or practically invisible entry wounds, especially in fatty tissue or with heavyset victims.

Of course, none of this ballistic data bears any resemblance to its portrayal in film and television – whether the Hollywood "flesh wound in the left shoulder", the special-effect exploding blood pack, or even the sound of gunfire – all very different in real life. The shock of a bullet wound, the months of recovery, the frequency of spinal injury and paralysis – hospital wards bearing no resemblance to movie sets.

The two main differences between Hollywood and actual shooting scene most often noted by police and military personnel: *first*, either shooting victims are initially unaware that they have even been wounded and keep running or else drop like a sack of potatoes when hit, their legs suddenly buckling under their own dead weight and, *second*, many of the wounded subsequently cry out in pain and scream for help, unlike Hollywood, Xbox, and PlayStation victims – "extras" who, once disposed of, die quickly, quietly, and conveniently, off-camera and out of sight.

Real-life witnesses often report gunshots as sounding like cap guns or backfiring cars, bodies do not really fly through the air upon impact (not even from a twelve-gauge shotgun blast), and victims are often maimed for life.

In real life, the victim or enemy is not just a target or a prop, but a human being with a life context, a story behind them, family and friends, weaknesses, character flaws, and extenuating circumstances.

In addition to the rifle and ten magazines carried by each Dreg (which weighed remarkably little), Leon now quickly added three other items of Spitzer commando gear: a walkie-talkie, a watch, and a Dregcam.

The walkie-talkies were basic – UHF, seventy-five voice channels, three kilometre range. Small rural property usage, really, but Leon didn't *want* them to have extensive broadcast range and thereby increase the chances of having any Dreg conversations intercepted – didn't want them used *at all* if possible – but, within the school building, they would do fine for brief and urgent communication.

Leon distributed the watches at the last minute, insisting that he synchronise them himself, so critical was timing to the success of the operation. Leon was already wearing his as he handed out the first one to Slave – who smiled his rare Slavic smile as he noted, with great amusement, the Mickey Mouse cartoon figures pointing out the time on all the watch faces.

Once the watches were on, Leon handed out three Dregcam head units. Leon could have easily afforded the type of miniaturised headsets with temple-mounted cameras, tiny earpieces, and jawline mini-mikes currently utilised by the police and military – compared to them, the forehead-rigged GoPro Hero wired to the Immortal Mic ears looked home-made and clunky – but the Dregcams were intentionally reminiscent of the Borg enemy aliens from Star Trek.

The Borg was a huge alien spacecraft, an unstoppable black cube on a mission to conquer the universe, consuming all in its path and linking each captive mind to itself via clunky wires and implants to the head – each new cyborg/drone thus becoming an organic yet programmed cog in a killing machine, a hardwired and cold-blooded member of one murderous body.

Leon had played the Borg episodes for his Dregs, over and over again, in their tree house lair – the concept, the message, and the programming now ingrained.

Wade pulled the fifth and final Dregcam out of his raincoat pocket – the head unit that Leon had so reluctantly allowed him to take home the night before to get the adjustment just right. It seemed to fit fine now. They were right to go.

Four black hoods were pulled back up over their heads to shield their new Dregcams, and their eyes, from the pelting rain. Leon closed up his Jeep for the last time.

The armada of Doc Marten boots then sloshed its way through the flooded parking lot and towards the entrance of Hunter High.

At the foot of the ten front concrete steps, they checked their watches. 11:45 Mickey Mouse time, just about exactly as planned.

For Leon knew that fifty minutes was the optimal duration for all television documentaries, worldwide – allowing ten minutes for commercials, and still fitting within the most highly marketable sixty-minute time slot.

Leon's camera already contained the initial tree house introductions and, now, their parking lot arrival, so that a 12:30 conclusion could all be edited together into a neat, fifty-minute package – 12:30 and not one minute later.

Leon had previously recorded hours of extra footage documenting all Dreg training and preparations for the assault, leaving those micro SD cards back in the tree house for the police to find in their subsequent searching – and, hopefully, for producers to use in their subsequent documentaries. But the master video, now on his head, should run no more than fifty minutes in total.

That moment when the other four Dregs turned on their cameras at the foot of the steps was the culmination – for each of them – of sixteen or seventeen years of circumstances, relationships, responses, choices, and decisions. The finale – for all of them – of a secret mission, plotted and planned for months. And the beginning – for a potentially global audience – of live video coverage, at a major crime scene, recorded from five different camera angles. It was Leon's vision, a detective's dream, and a coroner's nightmare.

Anton Spitzer owned a seven-hundred-acre country estate fifty minutes away from his Newcastle home – indoor pool, tennis and squash courts, bowling alley, twenty-seat cinema, helicopter pad, man-made lake well stocked with trout, award-winning vineyard, nine-hole golf course, and go-kart track built to international competition standards – with a three Michelin-starred chef on call to prepare the fruit, vegetables, meat, fish, and poultry grown and raised right there on the property.

Anton only ever went there to entertain business contacts and flaunt the recreational fruit of his labours. Well, for his guests it might have been recreation but for Anton it was, in truth, all business strategy investment and tax write-off.

There Anton plied them with food and drink, tennis and go-karts, golf, skeet shooting, hunting, fishing, mergers, proposals, and profit potential. Anton boasted to his confidants that the estate, ultimately, earned him more money in sales and contracts than all of his five overseas offices combined.

The Great Anton Spitzer complemented his estate's well-stocked lake and well-stocked wine cellar with a well-stocked arsenal. Many Australians own gun safes – Anton owned a vault.

But, all alone on the estate, just him and the staff, it was Leon who actually played with his father's toys. Not only was Leon taught to handle guns, he was also expected to keep the armoury topped up with ammunition, and all weapons well maintained. When only a boy, his shooting was supervised by the staff of the estate. But, by the time he was fourteen, Leon ran the armoury autonomously and anonymously, ordering weapons, ammunition, and cleaning products at will via email – all backed by his father's platinum credit cards. Leon knew guns, and he knew how to get them.

The Ruger model 10/22 was one of the best-selling .22 calibre semi-automatic rifles in America, and around the world, since its initial release in 1964. The 10/22 was tough, reliable, highly respected, and famous for its unique, ten-shot rotary magazine that fit flush into the stock – but Leon wanted even more firepower for his Dregs.

Cheap, curved, thirty-shot magazines were available in plastic through a number of manufacturers, but consumer feedback provided only mixed reviews, with ongoing complaints of jamming. So Leon did his homework on the internet and found instead a more expensive, twenty-five-shot, metal "steel lip" magazine, the TI-25 by Technical Innovations in America, precision-tooled and machined in lightweight aircraft-grade aluminum with adjustable mounting screws that assured a perfect, customised fit.

Bullet-jamming was always a possibility with any semi-automatic – and especially with the .22 calibre, because the ammunition was so small and the cheaper brands notoriously dirty. But the Ruger's reputation for reliability, enhanced by the precision-made TI-25 magazine, and loaded with high standard Winchester Power-Point ammunition, meant that flawless feeds were virtually guaranteed.

In fact, so flawless was the TI-25's bullet-feeding capability that it was rated and recommended not only for semi-automatic, but even fully automatic (machine gun) applications. Once his concern over bullet-jamming was eliminated, Leon began placing orders.

The TI-25's were, ironically, available in nine designer colours. Leon bought standard matte blue-black metal for all the boys but, for Weed, he purchased metallic red, green, orange, and purple to match the fluorescent streaks in her hair.

After a 1996 shooting spree that killed thirty-five people and wounded twenty-three in Tasmania (the most southerly of Australia's seven states), public outcry demanded, and parliamentary lawmakers implemented, severe restrictions on gun ownership, calibre, semiautomatic capability, and magazine capacity.

Australia, like its Commonwealth cousins New Zealand and Canada, was trying to insulate itself from a growing tide of violence in the world by legislating firearms restrictions – perhaps inspired by the legendary unarmed London bobby, perhaps just a vain attempt to maintain the façade of peace, civilisation, and the containment of evil – but a tougher response of some kind was demanded by an increasingly-nervous electorate in the face of rising crime rates, the declining value of human life, and the judicial undermining of personal accountability.

The logic was simple: a gunman was much easier to evade or overpower if he had to reload after every few shots. Body counts and electoral anxiety could both be lowered, simply by the signing of one bill in parliament. The pen, at least in this case, *was* mightier than the sword – unless, of course, you could access illegal suppliers in the name of Anton Spitzer, a registered gun collector.

Only professional, contracted shooters and specially authorised primary producers with a Category D firearms licence – closely vetted and monitored by the police – were now able to own .22 calibre semiautomatic rifles with a magazine capacity beyond ten shots and larger calibre, centrefire, semi-automatic rifles.

Although Leon enjoyed a certain freedom of access in his father's name, ordering four restricted semi-automatic rifles and receiving delivery of forty prohibited magazines would guarantee a raid by the police.

So, over the course of three months, Leon contacted twelve different gun dealers in Australia and overseas who had all enjoyed significant Spitzer patronage in the past, dealers who were willing to circumvent Australian gun-importing laws themselves or knew people who would. Leon had them all deliver by early September – the smuggled items redirected through middlemen so that no restricted firearms whatsoever passed through Australian Customs bearing the name of Spitzer.

All the gun dealers charged exorbitant black market prices, several demanded cash payments that generated no electronic banking records, a couple of others were willing to risk Leon's offer of delayed Spitzer credit card payment by the end of October at triple the cost. Whatever they wanted, Leon gave them, but secretly recorded their phone conversations and kept copies of every email to ensure they were all subsequently charged. Leon wanted proof, glaring shameful evidence, of his father's ignorant complicity in funding such illegal arms trafficking.

The September delivery allowed several weekend field trips to deserted bush areas to train the Dregs with their new weapons. And it was not just *skill* that Leon wanted to develop in his Dregs – it was *confidence*. The Dregs saw that the Rugers were fast and faultless throughout the thousands of practice rounds fired. They soon came to realise, then to appreciate, and finally to relish, the sense of *power* that bolsters a four-member team able to dispatch one hundred bullets in under ten seconds – and then reload in another five.

But even that wasn't enough for Leon Spitzer. He wanted to further endow his Dregs with the ability to control and manipulate people such as he himself enjoyed every day. And, so, to their quivers he added two additional weapons of psychological warfare intended to physically immobilise and emotionally paralyse their hostages.

The first was *bondage*. In each of their army ammo pouches was placed two hundred plastic cable ties weighing and costing almost nothing. The four Dregs now had the ability to bind every set of wrists in the high school. The staff of local hardware stores sold hundreds of such plastic "ziplock" cable ties each week to dozens of tradesmen, handymen, and gardeners, without batting an eye. They certainly didn't bat an eye when Leon bought his – he was such an exceptionally polite young man that the saleswoman recognised his photo immediately, when questioned later by police.

The second was *threat*. Leon knew the intimidating power of a loaded weapon – the aimed muzzle, the dark cave at the end of the barrel from which death could flash at any instant, the black hole threatening to engulf its victim in blackness. But, for Leon, that wasn't enough. Simply by mounting a laser sight on each of their rifles, every hostage would see themselves – even *feel* themselves – repeatedly touched by the red dot of death. Cost was never an issue with the Spitzers, but value was always paramount. Leon had to pay hundreds of dollars for the top-quality lasers, but he would have gladly paid thousands because the lasers were integral, non-negotiable – and inspired by the Borg drones who had theirs embedded near their temples.

True, the lasers did improve and quicken target acquisition without the need to rely on the gun's own metal sights, but their real value, their true power, lay in their ability to magnify the threat – to visualise, personalise, and realise it. To drive it home, like hitting a nerve. Whatever that red dot touched could be hit by a bullet, might be hit any second, the bullet perhaps even now on its way at the speed of sound. And the red dots constantly dancing, and bouncing, and flitting around the room, graphically illustrated that no one was safe should a rifle ever be discharged accidentally.

Another psychological torture rarely even admitted by survivors was the sense of relief, and subsequent guilt, experienced by each hostage whenever he or she saw a red dot on someone else – because any red dot on anyone else, was one less dot on them.

The blinding brightness of the lasers also caused hostages to squint and turn away, yet another form of control. The manufacturers of green laser sights claimed that theirs were four times as bright as their competitors' red, and much more effective in daylight – and they probably were. But Leon quickly recognised, and embraced, the superior emotional – and almost hypnotic – power of the red dot. Blood red.

And, as it turned out, Leon was right. Even under the institutional glare of the high school fluorescents, the red lasers were blinding and surely no green one could have been more terrifying.

Another interesting psychological, or psychosomatic, observation noted by a Melbourne university criminologist: green is considered a "cold" colour, while red is "hot". It was fascinating to hear the number of survivors who later reported the hot, even burning, sensation they felt whenever the red dot fell upon them. Would green have felt any less so, I wonder?

Now, at the foot of the steps, Leon stood in front of his squad of identically-clad and armed Dregs. Identical to each other, that is, but not to him. For strapped over his shoulder and under his coat was the .30 calibre M1 carbine that his father had owned and loved for years. It was, historically, considered more of an officer's rifle than an enlisted soldier's – fitting, perhaps, as Leon was the "officer" in charge.

The M1 carbine was designed by Winchester during the Second World War as an alternative to the heavier M1 Garand battlefield rifle with its much more powerful .30-06 ammunition. The compact, lightweight carbine was often favoured by jungle troops but was designed specifically for paratroopers, officers, drivers, medics, radio operators, and tank crews – for fighting men facing weight and size restrictions, as well as support troops who needed a compact rifle or whose lives didn't depend on it daily. Bigger than a pistol, smaller than a full-scale rifle, the M1 carbine was never intended to replace the Garand, which was just as well, because word spread quickly among Allied infantrymen that an enemy soldier hit several times by a .30 calibre carbine could still shoot back – not nearly as likely with a .30-06.

But firepower comes in many forms, and what the M1 carbine lacked in knockdown power it made up for in ammunition supply. The Garand held only eight bullets in its clip, the carbine offered fifteen and thirty-shot magazines. And so the little carbine appealed to many a soldier, police officer, recreational shooter, guerrilla fighter, and bank robber as it made its way around the world after the Second World War. In fact, the .22 calibre Rugers carried by the four Dregs were originally inspired by the M1 design.

Over six million M1 carbines were manufactured – initially by Winchester and subsequently by Underwood, IBM, and General Motors. In fact, "civilian" companies like Boeing, Lockheed Martin, Honeywell, Goodrich, Pratt & Whitney, Samsung, and General Electric continue to sell billions of dollars worth of military hardware and software each year, with total annual global arms sales from all sources now reportedly approaching two trillion dollars – almost five billion per day. Killing is big business. Always has been.

Leon emphasised to the Dregs that he was only using the M1 as icing on the scandalous cake that he was baking for Anton Spitzer – his son using his father's name, tree house, credit card, and even his very own prized rifle, to mount the siege. (Anton had defied Australian legislation banning centrefire semi-automatics, by not surrendering his unregistered M1 years ago during the government's buy-back campaign – Anton thought it was retired and hidden forever, but it was now resurfacing to haunt him.)

All their weapons looked similar. The Rugers and the M1 were all fed by similar banana-curved magazines, and Leon carried an identical black army ammo pouch with extra magazines – but only four extras for him, compared to each of his Dreg recruit's nine, because Leon's thirty-shot M1 magazines were much bulkier than the .22 calibre TI-25's.

Leon repeatedly highlighted to his Dregs that he was armed with only 150 rounds, compared to their one thousand in total – but never once discussed with them the fact that his .30 calibre bullets were three times as heavy as their .22s, one and a half times their speed, and seven times as powerful upon impact.

Now, at the foot of the school steps, the five Dregs moved as one body. First, they all turned on their laser sights, then the four recruits pressed the record buttons on their video cameras. Live, non-stop, unedited action – high-definition video, 3-D sound, five camera angles.

Five hooded and faceless Dregs in the storm, clothed in black from head to foot. Each hood a darkened cave now inhabited by a red-eyed, blinking cyclops. Blink, blink, blink.

The four Dreg disciples looked to their leader, and all their cameras recorded Leon Spitzer's sneering tone. "Show time, boys and girls. Remember: I'm counting on you – and the world is watching. The Revenge of the Dregs, Take One." Sneering – yet calm, and almost soothing.

Following his lead, five bolts were pulled back and released. Five bullets slid into five chambers. Five safeties clicked off.

20

Gary Dixon was passionately dedicated to the police commando training scheme – and utterly frustrated by each week's batch of new conscripts.

The rigid way in which the general-duty officers handled their Glocks, their ingrained dependence on backup and superior numbers, their lack of initiative and independent thinking – all of these were big hurdles to overcome in the five short days of his crash course. These were street cops, beat cops, patrol car cops, who rarely drew their guns – yet the SAS sergeant sought to develop in them that fluid, instinctive, and reflexive appreciation of their weapon as an extension of their arm, and eye, and will.

Dixon was soon respected (if not feared) as a relentless, hands-on instructor who played the hostile gunman himself in every scenario. Initially disgusted with the poor reflexes of his first week's trainees, Dixon quickly exchanged everyone's blank-loaded, service-issue Glocks with the carbon dioxide-powered Glock-replica paintball guns that he used from then on – the red paint graphically simulating a gunshot wound, and leaving his recruits black and blue with paintball welts by the end of the week, though Dixon himself was rarely hit.

When any of his disgruntled victims complained to their police union, they were told to quit the training or improve their skills – that there was far worse than welts awaiting them in a real-life gunfight.

But if Dixon was disappointed with the weekly results, he was at least encouraged by Rod Stanwych's enthusiasm and monthly reports that police firing ranges recorded a threefold increase in attendance rates by his graduate police commandos, compared with their untrained colleagues.

When Dixon finished with all the Newcastle officers, he took his training program on the road to other centres in the state.

In fifteen months, Dixon established his reputation, trained over four hundred commandos, created serious opposition amongst police and political proponents of the antiquated and centralised SWAT siege mentality, and lost the state election.

Well, *Dixon* didn't actually lose the election, but all his political allies did. The New South Wales Premier lost the governing majority, the Minister of Justice lost his portfolio in the cabinet, the Police Commissioner lost his appointment – and Rod Stanwych found himself alone, surrounded by political opponents, and saddled with blame for the expensive and unproven commando training scheme.

But the biggest losers were the citizens of the state of New South Wales themselves. Once again, they lost time and money – both devoured by the four-year-election monster. Each state and federal government rode these electoral monsters in jousting matches against their opposition. And all because Western culture, media, and education had indoctrinated voters to demand (and their politicians to provide) simple solutions quickly – short-term vision, sound bites, three or four-year office terms – a warped type of Immediate Action, Rapid Deployment that could never provide any genuine long-term vision, progress, or momentum.

The primary goal of even the most honest, passionate, and committed politician could never truly be the *long-term* benefit of the electorate – it always had to be, first and foremost, his or her re-election.

Did Australia, the driest continent on earth, need a decades-long, multibillion-dollar plan to pipe fresh water from the northwest corner of the country, with its yearly torrential monsoon floods, down to the ever-thirsty population centres of Melbourne and Sydney in the southeast, while irrigating parched farmland all along the way? Of course it did – a pipeline had been proposed by scientists for years – but no politician, it seemed, would ever risk telling the truth and losing his bid for a three or four-year office term, just for the sake of Australia's long-term future.

Voters didn't want to pay taxes and politicians didn't want to lose votes, so politicians continued to lie and voters continued to complain.

And what about a long-term financial plan to truly brace Australia for the economic drain of the aging Baby Boomers – the Age Wave that all politicians knew was due to hit in the coming decades? "Surely voters deserve a brighter, short-term forecast," the politicians lied to themselves, and anyone else who would listen, as they feebly extended the retirement and pension-eligibility age.

Bereft of any strong political leaders with clear vision, Australians had to stand by and watch their resources sold out from underneath them for short-term profit and debt reduction – asset by asset, and hectare by hectare – while "economic health and growth" figures were buoyed by mass immigration and the transfer of hyper-inflated real estate from one indebted citizen to another.

Foreign investment and trade deficits were rife, Australian manufacturing declining or defunct.

Always band-aids, never cures. And so, too, with tactical squads.

When the newly-elected state government needed a culprit for police budget blowouts, the new premier pointed his finger of blame at the commando training scheme – it was colourful, costly, and controversial.

The program was mothballed, Superintendent Rod Stanwych decided to take early retirement, and Sergeant Gary Dixon was left hanging in limbo – dividing his time between weapons training instructor at the police academy in Goulburn, relief and support officer with the Sydney-based tactical squad (State Protection Group / Tactical Operations Unit) and commander of the Newcastle tactical squad (State Protection Support Unit).

The new state government had wanted to dump him completely, but the police union raised a stink because of their members' almost unanimous respect for, and appreciation of, Dixon and his training.

So the public missed out on improved police training and tactics, and was then hoodwinked again, seven months later, when the new government rolled out its newly acquired, one-million-dollar mobile command centre for the Sydney-based tactical squad – called "Siege Buster", but nicknamed "Buster" for short.

The armoured vehicle was bulletproof, bombproof, fireproof, and gasproof (with its own sealed air recirculation system), capable of transporting eight fully-armed tactical squad members, fitted with water cannon and weapon portals, bristling with high-tech surveillance, communications, thermal imaging, and night vision equipment. But it was slow, very slow – its Belgian manufacturers installing a suspension system suited for ramming roadblocks, crumpling any burning cars in its path, and even climbing stairs, but not for highway driving.

With a top speed of only one hundred kilometers (sixty miles) per hour, Buster was a complete reversal of the previous government's commitment to immediate action and rapid deployment. So the premier knew that he had to resort to one of the three present-day scapegoats in his political barnyard to pacify the voters: economy, environment, or technology.

Government ministers either blamed them, or exalted them, as required – depending on the circumstances. Circumstances and labels changed quickly, making it difficult for the voters to keep up – which was also part of the plan, whatever it took to avoid personal responsibility. Ineffective and dishonest, to be sure. But the voters only had to be deceived for a few years, before again being promised radical improvements by their repentant leaders during the next election campaign.

The new government promoted Buster's techno-wizardry in a sleight-of-hand propaganda campaign to divert criticism from their cost-cutting restructuring of the state's tactical squads. For policing purposes, the huge state of New South Wales, covering over 800,000 square kilometres (310,000 square miles), had long been divided into eighty Local Area Commands – forty-six of them in the greater Sydney Metropolitan Area, eleven in each of the state's sparsely populated South and West, and twelve in the North (one of these twelve being the Hunter Valley Area Command).

With great media fanfare, the newly unveiled Buster was garaged in Sydney where the vast majority of the State Protection Group's call-outs originated and were handled by the Sydney-based, full-time, highly trained specialist tactical squad members – that was *logistically* obvious to the public. But *politically* obvious, to the premier, was the potential for Buster's presence in Sydney to inspire a sense of increased police security (and electoral satisfaction) within those forty-six Sydney Metropolitan Area Commands – inhabited by more than sixty per cent of all New South Wales residents, with that percentage rising every year.

And, since governments are re-elected by majorities, if the majority of the state's voters *felt* that Buster provided them better protection, then that would free the reigning politicians to tighten their belts and cut back on their costly commitment to training, equipping, and supporting the three hundred volunteer, part-time, members of the State Protection Support Units scattered around the smaller cities and more rural areas of the state inhabited by the minority of voters. There would be no expansion in these areas, departing officers would not be replaced, and natural attrition would eventually save millions.

The premier argued that, since almost all State Protection Group call-outs originated from within the Greater Sydney Metropolitan Area, centralisation was the way to go and, at their press conferences, government officials repeatedly and pointedly referred to a recent standoff in a rural area where "part-time, volunteer State Protection Support Unit officers had killed an armed father in front of his children" – and thereby ignited media criticism about poor training of support units, as planned.

But one government was no different than another, really. It was just the unstoppable twenty-first century trends of centralisation, urbanisation, population growth, and cost-cutting, all over again. Global. Depersonalised. Efficient. And heartless. It was technology, it was a machine, it was the way of the Borg, and no *one* politician or political party was to blame, over the last twenty years, for closing dozens and dozens of small local police stations around the state while voters were mesmerised by the media glare of "sexier" issues like DNA evidence, armoured vehicles, and taser stun guns. The natives, yet again, pacified by trinkets and baubles while their land was plundered.

Costs were always rising and the new government, just like the old government before it, knew that there was rarely a solution both effective and affordable – they only needed a media-friendly band-aid that would suffice until the next election. Just one good siege where Buster saved the day and rescued some hostages, fully covered on the evening news.

And so, whatever the complex political reasoning and strategy behind the scenes, the simple fact remained that on Black Friday the Dregs were confident that the Newcastle-based State Protection Support Unit would be held back and ordered to wait for the Sydney-based State Protection Group – which would not arrive until well after 12:30. And even if the Sydney tactical squad *could* somehow get to Hunter High by 12:30, they had been trained in, and were committed to, containment, control, and risk minimisation, so there would probably be no rapid deployment – certainly no immediate action.

They would be too late and Leon knew it – simply from watching the news, appreciating the politics, and betting that the new state government would insist on waiting for Buster to rumble up in front of the gathered media before launching any police response.

21

There was really nothing fresh, creative, or innovative about Hunter High School. Nothing. And that included the architecture.

The building was only one storey high – all ground level, no second floor – and it was shaped like an unused staple, or squared-off letter "U". Some students called it "the horse shoe", adding that you'd have to be lucky to ever graduate from the place.

The building's designers were obviously thinking "practical", "efficient", and maybe even "cost effective" (as in the real world outside) when they placed all "communal facilities" in the horizontal bottom of the "U". Admin offices, teachers' staff lounge, student council and department-head offices, gym and showers, auditorium, science/language/music labs, and toilets – they all ran off the main corridor that formed the base of the "U".

Any visitor entering the lobby, centrally located at the bottom of the "U", need only look left or right along the length of the main corridor to see the entrance to each of these rooms clearly identified across the hall.

At each end of the main corridor a vertical arm, or wing, branched off at a ninety-degree angle. Each wing of the building contained six classrooms on each side of a locker-lined corridor, twenty-four classrooms in total. But no toilets or taps in the wings, only sprinkler systems – thereby saving on plumbing costs.

The library and small cafeteria were also located just off the main, horizontal corridor but both were closed due to renovations that had dragged on for months longer than planned – although rumour had it that their postponed completions were due more to politics than to construction delay. School cafeterias were under constant media attack from nutritional critics, and the library was being downsized to make room for modern classroom "labs" as literacy was, again, sacrificed on the altar of technology.

The building was painted in unimaginative and impersonal institutional colours, with only a half-hearted attempt at the occasional pastel. Fluorescent-lit halls led to fluorescent-lit classrooms which led, ultimately, to fluorescent-lit factories, offices, and shops.

The Dregs stepped out of the pouring rain and into the lobby, walking past the trophy cases that paid homage to the school's glorious exploits of the past – and ignoring the gaze of dozens of graduating classes in framed photographs on the wall.

They all dropped their sopping wet hoods, so as not to obstruct their camera lenses. Druid's Dregcam looked up at the ceiling lights passing by overhead, then down to the floor as their dripping black raincoats left water trails across the lobby's carpeting. Five red laser dots danced and flickered across the floor as they walked.

"Fireflies," whispered Druid slowly while exhaling. "Five little fireflies." Druid stopped in the lobby and stared at his own red dot, while the other four dots continued on.

> "Fireflies, fireflies, in from the wet,
> fireflies, fireflies, take what they can get,
> fireflies, fireflies, swat them if you can,
> fireflies, fireflies, fight to the last man."

The four other fireflies reappeared on the carpet next to his.

Druid looked up, and into the faces of his comrades.

"Are you okay, Druid?" asked Leon.

"Never better, mon capitaine. I was born for today. Druid MacDreg – born October the thirteenth, died October the thirteenth. Did you know that fireflies only live for one day?"

It was a powerful and poignant comment – but untrue. Fireflies actually live for about two months, only proving what the propagandists have always known – words do not need to be true to be inspirational, just emotive.

"Let's do it," Leon focused the team.

Slave and Druid headed for the left wing, Wade and Weed for the right.

"Keep an eye on him," Leon advised Slave in lowered voice.

Slave nodded silently, Druid flashed his smile and the thumbs up sign back to Leon. "Carpe diem, mon capitaine."

Leon headed into the heart of the school – the admin office – dead centre, and dead ahead, in the horizontal base of the horseshoe.

For those first few minutes in the car park, at the steps, and in the lobby, because of the weather and the class schedules, no one in the school had yet even seen the Dregs, with their five black coats and their five Dregcams. So far, so good.

Leon made sure he closed the two sets of heavy doors behind him – first to the admin area, and then to the reception office itself.

Pam Blain, the only secretary in sight, looked up from her desk beyond the reception counter. Pam was renowned around the school for always being gracious and friendly to all the students.

"I give up, Leon, what *is* that on your head?"

"I call it the Pamcam, I just want to film your reaction."

"Reaction to what?"

"To this," replied Leon as he drew the M1 from under his black coat and laid it on the counter.

Leon's high-definition lens was literally able to capture the blanching of Pam's face as her mouth dropped and her eyes widened.

"I'm afraid I have to ask you to step into the auditorium please, Pam."

The secretary rose quickly to her feet. Leon spoke gently, "Not *now*, Pam, in a minute. Right now I want you to stay there at your desk, call Mrs. Forman, and tell her there's a student out here that she really needs to see."

As he spoke, Leon made his way around the reception counter and picked up a pair of scissors from the top of Pam's desk.

Pam stared at the scissors as she sat back down and picked up the phone. "Mrs. Forman, there's a student out here that you really should see."

There was a pause. Leon playfully snipped the scissors open and closed.

"No, I really think you need to see him *right now*." Pam hung up.

"You were always nice to me, Pam. And I'll never forget that – as long as I live." Leon cut Pam's phone line with her scissors. "Mrs. Forman, on the other hand, was always a very snippy woman." Leon snipped the air playfully. "Snip, snip, snip. Mind if I keep these?"

Leon pocketed the scissors without waiting for a reply.

22

Slave had stopped at the junction of the main corridor and the left wing as planned, with Druid instructed to station himself at the far, upper end of the left wing, near the double exit doors.

Slave and Wade were Leon's right-hand men. They were each to station themselves at the junction points, responsible for keeping watch over their own (vertical) wing, as well as staying in visual contact with the main (horizontal) corridor.

Druid and Weed were to station themselves at the top ends. Druid had almost reached the top exit doors, when he turned around and headed back towards Slave.

"I've been walking in the rain for three hours – I need to do a wee-wee," Druid explained. But Slave was incredulous.

"I need you at your post!"

"Thirty seconds," promised Druid as he hustled off to the toilets in the main corridor. Slave didn't like it, and he didn't like Druid.

Weed walked quietly up the right wing and stopped two classrooms before the double exit doors, at the top end. There stood Treena Carr and Zoe Moustakis, gossiping at their lockers. Zoe was Weed's age in Year Ten, Treena one year older.

Together the girls had uncovered Wendy's secret attempts to create a fictitious on-line identity and establish virtual friendships. So they cruelly ignited and stoked a Facebook hate campaign against her – a campaign in which Wendy was repeatedly insulted, taunted, tormented, and even challenged to commit suicide, by strangers from across the globe – until she was forced to close all her social media accounts.

"Whatever that is on your head, Weed, you look like an idiot." Treena, a little cobra with a school uniform skirt that could be neither tighter nor shorter, spat the words like venom.

Contempt was written all over Zoe's face.

"Could you please be quiet, Treena?" Weed spoke softly.

Treena whispered back, mocking her, "Don't you even care about my opinion, Weed?"

"You *have* no opinion, Treena, you just follow the crowd. You don't really exist on your own. But you really *do* have to be quiet now – we're trying to sneak up on everyone."

"Who's 'we'?" whispered Treena.

"Me and Wade."

Weed pointed down to Wade at his junction with the main hall.

Treena and Zoe turned just as Wade shouldered his rifle, the laser sight gleaming. Treena gawked down at the red dot targeting her heart.

"Has he got a real gun?"

Weed opened her black coat. "I've got one, too."

Zoe remained silent.

Treena's sneering face melted into a mask of terror, as though her worst nightmare was finally being realised. "Oh my God!"

Treena looked down again at the red dot on her chest. It was now bouncing wildly as Wade hustled up the corridor towards them.

She began to wet herself, urine streaming down her legs and forming a frothy yellow pool at her feet.

Zoe hopped aside to avoid the splashing.

Wade arrived and watched for ten long seconds until she finished.

Treena was shaking.

"I'm disappointed in you, Treena, I always thought you were such a cool chick." Wade lowered his voice, "This will be our little secret, Treena, just the four of us – and a worldwide TV audience."

By now Treena had closed her eyes and it didn't look like she was going to open them again any time soon.

"Sit down." Wade shared none of the compassion that seemed to furrow Weed's brow.

Eyes still closed, Treena's back slid down the locker as she slowly sat in her own puddle.

Wade shifted his laser dot to Zoe's chest. "Sit next to her."

Zoe took one step aside and began lowering herself.

"Sit NEXT to her," Wade repeated the command as he pulled her back to her feet to try again.

Zoe was a little firecracker, trained by her single-parent mother and brought up, like her sisters, to trust or fear no one – especially men. "I'm not sitting in *her* pee!"

Wade placed his muzzle under Zoe's chin and tilted her head back against her locker.

He moved in, eye to eye, and whispered in her ear while nodding his head towards Weed. "You and Treena were bound together by your cruelty to this girl. And now you're going to let that bond be dissolved by a little puddle of pee?"

Zoe dared not move.

"Are you a pretty girl?"

Zoe just swallowed.

"ARE .... YOU .... A .... PRETTY .... GIRL?" Wade emphasised each word through gritted teeth.

"Whatever you say." Zoe was now like a dog exposing its throat in submission, all fight gone, seeking only to appease.

"Do *you* think you're a pretty girl?"

"Yes. I do."

Wade shifted the Ruger's muzzle from Zoe's throat, to the side of her nose. "How pretty would you be without a nose?"

"Don't do it, Wade, please. Just let her sit," Weed pleaded weakly.

There it was, proof that Wade's relationship with Weed – that precious relationship – offered Wade his first opportunity in life to demonstrate the mercy and protection that he had never received himself.

Wade stepped back and levelled the Ruger again at Zoe's chest.

"You need to thank this girl for saving your nose."

Zoe looked down at the rifle as she spoke, almost as though she was trying to see if a bullet was on the way. "Thank you, Wendy."

She didn't sound insincere.

"Don't you have anything else to say?" Wade prodded.

"Thank you, Wendy, for saving my nose."

"What about the way you always spoke to her?"

"I'm sorry, Wendy, for the way I spoke to you."

"Look her in the eye when you say you're sorry."

Zoe turned to Weed, who was now crying silently.

"I'm sorry, Wendy, for the way I spoke to you."

"For years," added Wade.

"I'm sorry, Wendy, for the way we *all* treated you, for years."

"That's okay," Weed whispered gently, eyes downcast.

"Look at that, isn't it amazing what an apology and a loaded gun can do to heal a relationship? Now sit in your puddle like a good little girl."

Zoe took her appointed place on the floor next to Treena, who was still shaking violently with her eyes closed.

23

"Mr. SPIT-zer …. I should have known."

Even your name can be used as a weapon against you, when spewed from the mouth of an enemy.

Mrs. Forman, the deputy principal, had emerged from her office in response to Pam's phone call. As usual, she split Leon's name into two distinct syllables and emphasised the "Spit". She had taken an instant disliking to Leon as soon as they met, and they had crossed swords on many occasions over the last eighteen months.

"What is it *this time*, Leon?"

Leon waited humbly at the reception counter, no rifle in sight. Pam was still seated at her desk, her back turned to the emerging deputy principal.

"Sorry, Mrs. Forman, I thought it was a mufti day, so I didn't wear my school uniform. And now I need a permission note to get into class."

"It's almost lunch time – are you just arriving now?"

"Lunch time? Oh no, my new watch must have stopped! I guess that means I'll need two permission notes now, Mrs. Forman."

"And what exactly is that on your head?"

"It's part of a school project, Mrs. Forman. Can you give me a note so I can wear it to class?"

"So that's *three* permission notes now, Mr. Spitzer. Anything else while we're at it?"

"Not unless I need a note to bring this to class, do I?" Leon slipped the M1 from under his coat and laid it on the reception counter.

"That thing isn't loaded, is it?" Mrs. Forman's sarcasm was suddenly mixed with serious concern for everyone's safety.

"Oh, absolutely." Leon rested his hand on the carbine, almost as if to soothe its hurt feelings at being called a "thing".

Because Leon's tone was so naive and non-threatening, Mrs. Forman resumed the upper hand. "You're lucky that someone hasn't been killed already, bringing a loaded gun to school like that."

"Fear not, Mrs. F, couldn't have happened – we all agreed that you'd be the first to die today."

Leon picked up the rifle and aimed the red dot of death at her chest.

Both their demeanours changed – quickly. He was now confidently, arrogantly in command. She was livid.

"You're about to step into a whole world of trouble, young man, that even your father can't buy you out of."

"Any more advice, Mrs. Forman? You've always been like a grandmother to me, or an evil stepmother – you're such a sour old bat."

"You're an arrogant little boy, a spoilt little brat ...."

The .30 calibre gunshot was deafening within the confines of the office. A splash of red appeared on her blouse before Mrs. Forman crumpled behind the counter.

The bullet tore through the deputy principal's chest and esophagus, exiting below her left shoulder blade, and shattering the framed "Learn to Live" school motto hanging on the wall directly behind her.

Leon looked down at the body. "Maybe we should drive a stake through her heart – I don't want her coming back to life at the next full moon."

It sounded like Pam was laughing at his black humour, but when Leon turned she was actually sobbing, her head lying on her desk, her arms trying to blot out all sight and sound.

Earl Kennedy burst from his inner office, shouting "WHAT WAS THAT?"

Earl looked at Leon and his rifle, then he bent down to Mrs. Forman and felt for a pulse in her neck. "Pam, call an ambulance. Leon, put that gun down. We'll try CPR."

Earl knelt beside his deputy principal, his friend of twenty-one years. Eva Forman was a much-respected English teacher from Sydney. When her husband's four-year fight with cancer required too much of her time to carry on the classroom workload, Earl offered her the deputy's job at Hunter High – 8:00 a.m. to 4:00 p.m., no classroom stress, no lessons to prepare, no work at home.

It was only after she arrived in Newcastle, that Earl realised the toll that the cancer had taken on her, too. Eva was no longer a light and inspiration to the students. She was pessimistic and short-fused. And then when her adult son, their only child, was killed in a boating accident, Earl helplessly watched the final souring of a once-sweet heart as he tried to keep her busy in the office and away from the students.

Earl once painfully overheard her discussing Leon with one of the other staff members – bitterly referring to him as "The Golden Boy".

She jealously assumed that the Spitzer heir had no problems of his own, while Leon never considered the context of her life outside the office.

Leon now promptly rescinded each of Mr. Kennedy's three directives. "Pam already made her last phone call for the day, I'm not finished with my rifle yet, thank you, and resuscitation is hopeless."

"We don't know that," said Earl, placing his hands upon Forman's chest to begin CPR.

Leon shot her in the head where she lay. "We do now."

Earl vaulted to his feet, fists clenched, Eva Forman's blood and brain matter now splattered all over his face and shirt.

Leon pointed his M1 at Pam's head. "Your job description has just been changed, Mr. Kennedy. Your number one priority as principal here today is to keep the body count down and to help save lives."

Pam, back turned and still covering her head, didn't even know she had just become a pawn.

"What do you want me to do?" Kennedy was inquiring, not necessarily submitting.

"Get on that public address intercom of yours and instruct all staff and students to remain in their classrooms – no exceptions. Tell them you have to do a brief security check, and then each class will be escorted to the assembly, in turn."

When Hunter High School was first built, the Department of Education had installed an internal intercom system as a state trial, similar to those used in many North American schools. Admin staff could make announcements to any or all of the classrooms, conduct two-way conversations, or even eavesdrop electronically – enabling many teachers in Canada and the States to leave their student charges unattended, under threat of monitoring any classroom antics from the office.

But the expense, and the subsequent complaints by the Australian teachers' union over potential abuse of workplace surveillance by admin staff, halted any widespread installations – despite the Department of Education pointing out that a red light was illuminated in the classroom whenever the intercom was activated and, therefore, no truly *covert* eavesdropping on teaching staff was possible.

Leon's instructions to Earl Kennedy were meant to eliminate panic. If only all teachers and students could be contained in their classrooms for twenty minutes, then the Dregs could go calmly from room to room, flexi-cuff everyone with their cable ties, locate and segregate the targets on their blacklist, and begin the judgement around 12:10.

"Instead of concentration camps we're using auditoriums now, are we? And you expect me to be an accomplice to this massacre?"

"I was hoping you'd assist us in *avoiding* a massacre, and carrying out a surgical operation."

"I see no surgeon before me now, just a butcher. Up until today I've always admired you, Leon. I think you have huge potential in life – for good or for evil. It's not too late for you to stop all of this."

"*I'm* giving the lessons here today, thanks just the same, Earl. So what do you say?"

"Nothing," Kennedy muttered to himself, almost indecipherably.

"What was that?"

Conviction and resolve were suddenly etched into Earl Kennedy's face. He looked Leon in the eye and announced his decision clearly. "NOTHING. The only thing necessary for the triumph of evil, is for good men to do nothing."

Earl threw himself towards the wall, and his hand shot out for the red fire alarm behind him.

Leon fired the M1 from point-blank range and the 110 grain bullet entered the principal's abdomen at 600 metres per second, one inch below his beloved tie clip. Impacting with a force of 967 foot-pounds, it shattered the principal's liver, deflected off his eighth rib, and severed his spinal cord.

No one can say for certain whether the still-living Earl Kennedy pulled the alarm in the last heroic moment of his life, or whether the momentum of the already-dead Earl Kennedy pulled it while collapsing unconscious to the floor.

The only thing we *can* be certain of is that all of Leon Spitzer's hopes for a precise and surgical operation were dashed at 11:49 when that fire alarm was activated.

24

With very few exceptions, New South Wales police officers are prohibited from bringing their firearms home. Ronnie MacDonald was one of those exceptions, because of his constant travelling to present tactical seminars around the state. So, ironically, Ronnie – who never carried a gun "in the streets" himself – regularly brought home a vast array of weapons, while officers who carried them daily in self-defence were not allowed.

Alison had always suggested that Ronnie segregate his police work from his family life – and Ronnie always listened, agreed, and complied. A tiny rudder can alter the course of a huge ship, and the smallest of decisions can save a thousand lives.

After their first child Drew was born, and while he was still only crawling, Ronnie MacDonald's wife Alison insisted that he unload and lock up his police handgun each night when he came home – initially his .38 calibre Smith & Wesson revolver and then, with the upgrade to semi-automatics, his .40 calibre Glock – along with any other items from the police arsenal that he might be transporting.

And, a few years later, when their boys grew old enough to understand his work details as shared with Alison over dinner, Ronnie stopped discussing them.

So Ronnie could never remember a time when there was not this safety barrier between his police business and his home life – whether that was firearm safety or keeping criminal activities and gruesome details away from little ears – for the purpose of protecting his family.

But Ronnie's thinking changed around the time that Drew, his oldest son, enrolled at Hunter High. The boy's descent into darkness was like a chronic disease plaguing the family – always there, hovering, central but unmentioned, setting the tone, determining the agenda, stealing life from the other children.

Ten months before the siege, Ronnie had confided in a police counsellor (but not in his wife) a sense of foreboding that Drew no longer needed to be insulated from his father's police work, but vice versa.

Ronnie was not worried that the sullen teenager might use the Glock on himself in depression but, rather, against the world in anger. Ronnie was no longer afraid that the details of criminal activities and gruesome assaults would frighten his son but, rather, inspire him.

And so, when the Department of Education called in Technical Consultant Police Inspector Ronnie MacDonald to advise them on high school security and surveillance around the state, he didn't tell his son Drew. Nor did he share with Drew his advice and directives about Hunter High School specifically, nor about the private security contractor's secret installations there during the Easter school break as advised and overseen by Ronnie himself.

Little rudder, small decision.

And thus when Druid returned to Hunter High in April, he smirked along with all the other students at the new little ceiling-mounted cameras with their tiny red blinking lights now positioned at each end of the main corridor – unaware that they were dummies, fake cameras with battery-operated lights, wired to nothing and transmitting to nowhere.

Technologically worthless but strategically priceless, their purpose was twofold. First, to discourage students from minor misdemeanours with the knowledge that they were being watched. And, second, to outsmart serious felony offenders who thought that destroying the dummy cameras ended all surveillance. It did not.

25

The four Dregs outside the central admin office had heard nothing for the first couple of minutes, according to plan – followed by Leon's first muffled gunshot, which was totally unplanned and came as a surprise to the four of them.

Leon was *supposed* to enter the admin office (before the CCTV monitors alerted staff to call the police), cut the phone lines, coerce Earl Kennedy at gunpoint to make a schoolwide announcement over the public address system (keeping staff and students in their classrooms), handcuff all admin staff, and bring them out to the corridor.

The four Dregs knew that Leon had put Forman on the blacklist, but he had not informed them of his plans to execute her immediately. That information he had noted only in his secret diary.

At 11:47 the only thing they knew for certain was that the admin office's double set of doors had muffled the shot sufficiently so that none of the occupants in any of the classrooms or other offices would have heard a thing through their closed doors – the Dregs themselves barely did in the open corridors.

Wade and Weed could do nothing more than hold their appointed positions in the right wing. Treena and Zoe were sitting in silence, and no one emerged from any of the classrooms, so Wade ran back to his assigned sentry point at the right junction.

Druid finally emerged from the toilets and enraged Slave by heading over towards Wade, possibly to discuss the gunshot.

Wade signalled him to return to his post in the left wing and, when he didn't, Wade aimed his laser in the redhead's general direction. Druid mugged a terrified expression, raised his hands playfully into the air and kept them up while returning to Slave.

Next came Forman's fatal second shot and, less than a minute later, Kennedy's.

The once-quiet corridors then erupted with the deafening blare of the fire alarms.

The closest Newcastle fire station was only four minutes away from Hunter High at top speed, perhaps less once the dispatcher notified firefighters that the alarm originated at a Priority One location – multiple lives at risk – such as a school, high-rise building, cinema, shopping mall, hospital, nursing home, chemical storage facility or the like. All Priority One alarms were overseen by district superintendents who typically dispatched at least a dozen vehicles – including police, fire, rescue, and ambulance – even before fire captains on the scene had a chance to call for support.

Besides for the main entrance of Hunter High, there were double access doors at the top of each wing. In order to contain fire, cut off oxygen supply, and limit fatalities, each wing was also fitted with a set of fire doors at the point of junction with the main corridor.

These fire-resistant doors were very heavy and hinged at an angle so as to close of their own accord. They were, however, held open by electromagnets. Pulling any of the fire alarms throughout the school initiated three immediate and simultaneous electronic responses: the fire bells throughout the school were loudly activated, the Newcastle Fire Department's alarm-monitoring system received notification, and power to the electromagnets holding open the fire doors at the two wing junctions was cut off. The heavy doors, thus released, swung closed by their own weight and could only be reopened from *inside* the wings.

In theory, the fire threat was thereby contained and limited to only one third of the school and no one from the main corridor – the base of the horseshoe – could go running off into the building's extremities. The oft-repeated drill instruction for all staff and students was "when the fire alarm sounds, immediately vacate the section of the building where you are located, through that section's external exit doors."

The four Dregs, now surprised by the unexpected fire alarms, shot panicked glances back and forth between each other. The electromagnets let go their grip, and the heavy fire doors swung closed to seal off the two wings.

Wade blocked the fire door open with his body, signalled to Weed to prepare for the coming tidal wave of fleeing students, and positioned himself to cover both the right end of the main corridor as well as their own right wing.

Seething at Druid's antics, Slave had left his junction and stepped toward the returning incompetent. When the alarm sounded, they both bolted back towards their left wing junction. Druid, ice-empowered and judgement-impaired, got there first and jammed his left hand between the heavy fire doors.

Druid screamed as the closing doors sliced off the tips of his pinkie and ring fingers.

The stealth and surprise attack of moments before was now replaced with alarm bells, Druid's howling, Slave swearing Slavic curses at the doors that had locked themselves before him, and the clamour of two dozen classroom doors being flung open and 710 students migrating towards the exits.

Leon emerged from the admin office, gently leading Pam by the hand, with an ironically placid grin on his face. He seemed deeply gratified to be surrounded by all this chaos of his own creation.

Roughly half of the emerging students from the right wing looked up to Weed's exit and half down to Wade's, everyone wondering whether it was an actual fire or just a drill.

Wade opened up with a magazine load of bullets. Fired first into the ceiling-mounted surveillance camera right above his head, the deafening shots were amplified and echoed in the enclosed space, each of the twenty-five mini-explosions setting off a little shock wave of its own that was felt thudding against each person's chest.

The Dregs had agreed that the surveillance cameras installed last Easter had to be top-priority targets, to be crushed quietly with rifle butts after Kennedy's intercom announcement. Situated inside their smokey-grey perspex bubbles at the two junction points, the cameras were rumoured to cover all corridors and might even transmit a live feed to the police.

Then Wade aimed for the large windows that ran the length of the right wing, above the lockers. These windows were intended to allow light from the classrooms into the corridor – and only light, they were too high to provide a view of anything or anybody in the classrooms.

Their large panes of glass at first registered only small .22 calibre bullet holes, but soon they exploded under the barrage of semi-automatic gunfire.

Wade had accomplished his mission – to rip everyone's attention from the fire alarm and the attempted exodus. Glass smashed, flew, and fell everywhere. Students screamed, and a dozen began bleeding from flying glass debris.

One pretty little Year Seven girl, Tessa Briggs, was hit by small shards in both eyes and subsequently became a media sweetheart as Australia followed her medical battle in the news – first losing one eye, and then fifty per cent of her vision in the other.

After the first three weeks of daily media attention, she vanished from the newspaper pages and the television screens altogether as the news editors moved on to newer, fresher, human interest stories. She wouldn't have lasted even those three weeks, had she not been so photogenic.

"I've got some good news and some bad news," Wade yelled above the fire alarm. "The good news is that it's a false alarm. There *is* no fire. No one is in danger of being burned."

The acrid smell of gunpowder hung in the air. Wisps of smoke curled out of the Ruger's muzzle.

Wade dropped the empty magazine onto the floor, loaded another from his black pouch, and cocked the bolt.

"The bad news is that if you all don't turn around and head right back into the classrooms you just left, I'm going to start killing people – and I'm not alone. Weed!"

The always-quiet girl, who never raised her voice, now raised her Ruger as she shot out the as-yet-untouched windows on the other side of the wing, but much more slowly and meticulously than Wade had.

"Leon!"

Spitzer, still outside the admin office, responded to Wade's call by first shooting out the surveillance cameras above the left wing junction point with two direct hits from a four-shot volley.

The perspex dome covering the cameras was a very small target at such a distance, and Spitzer's accuracy reflected years of practice.

Then Leon swung his M1 around behind him, aimed into the lobby, and shot the glass trophy cases and framed photos of sports teams and graduating classes to bits with the remaining twenty-three bullets in his magazine.

For a moment, the 348 students in the right wing stood stunned, and the dozen teachers among them just as shocked.

Weed loaded a fresh metallic green magazine into her Ruger and thoughtfully placed the empty orange one back in her ammo pouch – choosing not to add to the glass debris already littering the corridor.

Then Mr. Sartor, the science teacher, began issuing commands above the cacophony of alarm bells, "You heard Aron. Keep quiet, cooperate, return to class now, and no one will get hurt."

"*I'll* decide who gets hurt – *not* Mr. Sartor!" Wade yelled out to the students. He turned to Sartor and lowered his voice, though his threat was still captured by the Immortal Mics, "I've asked you for years not to call me Aron – do it again and I'll kill you."

Then Wade raised his voice again to continue addressing the crowd, "And before you return to your classrooms, every one of you drop your phones – right now, right where you are, right on the floor."

According to school rules, all mobile phones were to be turned off and left in the students' lockers until after the dismissal bell at 3:10. According to the rules.

But dozens of prohibited phones now dropped to the floor. Three or four brands, in a dozen different colours – perhaps forty phones in all.

Wade reinforced his threat, "Possession of a phone has just become a capital offence in this school. And capital offence means capital punishment."

Many students had grabbed their school bags and backpacks when the fire evacuation began. They weren't supposed to, and that had been clearly explained to them in previous fire drills – "stop what you're doing, take nothing with you, evacuate your section of the building as quickly and calmly as possible, through that section's external exit". Some students had forgotten the directive, others just chose to ignore it.

And, now that Wade had just announced the death penalty, more phones were dug out of bags and pockets and dumped on the floor.

Expensive and once-treasured toys – now just so much multicoloured techno-litter atop a crystalline base of broken glass, about to be trampled by 360 pairs of feet.

Phones surrendered by students who, just minutes before, would have sworn they could not live without them – easily discarded now because they were told they could not live with them.

Sudden re-evaluation. Instant currency conversion in the kingdom of the Dregs. Values clarification at the muzzle of a gun.

In the face of death, priorities suddenly change. Options are fewer, and decisions easier.

As the now-decellularised students and faculty headed off to their appointed classrooms, Wade called after them, "And that goes for all tablets and laptops as well as phones – in your pockets, in your bags, in your classrooms – I want them all tossed out here in the corridor within the next two minutes."

It was all part of Leon's master plan.

Certainly Leon wanted to sever all communication between the hostages and the police outside – for any intelligence passed on could and would be used strategically against the Dregs.

But Leon had also emphasised the demoralising power of hostages *feeling isolated* from the outside world and distanced from any potential rescuers. "The greatest weapon to be confiscated from the enemy in any battle is hope," Leon had told his Dregs.

An ironic comment from a commander who had himself given up all hope in the future. Ironic but not exceptional, for often the only aspiration of the hopeless is to crush the hope of others – dwellers of darkness, whose mission it is to extinguish all light.

Wade's final command up the wing, "And we need every curtain and blind closed in every classroom *immediately.*"

Leon's three-part directive being enforced: physical, auditory, and visual containment – detained in classrooms, communication devices confiscated, all windows covered.

Closing all the classroom curtains would frustrate immediately any police officers watching through binoculars, and eventually those armed with telescopic sights. Leon knew that the tactical squad, if they ever arrived, would err on the side of caution. But if they happened to line up all five Dregs in their sights at any one time, they might just risk five simultaneous shots.

And there was also a second, psychological, reason for closing the curtains. Leon had referred his Dregs to a laboratory study of rats placed in buckets of water to face certain drowning. Those nearing exhaustion that were lifted, even momentarily, out of the water to see beyond the bucket, and then returned to the water, continued swimming for much longer than those who were never even given a glimpse of freedom. Closing the classroom curtains removed from the hostages the sight – and therefore the hope – of a world outside of Hunter High.

I am familiar with that study because I was the one who originally told Leon about it.

Weed and Wade's forehead-mounted Dregcams, positioned at opposite ends of the right wing, each recorded the haunting image of two hundred more phones, tablets, and laptops, being tossed from twelve different classrooms and onto the growing pile of digital debris strewn along the length of the hallway.

Then the corridor grew steadily darker as the closing curtains and blinds in a dozen classrooms eerily blotted out more and more of the outdoor illumination.

The black stormy sky had contributed little external daylight into the right wing but, now that all blinds were being closed, it appeared as though the weakened sun had set in sixty seconds – and darkness, indeed, had fallen on Hunter High.

26

But while Wade and Weed had been regaining control, Slave and Druid had been losing it.

Half the students in the left wing were filing calmly towards the fire doors of the main corridor (forgetting their fire drill instructions to exit externally at the top of the wing) and would have quite happily opened them to walk right into the waiting arms of Slave.

But Druid went berserk, yanking on the locked handles, screaming wildly, and hammering his fists on the glass windows of the door. The windows quickly became smeared with the blood spurting from the stumps of his amputated fingertips – and then the students heard the roar of Leon's M1 above the blaring fire alarm, and stopped in their tracks.

They stepped back from the door. Druid screamed and pointed his Ruger at them through the window.

The students turned and fled, joining their peers who had begun exiting at the top end of the left wing.

Druid opened fire at the window. It was made of double-paned, fire-resistant glass and reinforced with internal wire mesh. His .22 calibre bullets first cracked, then shattered the window but Druid's muzzle was still obstructed by the undamaged mesh. His first shots ricocheted dangerously off the wire, so Druid wriggled the muzzle between the mesh grid and fired erratically from weird and restricted angles. With each passing second he grew more crazed, and his firing more erratic, while his screaming targets fled further up the wing.

"We're losing them!" shouted Slave as he ran towards the glass-strewn lobby and the school's front doors. Druid now abandoned his vendetta with the mesh and was hot on Latska's heels growling, literally growling, in anger that hostages should be so uncooperative.

By this time, Leon was standing with Pam Blain at the door of the staff lounge, greeting the emerging teachers, smoke curling from the muzzle of his M1, as he called out after Slave. "Be back in two minutes, no longer — we need you *in here*!"

Slave shouted back "Okay!" before exiting. He and Druid ran down the front steps and to the right, through the blinding rain, along the grassy slope at the front of the school building, and turned right again at the end of the main block.

In the distance Latska could see the last of the 362 students and twelve teachers pouring out of the fire exit at the top of the left wing and into the waiting storm, obscured by poor visibility and dispersing in all directions.

27

Once the commando training scheme was mothballed across the state, the eleven-man Newcastle State Protection Support Unit asked to meet with Dixon off-duty, off the record, and over a beer.

The eleven Newcastle officers felt undermined by the new state government's funding cuts and feared, more than anything else, that their full potential to save lives in a crisis might never be realised. So they called a meeting to talk with the only man who seemed a kindred spirit in their passionate commitment to protect Newcastle — and in their betrayal at the hands of state politicians.

Dixon calmed their fears by sharing with them his as-yet-unannounced appointment as their commander. Any training and support to be cut back from the police budget would be more than compensated by their new SAS instructor, with two decades of combat training and experience.

Unlike the full-time State Protection Group based in Sydney, the Newcastle Support Unit was comprised of volunteer officers, on-call twenty-four hours a day, who might or might not be working other duties when a local crisis required an immediate tactical response.

Each of the eleven men carried his black tactical uniform, kevlar helmet, bulletproof vest, communications gear, weapons, ammunition, and explosives in two black sports bags, locked in the boot of his personal or on-duty vehicle. Their mobile phones were always to be left on – but they were never to act other than as a support to the State Protection Group from Sydney, and only as ordered. Just like every other Support Unit around the state.

But, unlike any other Support Unit, they now pumped the SAS officer for *his* take on things.

No member of any New South Wales tactical Support Unit had undergone Dixon's five-day commando course – it was geared for general-duty officers only – nor had any of his graduate police commandos (they called themselves "paintballers") ever had the chance to participate in his proposed follow-up team-building exercises.

Dixon's ultimate vision for local commando tactical squads was a hybrid – *a team of individuals,* each trained and ready to execute Immediate Action, Rapid Deployment on their own.

The potential was awesome. Even if several suicidal gunmen were to fan out (in a shopping mall, for example) and each head off on their own mini-rampage, several police commandos could coordinate themselves in seconds and, conceivably, kill all gunmen within minutes – a vast improvement over the original SWAT containment tactics.

But even though the *potential* of such local police commando teams was awesome, its *implementation* had been tethered, and mired, and muzzled by government policy – because, if such IARD tactics worked, it was a political slap in the face to Buster and its proponents.

The Newcastle team listened – to every word – and caught his vision. Then, after that initial beer, in their own free time and paying their own expenses, the eleven volunteer officers, led and trained (and paintballed) by Dixon, went on to become the first twelve-man IARD team in the state, and the only such team in the country – albeit unrecognised, unauthorised, and renamed.

Under the radar, and among their colleagues, they were now referred to as the Newcastle Swat team – "*swat*" as in "squash an insect fast – before it stings".

Their police overseers eventually got wind of their commando-style training, and begrudgingly allowed them to continue their off-duty "war games". But, they were warned, while on-duty all twelve members of the Newcastle Support Unit were expected to toe the line and follow orders – or risk dismissal.

And that was their mandate at 11:52 on Black Friday, when Acting Police Sergeant Gary Dixon was investigating the risk of lead poisoning due to improper ventilation at the Newcastle indoor police shooting range – doubly ironic, thought Dixon, that cops trained there to kill yet worried about their own health risks and, also, that "lead poisoning" was an old Hollywood euphemism from the 1930s for getting shot.

Dixon had authorised exhaust and airflow analysis of the lead levels in the building, and was now driving away, when his mobile phone beeped to signal its long-anticipated, yet much-dreaded, text message: "multiple shooters, hunter high, respond immediately".

28

The staff lounge was located just to the right of the admin office. The doorway to the lounge now jammed with eight teachers, admin office assistant Carol Spargo, and Mrs. Argyle the librarian – most of them holding mugs, and all of them stunned by the speed with which their school had been transformed into a battleground, by the apparent ease with which all control and authority had been wrenched from their hands.

The teachers stared at Leon's M1, and its laser sight, while the fire alarm continued to blare. Leon just ignored it while he smirked back at them all. The scene was quite surreal.

"You're probably all wondering why I called this little meeting – there are a number of serious student grievances that require urgent discussion. First and foremost, there's the issue of the school uniform. As substitute principal, I have declared this a reverse mufti day, which means that all students can dress in the clothes of their choosing while you, the staff, must all wear those stupid school uniforms and see how *you* feel."

Dr. Suman Khoury, mathematical genius from India and head of the math and science departments, pushed himself forward from the inner sanctum of the staff lounge and into the corridor. "Where is Mr. Kennedy?"

"I had to terminate him, and the deputy principal. Didn't I, Pam?"

Pam shook her head, perhaps trying to dislodge the nightmare of the double murder she had just overheard, perhaps signalling her inability to respond, or her unwillingness to confirm the reality she was trying to deny.

"What happened?" Dr. Khoury pressed for details.

"Hunting accident," replied Leon, "I was actually stalking *you*, Dr. Khoury."

Khoury was visibly shaken by the threat.

"Just kidding!" Leon erupted into laughter, impressed by his own performance as emcee to a global audience. "And while you are all so rudely staring at my forehead camera and plastic ears, the world is staring at you. Now let's see how *you* like being under constant observation and scrutiny for a change."

"Why are you doing this?" asked Dr. Khoury.

"I didn't see a hand," Leon shook his finger at Dr. Khoury in reprimand, "you really *must* raise your hand when you have a question, otherwise there will be chaos in the classrooms and I won't stand for it."

Dr. Khoury raised his hand and prepared to ask again.

"I'm not going to answer your questions, Doctor, because I am in a bad mood, and when teachers are in a bad mood they take it out on their students. The good news is that you will only have to suffer my bad mood until 12:30."

Leon pointed to the little librarian behind Dr. Khoury. "Mrs. Argyle! Would you please be a dear and escort the Pamburger here to the auditorium? She's just now suffered quite a shock and the quiet of the auditorium might settle her a bit. We all know that you're obsessed with quiet, Mrs. Argyle, so I thought of you right away."

Mrs. Argyle sought clarification. "But what …. ?"

"SHUT UP, Mrs. Argyle, PLEASE!! I'm very disappointed in you, as a librarian you should know better – I can barely hear that fire alarm with all your chatter. Now off you go, the two of you."

Mrs. Argyle complied without another word.

Leon called after them. "Oh and, Pam, I expect a fifteen-hundred-word essay about '*Escalating School Violence*' – on my desk, first thing Monday morning. That should ruin your weekend."

Suddenly Leon looked up, pressed the earpiece further into his right ear and said to himself, "The fire trucks have arrived."

The police scanner in the right hip pocket of his Driza-Bone was yet another perk of leadership denied the other Dregs.

"I'm afraid I'll have to ask you all to step back into the staff lounge for a minute while I handcuff you, confiscate your mobile phones, and adjust your landline." Leon herded the nine staff members with his outstretched arms – as if they were chickens, or sheep – while pulling Pam's stolen scissors from the pocket of his long, black raincoat.

29

Slave and Druid had to cover ninety metres of very soggy, sloping grass to reach the outside junction of the left wing. Druid stopped at the corner of the building, still eighty metres short of the fire exit, and yelled at the fleeing students, "Get back in your dungeon where you belong!"

While Slave ran ahead, Druid shouldered his Ruger and prepared to fire, but he was panting heavily, trembling with anger from all his door pounding, and at pains to hold the rifle stock with his two amputated fingertips. He pulled – and jerked – the trigger five times, instead of squeezing it.

The bullets went wild, he ran out of ammunition, Slave stopped and yelled back that he had just almost shot him – a fellow Dreg.

Druid had, so far, wounded no one inside through the wire-meshed window, nor outside through the storm. By the time he had loaded a new magazine, the red dragon had arrived.

The two-man crew of Pumper 57, the first of six fire trucks racing to the scene, could see no smoke emerging from Hunter High School as they approached. But visibility was limited by the heavy rain, windscreen wipers, their speed, and the need to keep a lookout for civilian traffic. Firemen Harvey Pitkin and Jordan Reece were heading towards the school's front entrance when they noticed dozens of students bursting forth from an exit almost a hundred metres away and off to their left.

Pitkin steered well clear of the deserted construction shed in the parking lot and headed towards the exit, hoping to question the students and assess the situation. They still saw no signs of fire, but mentioned between themselves that the kids were obviously terrified of something to ignore the rain like that.

Slave and Druid only heard the siren of Pumper 57 as it pulled into the high school parking lot, in auditory competition as it was with the fire alarms ringing beside them.

Slave turned to look at the vehicle, but resumed running. Potentially half of the faces on their blacklist were escaping from their clutches, and a fire truck posed them no real threat.

Druid, however, pointed his freshly-loaded Ruger at the truck and started yelling "Dungeons and dragons! Dungeons and dragons! Behold the red dragon!"

Pitkin and Reece had initially dismissed the running Dregs as just two more students fleeing in the rain, never even seeing their rifles due to the poor visibility. But now the firefighters skidded to a stop – the front wheels of their truck mounting the curb of the parking lot near the corner of the left wing – thinking that Druid was yelling out directions or information about the emergency.

Reece turned off his siren, rolled down the passenger window, stuck his head into the downpour, and yelled, "What's up?"

Druid yelled back "Beware the eyes of the dragon – and behold the dragon slayer!"

Druid emptied his magazine, all twenty-five shots, towards the big glass eyes of the fire truck's windscreen.

His first shot went wide as he brought the rifle up to his shoulder, and the bullet passed through Reece's neck – narrowly missing his larynx, carotid artery, and spinal cord.

Within seconds Reece had grabbed his wound and Pitkin had pulled him back into the cab and down to the floor, while their heat-and-shock-resistant windscreen was peppered with bullet holes, then crystallised, then turned flaccid under the barrage.

Glass particles rained down upon the two huddled firefighters but the windscreen remained intact for the most part, though now totally opaque.

"Have you got the bleeding?" asked Pitkin.

"Pretty well," Reece whispered back, both hands around his throat and covered with blood, "but I don't know about the carotid and I'm not moving."

Pitkin grabbed the radio mike. "Pumper 57, Mayday, Mayday. Shots fired, repeat, shots fired at Hunter High School – keep out of the parking lot! Reece is already hit."

30

Dixon activated the red and blue strobe lights mounted on his dashboard and hidden within the front grille of his black, unmarked police Landcruiser. He allowed his siren a five-second warning blast before he slammed on the brakes, waited for a momentary gap in the traffic, then mounted the grass median and roared down the highway in the opposite direction.

Even as the oncoming cars swerved to avoid his daring U-turn, Dixon did the math. Of the eleven men under his command in the Newcastle Swat team, he knew that two were out of state together on a fishing trip, a third was recovering from surgery on sick leave, and a fourth now in the labour ward with his wife – Dixon had spoken to him not even thirty minutes earlier.

That left seven, but Dixon remembered that three of those seven had immediate or extended family members attending Hunter High as students or working on staff – he had previously discussed his team's links to Newcastle schools with this very scenario in mind.

While en route to the scene, he called their mobile phones which, he knew, would have each received the same "multiple shooters" text message that he had.

Dixon spoke to each of the three empathically, yet with uncompromising authority, and leaving no room for discussion – next of kin, conflict of interest, stand down immediately, attend at the scene only as a family member *after* logging off-duty at the station and stowing all weapons there.

The conversations were brief. Two of them were already off-duty and about to call Dixon to disqualify themselves. The third agreed to sign off at the police station before meeting his wife at the high school.

That left Dixon himself and four of his commandos – the best that Newcastle had to offer, each one personally trained, well-equipped, and surely racing to the school right now.

High school shooting, hundreds of targets. Dixon knew the stats: there was not one record of successful hostage negotiation at any school shooting, ever, anywhere around the world. That's because it was never *about* hostages or lists of demands, the motive was always revenge against offences real or imagined – the shooters usually roaming the halls, stalking their prey.

Eight minutes to Hunter High even with lights and siren – 480 seconds – and he would need every one of them. A surgeon has to clear his head before a major operation, a soldier has to focus. Remember the training, visualise the drill, slow the breathing, still the pounding heart, think "surgical operation, surgical operation" – not "slaughter" or "bloodbath".

31

Slave finally reached the fire exit at the top end of the left wing. Too late, he scanned his laser dot across the backs of the last twenty fleeing students and staff.

They were already thirty metres away, running into the storm, dispersing in all directions, most of them girls from Years Seven and Eight, a few stragglers being helped and guided by senior boys and a couple of female teachers.

Slave would never shoot a female, nor anyone in the back. It was, specifically, his senior male attackers that he had signed on for, and these boys weren't about to stop and identify themselves.

He lowered his rifle.

"I already told you, Brutha – you can't win this game."

Slave spun around to the voice behind him and his red laser dot came to rest on the heart of Luke, the school janitor and maintenance man.

Wearing his fluorescent yellow rain suit, Luke had been on the school's little tractor, in the farthest corner of the farthest playing field, digging up a plugged drain that only ever reared its head in serious downpours.

He had barely heard the fire alarm through his industrial earmuffs but, when he finally did, he tossed them aside, abandoned the tractor with its motor still running, and ran towards the school. On the way there, he heard several barrages of gunfire.

He had arrived at the fire exit just after a panicked herd of students burst forth. Luke had then held the heavy door open as he repeatedly directed the emerging students to disperse as far and as fast as possible, and to bob and weave while doing so.

Slave instantly recognised the tattooed face within the yellow fluoro hood. "And I told you, I am playing no game."

"I was young once, too, and angry. So I joined a gang, itching for a fight."

"And?"

"I fought – for years. Until I finally realised that no knife or bullet can ever win a battle that's raging inside here." His tattooed fist tapped his tattooed forehead.

"And inside here." His fist pounded lightly against his chest, ignoring Slave's red dot.

Slave lowered his rifle, ineffective as it was against a fearless man.

"The race is not to the swift, nor the battle to the strong," Luke finished.

"You go now." Slave jerked his head in the direction of the recent exodus.

"Don't you want to keep me as a hostage?"

"So you can help the other three hundred escape? I don't think so."

Slave placed the red dot back on the janitor's chest. "Three hundred I forgive you, seven hundred would make even *you* my enemy. I prefer to keep you as my friend. You go now, I have business to finish."

The two warriors stood toe to toe, staring at each other in silence for a few seconds until the stronger, the older, and the wiser, surrendered and turned to walk away in the downpour.

Slave called out after him, "How do you turn off this fire alarm?"

"You need two codes. Mr. Kennedy has one, fire department has the other."

But, at that very moment, Slave's partner in the rain was worsening an already bad relationship with the fire department. Druid, not satisfied with merely blinding the red dragon, decided now to cripple him. He loaded a full magazine and began circling the wounded fire engine, shooting each of its ten tyres two or three times until he was empty, then he reloaded.

Inside, huddled on the floor of the cab, Jordan Reece clutched his throat and wondered, should he die today, whether his wife Julie would remember their twelve initial years of relatively happy married life with the two boys, or just the last nine months of bickering with each other, stressed out as they were with baby Aimee and her seizures.

Tanker 16 received Harvey Pitkin's "Mayday" just as they pulled into the parking lot. The tanker stopped. Reversed. Stopped. Inched further into the parking lot. Stopped again.

The four firefighters inside the cab were willing to risk their lives for the stricken crew, but what to do? Risking and foolishly wasting were two different things. Their discussion was cut short by the first police vehicle on the scene, a dual cab Ford Ranger paddy wagon.

Sergeant Darren Hayes was behind the wheel as he pulled up alongside the second fire engine. He rolled down his window and yelled above the storm, the fire alarms, and all the converging sirens. "We don't want any more firefighters getting shot, get out and stay out – we'll call you in when we need you."

Sergeant Hayes headed over to the ambushed pumper. A uniformed street and patrol car cop for over two decades, Darren Hayes sometimes felt like he was getting too old for this job – a bit long in the tooth. But his current three-month stint as orientation supervisor to Probationary Constable Debbie Wassler had refreshed and energised him.

They were a perfect match – graduate-cadet Wassler eagerly tapped into his wealth of experience, and Hayes was reminded of his oldest daughter Rita every time he looked at Debbie. Rita now lived five hours away in Canberra, too busy and too distant.

Hayes had heard the initial Priority One call on their radio and volunteered to back them up – Debbie had not yet attended at any fire scenes. Then, when the "Mayday, shots fired" call came through, Hayes quickly tried to balance his responsibilities of training and support – and he had less than thirty seconds to do it before they reached the high school.

He and Wassler each carried the standard, service-issue .40 calibre Glock Model 22 semi-automatic pistol. With fifteen shots in the magazine the Glock was lethal enough but, compared to rifles, all handguns are limited in their effectiveness because of their shorter barrels.

The grooved rifling inside gun barrels causes bullets to rotate and spin as they race down the barrel. The longer the barrel, the greater the velocity created by pressurised gases, and the more controlled the spin – resulting in a much truer flight path, greater accuracy, and longer range. Even modern shotguns with their smooth-bored barrels, although powerful enough, can never really be relied upon as accurate or lethal beyond twenty metres.

In addition, the one or two-handed gripping of a handgun and limited sighting length down a relatively short pistol barrel can never match the extended arm support and the longer barrel sighting length of a rifle.

Repeatedly, when hearing testimony at the inquests, I was struck by these ballistics illustrations and I thought of the Dregs, indeed, thought of all teenagers.

I came to appreciate that each parent and teacher leaves unique and indelible "rifling" marks on each child – each "bullet" sent out into the world for good or for evil – and I wondered how much better off their lives would have turned out if only they had been given more time within the "rifling" influence of good parents and adult mentors.

How much better might their lives have been with more controlled spin, truer trajectory, greater accuracy, more power, longer range, extended arm support, and longer barrel sighting – instead of the sawn-off lives they had been dealt in the time-poor twenty-first century with its ever-deteriorating standards?

And, besides for the limitations of a handgun, there are the limitations of the officer holding it. An inexperienced young cadet like Wassler could only yet be expected to relate to her gun as a tool on a shooting range, not as a weapon in a fight for life.

True, most police officers around the world never discharge their weapons in the course of their whole careers, but even having to *draw it once,* in response to a potential threat, changed a cop's thinking and reflexes forever – and Wassler had no such prior experience.

But, since a green cadet with a Glock was all Hayes had to back him up, he had reminded Wassler to draw her weapon before they entered the parking lot and keep her finger off the trigger until aimed and ready to fire. That was good gun-handling technique generally, but *especially* with the Glocks and their three in-built safety mechanisms – trigger safety, firing pin safety, and drop safety – three independent safeties, automatically deactivated one after the other when the trigger is squeezed, and reactivated when the trigger is released. With a Glock there is no hammer to cock, no safety switch to operate, no possible accidental discharge when dropping the gun, no delay when lives are at stake.

"And no matter what happens out there, make sure you keep the Ford's engine between you and the shooter – cops crouching for cover behind car doors might look good in the movies, but its useless out in the street – only the engine block can really protect you."

Hayes didn't burden the young cadet with the fact that even an engine block would not stop the bullets from some magnum handguns and high-powered rifles – there was no time for such details, they didn't know what firepower they were about to face, and they were both scared enough already. Instead he reached out to squeeze her hand, to reassure her, and quell her trembling. Then he spoke harshly to her, "I'm depending on you, Wassler, don't you let me down."

"I won't, Sergeant," she replied, without taking her eyes off the stricken and fast-looming fire truck.

Hayes yelled into the radio mike before throwing it down, "Unit 11, returning fire at the high school."

32

During the course of his military career, Gary Dixon had handled hundreds of different weapons from all over the world – and mastered many. Yet he was without hesitation or reservation in supporting the State Protection Group's initial selection of the 5.56mm Colt AR-15 A3 Tactical Carbine as their weapon of choice – the compact semiautomatic with its adjustable, fully-retractable stock butt and thirty-shot magazine was actually one of his favourites. Finally they agreed on something.

Originally manufactured by ArmaLite in America, the AR-15 was an exceptionally light, powerful, accurate, and reliable semiautomatic – and Colt Firearms knew it, buying out the name "AR-15" and the manufacturing rights from ArmaLite just prior to America's involvement in the Vietnam war. The AR-15, renamed the M16 for issue to the U.S. Military, swept the world and proved to be hugely successful – eventually morphing into many different versions and models (including the smaller M4) as it offered not just semi-automatic, but also three-shot-burst, or fully automatic (machine gun) modes of fire.

Faced with the growing threat of urban terrorist attacks, Australian police were beginning to follow the lead of their international colleagues in arming specialised, highly mobile, anti-terrorist teams with M4 machine guns. That was alright for full-time tactical officers who trained constantly, Dixon argued, but regional Support Unit officers and IARD-trained street cops would be more effective staying with semi-automatics – he already faced enough challenges training general-duty officers to perform like commandos, without handing them automatic weapons to practise with on the firing range. (Into his crash course Dixon had incorporated a few hours training with AR-15's to provide foundational instruction, in anticipation of the day when such carbines might be standard issue in every police car.)

Dixon *always* argued passionately for precise, semi-automatic fire – because he would never forget what it was like to enter darkened rooms filled with innocents, and have only seconds to identify and neutralise a gunman.

When his statewide IARD vision was eventually quashed, Dixon had no choice but to funnel all that passion into his Newcastle team of eleven personally-trained police commandos – each armed with a small, black AR-15 carbine (its stock adjusted for a perfect body fit), and confident of placing single shots precisely where intended, every time.

To bolster such confidence, atop each of Dixon's AR-15's (standard issue to all Support Unit officers) he mounted a 4X Trijicon ACOG Scope (Advanced Combat Optical Gunsight). It cost his Swat team members fifteen hundred dollars each to purchase their own Trijicons, but it was worth it – far excelling the optics supplied by the state.

The ACOG was a rugged little telescopic sight designed for military and tactical applications, best used with both eyes open to allow coverage of constantly changing target ranges in all lighting conditions, including total darkness. Tough, cutting-edge, and even waterproof to a depth of one hundred metres. Fibre optics and self-luminous Tritium amplified ambient light and replaced the need for failure-prone batteries, while the scope's reticle included a bullet-drop compensator with range markings calibrated at one hundred metre intervals for targets between one hundred and eight hundred metres, eliminating the need for any scope adjustments while delivering both precise distance marksmanship and close-in aiming speed – near or far, wet or dry, day or night.

The ACOG sights were a battlefield breakthrough and quickly became standard issue for all U.S. Special Forces (Green Berets), with an additional 800,000 ACOG's (retail value one billion dollars) ordered by the U.S. Military and issued to troops in Iraq and Afghanistan – although such military contracts were only secured after the religiously and politically conservative Trijicon manufacturers agreed to refrain from inscribing any more Bible verses on their army-issued consignments.

I remember high school student Barbra Burser once commenting to me that although many combatants, politicians, and athletes, across the globe, seek after or boast of God on their side, very few ever seem to consider whether they are on His.

33

Hayes fishtailed to a stop in the flooded parking lot, between the dragon and the dragon slayer. The veteran cop had hoped to hit or kill the gunman with his paddy wagon, but Druid ducked quickly around the far side of the stricken pumper.

The two officers jumped out into the rain, shielded themselves on the left side of their vehicle and aimed towards the fire truck on their right – waiting for Druid to reappear.

Suddenly, gunfire erupted on their left, from the top of the grassy slope – Slave was trying to pin them down while he yelled for Druid to run back towards him and the fire exit. Both officers dove to the rear of their Ford Ranger as fifty .22 calibre bullets rained down upon them in crossfire from the two Dregs.

Photographs of their bullet-riddled paddy wagon would be broadcast around the world in only a few minutes – with Australian police, parents, and teachers shocked that such firepower could end up in the hands of their teenagers.

Hayes yelled into the mike on the shoulder epaulette of his uniform. "Unit 11, TWO shooters, not one – semi-automatic rifles."

Druid, firing on the run, had almost reached Slave at the top of the slope by the time they both ran out of ammunition. Hayes and Wassler emerged from the cover of their vehicle, and were about to start squeezing off .40 calibre return fire of their own, when the M1 opened up on their right.

Leon had been following Hayes' commentary on his police scanner and now stood waiting, unnoticed, at the high school entrance. When the cops took aim at the fleeing gunmen, Leon started laying down covering fire of his own so that Slave and Druid could dash back in through the fire exit. Leon had yelled instructions into his walkie-talkie, and now the boys were obeying them.

The more ferocious bark and bite of the M1 were immediately evident to Hayes and Wassler as they retreated back to the left side of their vehicle and crouched behind the engine block.

Leon was eighty metres away from the police, holding his carbine freehand – unable to support it on a wall or tree branch – and forced to squint through the rain, so the accuracy of his fire was not great. Not efficient, perhaps, but very effective – for his purpose was to cover the retreat of his two young recruits, not to kill the police. The .30 calibre slugs slammed into, and right through, the metal chassis and fibreglass cage of the paddy wagon and kept the officers' heads down.

Hayes grabbed his shoulder mike, "Unit 11, we've now got a THIRD shooter – heavier calibre – how long till reinforcements?"

The dispatcher responded immediately, "Two more cars, ten blocks away. How's your rookie?"

"She's a veteran now," Hayes smiled at Wassler, "just survived the experience of a lifetime."

After emptying his thirty-shot magazine, Leon had turned on his heels and ducked back into the cover of the school lobby.

Hayes and Wassler rose to their feet just in time to see Leon stick his head back out the front door, toss his empty magazine into the "Please Don't Litter" garbage bin, and wave good-bye to them.

34

People rarely tell you about their failures. So, too, their premonitions, forebodings, and hunches that never come to pass.

But if one *is* perchance realised, if it does materialise, if their "premonition" proves prophetic – then they reckon that their special gifting is confirmed, and they are just as likely to publicly announce it as they were to suppress and forget the details of all their past unfounded inklings.

And so it was that, not long after Ronnie MacDonald pulled off the M1 Pacific Motorway from Sydney at 11:25 and began navigating the outskirts of Newcastle, his police radio began crackling reports of fire alarms, and then shots fired, at Hunter High School.

The police computer time log of the GPS in MacDonald's van confirmed that he had turned off towards the nearby Hunter High at the first police broadcast regarding the fire alarm, and had stomped on the accelerator at the first mention of shooting when he was only blocks away from the school.

Ronnie was already certain of Drew's involvement – and the realisation of his own precognitive fears – well before his police radio began broadcasting reports of three unidentified, but identically clad, shooters wearing long black coats.

Ronnie just *knew* it was Drew and his gang of Dregs, of that he was sure – what he wondered, as Drew's father, was how much more he could have or should have done to prevent it. They had known about the deepening darkness in their son's heart and mind for years. This violent outburst now – was it a case of parental irresponsibility, or actual criminal negligence, on their part? If they couldn't control their son, they should have at least reported him.

As Ronnie approached Hunter High (and the gathering horde of emergency vehicles around it) the visibility was poor, the radio communications chaotic – and prospects for the school, his family, and his police career all bleak.

35

Chronologically, biologically, and experientially, Wally Martin was forty-three years old. But emotionally, interpersonally, and in all areas requiring discipline, he was little more than seventeen.

I guess that's why all the chemistry students at Hunter High could relate to him so easily.

Wally grew up in Newcastle, long before Hunter High School was even built, and not far from where it now stood. He was one of the thousands of teachers around the state hired by the Department of Education to meet the demographic demands of the growing and aging population.

Essentially, the state government recruited him, offered to pay for his education, and guaranteed him a job for life – with an enticing retirement package awaiting him after forty years of service.

Wally was never much of a student himself, but the offer was too good to refuse, and he had absolutely no other plans or ambitions. Since he was always blowing things up and setting them on fire as a kid, he decided to get his Bachelor of Science in Chemistry.

His chemistry lab was the one classroom at Hunter High where students knew they would never come under any pressure from the teacher. Chemistry was an elective subject, it was optional, and therefore Wally always assumed his students had either a personal interest, or a career requirement related to chemistry, in order to choose it. Any student was free to sign up for his class, or free to drop it at any time.

Wally was always available after class for chemistry advice or direction but he generally let the text do most of the teaching and used class time for his good-natured, entertaining, and very insightful illustrations and explanations of the atomic and molecular kingdoms. These illustrations usually hinged on demonstrations and experiments that might, or might not, work out as planned – but they were never short on laughs, smoke, noise, and light.

Wally was certainly no model of academic excellence or career ambition, but nor did he bore, disrespect, or abuse his students, and never did he stifle their curiosity or extinguish their fascination with science. He also taught them to think critically, evaluate the world around them, and take responsibility for their lives while they were still young – often implying that he himself had thought through his own life too little, and too late.

On the wall of his chemistry lab classroom was affixed a dog-eared old poster that read:

> "Excuses are often used to say that bad choices are okay.
> Your past, your home life, and the way other people treat you,
> may influence the way you behave
> but none of these are excuses for bad behaviour.
> At this school, and in society, we expect you to be responsible
> for whatever you choose to do, no matter why you do it.
> Excuses do not cover up the fact that you choose to behave badly."

It was to that poster's challenge that Wally often referred students in classroom discussions. It made most students think, but it only made Leon Spitzer angry, and he took on an instant dislike and contempt for the charismatic chemistry teacher.

One day Wally arrived in class late, went straight to the blackboard without a word, wrote this equation: "1 Aussie = 10 Britons / Americans = 100 Indians = 1,000 Chinese", and then asked the students what they thought it meant.

After ten minutes of wild suggestions, Wally explained that it was a Sydney news editor's personal quota of lives that had to be lost by various nationalities in order to qualify for front page headlines in an Australian newspaper. Then he opened the class up for discussion. Chemistry was never mentioned at all, that day.

Wally had unkempt, shoulder-length hair. He never let it grow any longer, but maintained its dishevelled lack of styling for decades – long after it may have enhanced his appearance. His clothes were often unironed and he shaved irregularly. His wardrobe was limited, varying little from day to day and, indeed, from year to year. So predictable was it, that everyone commented when he bought a new shirt or pants. He excused himself by blaming the white lab coat that he wore daily.

"Why spend a fortune on clothes, when all you're going to do is cover it up with a lab coat?"

Such practicality and frugality, he joked, allowed him the luxury of buying and wearing the most expensive underwear in the world. When his students, invariably, asked him which brand, he explained that he was professionally prohibited from involving himself in product endorsements of any kind.

But perhaps the true purpose of the lab coat was the persona that it provided. For, despite his façade of apathy, Wally Martin was actually a shy and sensitive man, who habitually buried his hands in the pockets of his lab coat, and wrapped himself in that identity.

The only three personal details that he ever really shared about himself were that he was a Newcastle boy, a fanatical supporter of the Newcastle Knights rugby team, and a chemistry buff.

But there were two, more telling, disclosures that he also permitted. Two rare glimpses into his heart.

The first was his self-introduction to each new class of Year Ten chemistry students, when he faced them for the first time. Wally projected his own Year Ten high school photo on the overhead screen, and they all had a good laugh at the very unflattering image. Without saying a word, he had given each student permission to be who they were – unconditional acceptance in a school system whose very heart (or lack of it) was marking, judging, and evaluating.

The second disclosure began in his early thirties, when he confided to fellow teachers in the staff lounge one day, that the girlfriend he had never even mentioned before was now pregnant. Month by month he let his colleagues know of their wedding plans and, eventually, their little girl's birth. And then came the baby photos – weekly.

After one year, the photos stopped. His wife had filed for divorce, and his family updates ended, except for occasional school photos of the girl growing up in New Zealand.

At 11:49, Wally Martin was in his chemistry lab with the door closed, reviewing students' homework, when the fire alarm erupted.

"It's probably just the biology students next door, burning their animal sacrifices again – but let's quickly recap those fire procedures just in case:

Rule Number One: Don't panic – that's my job, and I've been specially trained for it.

Rule Number Two: Save your teacher at all costs.

Everyone line up at the door. When you're all ready, we'll walk straight out through the lobby, and into the parking lot."

From the back of the room, an objection, "But, Sir, it's pouring rain out there – we'll get soaked!"

"*Anything's* better than chemistry homework, I reckon," Wally assured them.

Then, above the clanging of the fire bell, gunshots and smashing glass. Sounded like it, anyway.

The lining-up had only just begun when Wally redirected them.

"Everyone back to your seat."

Then a second twenty-five-shot volley began – the .22 calibre explosions from around the junction of the right wing almost muffled by the closed classroom door and the blaring fire alarm. Almost.

The class, as one body, turned to Mr. Martin in his white lab coat for direction – while any students, who hadn't yet realised they were trapped in the middle of a school shooting, were quickly brought up to speed by their neighbours.

Wally spoke as quietly as he could while still making himself heard above the fire alarm, "Clear your desks, sit on the floor, hide behind your cabinets so you can't be seen from the doorway, and keep your eyes on me."

While the whole class complied, Wade's voice rang out clearly from down the corridor, "Leon!"

And then the M1 roared, much closer and louder than the .22s.

It seemed like Leon, and his rifle, and the Dregs, and perhaps Death itself, had all gathered just outside the door of their chemistry lab.

36

If you had asked me, before Black Friday, what crime scene witnesses were most likely to report, I would have said descriptions, actions, and events. And that's certainly true – visual images, burned so indelibly in the memory, that many survivors experienced vivid flashbacks even years later.

But sounds and noises echo loudly in the brain, and were reported at least as frequently – fire alarms, gunshots, smashing glass, sirens, screeching tyres, police radio chatter, helicopters overhead, police dogs barking.

And then there were the memories of smaller, commonplace sounds like pelting rain, crying, whimpering, the crunching of broken glass underfoot – ordinary, everyday sounds that often brought the trauma flooding back. The latch on one teacher's backyard fence at home sounding exactly like a rifle bolt being pulled back and released, coins dropped and rolling on the kitchen floor reminding one student of spent and ejected bullet cartridges landing in the school corridor.

The sounds of the siege. Sensory overload. A cacophony of noise. A symphony of chaos. All of which I am incapable of ever truly communicating to readers who weren't there that day.

And, in addition to all of that, there was the electronic noise that even *I* didn't hear.

Although the student cellular airwaves were flooded daily before and after school, mobile phones were not even allowed *on* during class time. But laws always inspire law-breaking and, because all cellular communication was prohibited during classes, its illicit use was limited to texting – which required smuggling, muting, stealth, touch-typing skills, codes, symbols, abbreviations, lightning-fast reflexes, and a certain proficiency at acting and lying.

When Earl Kennedy pulled the fire alarm at 11:49, six fire trucks were dispatched from three different suburbs and Sergeant Hayes volunteered for support duty, but no media were alerted and the outside world was not officially informed of the emergency.

Not officially – but even as the students filed out into the corridors in response to the fire bells, their texting had begun. Parents, friends, and siblings at work, home, and other schools – dozens of them received notification within seconds. "Fire alarm." "Fire drill?" "Maybe classes cancelled?!?" "I'll let u know."

Between 11:49 and 11:55, over two hundred texts and calls were made by terrorised staff and students – initially about the fire alarm, but then to spread the word that Wade and Druid were opening fire on the two wings. Seventeen escaping students and teachers dialled Triple Zero and spoke to emergency operators, while forty-two further calls were received from off-campus contacts passing on the news to police.

When firemen Reece and Pitkin pulled up at 11:52, no word of any shooting had yet been conveyed to emergency vehicles, but police officers Hayes and Wassler heard the "Mayday" call before they arrived at 11:53.

By the time the next two police units pulled up alongside Hayes and Wassler's bullet-riddled paddy wagon at 11:55, all the outside shooting was over, and the Dregs were back in the building.

Leon was monitoring his police scanner, and therefore knew to lay down covering fire for the retreating Druid and Slave. He soon learnt that five fire trucks were idling just outside the school parking lot, that ten more police units were on the way, and that support calls had already gone out to the police dog squad and helicopter, as well as the Sydney-based tactical squad – the State Protection Group.

Ten ambulances were sent racing to the scene, the first arrival volunteering to retrieve the wounded Reece from his crippled fire truck while ringed by police escort.

By 11:53, Newcastle radio was broadcasting reports of a rumoured incident at Hunter High School and, before noon, local TV news crews were on-site – and setting up live feeds to the national networks.

Only sixteen minutes after its commencement, the whole world was being made aware of the siege at Hunter High.

Amazing that no one had noticed its build-up for sixteen years.

37

Ronnie MacDonald knew better than to drive into the Hunter High School parking lot – some of the cops there would have recognised his face, and none could have missed his black van with "POLICE Technical Support" displayed clearly in white letters all over it. And, besides, the front entrance wasn't his objective.

So he skirted the parking lot, drove two blocks away to the corner of Loftus and Alcorn, and turned into an unpaved council workers' service road.

Ronnie's van slowly crunched over the gravel, past a municipal park and kiddies' playground, and next to a small power substation amidst the bushes before stopping at a chain-link fence that marked the boundary of Hunter High School property.

Ronnie opened the school's rear gate, that he knew was never locked, and drove slowly through the bushes. His intended parking spot was a small brick shed with a corrugated tin roof that was sandwiched between the school's industrial-sized metal garbage collection bins. The shed was used for storing mowers and a tractor and hopefully had enough space for the van. Luckily the tractor was gone and Ronnie had plenty of room.

He was now on the right rear side of the school, just beyond the external junction point of the main corridor and the right wing, but around the corner and not visible from the front parking lot. It was perfect. His van had only been exposed on school property for seconds, and only at a point of little interest to the police.

Ronnie's pounding heart seemed to somehow sync with the rain pounding on the tin roof overhead. This was not his style, not his scene. Perhaps it was not too late to drive away. He was a technical adviser, a resource, even an armourer of sorts. But a true police officer he was not.

He remained in the van for thirty seconds, even timing it on his watch, to ensure that he was not approached or challenged by police guards. And it was during those seconds that Ronnie recognised the voice of an inexperienced young constable broadcasting on the general police band – regularly monitored by curious civilians and predatory tow truck drivers, and now also being recorded by a few resourceful reporters – confirming the names of the two Dreg shooters involved in the assault on the left wing, the fire truck, and the paddy wagon, as identified by left wing escapees.

"Slave Latska and Drew MacDonald."

It was a breach of fundamental police protocol. Such details were *never* to be transmitted or released to the public in siege or hostage situations because gunmen hearing, directly or via a third party, that they have been identified become immediately more desperate and dangerous as they realise that they have now lost all hope of anonymous escape.

This errant announcement of suspects' names resulted in a subsequent written reprimand in the young constable's file, and an immediate confirmation to Ronnie MacDonald that he had been right, after all, in sneaking up to the school's rear door.

According to police regulations, being related to any student or staff member inside the school would have constituted a "conflict of interest" and "emotional prejudice" that required immediate disclosure to a commanding officer and subsequent disqualification from decision-making and line-of-fire duties at the scene.

And if, as the father of one of the actual gunmen, Ronnie's *involvement* in the siege would have been quashed, how much more so his *infiltration*? For him to enter the school on his own – without authorisation, without permission, without even informing the crime scene coordinator and supervisor – was way beyond negligent, it was, in fact, criminal.

Ronnie knew all that when he parked his van under cover by the rear entrance.

But he also knew that, once inside the school, he could provide invaluable intelligence to the police – intelligence that he was unwilling to let any other cops risk their lives to obtain.

Perhaps, in some small way, he could make atonement for his failings as a husband, father, citizen, and police officer.

Perhaps it would be too little, too late.

38

Druid made it safely to the top of the hill and dove for cover around the outside corner of the left wing junction, well before Leon had completed his thirty shots of covering fire from the school's front entrance.

Slave was waiting for him up ahead at the top of the wing, holding the fire exit door open while scanning the playing fields for any more emergency response vehicles.

"It was so important for you to shoot that fire truck fifty times? We lost half the hostages through this door – you could maybe have helped me to hold some back."

Druid loaded his fifth full magazine as he entered the building.

"The only way to defeat a red dragon is to blind and cripple him."

Slave's mouth dropped, and he froze for a moment, still holding the door. "You've been taking drugs!"

"I need to see things that you can't see!"

"I am trusting my life into your hands – and you take drugs?"

"I am a druid, a seer, a wizard."

Slave slammed the door closed behind him and caught up to Druid, wrapping both his hands around the magician's throat.

Druid fixed his bulging blue eyes upon his attacker. His wounded left hand clawed at Slave's grip while his right fumbled down the guitar strap seeking his Ruger.

"Why do you need a rifle, wizard? Does it contain magic bullets, maybe?"

Three deafening shots echoed down the corridor, and then a sudden quiet.

The barrel of Leon's M1 protruded through the meshed, shattered, and blood-smeared window of the fire door at the base of the left wing. Spitzer had finally silenced the clamouring red fire bell on the wall near the junction point and, in so doing, gained the attention of the two brawling brothers.

Leon's raised voice now carried down the silenced corridor.

"Take a good look at him, Slave, I see no rubber mask. He is not the enemy you came here to fight."

"Maybe not – but he just let half of them get away."

"That means we've still got half of them left. We don't have much time, let's not waste it."

Slave loosened his grip of Druid's throat a little as he deliberated.

Druid stopped clawing with his mangled fingers, and raised both hands, palms forward, as a sign of peace.

Slave took his eyes, momentarily, off his prey and turned to look at Leon – Latska's camera recording the surreal and almost comical image of

Spitzer's little face behind the battle-scarred window at the far end of the wing. Two other fire bells were still ringing around the building – strong, but distant.

"Obeying the king is the honourable thing to do," croaked Druid, as clearly as he could.

Slave looked back to Druid, who added "He's the king, I'm just a joker." Druid flashed one of his crazed, wild-eyed smiles.

But Slave wasn't smiling as he let him go.

Leon resumed command, "We'll abandon this left wing immediately. Now with only half the hostages and two-thirds of the building to control, our position is even stronger. Druid, I need your eyes in the lobby."

Druid whispered, "He knows I can see things that others can't," and walked off towards Leon's little face.

"How's your hand?" Leon asked the redhead as he drew nearer.

"The pain helps me focus," replied Druid.

"Come on, Slave," Leon called out, "you and I have an assembly to organise."

Druid opened the door to Leon, the door that had cost them 374 hostages, crunching over the broken glass as he went – much of it, already smeared with his own blood from a few minutes ago, now splashed again with even more as it dripped freely from his hand.

"Kennedy and Forman are dead," Leon announced quietly to Druid, as if to test his response.

"Their throne is now yours – and rightfully so, my lord," replied Druid without missing a beat.

"Before you take up sentry duty at the front doors, do me a favour and kill those other two fire bells, will you?"

The fire alarm had served to focus both the Dregs and the hostages – to establish the sense of urgency, and to shatter the illusionary world of academics. It had served a purpose, but now it was just a nuisance, and Leon ordered its execution.

Druid saluted his commander and set off.

Leon held the door open, Slave walked up to him and barked, "Do you know that he's hallucinating on drugs, *right now?*"

"And this comes as a *surprise* to you, does it? That boy's *permanently* drug-affected – they've fried his brain, they're flowing through his veins, they've become part of his DNA."

Leon stopped Latska with a hand on his shoulder and looked him in the eye. "I had to kill Kennedy and Forman."

Though death was never a shock to the young war veteran, he was yet to be numbed by the familiar sense of loss. "Kennedy was a good man. He always spoke the truth."

"I had no choice – he grabbed my rifle, and she pulled the fire alarm," Leon lied.

"What about this surgery precision of yours, Leon?"

"I think it's become more like Accident and Emergency now, don't you? Our mission remains unchanged, the world is just aware of it sooner, rather than later – that's all."

"Okay, but I cannot risk something else to go wrong. I am going to first bring together my targets into the gymnasium right now – exactly like we agreed. I won't be long – then I can support your assembly. I just need Wade to referee."

Leon exercised his authority and refined the plan. "Help Wade to clear out the right wing first, then the two of you can have five or ten minutes in the gym – no longer. *Then* the assembly."

The fate of four hundred people, in and around the school, decided in seconds.

39

Dixon had always spent a half day of his five-day commando training – ten per cent – on hand-to-hand combat and killing with a blade, and he extended that training with his Swat team.

He knew chances were slim that any IARD action would involve such close-quarter engagements, but his students needed to fully appreciate the eye to eye, life and death, sweat and blood, seek and destroy nature of the mission for which they had volunteered.

This was no video game, no antiseptic kill through a telescopic sight. They would ultimately have to look into their downed target's face, feel for a pulse, ensure their kill, and wipe the blood from their hands onto their clean black tactical squad uniforms.

They were being trained for mortal combat. This was brutal, this was justice, this is what the public demanded when their loved ones were held hostage – victims had to be saved, even if their rescuers were scarred and haunted by the ordeal for the rest of their lives.

When the eleven members of the Newcastle Support Unit enlisted Dixon to train them as commandos, they sacrificed their free time and paid for their own ammunition. Their SAS sergeant brought along the paintball guns, and bought them each a black "knuckle knife" – originally developed for close-quarter combat in confined First World War trenches, the handle incorporating a set of brutal brass knuckles that ensured an unbreakable grip in a fight to the death.

He paid for them himself, handed them out to his Newcastle team, and told them that he couldn't entrust his life into the hands of men who weren't fully armed. "If you're not prepared to have your enemy breathe his last breath in your face – you're not prepared."

They accepted the cold steel blades in silence, and trained with Dixon even more intently from then on.

40

The cardinal rule of physicians, included within the original Hippocratic Oath, is "first do your patient no harm".

Such was the thinking of Ronnie MacDonald when he left his .40 calibre Glock pistol behind in the locked console of his van, still sheathed in its black leather clip-on holster.

It was a Glock 27 – much smaller, lighter, and easier to conceal than the Glock 22 carried by uniformed officers. The subcompact Glock 27 – often called the "Baby Glock" – was generally carried by detectives, undercover, or support officers like Ronnie. It held only nine rounds compared to the fifteen held by the Glock 22, but nine rounds of .40 calibre semi-automatic fire still qualified it as a formidable little weapon – especially in the hands of a Dreg. If Ronnie failed to defuse the siege, and was captured or killed in the process, at least he could be certain that he would not provide the Dregs with any additional lethal weapons.

Ronnie was authorised to carry the full range of police and tactical squad weaponry for display, demonstration, discussion, and training at various police stations throughout the state. (It was ultimately cheaper for him to travel alone to regional seminars, than it was to transport and accommodate officers from all around New South Wales to some central conference). This arsenal included shotguns, handguns, rifles, specialised ammunition, capsicum spray, taser stun guns, night vision and telescopic optics, bulletproof vests, ballistic shields, and concussion grenades.

Ronnie was carrying only a half-dozen of these in his van when diverted to Hunter High. From them, he chose a few LTLs (Less-Than-Lethals) and made his way towards the rear entrance of the maintenance workshop, black leather satchel slung over his shoulder.

41

At 11:51, the Triple Zero emergency operator offered Wally Martin the choice of "police, fire, or ambulance".

Ironic question that really, because thirteen, six, and ten of each vehicle, respectively, were now racing to the scene.

Wally requested the police, and waited.

And waited – while the approaching sirens grew louder.

At 11:53, Wally finally spoke to an obviously stressed police operator, already overwhelmed with calls concerning Hunter High.

Wally spoke fast, "I am a school teacher hiding with my students in a classroom at Hunter High – can you connect me with someone in charge of coordinating the police operation here."

But, at 11:53, there *was* no coordinated police operation because the Newcastle State Protection Support Unit commander had not yet arrived, nor was he *truly* authorised to coordinate once he even got there.

Here was a perfect illustration of the subjective perception of time. For hostages and victims inside the school, each terrifying moment seemed like an eternity, each heartbeat a further loss of precious lifeblood, a deepening of shock. Yet, for emergency response teams racing to the school, moments were lost and minutes flew past.

For most of us most of the time, time itself seems like an enemy, marching on without mercy or compromise – a heartless taskmaster pressing in from all sides. While somewhere deep within ourselves we harbour a taste, a craving, for eternity. Always feeling young at heart – ageless, yet trapped within aging bodies – constantly frustrated, constrained, chafed, and shackled by time.

Wally hung up, closed the classroom curtains, turned off the lights, and hid in the dark with his students – listening to the fire alarm, the sirens, and the gunfire out in the parking lot.

42

The two minutes allotted to Slave and Druid for rounding up escapees had stretched out to almost five by the time they returned to the main corridor at 11:55.

True, the Dregs had a plan and were well prepared, but they are really best portrayed as reacting, moment by moment, to ever-changing circumstances.

What might seem now like cowardice on the part of hostages was simply gut-wrenching fear at the time, and the "heroic" acts of a few were but feeble attempts at decency by desperate people in a hopeless situation.

And where was I during those first five minutes, from the sounding of the fire alarm until the Dregs returned from the parking lot shooting? In my office, on my hands and knees, hiding under my desk.

My diary, like all diaries, had my day laid out for me in neat, stress-inducing little boxes. I had booked 11:30 to 11:45 for a run-through meeting with Barbra Burser and her Scripture Union group, but we were running late.

"Barb" was a Year Ten student whose petite frame belied an internal furnace of enthusiasm, energy, and a maturity beyond her years. Barb was regularly criticised for being sickly-sweet, but her integrity, persistence, and mettle had stood the test of time. She was constantly slandered, yet consistently asked to contribute and lead.

Throughout the year, the responsibility for the organisation and emceeing of Friday school assemblies was rostered out to different classes, and various student groups.

The year's last full-school assembly, just before the seniors of Year Twelve began their final state exams and departed forever from high school, fell on the thirteenth of October – its programming and presentation placed into the hands of Barb's Scripture Union group.

Barb and her boyfriend, Kieran Thredbo, were well known around the school for their Christian stance. Well known, and perhaps even begrudgingly respected – but not much appreciated.

Had Kieran been a nerd or a geek – as well as a Christian – he would surely have been martyred by his peers. But he was tall, strong, and a star basketball player with a great sense of humour, who readily shared his academic giftedness with any student, anytime, who was struggling.

And Barb's childhood years, spent travelling the globe with her medical missionary parents, had tempered her naturally buoyant personality with a backbone of steel, and a burnished sense of responsibility.

One wintery afternoon, only months before the siege, Barb and I had remained in my office for hours after the last bell, drinking hot chocolate as she first discussed her frustrations with high school leadership, and then recounted some of the atrocities and suffering she had seen around the world with her parents.

As the school fell quiet and the sky grew dark, Barb began sharing about the supernatural occurrences they had witnessed and experienced in primitive cultures, without modern comforts or distractions, where spiritual powers – both light and dark – seemed to walk the streets and enter the houses. Barb emphasised her culture shock in returning to an increasingly materialistic Australia where the spiritual was rarely expected, experienced, or discussed – perhaps at times of crisis or death, but probably never.

Barb's father was her hero, having challenged and inspired spiritual growth and discernment in her own life. Yet in light of all that experience, in the shadow of her father's accomplishments, in contrast, she had to fight feelings of frustration and failure at Hunter High, where her Christian leadership had proven largely ineffective in a digitalised Western world addicted to technology and obsessed with success and happiness as portrayed in the media.

I sat simultaneously inspired and discouraged as her life experience seemed to expose high school curriculum and culture as trivial in comparison – depressed as her wisdom seemed to shame all my training and advice as a sham. If Barb's father was her hero, then she was mine.

And if discouragement and depression were the two emotions that enveloped me as I drove Barb to her house and dropped her off – once she stepped out of the car they turned to fear. Driving myself home, locking my apartment door behind me, even lying in bed that night – it wasn't the dark that I was afraid of, it was the darkness. Barb talked about a spiritual enemy of whose existence I had never even known. And if all that she had said was true, perhaps I was safer not knowing.

It was only a matter of time until the young couple – Kieran and Barb – became known as "Ken and Barbie" because of their squeaky-clean reputations. There was a good deal of affection in the "Barbie" branding, though it was also satirical – with Barb's short, dark hair and five-foot stature contrasting starkly with the tall blonde Barbie and her flowing locks.

The actual Barbie doll was released into the world in 1959, eventually selling over one billion units in 150 countries. With her flowing blonde hair, long lean legs, no excess body fat, good-looking boyfriend Ken, wardrobes, vehicles, and houses to die for, Barbie inspired decades of fantasy, envy, anger, frustration, and anorexia for generations of young girls around the world.

Years later I realised how ironic it was that Leon Spitzer was himself a real-life, male version of Barbie with his good looks, wealth, and ability to inspire envy and jealousy – ironic that he was so envied when, in fact, he was such a distant loner, apparently ill-equipped for intimacy, an only child of divorced parents with an absentee father, a suicidal mother, no real friendships, and never a girlfriend as far as anyone knew. Leon was forced to repeat his first high school year over again in Australia because of all his father's previous international moves and constant uprooting of the family – often the "new kid" at school, displaced and disoriented almost annually, torn from old friends and unskilled at making new ones. Now, at almost eighteen, he was a year older than all his peers in Year Eleven.

So "Ken and Barbie" headed up the Scripture Union group at Hunter High as much by qualification as by default – no one else wanted to. And though dedicated as they were, the group never caught fire, never really grew, and the thirty or so members didn't seem to mature as Barb and Kieran had hoped.

Most were from Years Seven to Nine and came from Christian homes

– theirs seemed almost a faith by inheritance, entitlement, or parental expectation, rather than choice and decision. When any high school students *did* decide to become Christians it was almost always the younger ones. Years Ten through Twelve, it seemed, brought greater responsibilities, distractions, and temptations that competed and usually won.

The only person in Scripture Union more committed than Barb was Ricky Russell, a tender-hearted student with Down syndrome. Ricky accepted Barb's initial invitation to attend, without hesitation – he was rarely invited anywhere – and he quickly embraced the Bible, and the Jesus that Barb and Kieran endorsed. In two years, Ricky never missed a single Scripture Union meeting. Eventually Barb computer-designed and awarded Ricky with an honorary Master of Hospitality certificate for tirelessly inviting anyone and everyone to join them.

43

Ronnie MacDonald had initially heard the bellowing fire alarm even before he saw the school parking lot, but it was only when he emerged from his van at the rear of the school that he appreciated its full volume as it clawed into his ears and assaulted his brain.

The dash required only a dozen paces from van to rear entrance but that was about a dozen more than Ronnie would have liked – what with all the police and media eyeballs, cameras, binoculars, and helicopters converging on the scene.

When Ronnie arrived at the door to the maintenance workshop his momentum was halted by the security keypad. Ronnie was certain that he remembered the initial installation code, but had no idea whether it had since been changed.

He tried to slow his hammering heartbeat as the rain pelted down and a helicopter circled overhead. He felt like Dr. Frankenstein as he looked upon the keypad – now at the mercy of his own heartless technology.

He punched the numbers in slowly, and was ashamed of his gut response when the lock opened – disappointment. Had he been locked out and forced to flee the scene, he could have at least faced Alison with an excuse.

Once inside the school – alone, enveloped by the gloom and unpainted concrete walls of the maintenance workshop, navy blue police coveralls and bomber jacket soaked from his dash through the downpour – the waves of doubt assailed him, and he reviled himself out loud. "Who do I think I am, anyway?" "I'm not even a real cop." "No one even knows where I am." "I feel like a drowned rat." "I would have been more useful if I had just reported in to the command post." And, finally, "God, please help me!"

He sighed deeply in despair. Twice. Then the two sighs evolved into a few deep breaths. He managed to get a grip on himself, he raised his sights, elevated his vision, looked up to the ceiling air conditioning duct, got his bearings, and began searching for a ladder.

44

Druid had his orders and he followed them – seek and destroy the fire alarm bells outside the admin office and at the base of the right wing, just beyond its junction with the main corridor. On the way, he ducked his head quickly into each room to seek and apprehend any potential hostages who might be hiding.

He turned left into the main corridor and began to search the biology lab, with its tables for four each built around a sink.

Next, the chemistry lab – countertop desks for two, each with its own sink, bunsen burner gas tap, and enclosed cupboards from counter to floor for storing utensils.

Lecture theatre with full audiovisual facilities, large enough for two classes, with sixty fixed seats and hinged-tray writing tables on three tiered levels.

Language lab – twenty cubicles, each with a set of bluetooth headphones ready and waiting on its own hook.

Music studio with piano, keyboards, drum kit, twelve desks, and a tiny soundproof booth with window.

Computer lab with eight laptop and twelve desktop computers, all equipped with wireless internet and web cams.

Six specialised classrooms, used only when specifically booked and required, with their doors never locked but always closed.

Druid only took time enough to swing each door open and quickly scan each room to confirm that they were empty.

Midway down the main corridor was the door to admin on Druid's left and the smashed lobby on his right. Druid approached the fire bell clanging high up on the wall just past the admin office and raised his rifle.

45

At 11:35, while Druid waited outside in the rain for the arrival of Leon's black Jeep, my office was crammed with the ten students responsible for running the assembly. One of the ten was recording it all on her phone.

We tweaked the schedule one last time, and were running through the students' allotment of responsibilities. Foureen minutes later, the fire alarm was the first indication of our plan's demise.

It's funny, but people don't think of buildings burning down in the pouring rain, so Ricky said, "Maybe it's a fire drill."

"I don't think the office would send us all out to stand in the wet, and surely not ten minutes before the final assembly," Barb just couldn't see the sense in it.

Kieran's hand was on the doorknob when Wade's twenty-five shots rang out, followed by the smashing of glass, and the screaming of students.

Everyone in the office knew immediately that it was a high school shooting. Gunman or gunmen on a shooting spree in a school, or a shopping mall, or an office – we had all seen the news reports and wondered, at least subconsciously, if it would ever happen to us. Well, the wondering was now over.

My office was located in the main corridor, two doors to the right of the admin office upon entering the building.

Wade's shouting, at the junction with the right wing, was barely audible through the closed door and in competition with the fire bell ringing on the wall just outside the admin office.

"The good news is that it's a false alarm. There *is* no fire. No one is in danger of being burned.

The bad news is that if you all don't turn around and head right back into the classrooms you just left I'm going to start killing people – and I'm not alone. Weed!"

The second volley of shots and shattering of glass began.

None of us had recognised Wade's voice, but then we heard that name.

"Weed?!" Kieran couldn't believe it. None of us could.

"Leon!" Wade shouted from the junction.

Up until then, Kieran, Barb, and I had been craning our ears to the door. We all jumped – and I think I even yelped – as Leon's much louder and much closer M1 began shooting up the distant surveillance cameras, and then the trophy cases just across the hall.

"Leon and Weed?" I asked myself out loud.

"And whoever's calling out their names," added Kieran, referring to Wade's as yet unidentified voice.

"The Dregs." Barb was one step ahead of us, and we knew immediately that she was right.

"Then there's probably five guns out there," said Kieran.

Karen Whitaker from the back of my office whispered – or sounded like she was whispering in contrast to the M1's roar, and the fire bell's clanging – "What should we do?"

"Pray." All eyes turned to Ricky Russell.

He wasn't embarrassed. He didn't repeat his suggestion, he just underlined it, "What else?"

Barb backed him up, "If not now, then when?"

Barb dropped to her knees. Some stood, some sat, some knelt. I even knelt – me, with a really sore knee from field hockey, who hadn't knelt to pray for over twenty-five years.

I've often thought back on that. Did I really want to pray – or was I just going with the flow, and bowing to peer pressure? I must have wanted to pray – I know that I wouldn't have started chanting or burning incense if anyone had suggested it. Would I have thought of it on my own? I don't think so – I certainly wouldn't have admitted it out loud, or knelt there in front of everyone by myself.

I have since wondered greatly about how our decisions form our character, forge our destiny, and change our lives. A momentary decision to cement some bricks together results in a wall that stands for a lifetime. So, too, perhaps my deciding to pray that day opened up my mind to the possibility – even the expectancy – that there was a God listening, perhaps even ready, willing, and able to help me.

I do remember thinking pragmatically that a kneeling target is only half the size. Then I felt guilty for thinking it. Then Kieran suggested, "Let's pray *and* take cover," and I didn't feel so bad any more.

Students began to kneel behind the sofa and chairs in my office, I crawled under my desk.

Silly thoughts. Random recollections. I remember thinking how grateful I was that I hadn't worn a skirt. Then I thought that my old wooden desk was better cover than the students' sofas – harder for a bullet to penetrate wood, than it is to penetrate foam. Then I felt guilty again. Then I wondered if perhaps I should offer my hiding place to someone else. I finally decided that it was *my* desk, after all, and they should be grateful that I was even letting them hide in my office.

Never mind my *life* flashing before my eyes – there goes my maturity, my compassion, and what about all my responsibility? I *am* a staff member, after all. What about my duty of care?

Such are my snatches of memory bits. But what I do recall in vivid detail is noticing, really noticing, the pattern of the carpeting under my desk for the first time ever, and how I wished I could just burrow into it.

The gunshots and smashing glass had started me trembling. Not constantly, but in waves, and I couldn't stop. It wasn't even a plush, deeper pile carpet that I could sink my fingertips into. It was just government institutional-issue. So I closed my eyes and prayed with the students – at least I nodded assent to *their* petitions, and whispered "please" and "yes" as *they* prayed. I never said "amen" though – it just seemed too sanctimonious.

As expected, there were requests for protection and deliverance. One of the Year Seven's prayed for all the guns to jam.

Ricky Russell prayed "I like Wade – Aron Wade – he's my friend. He's one of the Dregs, and he always looked out for me. Please forgive them."

There were many more – four or five minutes of intermittent prayer and silence while Druid shot up the meshed window of the fire door, Leon yelled outside the staff lounge, and the fire alarm rang, and rang, and rang.

I remember Leon laughing with the teachers. Then sirens and shooting in the parking lot.

And then Barb prayed. I transcribed it word for word from the recording, and have read it countless times since: "Thank you, Father, that

You are in control even amidst the apparent chaos. No one and nothing is outside Your knowledge, Your care, and Your power. We acknowledge that *You* are in charge here today, not the Evil One – he would use people as puppets and then dispose of them, whereas You would inspire and empower them, as sons and daughters, and cherish them always. It is no accident that each of us is here today. Please help us to learn what You want us to learn. Help us to learn how to live, and how to die – never alone and always trusting You, just as we were taught by Your Son, Jesus Christ, our Lord. Amen."

And then Barb turned to me, reached out to me beyond her little flock, squeezed my ankle, and said "Danielle Marie Bennetton, God knows your name, your thoughts, and your fears. He has always been watching over you, and drawing you to Himself. He is with you even now."

Never in my life had I heard more comforting words. Never in my life were they more needed.

And then, without another word, everyone got to their feet and headed for the door. I don't know if we all thought that hiding in the office was the cowardly thing to do or if we just thought that it was futile. But I do remember, at the time, feeling exactly like I used to when I was a little kid, and a game of hide-and-seek was declared over just after I had found the best hiding spot.

I was the last to my feet as Barb opened the door.

46

At 11:54, Wally Martin turned to the young men and women sitting beside him in the dark, his fellow hostages, and started consulting. In so doing, he broke the number one rule of classroom management theory and spoke to them as equals.

"We can't depend on the police to rescue us, they might not even enter the school for another hour. If the Dregs check this room, I think the lights being out might cause them to search behind the desks. I suggest we turn the lights back on, but keep the curtains closed in case they go back outside and look in. It's got to be a group decision. Light or darkness?"

There was a brief discussion, but Wally had thought it through, and his opinion was respected. The students agreed, so Wally made a dash for the light switch, illuminating his way there with his cigarette lighter.

Just as the fluorescents flickered back to life, three shots rang out. It was Leon killing the first fire bell in the left wing, and ending Slave's threats towards Druid.

Sixty seconds later, Druid flung open the chemistry lab door as he checked every room between the left wing junction and the admin office. He quickly stuck his head into the room and then moved on, leaving the door open.

47

Barb opened my office door just as Druid fired his rifle four times in her face.

He was aiming up at the fire bell outside the admin office, so Barb had to step back to avoid the hot spent shells ejecting from the chamber.

The deafening fire bells were now only one third their former volume and people no longer had to shout to be heard, so Druid could speak quite softly.

"Ken and Barbie – and all their friends! Come out, come out, whoever you are!

Miss Bennetton! While you've been having group therapy in there, I've been out here experiencing an overwhelming urge to kill and destroy – it's the most powerful drug I've ever tasted."

Druid turned his head back towards the left wing, "Leon! Some late arrivals to the party!"

Suddenly Druid's smile disappeared, and he wasn't kidding anymore. "Stay inside the office!" he commanded, before walking off towards the right wing and the final ringing alarm bell – checking for possible hidden prey in the offices, gym, and auditorium along the way – leaving the eleven of us to Leon.

And in that thirty seconds – the changing of the guard – while Leon walked slowly to my office, my brain amazed me with its speed and capacity for assessment. The rifles, laser sights, black uniforms – even the forehead

Dregcams. Suddenly the unimaginable seemed obvious, predictable, even inevitable, and immediately ignited the self-recrimination and guilt – that I should have foreseen, and ought to have prevented.

I had long understood in theory – but now came to fully appreciate in a split second – the power of the military uniform: to fortify a soldier with the confidence that he has become part of something greater than himself, to terrorise his enemy as a member of a faceless and nameless yet instantly recognisable horde, and to alleviate each combatant of his or her individual culpability for the atrocities that are always committed in the name of war by "us" against "them".

As Druid headed off towards Wade at the right wing junction, and Slave appeared in the distance behind Leon at the left junction, we seemed suddenly surrounded by black coats – engulfed in blackness.

Broken glass underfoot, fire bells being shot out, dozens of empty shell casings, and sirens in the parking lot. I was surprised, looking left and right along the main corridor, that there were no bodies and no blood except for what was dripping from Druid's mangled fingers.

Maybe we could all get out of this alive and without injury after all, I tried to encourage myself.

While we huddled together back in my office as ordered, we could hear from his approaching footsteps that Leon was only a moment away, and I wondered if it was too late to crawl back under my desk.

Leon poked his head in, playfully – all confidence and smirky smile. His eyes fell upon Barb and Kieran and the eight students cowering behind them.

"I've uncovered the catacombs, have I? That's where Christians hid to avoid the death penalty, wasn't it, Barb?"

"It was, Leon."

"Well, didn't work this time, because *I am* the death penalty."

48

Two blocks out from the high school, Sergeant Dixon cut his siren and pulled into a suburban side street to change into his black tactical uniform.

For him to be seen arriving without his uniform on, or having to get changed in the school parking lot during the deluge, would be sloppy both physically and professionally – as if the Dregs and the weather had the upper hand, and the police had been caught off guard. Better to be seen arriving in control, in charge, and in uniform.

Only a seasoned soldier like Dixon – a bloodied and muddied veteran – can truly appreciate the power of a uniform, discipline, and self-control to inspire instant respect from civilians, subordinates, and the enemy, especially amidst the carnage and panic of battle. Guardians of law and order are only ever truly appreciated amidst lawlessness and chaos. The light shines brightest in the darkness.

He was just a man as he stripped to his underwear in the pouring rain near the corner of Loftus and Alcorn, only a sopping wet man in black as he jumped back into his Landcruiser, but the commander of the Newcastle State Protection Support Unit as he emerged in the parking lot of Hunter High School, two blocks away.

Dixon knew that all eyes would be looking for him – and looking to him – as commander of Newcastle's initially much-publicised, but now only rumoured, IARD team in this hour of crisis. Most of the police officers assembling in the parking lot were "paintballers" – survivors and graduates of his five-day commando training – and everyone in Newcastle recognised him. Dixon intentionally chose not to wear his tactical uniform-issued black woollen watch cap, so that his trademark glistening bald head would stick out in the crowd – combatants need to know that their commander is leading them into battle.

Dixon retrieved only his AR-15 carbine from the back of his Landcruiser – it was a symbol of authority and power, and all his colleagues were watching.

Throughout his long military career, Dixon had habitually refused to wear body armour himself until he had confirmed that all those under his command had first donned their own. His first order of business, therefore, would be to demand that all police officers on-site, not wearing their standard-issue bulletproof vests, were to immediately retrieve them from their vehicles and get them on. Extra vests were to be raced to the high school for any fire, rescue, and ambulance officers, relatives, reporters, or officials who might be called in to the immediate danger zone.

Dixon – in command and now on the scene, AR-15 in hand, Glock 22 strapped just above his right knee in its thigh holster – made sure he wasn't seen by his colleagues to flinch or cringe, bow his head, or run through the Newcastle downpour. He walked slowly. The rain was his adversary – hostile, opposing – and Dixon's adversaries *never* made him flinch or cower. The enemy would not prevail, but only serve to make him stronger. Water off a duck's back. Bulletproof.

Paratroopers, Special Forces, SAS troopers, commandos, and tactical units were often sneered at in their distinctive uniforms – but always envied. Special weapons, training, tactics, and warriors, called in to get the job done – in and out – while regular officers often resented their own limited responsibilities to set up before, and mop up afterwards. But, then again, none of the regular officers were trained or willing to enter the rooms, or face the odds, that awaited the elite warriors.

At 12:01, Sergeant Darren Hayes, having survived eighty gunshots and 123 bullet holes in his paddy wagon only eight minutes earlier, hustled over to meet Dixon and shake his hand, followed closely behind by the first two of Dixon's commandos to arrive.

"Glad to see you, Gary, but we really could have used you and your boys about ten minutes earlier."

"Is that *your* paddy wagon, is it, Darren?"

"It *was* – I stayed behind the engine block."

Dixon laughed and slapped Hayes on the shoulder. It was Dixon who had drilled into him the engine block advice eighteen months ago in commando training. "I've cleared out the construction shed for your command post," Hayes yelled in Dixon's ear above the clamour of overhead helicopters, encircling police radio chatter, and Newcastle storm, as he led the commando chief by the arm.

Hayes was guiding Dixon towards the white, portable, on-site construction office and lunchroom that had sat now, for months, in the school parking lot while the future mandate of library and cafeteria were debated. Only minutes before, Hayes had borrowed a pair of bolt cutters from a fire rescue truck and snapped the padlock that barred the door.

"I'm not in command, Darren, Sydney tactical squad is."

"That's what *they* think," said Hayes as he followed Dixon and his two commandos into the construction office. Hayes knew Dixon, and he knew chain-of-command protocol – the Newcastle State Protection Support Unit commander was, in fact, in charge of the siege operation until physically relieved by the Sydney tactical squad commander.

Once inside, one of Dixon's commandos reported, "We just got the word – Buster's on the road and heading our way." They all had to raise their voices to speak, with the rain pelting down on the thin roof.

"ETA?" asked Dixon.

"Even with their Highway Patrol escort, well after 1300 hours – maybe 1330, visibility terrible all the way from Sydney."

Dixon made no reply and, when he spoke, it was only *towards* the three other officers, and not specifically *to* anyone. "We'll need the school building plans from the municipal council."

"I've got a patrol car on the way with the plans – should be here any minute," reported Hayes proudly.

"Excellent, Sergeant Hayes, thank you."

Hayes continued, "…. and along with those plans, you need to talk with Luke, the high school maintenance guy – he escaped with half the students."

"How many got out?"

"Over three hundred."

"So there's still another, what? Three hundred hostages inside?"

"Closer to three-fifty – we're trying for an exact number. And Superintendent Stanwych wanted you to call him as soon as you arrive."

49

So far, so good.

Well, "good" might be too optimistic a word.

True, Ronnie had made it into the school and now he had a plan of sorts, a direction, a goal, a destination, a covered conduit to take him there, and a leather bag small enough to tie around his ankle and drag behind him as he crawled along in the dark.

But three unexpected disappointments gnawed away at his optimism, and everyone knows that a tiny gnawing worry or disappointment can soon devour a great initial optimism – can swallow up even a confident expectation many times its size, over time.

First was the size of the air conditioning shaft itself. It was smaller than Ronnie had remembered, or maybe it was just that Little Ronnie MacDonald had forgotten for a moment that he was now a mountain of a man – six-foot-three-inches, huge feet, fiery red hair, booming Scottish brogue. Or, most probably, the giant looming crisis had simply caused him to see himself as a smaller, weaker man.

Claustrophobia was not so much the problem, Ronnie had dragged audiovisual cables through conduits much smaller than this. The problems now were the slowness of the cramped crawling, and the need to be quiet – if and when the fire alarm should ever stop.

While it rang he was sonically camouflaged, though almost deafened inside the conduit by the amplifying effect of the hollow tin shaft on the alarm bells. But should the alarm stop, for whatever reason, his crawling and scraping noises would likewise be amplified, and echoed, all along the school corridors.

The same architects who saved money by not plumbing the building's two wings, had then turned around and installed air conditioning conduits inside the ceiling and running the entire length of the school's corridors.

No school had *ever* been air conditioned in the Newcastle area, but the architects had allowed for its possible future provision at much lower cost than would be the case were ducting installed post-construction. Clever, but never appreciated or taken advantage of by the Department of Education – perhaps because all the offices of the bureaucrats who made such budgetary decisions were already air conditioned and, therefore, they found it difficult to empathise.

So, naturally, when Inspector Ronnie MacDonald was asked by the private contractors installing his recommended covert mini CCTV cameras at Hunter High where to run the cabling – he suggested the unused air conditioning conduits. And, being the hands-on adviser that he was, Ronnie became quickly familiar with the confines of the ducting. They were made of cheap but strong tin sheeting, easily capable of supporting a grown man, but prone to loud buckling noises if negotiated too quickly.

The *second* disappointment was that he had neglected to take a portable police radio along with him that morning when he went to Sydney. So if he *did* manage to obtain the information inside the school that he hoped to, his only way of conveying it to the tactical squad outside was by telephone – but the school phones could be easily monitored by the Dregs, and his mobile phone had only one bar remaining on its battery, only a third or a quarter of a full charge.

Ironic that although the provision of a million-dollar Siege Buster might not be able to rescue the school hostages, the lack of a ten-dollar battery charger might doom them all.

The only source of illumination inside the ducting was by way of the air vents, each twice the size of a man's face and spaced every three of Ronnie's body lengths apart. Each ceiling vent in the corridor aligned with a corresponding air vent cut in the floor of the ducting to allow the passage of the air-conditioned breeze which never came.

From the corridors looking up into the vents, only blackness could be seen, as pupils contracted in the glare of the ceiling fluorescents. But from the conduit looking down, the viewing was clear.

As Ronnie hoisted himself inside from Luke's ladder, the initial protests of the buckling tin conduit were, indeed, camouflaged by the school's remaing two operational fire alarms. But before he had crawled even three body lengths, Ronnie heard the four gunshots and felt the shockwave of Druid's execution of the second fire bell outside the admin office – amplified and echoed down the tin shaft. Ronnie could feel, as much as hear, the protective wall of noise around him beginning to crumble as he now faced his *third* disappointment and his greatest fear – the silencing of the fire alarm.

Ronnie had crawled another ten times his body length and was bathed in the sweat of exertion and fear when he came to the first junction point – about two minutes later. He knew that he was now leaving the confines of the maintenance workshop (with its electrical and plumbing central control areas) to merge with the main corridor, and he had slowed down considerably from his initial pace – partly due to exhaustion, partly because the alarm bells were now only one third their initial volume and he could no longer risk buckling the tin, but mainly because he was about to crawl above the heads of 387 people whose nerves were taut and whose senses were heightened. One hostage looking up at the ceiling suspiciously could mean Ronnie's sudden death in a hail of bullets.

The conduit straight ahead would take him towards the lobby, the conduit to the right headed up the right wing and towards the classroom only metres away where his second son Marty sat captive – but, of course, Ronnie didn't know that.

He didn't know exactly where Marty was, and he was very worried about him.

Ronnie was about to pass the junction vent on his journey towards the admin office – if you could call such crawling a "journey" – when he looked down through an air vent and directly into the face of his firstborn son, although it took Ronnie a moment to recognise him with that GoPro strapped to his forehead and an even weirder than usual expression on his face, obviously drugged out. As Drew looked up towards his father, his furrowed brows melted into a fiendish grin. Ronnie stared, transfixed like a kangaroo in a car's headlight, mesmerised by the red laser sight, as Drew raised a .22 calibre rifle towards him and squeezed the trigger.

50

Leon held his M1 at waist level, the blood red laser dot scanning all ten Scripture Union students.

"Whoever's not ready to die for their faith right now, get out of this office. Miss Bennetton, I know you are not a Christian counsellor – you are very much a *secular* counsellor. You may step outside."

Without any hesitation I was halfway out the door, having already decided to cooperate with the gunmen as fully and as quickly as possible. So quickly, in fact, that Leon, still inside, had to slow me down.

"But don't go away though, Counsellor, when I come back out I will still need you right there by my side in this time of crisis."

Four of the students exited with me. Three more jumped out as they saw Leon beginning to close my office door.

"Time to move, Ricky," Leon suggested gently.

"No, it's time to stay. Barb told me right from the start that being a Christian means laying down your life. All this is no surprise to me, Leon. I was expecting it."

"Do you really understand what you're choosing?"

"I always understand simple things, but thanks for giving me the choice. I like your video camera, Leon, it's cool."

"You know you're free to go, Ricky?" clarified Kieran.

"I know God's not holding a gun to my head." Ricky turned to Leon. "Only Leon is."

The last thing I saw from the corridor, as Leon closed the door, was Barb hugging Ricky. He patted her shoulder in awkward response. Kieran stood defiantly behind them both.

Then, only slightly muffled through my office door, came three rifle shots – evenly spaced.

If there was ever a time in my life when I felt lost and hopeless, weak and helpless – that was it.

Only a few minutes before, I had heard Barb's prayer and felt like her faith was maybe a bridge between God and me. Now, only minutes later, Barb was dead, the bridge had collapsed, and I was falling.

For a few seconds there I couldn't speak or scream, run or hide. The corridor seemed to grow or I seemed to shrink, or both. In a strange kind of out-of-body experience I looked down on myself, surrounded by the seven Scripture Union students who had fled the execution site with me.

The four girls were holding on to each other. Each of the three boys stood alone, avoiding all physical contact. One stared at my office door as though by looking hard he might see through it, one hung his head in shame and cried, the third kept looking up and down the corridor – whether fearful of attack or hopeful of rescue, he could not remember when I queried him later.

Some people report that their lives flash before their eyes when facing imminent death or the threat of it. But, instead, I imagined my two teenage brothers from years gone by, target shooting with their rifles, and I longed, and ached, and willed for them to be right there in that cavernous corridor, at my side, with their guns. Or, better yet, standing in front of me so that I could hide behind them.

Then, suddenly, my office door was flung open and Leon reappeared with his smirk. "Just kidding! We're all fine, really. Just a little ringing in our ears, is all. I bet we had you going there, for a minute!"

We eight in the corridor could clearly see that the three earmarked for execution in my office were still very much alive.

"Counsellor, although your office *is* big enough to swing a cat, it's much too pokey for semi-automatic gunfire – gunshots *really* reverberate off those walls. Tell you what I'm going to do, I'll take you into the principal's office with me, right now, and *demand* that they give you a bigger office. Come with me, kids."

I was amazed at how much stronger I felt, reunited with Barb.

The three Christians followed Leon out into the corridor where they were welcomed with hurried hugs, tears, and apologies.

"Behold the world you're trying to convert, Barb – abundance of emotion, shortage of guts." Then Leon turned to me, "Counsellor, I'll need you to chaperone Barbie if you don't mind, I don't think Ken here is quite the gentleman he makes himself out to be."

Leon caught Ricky's eye. "Ricky, you can escort these seven backsliders to the school assembly. You won't be needing a ticket, but we do require handcuffs, so please see young Mr. Wade down the hall there before you enter the auditorium – and he'll fix you up."

"I want to stay with Barb and Kieran." Ricky was adamant.

Leon's light banter ended. "I like you, Ricky – you've got guts. But *I'm* in charge here, and you'll do as you're told or they'll have to hose that tiny little brain of yours off these walls. Did I say that slowly enough for you, Rick-eeee?"

For the first fourteen years of his life, Ricky Russell had been weighed down by his handicap while swimming upstream against a current of prejudice. Then, for the next two years, as a Christian with Barb and Kieran, he had enjoyed a new identity, value, purpose, belonging, and hope – in the last two minutes, he had even vaulted to death-defying hero status.

But now he was suddenly deflated. Not by Leon's death threat, but by this reference to Ricky's handicap, this cruel reminder, embarrassment, and ridicule. For Leon knew the essential technique of judo – knock down your opponent, using his own weight and momentum against him.

Ricky took a few moments before answering. "Nothing you can say or do is beyond the forgiveness of God, Leon."

Leon looked for a moment like he was profoundly touched. "Really? Reeee-leee? You mean there are no limits of space or time with God?"

"None," Ricky beamed.

Leon placed the muzzle of his M1 against Ricky's temple and pushed his head up against the wall, leaned closer to the young man, and whispered hoarsely in his ear. "Well I'm not God, and neither are you, Rick-eeee, which means we *are* limited by space and time, you and I – the effective killing range of *my* rifle is one hundred metres, and *you've* only got sixty seconds to get yourself into that auditorium, and out of my sight, without saying another word. Fifty-nine, fifty-eight, fifty-seven …."

Ricky walked away silently, his seven friends following.

51

At 12:02, Superintendent Rod Stanwych took Dixon's phone call in his office and immediately apologised for being there.

"Gary, the only reason I'm not there, on-site, is because you are. You're best suited to the front line – and at this late hour in my career, seventeen days from retirement, I'm best suited to the office and the phone. I just reached way over my head and tried to contact the state premier to see if he would authorise IARD action if needed."

"And?"

"And his office had the minister of justice call me back to tell me that the premier is unreachable at the moment, and he ordered me to call him again in ten minutes with a thorough situation report – 'distance yourself from a decision, insulate yourself with facts'.

And I need to know how many men you've got on your Swat team today – they're bound to ask me."

"Four."

"Only four?"

"Plus me, makes five."

"Is that enough?"

"Any *one* of us is more than enough, trust me. I won't waste time now with details, Superintendent. I'll call you back in nine."

It was more than two years later, after I finished working with state and federal inquests and could again research as a private citizen, that I lodged a Freedom of Information injunction against the premier's office to examine his telephone records on the day of the siege.

The telephone logs prove that the minister of justice placed a three-minute call to the premier's mobile phone, immediately before calling Stanwych. I never sought to use that information as a weapon, and I never made it public. But, after years of being gagged and smothered by politics, I just feel that I now need some fresh air of truth.

By the time I unearthed the incriminating evidence, the premier and his justice minister were in the throes of a doomed election campaign. They are now both long gone. The names and faces of the players keep changing – but the game remains the same.

52

Though Wade and Weed's right wing had been contained and controlled much more effectively than had Slave and Druid's left, it still looked like a war zone and was a far cry from the orderly invasion originally envisioned with the help of Earl Kennedy's classroom intercom announcement.

While 348 students and their twelve teachers cowered at gunpoint, the Dregcams unceasingly recorded the incidental details – the little things.

As the last of the shell-shocked students headed back into their classrooms, Treena Carr and Zoe Moustakis were helped to their feet by Ed Zwick the economics teacher.

Wade wedged an empty TI-25 magazine and two discarded student phones under the junction's fire door, otherwise, once he let go it would swing closed, lock the other three Dregs out of the right wing, and splinter the team.

The crunching of glass underfoot from the thousands of broken shards, similar to the sound of munching on ice cubes, was almost blotted out by the clanging fire alarm, but not quite.

Weed replaced her metallic orange magazine with a metallic green one – only a little thing, a fleeting image caught on Dregcam that offered a powerful insight into Leon, Weed, and their relationship.

Once freed from the fire door's demands, Wade quickly regained control of the situation and thereby highlighted the irony of the stockman's riding coat as worn by the Dregs: stockman, cowboy, rancher – herding students, rounding up teenagers, corralling hostages.

Controlling, or herding, a large number of people requires systematic planning. I learnt – from decades of experience in the school system, first as a student and then as a faculty member – that the very essence of modern education is crowd control. And then later, as a psychologist, I found it fascinating.

And if herding crowds requires systematic planning, how much more so abducting and murdering them? There is a science to mass murder.

For example, killing one hundred people in a few minutes might be simple enough, but disposing of their bodies is a mammoth task. One thousand, ten thousand, one million almost unimaginable.

In the Second World War, the Nazis, with true Germanic efficiency, did their research: How many tightly-packed Jews could be killed with a single, high-powered bullet? How efficient was it to shoot Jews on the ridges above quarries or dirt pits and bury them in mass graves below? How long did it take for Jews to die, when crammed in the back of a sealed truck and gassed through a hose connected to the tailpipe – and how much fuel was used?

The Nazis soon realised that concentration camps were required and – even there, far from the eyes of the world – there had to be a science to their extermination.

The Final Solution was to ship millions by train to isolated camps, herd them into gas chambers disguised as communal showers, and burn the bodies in large incinerators that operated twenty-four hours a day.

Crowd containment and control, a lack of witnesses, efficient extermination in large numbers, and subsequent disposal of the bodies.

I remember discussing with Barb the science and psychology behind crucifixion as a means of crowd control. Barb's father, a medical missionary and himself a physician, had researched the subject extensively.

The Romans needed to maintain order throughout their vast empire, so they perfected crucifixion (initially developed by the Persians) as the simplest, most ingenious, economical, humiliating, wretched, sadistic, and horrifying method of execution available to them on a massive scale. It is from the word "crucifixion" that the English word "excruciating" is derived.

Roman citizens themselves were never crucified nor were females, the cruel and shameful torture reserved instead for non-Roman males – slaves, rebels, and contemptible criminals who did not bow to Roman rule and Roman law.

Despite all artistic and sacred misrepresentation to the contrary, the historical facts remain: no loin cloths were allowed the naked victims, nails driven through the palms would tear out between the fingers when made to support the weight of a human body, and the legs were bent at forty-five degree angles.

The seventeen-centimetre (seven-inch) nails were driven into the eight carpal (wrist) bones in the heel of the hand or between the radius and ulna bones where the forearm meets the wrist (damaging the median nerve and causing intense, burning pain or severing it and causing paralysis of the hand).

As he pushed himself upward to avoid this stretching torment, the victim was forced to place his full weight on the nail through his heels or feet – the latter causing the searing agony of tearing through the nerves between the metatarsal bones.

The condemned usually took from six to seventy-two hours to die, his arms sometimes stretched fifteen to twenty centimetres (six to eight inches) longer by the ordeal, with the initial and ongoing pain soon compounded and eclipsed by the difficulty in breathing – he needed to pull himself up by his nailed wrists in order to exhale. Then, when the weight and pain on his now-dislocated wrists, elbows, and shoulders became unbearable, he either fainted or rested his weight on his nailed feet. But, slumped in that position with his arms stretched above his head, carbon dioxide again built up in his lungs, exhaling was difficult or impossible and the pain in his feet excruciating, so that he had no choice but to pull himself up again by his wrists, or suffocate.

And on it went, second by excruciating second, minute by torturous minute, hour after interminable hour of writhing agony until the condemned was too exhausted to pull himself up, or until the Romans broke his legs. Either way it was slow, painful death by blood loss, exposure, shock, exhaustion, dehydration and, ultimately, asphyxiation.

The evil genius of the torture was fourfold: the initial crucifixion itself provided a powerful public deterrent to potential lawbreakers; it returned hours or days of torture from only minutes of nailing effort; the greater the threat to Rome, the more shocking appeared its punishment – with mass revolt or resistance resulting in hundreds or thousands of crucified rebels stretched out for many miles along Rome's famed roadways; and, finally, the bloated and rotting corpse of the crucified proved itself to be even more terrifying, as the days went by, than was the initial execution.

And the Dregs, like the Nazis and the Romans before them, had devised an efficient containment, control, and execution process of their own.

53

Gary Dixon always opened his five-day commando course with the same advice. "Life's greatest battles are fought in the mind and the heart – disciplined thoughts and emotions are the greatest of all soldiers, and focus is the greatest of all weapons."

But most of the police officers couldn't understand what he meant, and he could never hope to explain it, because the true meaning of some words is only ever really learnt in the classroom of affliction. In the modern Westernised world, most people spend most of their lives seeking comfort – undisciplined and unfocused, surprised and unprepared when they finally face crisis or death.

But so disciplined were Dixon's thoughts and so sharp his focus, that he was able to assess the strategic situation in the high school parking lot within seconds of his arrival at 12:01.

Number and position of police officers, their weapons, distances, lines of fire – he took it all in as he walked from his black Landcruiser to his command post in the construction shed, while exchanging greetings with Darren Hayes.

And, in those first few seconds, he recognised all the signs – it was just like his United Nations Peacekeeping nightmare all over again. Rebel gunmen outnumbered, outgunned, and surrounded by armed peacekeepers who were under orders to stand by helplessly – forced to oversee and overhear the settling of accounts and the slaughter of the innocents.

Though the gunshots from within the school were muffled – initially by the fire bells and subsequently by the building itself – the .22 calibre was still easily distinguishable from the .30, and everyone in the parking lot had cringed at the thought of the horrible wounds being inflicted.

In his lifetime he had seen enough and heard enough, and Gary Dixon couldn't stand being a silent witness anymore. He settled himself into his makeshift command post with little intention of re-emerging. Any information he needed to access, or officers he needed to consult, could be brought to him by phone, radio, or in person. Darren Hayes and the commanding officer on-site could maintain the perimeter and report to him any movement or developments.

After his very brief phone call to Rod Stanwych, Dixon decided to distance himself from the whole siege mindset and all the political manipulations.

He needed to focus solely on his training, mission, and mandate – as a hunter-killer – to lock himself away and prepare his team, while awaiting the bureaucratic go-ahead.

His third and fourth commandos, the school building plans, and Luke had all just converged around him – literally arriving in the command post within seconds of each other.

And even with precious little reliable information forthcoming on the Dregs – their location, movements, or plans – Dixon ordered his four commandos to begin memorising the layout of Hunter High with the janitor's help, in preparation for an IARD assault.

Dixon would get back to them and the building plans spread out across the lunch table in a minute, but first he had to clear his mind of clutter, had to make contact with the Sydney tactical squad (the State Protection Group), had to leave all siege thinking and responsibilities with them, had to wash his hands of any more innocent blood poured out due to inactivity, delay, and containment.

He retreated into the corner of the shed, pulled out his mobile phone, and called the Sydney tactical squad's commander, Dave Fisher.

Their relationship had always been adversarial – Dave knew that Gary disagreed strategically with everything he stood for. But all the animosity between them and all the tensions of the past were, surprisingly, absent from Fisher's voice as he answered Dixon's call.

Fisher confirmed that, yes, he was on the road to Newcastle with his hostage negotiator beside him trying, even now, to make telephone contact with the school – and that police on the scene at Hunter High were to secure the perimeter and nothing more.

And then Fisher's anger boiled over and he shared a bond of frustration with Dixon, as a comrade-in-arms shackled by bureaucrats and politicians – the commissioner's office had denied him authorisation to fly ahead of Buster in a police helicopter in order to establish electronic eavesdropping at the school and, hopefully, begin negotiations.

Fisher then had to *beg* for permission to load Buster onto the back of a police flatbed tow truck so that his team could cover the distance well in excess of Buster's top speed of one hundred kilometres an hour. Buster was now roaring through Sydney traffic, and towards the motorway, on the back of the truck at breakneck speed under Highway Patrol escort with sirens wailing, support vehicles following, and motorcycle cops racing ahead of them all to open any traffic bottlenecks. And yet, even for all that, their ETA would be well after one o'clock. Well after.

Fisher was furious and, ultimately, incredulous of the commissioner's final stipulation that Buster be seen driving up to the scene of the siege under its own power.

Dixon excused himself from the phone call, not wanting to waste precious minutes criticising the politics for which he already had no respect. Darren Hayes then brought Dixon and his men up to speed with the chain of events and intelligence gathered thus far.

The security ring around the high school was tight as a drum by the time Dixon arrived at 12:01. Ronnie MacDonald had managed to get inside only minutes before the building was locked down by Sergeant Hayes' conservative supervisor on-site at the school – Assistant Superintendent Vincent DeGroot, destined to succeed Rod Stanwych in seventeen days when he retired.

DeGroot was a giant of a man, a former rugby player and much-feared urban police commander from South Africa who had always been highly disciplined, and meticulously groomed. A fiercely dedicated police officer, proud of his uniform and bound by a strict code of honour – Vincent DeGroot was a crusader for justice with an instinct for self-preservation honed from years of duty in the ghettos of Soweto.

But even such youthful zeal as his was eventually worn down by the poverty, violence, and corruption all around him in South Africa – his flame eventually smothered by the darkness. First he grew tired and then he grew older – the years were catching up with him, his time was running out. His still-meticulous uniform bulged tightly around his burgeoning belly, he started losing his hair and then, eventually, he lost his nerve. He was threatened once too often by a criminal kingpin in Johannesburg, so, seven years ago, he broke and ran – to Australia.

Now a stranger in a strange land who hardly even recognised himself in the mirror – bloated, dreaming only of retirement, settling for security, feathering his own nest, bowing to the politicians – the instinct for self-preservation was all that had seemed to survive from his glory days. DeGroot was now chafing at the bit to make an impression as Superintendent – his plan: to toe the line in Newcastle and then be promoted to head office administration (and a higher salary) in Sydney before retiring, himself, in a few years.

Vincent DeGroot had been a passionate supporter of IARD until the new state government came into power – now he was the most vocal of advocates for Buster and containment.

Accordingly, he enacted a Hunter High lockdown with all Newcastle officers ordered to hold their positions and their fire unless emerging Dregs fired upon them. DeGroot then returned to *his* command post – at the extreme far end of the parking lot, right near the corralled media and their broadcasting vans, and readily accessible for interviews. But, before doing that, he had posted his sniper.

There was never the budget and rarely the need for a trained police sniper in the Hunter Valley Area Command – but what Newcastle lacked in funding, they made up for in the precious asset that was Detective Senior Sergeant Derek Pope. After a six-year stint in the Royal Australian Navy, Pope had promptly joined the New South Wales Police Force at the age of twenty-four.

Thirty years later, he was not only a highly respected detective but also a Commonwealth Games silver medallist (Fifty Metres Small Bore Rifle Prone) and three-time National Australian Full-bore (.308 Winchester) Long Range Match Rifle Shooting Champion (with a telescopic sight).

More than twenty years ago, an amateur cartoonist in the Newcastle station house had drawn a caricature of the ex-navy marksman dressed in a blue sailor suit with a white police cap, bulging forearms, bald, pipe in mouth, and one eye squinting behind his telescopic sight. Pope was not bald and had never smoked – artistic licence – but the cartoon was pinned on the bulletin board and, ever since, Derek Pope was affectionately called "Popeye".

When Pope retired from international Games competition, he began backing up the Newcastle tactical squad as sniper, and had trained with them ever since – now the unofficial thirteenth member of Dixon's Swat team. In the last twenty-two years he had attended over thirty siege and high-risk arrest call-outs, but had only ever fired twice – once shooting out the tyres of a getaway car when convenience store armed robbers tried to ram through encircling police cars with the cashier as hostage; another time, shooting the pistol right out of the hand of a man threatening suicide. (The video of that amazing feat posted on YouTube and since viewed millions of times.)

Vincent DeGroot had conveniently stationed the world-class marksman atop the roof of the construction shed because it was higher than the roofs of all vehicles in the parking lot, and afforded a direct line of fire to the school entrance. And there lay Derek "Popeye" Pope, now only inches above the Swat commander's head, under a black waterproof tarpaulin to shield him from the pouring rain, with only the tip of his muzzle protruding – ready and waiting.

Popeye had arrived at the scene four minutes before Dixon, having just visited his new granddaughter at his son's house not far from Hunter High when the text message came through. In the face of a high school shooting, he hadn't bothered to change into his black tactical uniform and was still wearing a baggy old track suit while wrapped within his trusty over-and-under tarp – his "cocoon" he called it, silver on one side to reflect the sun's heat, black on the other to absorb it – which had faithfully shielded him from hot, cold, frost, scorching sun, rain, hail, and wet rooftops for over twenty years, and countless hours of waiting with his eye glued to his scope.

Under the tarp, Popeye had his tactical team audio headset in place, a water bottle and a police radio beside him. He was lying on his stomach in the prone position with his Remington Model 700P Police Rifle supported by a front bipod. The American-made Remington was considered by many to be the world standard in bolt action sniper rifles, both police and military.

Mounted atop the all-black Remington was a state-of-the-art Schmidt & Bender PM II 5-25X adjustable magnification scope worth four thousand dollars. Loaded within the rifle's internal magazine were three .308 calibre Hornady A-MAX TAP (Tactical Application Police) red polymer-tipped bullets. The fourth round from the magazine was already chambered and ready to fire.

Statistically, more than half of all police sniper shots are taken through windows or walls, and the 168 grain A-MAX polymer tip was developed and proven to penetrate glass and plaster barriers intact with minimal distortion and then deliver "controlled and impressive soft tissue expansion without over-penetration" on the other side – thereby minimising the chances of travelling on through the targeted assailant to wound innocent civilians.

When initially partnering with the police, Dixon had to recalibrate in his mind the mission of the police sniper versus the military. The average military sniper shot is taken at several hundred metres – the mandate: to kill as many of the enemy (often moving) as quickly as possible without being targeted yourself with return fire. In contrast, the average police sniper shot is taken at sixty-four metres (seventy feet) – the mandate: to save as many civilians as possible and kill the perpetrator (usually stationary) only as a last resort, and often after a long wait. There is usually only one target, often wary of snipers, and only one chance to fire one bullet – return fire almost never an issue.

Popeye was positioned about sixty metres from the school's front doors – no target yet in sight.

Dixon had spotted his sniper as soon as he stepped out of the Landcruiser, but didn't mention or acknowledge him because he was focused on the greeting from Sergeant Hayes. Once inside the construction shed, however, Dixon knocked on the ceiling and Popeye knocked back.

Now feeling confident – and relieved – that DeGroot had assumed the mindset and total responsibility for an external containment-and-control-type siege, Dixon ordered Hayes to keep in constant contact with Popeye, to assign binoculars to several officers in the parking lot, and to report back to him immediately with any developments.

Dixon then huddled around the lunch table with his men as they poured over the interior building plans with Luke and asked for detailed descriptions of the Dregs inside – every sight and sound recorded by small, black bodycams attached to their bulletproof vests and mounted in the centre of their chests.

54

After securing the fire door, Wade turned to Weed as she drew near, "You were right on cue shooting out those windows. You holding up okay?"

All hostages had now returned to their classrooms and they could talk "privately", though still accompanied by the ringing alarm.

"I think so, I'm just looking to you for direction."

"You're doing great, I'm proud of you. Now I need your flexi-cuffs."

Weed handed over her bundle of two hundred cable ties.

"Just stand right here near the door and shoot anyone who's not following my instructions. Can you do that?"

"Yes, I can," Weed's tone was decided and determined, but certainly not confident.

"Even warning shots into the ceiling will probably stop most people in their tracks, and then I'll back you up."

Weed smiled, black mascara streaks staining her cheeks from her earlier tearful pleading for Treena and Zoe.

As per their original plan, Wade walked to the top end of the now-deserted, locker-lined, and glass-strewn right wing corridor and stuck his head into R12, the last classroom on the left. The desks were laid out so that the door was at the back of the room.

Wade passed a fistful of cable ties to the student nearest the door as he raised his voice.

"Listen carefully. The Dregs have hijacked the final full-school assembly of the year. We will be escorting this class to the auditorium in a few minutes. I want each and every person in this room – teacher included – to remain in your seat with your hands tied together and resting on the desk in front of you. I am now passing around plastic handcuffs. Pull them tight around your wrists with your teeth, or get your neighbour to pull them tight, without saying one word to each other.

When we march you out of this classroom, anyone found with uncuffed, or loosely cuffed, wrists will be shot through both hands.

Don't ask any questions, do what you're told. You have only a few minutes."

Weed stood guard at the junction while Wade repeated his instructions and handed out the cuffs to each of the twelve classrooms in the right wing.

When the Dregs were finally ready to move the herd, the students in the first of the classrooms, R12, with no questions asked, were ordered to stand on their feet and file out the door.

Of the 348 students and twelve teachers involved, not one of their 720 wrists was improperly bound, not one of their 720 hands shot. Even the Nazis would have been proud.

As always, much of the plan germinated in Leon's mind. It was *he* who had explained the mathematics of bondage to his fellow Dregs.

Binding the hands limited both the self-defence and the attack capabilities of an *individual* captive – that was certainly true. But exponentially greater was the power-sapping potential on a *group* of captives who came to see each other as bound and helpless. As their numbers increased and the minutes dragged on, the grip and the depth of despair only worsened.

And it was this demoralisation, this steady erosion of hope – more than anything else – that always proved overpowering in the end. How else could thousands of soldiers round up, intern, and execute millions of prisoners? And I'm referring here not only to the Nazis and the Holocaust, but also to the many hundreds of other genocidal purgings perpetuated throughout human history, both before and after the Second World War.

Leon illustrated with the example of how the old travelling circuses used to train their elephants. Baby elephants were restrained by a rope around their ankle tied to a stake in the ground. After the first few weeks of frustrated tugging, the infant gave up trying and eventually grew to be a giant, restrained by a tiny rope around his ankle – tied to nothing. The ingrained assumption of the hopelessness of escape hardened, over time, into a deceiving certainty of powerlessness.

And that's why a few Dregs could psychologically imprison the 360 hostages in the right wing.

The sheer force of their numbers would have guaranteed the success of a student uprising – five Dregs could never hold off 360 attackers – but successful escape required a leader, demanded that one was willing to die for the many in leading the charge to freedom. Of course, everyone wanted to be the *many*, and no one wanted to be the *one* – with the result that, together, they were all prisoners of their own fear, ultimately shackled by their instinct for self-preservation.

The captive students and staff of Hunter High chose to keep losing the Dregs' fight, rather than risk winning their own.

One of my brother's coaches used to say that the team trying to win, always beats the team trying not to lose.

And Barb once told me that a person's view of death, more than anything else, will influence how he lives his life – that the man willing to lose his life will always conquer the man trying to save it.

The students and teachers of Hunter High, more than anything else, feared the ending of the lives they'd always known. The Dregs, more than anything else, feared their own continuing.

Wade had already instructed and supplied seven classrooms with their cable ties by the time Slave entered the right wing – and Druid was trailing almost two minutes behind Slave, due to his thorough scanning of the gym and auditorium.

Slave walked up to Weed at her junction point.

"What was all the shooting about?" Weed asked him anxiously.

"Fire alarm locked us out of the left wing – students ran out the fire exit. We went outside to try and capture them, and Druid started shooting up the fire trucks."

"Anybody hurt?"

"Outside? No, I don't think. But the building is now surrounded by police."

"Inside?"

"Leon shot Kennedy and Forman when they tried to set off the fire alarm."

"How are they?" Weed asked with a wince.

"Both dead."

"But Mr. Kennedy wasn't even on the blacklist!"

"He died with honour – three hundred students escaped because of him."

Weed started crying. "But he had two daughters."

"*Three hundred* students he saved."

Slave's reference to heroism went totally unheeded by Weed. "They'll never be the same, it's a terrible thing to lose a father."

"I know," Slave replied quietly.

"A father is priceless – worth even more than one hundred and fifty lives, to each of his daughters."

"He died a hero."

"And who said Mrs. Forman wasn't a hero in her own way? We didn't even know her. She was precious to someone, even if she wasn't to us. How many lives will we ruin today? The ripples go on forever."

"Weed, *we* did not kill Kennedy and Forman."

"Oh, yes we did. We did when we signed that covenant. We're all in this together."

Slave gently shook her shoulders. "We *are* in this together – and we are depending on you, Weed. Me and Wade, we will start sending up students to go sit in the auditorium. You just have to keep an eye on them – that's all. Can you do that?"

Weed nodded as she wiped away her tears.

"Yes, you can. I *know* you can do that. *Your* job, Weed, is to save as many people as possible. Encourage people to cooperate. Keep things running smooth, and you *will* save people. Okay?"

"Okay," Weed sniffed.

"Who knows, maybe this is the total reason you were born, to be with us – here, today – to save many people."

She rubbed his shoulder. "Thank you, Slave. That's very wise."

He puckered his Slavic lips and shrugged his shoulders, then turned to join Wade.

"And why were *you* born?" Weed called after him.

"Maybe just to give you that advice. Perhaps maybe the first wise advice in my life."

55

As the story of the high school siege – and the viewing audience – grew, local Newcastle television reporters who had been the first on the scene were quickly upstaged by celebrity reporters from the national news.

Two of these "faces" (as they were called in the industry) were helicoptered into Newcastle, while several others "hosted" the live, on-site coverage from their studio anchor desks in Sydney – because viewers preferred their news coverage in bite-sized pieces and presented in familiar, instantly recognisable packaging.

Fast food for the busy masses. Authoritative coverage from warm and dry studios by familiar, trusted faces. Relentless, probing, celebrity journalists whose qualifications, character, integrity, and bias were never questioned or challenged – their personal lives and off-camera treatment of colleagues never scrutinised or broadcast.

In many ways, the media were better equipped and organised than the police, and the lone Newcastle police helicopter had to jostle for overhead airspace with three others from the national television networks, as well as two more diverted from local radio traffic-reporting duties.

56

Druid approached the third and last fire bell, located just beyond the junction point in the right wing.

His furrowed brows melted into a fiendish grin as he raised his Ruger towards the ceiling and silenced the final alarm with only one shot. It was 11:59.

Many hostages reported that with the silence came less stress, but more tension. Almost as if the Dregs had subdued the resistance, muted the outcry, stifled the objection, of the very building itself – stripping away the school's sonic camouflage of noise, and enveloping it instead with a sudden and contrasting hush that threatened to expose them all.

Every sound seemed suddenly amplified – each breath or cough, even just swallowing – drawing attention to itself, the last thing any hostage ever wanted.

In the eerie silence that followed the killing of the fire alarm could now be heard the occasional whimpering or sobbing of a captive student, the muted ring tone or vibrating of a discarded phone amidst the techno-litter strewn along the right wing corridor – the panicked call of a friend or relative as word spread about the siege. As none of the calls were answered, concern soon mounted, and the frequency of ringing, vibrating, and illuminating handsets increased exponentially.

As Druid walked past classroom R2, just next to the junction point at the base of the right wing, his younger brother Marty lifted up his two bound hands and called out, "Drew!"

Druid returned and stuck his head in the door at the front of the classroom as Wade and Slave looked to him from R5, two doors away and across the corridor, for an explanation.

"He used to be my little brother," explained Druid cryptically.

"Please, Drew, tell them to let me go."

Druid just stared at his red-haired sibling as if he were an alien – a noteworthy specimen and nothing more. "Do you promise to keep running and never stop?"

"Whatever you say," agreed Marty, desperate to escape and trying unsuccessfully to control the quiver in his voice and the tremble in his lower lip.

Wade now joined Druid at the classroom doorway, and peered in at the red-headed boy.

"Does your mother love you?" Wade asked the younger MacDonald.

"Yes she does," answered Marty.

Wade puzzled over the boy's response, then asked him, "What's it like?"

Marty just looked at Wade, saying nothing, *both* Dregs before him now too cryptic to understand.

Wade turned to Druid. "Let him go. Your mother doesn't need to lose two sons in one day."

Wade walked off to rejoin Slave at R5, and Druid called after him, "I'll escort him to the front door."

Druid turned back to his brother, "And then you'll run."

Marty MacDonald just nodded. As he rose from his chair, the student on his left touched his elbow and pleaded.

"Marty …."

But the boy on Marty's right beat him to the request, "Take me with you, Marty."

"Can I take two friends with me?" Marty asked his former brother.

Druid smiled patronisingly. "Course you can."

The boys on each side of Marty rose to their feet tentatively.

Then four or five other voices around the classroom whispered urgently, "Marty." "What about me?" "Me, too, Marty!" "Please, Marty."

"Can I bring *five* friends with me?" Marty requested meekly.

"No, none, just you," Druid reneged impatiently, overturning his previous ruling.

The two boys on either side of Marty sat back down, slowly, not wanting to upset the irrational gunman.

"But you said I could take these two."

"That was before you started negotiating. Never negotiate with a wizard."

"I'm sorry." Marty stood alone, at his desk, in the hushed classroom, and started crying.

Druid watched him. Wordlessly. For fifteen seconds. A very long time.

"Do you still want to take those two beside you?"

Marty wiped his tears with the back of his bound hand, and his chest heaved and shuddered when he responded.

"If it's …. if it's okay with you."

"Oh, it's okay with *me* – stand up again, you two …."

Marty's two neighbours got back to their feet.

"…. I was just thinking of *you*, little brother. When you asked to 'take' them with you, I thought you meant 'carry'…."

Druid raised his Ruger with its laser of death and, without a moment's hesitation, shot each boy five times in the chest.

The Year Seven classroom erupted in screams, gasps, and sobs.

Marty was left standing alone again, covering his head with his plastic-bound arms.

".... and I just thought that two was more than enough."

Druid had used the gunshots as punctuation for his sentence, like a writer uses exclamation points.

Both boys had fallen face down beside their desks, and one of them was now making gurgling respiratory sounds.

Druid, until now quite soft-spoken, suddenly erupted himself in response to the noise of the crowd.

"Shut up! Shut up!" he started yelling.

And when the silence was not absolute and immediate, he began pacing up and down the aisles screaming, "I SAID SHUT UP!" – his laser dot panning and scanning across the students, blood droplets spraying from his wounded fingers.

The class of emotionally shocked twelve and thirteen-year-olds fell silent. But the rasping continued.

"WHO'S MAKING THAT NOISE?!" Druid screamed.

Wade and Slave burst into the classroom and stood in the doorway so that they could still keep an eye on the corridor.

Thirteen-year-old Diana Mercer pointed towards the fallen boys and screamed back, "HE CAN'T BREATHE!"

Druid placed the burning hot muzzle of his Ruger against Diana's forehead in reaction to such insolence.

Diana just closed her eyes, not even daring to move.

Druid was shaking and breathing hard. "Which one is it?"

"I don't know," Diana answered, eyes closed, teeth clenched, voice lowered.

"WHICH ONE?!"

"I .... don't .... know!"

No one knew, and no one ever found out which boy was gurgling.

Druid lowered his rifle, leaving a red circular burn mark on her forehead.

"What do you think you're doing, Druid? They weren't on the blacklist!" Wade tried to restore some order to the insanity.

Druid drew five paces closer to the fallen boys and hammered ten more bullets into their backs and heads at point blank range, only stopping when the magazine was empty. The last gurgle ceased with a chilling, peaceful sigh.

All the other students in the classroom remained silent before, during, and after this final execution.

"Anyone else want to be carried out by young Marty here?" asked the crazed gunman.

Wade walked up to Druid. "They're only Year Sevens! What did *they* do wrong?"

Druid dropped his fifth emptied magazine of the day onto the classroom floor, and pulled his sixth fresh magazine from his black ammo pouch. "They'll be fine when they wake up."

Wade ripped the magazine from Druid's hand. "This isn't a dream!"

Druid opened wide his wild blue eyes and almost touched noses with Wade. "No, it's a *nightmare*, that's the whole point. The only way from this world of illusion to reality is through a nightmare – haven't you seen the Matrix?"

"This is not a movie or a video game!"

"And you are not God, the Righteous Judge! Is there no blood on your hands, my little blood brother?"

Leon's voice crackled over both their walkie-talkies, "What's going on with all the shooting out there?"

Wade hesitated before responding. Druid held up the silver Dreg ring on his finger with its overturned chalices of wrath, both the ring and finger now covered with blood.

"Discipline problem here in the classroom, Leon, that's all, bit of collateral damage," Druid responded to Leon.

"Everything under control?" Leon asked.

"I hope so," Wade responded as he glared at Druid.

Druid smiled and held out his hand for the return of his confiscated TI-25 magazine. "Just a little family spat, Leon, you know what families are like. I'm about to send my baby brother home to his mother, if that's okay with you."

"Escort him to the front door, Druid, and then stay there," Leon's final word.

Wade handed over the magazine, then led the way towards the corridor junction point. Slave returned to R5.

Druid headed towards the classroom door, beckoning with his index finger for his little brother to follow him.

Marty looked down on the floor, to his left, at Andy Stewart – thirteen years old, friend since preschool, always a nervous boy who clung on to him a bit, physically and emotionally. In kindergarten, Marty had complained to his mum that after all the other kids had confirmed an arm's-length distance from the student ahead in schoolyard line-up, Andy always continued to rest his hand, annoyingly, upon Marty's shoulder. Alison MacDonald just asked Marty to remember that Andy, as an only child, had always been wrapped in cotton wool by his parents and was probably just nervous beginning school.

On the floor, to Marty's right, lay twelve-year-old David Sheridan, a self-confident and talented young drummer who had only befriended Marty in this, their first year of high school. David's birthday was the twenty-third of October. His parents subsequently begged authorities for the prompt return of their son's body as they dreaded commemorating his birthday and funeral on the same date, but autopsy procedures took longer than expected and David ended up being buried exactly ten days after the siege, on his thirteenth birthday.

One of the two murdered boys had apparently lost control of his bowels, during trauma or after death, and the classroom soon filled with the odour of excrement.

With nearly twenty per cent of all battlefield wounds inflicted to the abdominal region, war veterans will often describe the smell of battle as a combination of dirt, gunpowder, blood, and excrement. This is especially so in the case of explosion from grenades, mines, aerial bombardment, and artillery.

So far, Hollywood has failed to appreciate, replicate, or communicate the odour – it being neither heroic, nor glamorous.

Druid had already stepped out into the corridor and reloaded. "Let's go."

Shocked and stunned by the sudden intrusion of death into his life, Marty dragged his feet of lead towards escape and freedom.

This time, none of his classmates asked to join him.

"Are you just going to leave them there to rot?" Druid asked with great contempt.

"I can't carry them." It was obvious that Marty was feeling guilty about deserting his fallen friends, but had already accepted his powerlessness.

"Okay, I'll give you a hand. You drag one, and I'll drag the other."

Marty looked back at the corpses. "I …. I just can't."

Druid raised his Ruger – inched his death laser around Marty's chest and up his throat, finally resting it in the middle of his forehead.

Young Marty followed the red dot with his eyes, as though it were a tarantula creeping over him, not daring to move a muscle. When it started crawling over his face, he just closed his eyes.

"What kind of a friend are you, anyway? Lie down beside your mates!"

Marty opened his eyes. "I thought you said I could go?" His voice was quivering again.

"Oh, gonna cry again are you, little sookie-baby? *Lie down!* I'm gonna drag you out of here myself just so you can save face – this way you can tell everyone that I had to drag you away from your dead mates."

Marty lay down beside the body of Andy Stewart, looking almost relieved that he didn't have to support his own weight any longer. One less task, one less burden, for the shaking knees that threatened to buckle beneath him at any moment. Druid, ice-empowered, moved quickly, grabbed his brother's ankles, and headed for the lobby.

"You make me sick, you little maggot. I'm ashamed to call you my brother. I'll cast you out of my sight as fast as I can."

Druid raved on, his rifle dangling by its strap, as he dragged his little brother to the front door – the red firefly darting around him on the floor, all the way.

At first Marty said nothing, busy wrestling to keep his shirt down with his bound hands so as to avoid carpet burns across his back. But as they entered the right wing corridor with its polished tile floors, Marty began crying out in pain, imploring his brother to stop, and then simply screaming as the broken glass from the shot-out windows and the piles of abandoned digital devices mercilessly ground into his flesh and ripped open his back.

Leaving the wedged-open fire doors and her post at the junction, Weed compassionately tried to lift Marty's shoulders to relieve the drag weight on his lacerated back, tried to keep up with the speeding Druid, lost her grip, lost her footing, and slipped in Marty's blood.

Wade stayed back to cover Weed's deserted post at the junction, then took a few steps towards following her, then returned to the junction – he could not and would not abandon Slave to cover the 357 remaining live hostages in the right wing all by himself.

Marty somehow managed to stop screaming as he was dragged along the main corridor, but began again through the carpeted lobby and over the shattered glass from the trophy display cases, leaving a smeared blood trail all the way – just as though some vandal had dragged a mop dipped in red paint.

Once through the lobby, Druid yanked him to his feet and pushed him out the front door. As Marty staggered towards the front steps and into the pouring rain – both his shirt and the flesh on his back in shreds – his brother called out after him, "And before you go tattling on *me* to Mum and Dad – make sure you tell them that *you* were just expelled!"

It was 12:02.

57

It's a good thing that Ronnie had managed to suppress his yell with the palm of his own hand, because Drew's execution of the final fire bell beneath him had snuffed out the last decibel of Ronnie's audio camouflage, and the yell would have surely given him away.

Below, Drew walked away from the vent and out of sight.

Above, Ronnie slowly crawled on towards the lobby – the almost-deafening din of the fire bell now replaced by the almost-paralysing fear of buckling tin – the black leather bag, his only hope, trailing silently along behind him in the dark.

With every inch that he dragged himself further away from the subsequent barrage of gunfire and yelling in the right wing, Ronnie MacDonald's conscience screamed at him, shouted his name, mocked him, wagged its finger, and shook its head.

The cop part of him felt duty-bound to assist at the scene of that shooting. The father part just wanted to get to the admin office, gather intelligence, and hasten his eldest son's safe containment and capture.

"Do your patient no harm". If only Drew could be arrested unharmed, and before hurting others. Extenuating circumstances, drug addiction, underage offender, no previous convictions – use of a prohibited firearm, sure, but hopefully no grievous bodily harm yet. And even if there was – God forbid – minors got away with murder these days. Literally.

Never mind a good lawyer, just get a great psychologist. Expert, clinical, forensic testimony. But, then again, even that would crumble if

the all-powerful media turned the public against the teenage offenders –
trial by television, verdict by viewers.

And how would Ronnie himself feel, he wondered, if it were one of
his own children being terrorised or shot in that classroom? Surely his cry
for justice would not be easily silenced, his thirst for vengeance not cheaply
quenched.

Ronnie crawled on past another three air vents, another ten body
lengths, another ninety seconds maybe, as he deliberated. Should he maybe
go back to the right wing, after all, back to the source of all that shooting?

But Ronnie's decision was soon made for him as the source – his own
son Drew – came dragging his younger brother down the corridor past
him, crying in pain. Their father looked down from above, watched in
horror through the air vent at the rifle strapped around Drew's neck, the
frenzied ranting of his madness, his grip on Marty's ankles, the helplessness
of his prey, and the trail of blood behind him.

Ronnie bit on his own fist to keep from crying out, and mopped
the tears in his eyes for fear of them dropping to the corridor below and
betraying his location.

But he missed two teardrops that dripped from the end of his nose.
He watched them falling through the vent as if in slow motion, the first
mingling with the smeared blood trail on the floor of the corridor, the
second one splashing onto Weed's shoulder, unfelt and unnoticed, as she
bent to lift Marty by the wrists and spare his flayed back from any further
dragging.

And then it happened. Through his tears, Ronnie suddenly saw things
clearly and, despite the whimpering, dragging, and grunting sounds from
below him, he somehow heard – or felt inside – a still, small voice or
bubble of hope. His pain was somehow eased by Weed's mercy, his burden
somehow lightened by her lifting of his son. They were, none of them,
alone. They were, all of them, somehow interconnected – hundreds of souls
in the building, thousands of family members around the state, untold
millions around the world hearing of their pain and cringing – somehow
all related.

His momentary flash of insight then just as suddenly over – like
lightning in the night – Ronnie crawled on in the confines of his darkness,
playing out his part in a much bigger drama, and dragging along his
contribution of hope in a black bag behind him.

And though the anguished cries of his sons may have led the way up the corridor before him, Ronnie knew that the best way to help them, and all the others, was to momentarily ignore their cries, pass them by, and press on to the admin office.

58

Gary Dixon was preparing his men, with Luke's help.

Ten stairs from parking lot to school entrance.

Fifteen paces across the lobby.

Admin office directly ahead.

Turn right – forty paces to the gym, thirty more to the auditorium.

Darren Hayes, finally wearing his yellow Hi-Vis police rain gear over his sopping wet uniform, burst into the construction trailer and motioned for Dixon to confer with him in the corner.

"One of our officers outside reckons that it's Ronnie MacDonald's son Drew that was confirmed as one of the shooters – I thought I saw Ronnie's van approaching the parking lot a few minutes before you arrived, but there's no sign of it now."

Dixon held out his hand. "Give me your radio."

59

"Why are you taking the three of us as hostages *specifically*?" asked Kieran. We had just been staring at the glass-strewn carnage that used to be the lobby – the symbolic destruction of the school's history, and all that we had ever known Hunter High to be.

And Leon let us stare, let it all soak in as the sirens approached and gathered together outside in the storm.

Then, behind us, Leon held open the door to the admin office for us to enter while he finally answered Kieran. "Don't flatter yourself, Ken, you may be my *special* hostages but you're certainly not my *only* hostages, I've got over three hundred – and would actually have seven hundred if Mr. Kennedy here hadn't made his fatal mistake."

Mrs. Forman and Mr. Kennedy remained unmoved in their respective pools of blood. I bent down and grabbed their wrists, feeling for any signs of pulse.

"Leave them, they're dead," said Leon, no emotion in his voice.

"Maybe not …." I was about to argue the case.

"They're dead because they made the mistake of thinking they were still in charge – and didn't follow instructions."

I caught his inference, and let go their wrists.

The third and final fire bell was suddenly, finally silenced – and Leon continued in hushed and threatening tones.

"There, you see, Counsellor, that's why you are one of my very *special* hostages – because you listen, you try to understand how people think, and try to develop your own understanding along with theirs. You, Ken and Barbie …."

"It's *Kieran and Barb*," Kieran corrected.

"Today, if I say you're Ken and Barbie, you're Ken and Barbie. You two are my special hostages because you have guts, and you're leaders. Most people follow the crowd in fear of walking alone – you two are exceptional. But you still need to remember that *I* am in charge here, and I'm about to teach you a lesson you'll never forget.

That's why I wanted you to take a good look at the previous administration here – to focus you. You need to pay attention because I can only teach today's lesson once – it's serious, it's urgent, and it's got to be brief. Blink and you'll miss it."

"Why so brief?" asked Barb.

"Because I'm tired. I feel like I've gotten too old, too fast.

There's a whole world full of consumers out there worshipping youth, beauty, and wealth. Well, it's not all that it's cracked up to be. Believe me, I know. I *am* young, and beautiful, and wealthy – but also old, and ugly, and bankrupt. Tired and empty. Stop the world, I want to get off – but I also want to go out with a bang.

Picture this now – those billions of little consumers come home from work exhausted, they turn on the TV – no patience, short attention span."

Leon pointed to his head-mounted Dregcam. "Sixty minute documentary, max – fifty minutes after the commercial breaks. I've been slaving all day to pay my bills, and this documentary better be riveting, or I'll switch the channel with my little remote here – the only real control I exert in my whole powerless life'."

"But your video is too graphic, they'll never air it," I blurted, then immediately feared I might have offended the young murderer before me.

"I think you overrate the taste of the modern audience, and underestimate their thirst for vicarious thrills. Give them bread and circuses – and Facebook – I reckon. They'll broadcast it – just think of the ratings."

"Fame is fleeting – you'll soon be forgotten," added Kieran.

"They won't even remember your name," emphasised Barb.

"Ahhh, but thirty minutes with the school counsellor here could be milked for years, as the masses turn to psychology for an explanation. Interviews, books, maybe even a movie."

"You never really struck me as a media hound, Leon, more of an enigma – tall, dark stranger, man of mystery," I said, honestly trying, like always, to understand.

"The spotlight's not for me, it's all for my father. Reputation means everything to him. I'm out to balance his books. For the rest of his natural life, the name Spitzer will be linked to Leon, and I will be linked to Hunter High.

The Dregs have the run of the place until at least 12:30. It's hunting season for another …. half hour? Less," he said as he consulted his Mickey Mouse watch. "We're abusing the abusers, and consuming the consumers."

"Like Robin Hood and his merry men," said Kieran.

Suddenly we heard a barrage of what sounded like ten or twelve shots from the right wing, muffled by the double doors to the admin office. But Leon continued, unfazed, as he smirked his Leon smirk. "Just lovable rogues."

"There's a much greater consumer power involved here than you even know. Do you believe in God, Leon?" asked Barb.

He pondered for several seconds before responding. "A good God? No."

"Do you believe in the devil?"

"Now, *him* I can relate to."

"Well believe me, Leon, he's stalking these halls today, too. Stalking our hearts and minds. Devouring his victims from the inside out.

You're right, it's hunting season – both for Satan and for God. All the distractions of youth, and the world, and the educational system have been peeled back, blasted away, for forty minutes.

This is not just the Dregs against Hunter High, Leon, this is darkness against light. Satan is out to destroy lives, and families, and futures – while God is determined to pour light into the darkness, and rescue all that seems hopelessly lost."

Barb was interrupted by a second barrage of gunfire from the right wing. Leon pulled the walkie-talkie from his coat pocket, "What's going on with all the shooting out there?"

"Discipline problem here in the classroom, Leon, that's all, bit of collateral damage," Druid responded.

"Everything under control?" Leon asked.

"I hope so," Wade responded.

Druid clarified, "Just a little family spat, Leon, you know what families are like. I'm about to send my baby brother home to his mother, if that's okay with you."

"Escort him to the front door, Druid, and then stay there," Leon gave the final word to his Dregs, but never responded to Barb's last comments – he just turned instead to Kieran. "She's a real firecracker, isn't she, Ken? She must be a lot of fun at a party. Tell you what – you stick with me, Barbie, and you can represent God's point of view in all of this.

Come along now, Counsellor, time to mingle with the students like you do so well. All the ones I've seen today are looking a little anxious – must be the pressure of those year-end exams, don't you think?"

Leon held the admin door open at arm's length for his three hostages. His right hand remained on the trigger, and his stance in the corridor provided him that extra moment's distance should any of the three of us try to rush him. It was a quick reminder to me – in case I had forgotten – that Leon was no more the gracious host, than we were his honoured guests. Just because we weren't handcuffed, didn't mean we were free.

We stepped into the main corridor only thirty seconds before Druid rounded the corner from the right wing, dragging his brother behind him, while Weed struggled to keep up with them both.

It was only when Druid had hauled Marty across the broken glass of the trophy cases in the lobby before us, and reached the front doors of the school, that he finally loosed his grip on his brother's ankles and let his legs drop onto the glass-strewn carpet.

"And before you go tattling on *me* to Mum and Dad, make sure you tell them that *you* were just expelled." Druid held open the front door as he shoved Marty, staggering, out into the storm.

My eyes shifted from Marty's torn back to the flash of recognition on Druid's face as he turned and saw me walking beside Leon.

"Hey, this whole situation reminds me of a Bible story, Barbie!"

"What, Cain and Abel?" cracked Kieran as he took in Marty's smeared blood trail down the corridor.

"David and Goliath?" Leon guessed as he pointed down towards the petite Barb.

"No," said Druid as he nodded towards me and Leon, "Danielle in the Leon's den. Get it? Daniel in the lion's den – Danielle in the Leon's den?"

"Yes, but God closed the mouth of *that* lion – and I'm still talking," smirked Leon.

"The day is not yet done, Leon, and God will do what God will do," Barb replied quietly.

"Well then, He'd better do it quickly, He's only got twenty-seven minutes left."

Druid whirled his red laser dot around Barb's head, and chest, and shoulders. "Fireflies, fireflies – what do you think of our cute little fireflies, Barbie? Beautiful, aren't they?"

Barb tried, and failed, not to squint at the blinding red light and not to wince as the loaded gun was flaunted recklessly in her face.

"Leon is lord of the flies," said Druid as he lowered his laser sight and turned to watch Marty collapsing into the arms of police officers, who ran over from behind their vehicles at the far end of the parking lot. "You want me posted right here, Leon, at the front doors – the portal?"

"We need to know you're there, Druid, covering our backs."

While Druid craned his neck and stepped aside to scan the parking lot, Barb turned back to Leon.

"Did you choose that title, 'lord of the flies'?" she asked him.

"No, just more of Druid's babbling. Why?"

"Lord of the flies – Baalzebub – it's from the Old Testament. Baal is the god of rain and storms, child sacrifice and death, false gods and oracles. Sometimes Baal is even used as a name for Satan himself. Many satanists believe that Baal is strongest in October, and the Celtic druids sacrificed to Baal on Halloween because that's when the veil was thinnest between this world and the kingdom of darkness."

"Druid doesn't know *what* he's saying half the time – it's just a coincidence," Leon assured her.

"Oh, I'm sure he doesn't know what he's saying – but it's no coincidence."

Leon's response was interrupted by Druid's return.

"I'll be too exposed – nothing between me and their marksmen but a glass door. I just have a premonition, Leon, mark my words as a seer and a prophet – great danger awaits me at a distance, by a faceless stranger. I fear their archers. Let me take ten students to use as a shield, around about me."

"Do you need ten?"

"I'll build a wall."

"You said a shield."

"I meant a wall of shields, like the Roman phalanx."

"Ten – no more. And you can't use anyone on the blacklist."

"I give my word to the king of the Dregs!" Druid walked off towards the first of the handcuffed hostages now rounding the junction at the far end of the locker-lined corridor.

"What blacklist?" I blurted out, not even trying to hide the dread in my voice.

"Don't worry, the three of you aren't on it – that's enough for you to know, isn't it?" asked Leon.

"No it isn't," retorted Kieran, his volume raised.

"Watch your tone, Ken, it's not too late to add your name," Leon threatened.

"You're not helping," Barb scolded her boyfriend, expecting more of him at a time like this.

60

Little Ronnie MacDonald's life – bizarrely, ironically, apparently – had now come full circle. His father had originally taken him to the Glasgow police station all those years ago to seek protection from teenage thugs, and now here was Ronnie – all grown up, halfway around the world, and several decades later – himself the avenging cop, his own sons now both bully *and* victim.

In the partial illumination provided by the air vents before him, Ronnie could see the point just ahead where the CCTV cables from each end of the main corridor met and then branched off to the right. That was the admin office.

And down through a vent beneath him, he could see Marty's blood trail veering off to the left – through the lobby, out into the storm and on to freedom. For a moment Ronnie fantasised about escaping *with* Marty, but it was too late for that, his heart now set on mass deliverance rather than personal freedom.

With hundreds of hostages still in the building, he turned right and crawled silently over the head of Leon Spitzer in the corridor below him, and on into the sanctuary of the admin office – refuge and relief *finally* from the terror of buckling tin and audio amplification that had dogged his every movement in the crawl space, and threatened to expose him.

So relieved was Ronnie, in fact, that he quietly kicked out the ceiling grille of the admin office without even first checking where it would land.

And therefore, when he finally did peer down through the open vent, he was shocked to see that the sharp edge of the grille had gouged a furrow in Earl Kennedy's right cheek. His pasty white cheek.

Inspector Ronnie MacDonald looked down at the first two fatalities of the Hunter High School siege to be confirmed by the New South Wales Police.

Ronnie quickly began searching for a way to defuse his panic, to lessen the gravity, to waken himself from the nightmare.

And he found it – proof, or the hope of proof, or the proof of hope – Ronnie MacDonald knew ballistics and these bullet wounds that had felled Kennedy and Forman were *definitely not* .22 calibre, of that he was sure. And the rifle that he had seen Drew carrying – the one the boy had used to shoot out that fire alarm beneath him – that *definitely was* a .22, Ronnie had no doubt.

Of course these observations did not preclude the possibility that Drew had used a second rifle to kill in the office – certainly not beyond all reasonable doubt in a court of law – but enough hope, for now, in the heart of a desperate father.

And as Ronnie wriggled his six-foot-three-inch frame out of the tin echo chamber and eased first his black bag, then his foot, onto the reception desk below him, he remembered hearing initial radio references to a third gunman in the parking lot – with a heavier calibre weapon – and he began, absurdly, hoping for as many gunmen as possible.

There were five Dregs? Hopefully then at least five gunmen – the higher the number, the lower the odds that Drew had pulled the trigger of the gun that killed Kennedy and Forman.

But by the time his feet were firmly planted on the floor, and Ronnie had knelt beside the corpses to take their pulses, and seek for signs of life – to hope for signs, and wish, and beg – the numbers had sorted themselves out in his mind, and began storming the parapets of his heart.

The facts were undeniable, immoveable even in the face of a father's will. Accomplice. Accessory before the fact. Aiding and abetting.

Even if Drew had not *fired* any fatal shots, he was still one of the Dregs, an accomplice to murder, and personally guilty of kidnapping, assault, and grievous bodily harm to Marty, as well as assorted drug and firearms offences.

Ronnie forced himself to shift emotionally beyond the despair, to step physically away from the bodies and towards the wooden cabinet inside the fallen principal's office – the cabinet that contained a large split-screen CCTV monitor, wired up to display the ten surveillance camera images being recorded from around the school.

He sat down on the floor, crossed his legs, and suddenly felt like a kid surrounded by his electronic toys. As the monitor sprang to life, his one brief lightning flash of optimistic clarity back in the air conditioning duct faded to black. And now, in the silence of the slain principal's office and under the glaring fluorescents, he could no longer hear the still, small voice of hope.

No order, no meaning, no hope – and little Ronnie MacDonald was once again helpless, alone, intimidated, and surrounded by school bullies.

Communications expert or just an overgrown child? Had he not been the man his son had needed?

Ronnie felt inside him, welling up, an overwhelming urge – an ache, a pang, a longing – to phone his wife and cry.

61

Once all the students and teachers in the right wing were back in their classrooms, and handcuffed, there was no escape and everyone knew it.

The architects of the high school building had designed each classroom with fairly narrow windows in order to combat the weather extremes of hot and cold. But although the windows were only ever moderately successful at insulating the elements, they did prove to be highly effective for restraining hostages. Even the smallest and thinnest Year Seven students could never have gotten their shoulders and hips through the openings.

When interviewing survivors, it was fascinating how many said that – although "trapped", "hopeless", and "helpless" would best describe their initial feelings upon capture – once handcuffed, other words like "inevitable", "accepting", and "fatalistic" seemed more accurate.

Like a fugitive finally apprehended, most hostages were not surprised at being caught or cornered, almost as if being human itself included an awareness of the ultimate need for submission, an expectation of a coming day of reckoning.

Hostages actually seemed somewhat calmed by the fact that the Dregs had a plan, a process, and a timetable to follow – perhaps partly because students were so used to being herded and processed from the age of three, or four, or five, when society began to usurp the role of the family and institutionalise them in day care centres, preschools, and classrooms.

Wade caught up with Slave at the doorway to classroom R12 – the last classroom at the top of the right wing, the first to have been issued their cable ties.

Slave stepped into the classroom, Wade stood in the doorway. Wade was the spokesperson, Slave the backup.

"Everyone on your feet, please."

As everyone stood and turned, they saw Slave and his rifle for the first time, standing between them and the door at the rear of the room.

Ever since the fire alarm had first sounded at 11:49, things had just gone from bad to worse for these students. They had worried about a fire, suspected a drill, were engulfed in a siege, deafened by fifty shots in an enclosed corridor, showered with shattered glass, threatened with shooting, confined in a classroom, handcuffed, and then horrified by the nightmarish sounds of Druid's classroom executions and Marty's being dragged away screaming.

Now they were faced with a fourth uniformed, well-armed gunman and about to be marched off.

"Single file down the corridor and directly into the auditorium, please."

That might have been twice in fifteen seconds that Wade had said "please", but no one had any illusions about the threat having diminished, because Wade checked the fit of every pair of flexi-cuffs that passed through the door before him and Slave was on sentry duty, rifle ready, laser glowing, no warmth or smile on his face.

And then the culling began.

After the first dozen students had passed through the door, Wade dropped his rifle to block the exit of Treena and Zoe.

"You two stand in the corner, you're not leaving yet."

Treena had been keeping her gaze fixed on the floor, avoiding all eye contact, ever since her earlier dealings with Wade when she wet herself in the hallway. Now confronted again, she silently took hold of Zoe's arm.

Zoe spoke for the two of them, in her new humbled and respectful tone. "Why can't we go stay with the others?"

The Dregcams captured in her eyes the terror, the racing mind, the fear of torture or abuse, the desperate longing to stay with the group, to blend in, to become invisible.

"You're both on the blacklist, we'll deal with you separately."

Wade's tone was much worse than angry or threatening, it was cold and procedural.

Slave spoke up, "Step aside, you're blocking the door."

Both girls obeyed instantly, and Wade resumed checking the cable ties of the students lined up behind them.

Zoe stepped to the other side of Slave, and the safe end of his Ruger, to ask him a question. Treena swung in behind her like an appendage. "What does the 'blacklist' mean?"

"Judgement day." If the girls were hoping for some form of reassurance, they were sorely disappointed – with Slave's lack of emotion and Slavic accent only magnifying the threat.

"What did we do?" asked Zoe.

"Abuse of power," answered Wade without taking his eyes off the cuffs that he herded quickly into the hallway.

"Look who's talking!" Zoe spewed.

Wade snapped back, "Ahhh, now *that's* the Zoe we've all come to know and love. Welcome back, Zoe, I didn't recognise you without poison on your lips."

The more submissive students were departing quickly now. At the very end of the line was Robyn Turner – personal development, health and physical education teacher. Miss Turner was wearing a green track suit, her plastic-bound but still-reassuring hands shifting between the shoulders of the last four students in line before her.

Robyn was only in her mid-thirties, but she had already mastered that mother-hen tone of voice usually employed by much older teachers. Miss Turner's plan was obviously to scoop Treena and Zoe up under her wing, and safely usher these last six students out in front of her. "Treena and Zoe can stay with me, Wade."

Wade lowered his Ruger, like a roadblock, immediately after Robyn's original four charges had exited.

"I agree," said Wade to Mrs. Turner, "you *three* can stay behind."

"You four to the auditorium," Slave instructed the confused students now standing out in the corridor and no longer under Turner's protective wing.

"We're separating all teachers from students. Once we've filled the auditorium, you'll be taken to the staff lounge," Wade explained to Robyn.

"Why?" asked Turner.

"To shatter the illusion that the teachers are in charge, have all the answers, and guarantee some kind of safe passage."

"And you just want to prove that to the students?"

"No, to the teachers – the students have known it for years."

62

Ronnie MacDonald was just about to punch Triple Zero into Earl Kennedy's desktop phone when he saw Leon Spitzer on the monitor before him, sticking his finger in his ear.

Ronnie peered closer at the split-screen image, confirmed his fear, hung up the landline before he even realised that it was dead, and reached for the speed dial on his mobile phone.

Now that he had a second to think about it, he decided to phone his own police station directly, instead of the emergency operator. In these days of centralisation and cost-cutting – when many "Australian" commercial call centres were now located in Mumbai, with Indian operators sometimes answering Australian queries in the middle of the night their local time – all Triple Zero calls were diverted to the next available emergency operator in the state, possibly located hundreds of kilometres from the site of the actual emergency and probably possessing no local geographic knowledge whatsoever.

Such displaced operators were therefore trained to demand street addresses, not directions or landmarks that were meaningless to them, which were then typed into a computer and electronically diverted to the closest local police dispatcher.

Recently a current affairs television show had sensationalised two accounts of distress calls from fishermen in sinking boats who could not be rescued until someone found the actual street addresses of the boat launching sites involved. Automatic GPS tracking of all Triple Zero cellular phone calls had since been authorised, but not yet budgeted or implemented.

And Ronnie knew that what he needed now was an immediate, local response. Human assistance. The last thing the renowned electronics wizard could afford was to be lost within the virtual world of a police telecommunications system – even if he had designed it himself.

Dave Lovell answered, "Newcastle Police, Central Station, Constable Lovell speaking."

"Dave, it's Ronnie MacDonald. I need to know who's leading the tactical squad at Hunter High – is it Gary Dixon?"

Ronnie hadn't specifically seen any signs of the tactical squad when he drove past the high school, but he knew they'd be there.

"Yeah, Big Mac, it's Dixon. But you know it's not the *official* tactical squad, and Dixon's not *officially* in charge."

"I know all about it, Dave. I need you to patch me through to Dixon's personal mobile phone, *don't use the police radio system* – we're being scanned. This is critical, Dave."

"Got you, Mac, hold on a minute."

It was a very long minute. Initially Lovell couldn't get through to Dixon because he was on the line with Dave Fisher, the Sydney tactical squad commander, so Lovell left a message on Dixon's voice mail. When he received no prompt return call, the young constable then radioed a patrol car on the scene and had officers go ask Dixon, still in the on-site construction office, to call the station – urgently.

When Dixon finally did, Lovell patched him straight through to Ronnie.

Dixon's new phone had come with the latest call-recording app, and he made sure it was on before he began speaking with Drew MacDonald's father.

"Dixon here, what's up, Ronnie? I've been trying to reach you on your radio."

"Police frequencies are compromised – they've got scanners."

"Reporters?" asked Dixon.

"No, the Dregs."

"How do you know, Ronnie?"

Tone, inflection, nuance – it was all there in Dixon's voice – and Ronnie could tell immediately that the SAS commander was already aware that Drew was one of the gunmen and was now asking what Drew's father knew about past, present, or future events relating to this siege. Good – Ronnie didn't have to waste time.

"I saw the leader, Leon – the kid carrying the M1 – using a scanner, he's got an earplug in his right ear."

Ronnie certainly didn't know the Dregs' names and faces because Drew had confided in him, but because Earl Kennedy had briefed him with class photos, when they discussed school gangs and the installation of surveillance cameras.

Ronnie had explained to Kennedy why the two weatherproof, light pole-mounted cameras in the parking lot with their wireless image-transmitting capability were so much more expensive to purchase, install, and maintain than were the eight mini-cameras wired along the corridors. But the principal had confided in Ronnie his secret sense of foreboding about escalating school violence, and spoke ominously about the terrible cost of doing nothing.

"Saw him how? Where? When? I need details, Ronnie."

"I'm inside the school, Sergeant."

Ronnie hadn't wanted to disclose or discuss his breaching of the police cordon or his infiltration into the high school – there just wasn't time – but he blurted it out because he needed Dixon to listen. Or did he? Maybe this was just his one chance in life to shine as a *real* cop. One chance for one hour. Ronald MacDonald, the hamburger clown, with his big feet in the principal's office. Little Ronnie, the techno-nerd, with his secret cameras outsmarting the Dregs.

"Why are you there, Ronnie?"

"Because I'm a father and my two sons are in trouble."

"Wrong answer. I was hoping you'd say it was because you're a police officer and three hundred kids are in danger."

"How's my son Marty – he get out okay?"

"He'll be fine – he's just now off to the hospital to get stitched up." (Accompanied by two detectives in the ambulance asking questions all the way, seeking intelligence to pass on to the Newcastle police commando team – but Dixon didn't elaborate on that.)

"How's Drew?' asked Dixon in exchange. Marty had been crying about his two dead friends all the way in the ambulance, and Dixon needed to know if Ronnie had yet realised that his son was a murderer.

"They're brothers, Gary. They fight, they've always fought, but I know I can contain him before he kills anyone."

Ronnie didn't know, and Dixon didn't need to snuff out that smouldering wick of hope – yet. But nor did he need a loose cannon. "And what if someone is killed *because of your infiltration?*"

"I've got four quick points, Gary – then you tell me if it was worth the risk," said Ronnie, ignoring Dixon's question.

"One: The principal and deputy principal are both dead in the next office. The Dregs have already murdered. We've got to move fast – not containment and negotiation – all the manuals are wrong and we both know it. Immediate action, rapid deployment – it's our only hope.

Two: I got in through the air conditioning ducts and no one knows I'm here. I'm in the principal's office right now watching eight live monitors that cover all school corridors from hidden cameras, and I can give you instant feedback.

Three: The Dregs are monitoring police frequencies on a scanner and, now that we know it, we can use it to our advantage.

Four: You wouldn't have access to any of this live intelligence if it wasn't for me being in here.

The bad news is that I can't use the landlines in case the Dregs are monitoring them, too, so I'm limited to a mobile phone with a low battery."

When Dixon finally replied, after a few seconds of silence, his tone had changed and he spoke as to a partner, "Well then we'd better start talking more quickly, hadn't we?"

Both officers resorted to staccato bursts of dialogue, now instinctive after years of talking on two-way radios and writing strictly factual police and military reports. "The Dregs have shot out my decoy dummy cameras and they think we're in the dark. But I've got eight micro-mini cameras covering all hallways – they're mounted on the fire exit signs at the end of each corridor, and outside the admin office. Two covering each wing, and two covering each half of the main corridor. But I'm blind in all classrooms, offices, toilets, lobby, gymnasium, and auditorium."

"Are your cameras recording now?" asked Dixon.

"Yes."

"All of them?"

"Yes."

"Good, we'll need all the footage later. Any sound?" asked Dixon optimistically.

"None, but each classroom and office has an intercom."

"Can we listen in?"

"Yes, but a red light comes on beside the speaker when any intercom is activated."

"Hidden video in the corridors, risky audio in the classrooms," Dixon summarised.

"That's it," Ronnie confirmed over his mobile phone.

A visiting British commando instructor had trained Gary Dixon and his Australian SAS mates to look upon each mission as a treasure hunt, each enemy position as an oyster, and each victory as a pearl. Prying open that oyster – access – was always the main challenge. And access – whether audio, visual, physical, or ballistic – was always the first step to victory.

"Two out of four," Dixon mumbled to himself.

63

Constable Dave Lovell was the duty officer on the front desk in Newcastle's Central Police Station, and Corporal Linda Minnetti was on dispatch.

Initial Hunter High calls at 11:50 were simply for fire alarm support, but things changed quickly once the wave of "shots fired" reports began flooding in.

Minnetti ordered Lovell to monitor Triple Zero dispatches and answer all local calls, while she frantically began coordinating vehicle and personnel response.

It was 12:05 when Ronnie asked Lovell to track Dixon down, and 12:08 when Dixon rang back and asked to speak with Minnetti.

"Sergeant Dixon?" Minnetti spoke quickly into the phone, juggling stress and responsibility.

"Linda, beginning now and continuing every five minutes until further orders, I want you on Channel One broadcasting a bulletin about the Sydney tactical squad's ETA of 1:10 p.m. – and then keep updating their progress every five minutes. Do the countdown: ETA one hour, ETA fifty-five minutes, ETA fifty minutes. Got it?"

"They'll be here at 1:10?"

"I don't know *when* they'll get here, but the high school shooters are monitoring police frequencies and we want them to think they've got an hour – it's very important that you get this right, Linda, I won't have time to call you back."

"I understand, Sergeant – every five minutes until you tell me otherwise."

Dixon hung up without another word, and Minnetti picked up her handset, "Attention all units at Hunter High, we have Sydney tactical squad confirmed for ETA in sixty minutes, repeat: sixty minutes. Further updates pending."

Leon cupped his earpiece with the palm of his hand – finally, the confirmation he had been waiting for. They were travelling quicker than he had estimated, and would arrive sooner than he had planned, but they would still be too late.

People watch too many action movies, and fail to appreciate that life's greatest battles are always first won or lost in the mind. The mission of the Australian SAS trooper is to create as much mischief as possible (usually behind enemy lines) through reconnaissance and surveillance, intelligence gathering, the dissemination of false information, disruption, sabotage, and attack.

With surveillance and the flow of false information now established, Dixon stepped back outside into the torrential rain and called out to his rooftop sniper, "Popeye!"

"Yo, Dixon," replied the ex-navy man, his protruding barrel unwavering.

"Do not underestimate these teenagers. Well organised, lots of ammunition – and they've got scanners. So don't use your radio or your headset. I know the Swat team's on a totally different frequency, but don't risk it – Sergeant Hayes can pass on any communication that's needed between us."

"Copy that."

"Assume they also have body armour, and aim for the apricot."

The "apricot" – the medulla oblongata, the holy grail of snipers – is an apricot-sized neuronal mass located in the lower half of the brain stem at the base of the skull and responsible for autonomic (involuntary) muscle movement and reflex actions. In a hostage situation, where even a mortally wounded gunman can still pull the trigger via muscle spasm, the quickest way of shutting down all neuromuscular function is to destroy the apricot with a "no twitch" kill shot that results in instantaneous incapacitation by flaccid paralysis and a total loss of muscle strength. Like flipping a switch, like turning off a light, like dropping a sack of potatoes.

There are four target areas available to the sniper that afford optimal access to the apricot with the least cranial (skull bone) resistance: the T-zone between the eyes (including the eye sockets themselves) and running down the bridge of the nose to the centre of the upper lip, the T-zone just below the bony protuberance at the rear of the skull and running down the spine towards the collar, and both ear canals.

"Copy that," replied Popeye.

64

It's funny – the memories that flash through your mind, the images that linger.

As I slowly approached Weed, the silent sentinel standing guard at the entrance to the auditorium, four images struck me.

The first image was waiting in line as a child to go to the movies. Saturday matinees at the Empress Theatre. All us kids lined up in the lobby, tickets in hand, keeping our voices down because the other movie was still playing in Cinema Two and we knew the manager would kick us out if we got rowdy.

My brothers, ahead in the line with their friends, me further back with mine. About to enter the door, and they checked our tickets.

There was, of course, no real need for Weed to check the students' cable ties as they entered the auditorium – Wade had already done that back in the classrooms of the right wing. But Weed's habitually downcast eyes just naturally fell on their wrists and the students, wishing to demonstrate the utmost compliance with their captors, started flashing their wrists for inspection as they entered the auditorium. Weed never asked them to, but one sheep followed another, after another, after another.

"Like lambs to the slaughter" – that was my *second image*. As I watched Weed, the usherette, Druid walked over and stood beside her, looking over her shoulder. Two guards in black, now supervising the humans being herded through the open gate and into the concentration camp.

Weed seemed to pay little or no attention, still the silent sentry. But Druid's eye burned into the herd like a laser sight. Like a Gestapo officer with a specific prisoner profile in mind, he began pointing out the ten shields of his choosing to build the wall of his fantasy. Culling the choicest of the herd, harvesting the best of the crop, pruning the strongest in the vineyard.

The brightest, the most respected, the most popular, the most gifted – all that Drew MacDonald was not, and never would be – targeted, singled out, uprooted from the crowd. And as I watched their numbers growing to ten, I realised that no high school counsellor – indeed, no human – could ever accurately measure, fully appreciate, or hope to replace, the unique potential of those ten. Just as no human could ever truly appreciate, or hope to fill, the emptiness that fuelled such jealousy in Druid.

My throat began to burn, my heart ached, and my stomach churned itself into a knot. I wanted to cry, but I had no tears. For a few blessed moments I stopped thinking only about myself and felt a great burden, a great sadness, for all of us there in the building. I longed to put my arms around us all – and not just as Daddy's Girl, The Nurse, or The Peacemaker – this was different, this was almost an out-of-body experience, again, where I saw all of us for the pitiful creatures that we were in our hour of crisis.

The crowd, the students, and staff – all gathered together, plucked from their safe and predictable roles and routines – felt fear and hatred towards the Dregs. For a moment it was as if I could actually *see* their emotions. But all I felt was pity. For the Dregs, and for their hostages, and for me. And it was unusual for me to think of myself last like that.

A *third image*, more of an impression really, suddenly struck me. Each of us was just a helpless infant – a few years older perhaps, but all still essentially infants – helpless and vulnerable.

And, finally, there flashed a *fourth image* in my mind: Hunter High as just a speck on planet earth – a beautiful blue globe spinning in the cold blackness of space – and I was relieved, *actually relieved*, that the mundane routine of our school and our lives had been peeled back and blasted away, just like Barb had said earlier in the admin office.

And then the sequence of four images ended as suddenly as it began. My perception returned to "normal", and I was once again just another hostage with Barb's prayer "learn how to live, and how to die" echoing in my ears. Words can't really convey the experience, nor can I explain it, but I felt obliged to at least recount it, so I have – for the first time ever, to anyone.

Once my focus had returned and Druid's conscription was complete, he directed his ten human shields to stand aside just a few paces from the auditorium entrance. Whether maliciously intended or not, the result was exquisite frustration for the ten, so near yet so far from their peers and the relative sanctuary of the auditorium.

The ten conscripts included: Year Twelve dux Murray Lewis, president and vice-president of the student council Donny Fairholme and Monica McLean, top academic achievers Victor Eng, Hui Tran, and Shujab Mukerji, state swimming champion in one hundred metre freestyle Bethany Schripp, and state representative soccer player Salvatore Perrino. The last two were Islamic girls who both wore the Muslim head covering –

the hijab – that left their faces completely exposed, Ishna Mahrmoud and Natalie Abrahim.

The media subsequently had a field day with the three Asian high academic achievers and the two Islamic girls. Druid specifically, and the Dregs generally, were portrayed as racists and white supremacist neo-Nazis. This was because the siege remained front page news around the world for two weeks, and such blinding media scrutiny drove reporters to uncover, or invent, unique angles and obscure "facts" to feed the ever-hungry masses.

But, based on all the events, evidence, and eyewitness testimony, it appears that Eng, Tran, and Mukerji were merely representative of a trend across Australia and around the world. Asian high school students in the West, both male and female, consistently attain a disproportionately high percentage of the top rankings in academic achievement. Research has repeatedly attributed this to family expectations, respect for elders, and a cultural emphasis on discipline, honour, and the family name. Considering also that many of these Asian high achievers tend to be first, second, or third-generation immigrants determined to "make good" – and Druid's sensationally reported "prejudice" seems more likely to be a simple reflection of societal trends.

Druid's bias and persecution were aimed at high achievers generally, not Asians specifically. The references to neo-Nazis seems to have been based solely on the Dregs' affection for Doc Marten boots, and nothing more. Beware: "racism" and "sexism", as reported by the media, is often actually more a case of sensationalism, readership acquisition, ratings, and political correctness.

But what of the two Muslim girls? No investigation or interviews revealed any previous relationship between them and Druid, certainly no clashes. The girls were not leaders or exceptional achievers in any way. I personally think it wisest to conclude that Druid, in his media and drug-fuelled fantasy world, chose Ishna and Natalie simply because they were the most exotically and mysteriously dressed in the school – and Druid was always drawn to other worlds, kingdoms, and ages.

Perhaps, again, because they were the most distinctly dedicated to their beliefs, and therefore fit his target profile as "exceptional". Or maybe his choice was merely motivated by jealously, because Druid himself did not feel committed to any particular spiritual belief, despite all his ravings.

Contrary to media reports, the girls themselves were not close friends, and did not "cling to each other, as sisters, in fear". Ishna had only recently arrived from Iran, while Natalie's parents emigrated to Australia from Malaysia before she was born – ironically, to avoid persecution and violence, and provide a safer environment for their children.

My feeling has always been that Druid chose his shields because of who he was – not because of who they were.

Druid's selection of his phalanx was a near-silent process without any objections from the ten, that has since intrigued many analysts. But it really shouldn't, if considered in context.

All the hostages were shocked. There was no warning of the attack, it began with sudden, deafening fire alarms and semi-automatic gunfire, and was obviously well organised by an efficient and well-armed team.

After many months of analysing the evidence, I can now present the facts in the context of the assailants' overall plan. But the hostages had no such luxury. They were swept along, powerless and afraid, in a fast-flowing torrent of unexpected events. Cooperation seemed the wisest option, offering their best – perhaps their *only* – chance of survival.

Therefore, to the handcuffed prisoners, being called aside by Druid seemed no more inherently dangerous than being herded into the auditorium – except that Druid's singling them out cast them into the spotlight of attention that everyone was trying so hard to avoid, just like that burning red laser dot. Thus ripped from the relative safety of grey shadowy anonymity, the last thing any of the ten wanted was to increase the attention by questioning or objecting.

Druid conscripted his tenth shield just as the last of the compliant students were being herded into the auditorium. But before he had a chance to steer them towards the lobby as per Leon's directive, the Power Brokers approached.

65

Wally Martin's first Triple Zero call at 11:53 had confirmed to him that the police themselves were just as surprised by the siege as any of the hostages, and no better informed.

At 12:01 Wally phoned the emergency operator to report Druid's bursts of gunfire in the right wing – and he was told to sit tight and await police rescue.

At 12:06 he rang again and spoke to the same operator. "That's *negative* on waiting for police rescue. We've heard *hundreds* of bullets being fired in the last fifteen minutes – hundreds, and you've refused to pass on any word of casualties. So we're assuming, here in this class, that the Dregs are not just shooting up the furniture, and we have to assume that we could be next. We've got a plan."

The operator's tone changed noticeably.

"What is your name again please, sir?"

"Wally Martin."

"And this is your mobile phone you're calling from?"

"Correct."

"I have your number noted here in case we get cut off. Which classroom are you in?"

"Chemistry lab."

"And how many students with you there in the room?"

"Twenty-six."

"Hold the line please, Mr. Martin"

The operator obviously wasted no time because Gary Dixon himself was soon on the line, fully updated.

"Mr. Martin, I'm Sergeant Dixon, commanding officer of the tactical team on the scene."

"*'Wally'* is quicker, and we may not have much time left."

"Wally, you have twenty-six students there in the chemistry lab and you've cooked up some kind of plan, is that right?"

"Our plan is not to die without a fight."

"Wally, there are five gunmen armed with semi-automatic rifles stalking the halls of the school right now. They've all got extended magazines, possibly thirty shots in each. Any one of those gunmen – any *one* by himself – could easily kill you and all your twenty-six students in seconds."

"How do you know how many bullets they've got?"

"One released hostage has given us details, and we have surveillance cameras operating in the school right now."

"You've got a live feed?"

"Yes." (Actually a live feed reported through a third party, but

Dixon was not about to endanger Ronnie MacDonald by sharing that information.)

"Well done, Sergeant. What's the body count so far?"

"One fireman wounded, two staff and two students confirmed killed – and we don't need another twenty-six dead chemistry students."

"How long before the police enter the building?"

"I'll lead them in myself as soon as I possibly can – I promise you. We're just outside preparing ourselves now – we'll only get one chance to do this right."

Wally was silent for a few seconds before replying. "I appreciate your honesty, Sergeant."

"You want honesty? And this conversation is being recorded, Wally – those students are minors in your legal care, and you have no right to involve them in a vigilante action. Do I need to repeat myself?"

"The four killed so far, were they violently resisting?"

Now it was Dixon's turn to pause before responding. "No, they were not – not as far as we know, the students certainly weren't."

"So therefore our cooperating with the gunmen does not guarantee our survival either, does it, Sergeant?"

Dixon was silent.

"Do the sixteen-year-olds in my classroom have no right to fight for their seventeenth birthdays?"

"They are *minors*, Wally."

"I wish they had another two years to decide, Sergeant, I really do – but they don't. Minors make decisions every day – long before they're eighteen – that greatly affect the rest of their lives. They are responsible for their futures, today. We can dispute it and deny it, or we can tell them the truth about the enemies they face, equip them as best we can, and fight alongside them. That's the responsibility of every teacher and every parent, every day – it's just more urgent and obvious here today at Hunter High."

"I've got to go, Wally. Put your phone on silent in case we ring you back."

"We won't be stupid, Sergeant, just prepared."

66

Wade and Slave, in their long black stockmen's coats, made their way up and down the right wing to all twelve classrooms, mustering the cattle and herding the sheep.

Considering that 357 captives were now involved in the operation, it is amazing that the migration did not get bogged down, but actually accelerated as the last of the hostages increased their pace to keep up with the human current flowing ahead of them down the corridor.

The procedure was repeated, class by class, until the assembly audience was ushered from the twelfth and final classroom. Then Wade and Slave did a quick sweep of the classrooms in reverse, beginning with the last, and gathering together all the teachers and those students, targeted on the blacklist, who had been culled and told to remain behind in their classrooms and wait to be escorted.

The Power Brokers, the leaders: twelve teachers, eight young men, and seven young women.

Weed had positioned herself at the doors to the auditorium so that she could ensure the serpentine line of students walked directly inside and took their seats – anywhere except the first two rows, which were reserved. As per the Dregs' pre-mission strategic planning, all hostage requests to visit the toilets were refused – the Dregs were so sorely outnumbered that the last thing they needed was another flow of traffic to monitor.

Although the range of reactions by those fifteen students who were culled, detained, and escorted at gunpoint was quite broad, the number was limited only to four that kept recurring (and which provided a profound insight, for me, into human thinking on innocence, guilt, and punishment). An illustration, once again, that perhaps our options are more limited, and our responses not nearly as unique, as we'd like to imagine.

When detained, some expressed shock and pleaded total innocence of any wrongdoing. These tended to be the girls apprehended for tormenting Weed. They dismissed their victim's pain as subjective overreaction, while yet expecting that their own subjective intent and emotions should overrule any absolutes of accountability or punishment. ("I didn't mean to hurt her", "we were only joking", "it was only a nickname", "I'm *sorry*, okay?")

For others, gang and mob mentality was so ingrained that even a serious physical assault on Slave was thought to warrant them each only a portion of the guilt, and a fraction of the punishment.

Still others neither denied their guilt nor disputed their well-deserved punishment, but their shock and surprise at being apprehended resembled a child caught with his hand in the cookie jar, or a kangaroo frozen in a car headlight. There was no attempt at denial, excuse, or escape. They knew they were guilty of wrongdoing, they just somehow thought they'd never get caught, or – if not *never* – then certainly not *today*. Whereas their grandparents were assured that justice delayed was only justice deferred, this generation, expecting and demanding instant results as they did, had little fear or respect for the value and importance of *time* as an essential ingredient in the recipe of life, and they had assumed that justice delayed is justice deceived, disarmed, or eluded – that the sins of the past were no longer able to catch up with the fast-moving and all-consuming *now* of their generation.

The fourth and final reaction, anger, spewed forth from those self-enthroned students who felt they were somehow entitled to dismiss their victims as worthless, while refusing to recognise anyone else's authority to pass judgement on *them*.

And, so, Wade and Slave mustered their growing herd of fifteen students and twelve teachers from classroom to classroom and on down the corridor, while their Dregcams recorded in high-definition video and 3-D sound the comments, facial expressions, murmurs, and body language of innocence, denial, excuse, guilt, surprise, pride, arrogance, anger, and fear, that one would expect on a day of judgement such as this.

But mainly the soundtrack recorded the footsteps of twenty-seven detainees crunching along on a carpet of broken glass and techno-litter, while Slave and Wade responded only sparsely with comments or grunts as they played their respective roles, and shouldered their escalating responsibilities.

Wade was a policeman raiding the high school, a sheriff cleaning up the town. Slave was a soldier enforcing martial law. And, between them, they escorted student leaders and lawbreakers who grew in numbers and in desperation with each crunching footstep. The teachers were also a mounting concern as their sense of helplessness and professional negligence intensified with each of the Dregs' additional threats, commands, and acts of violence.

A risky time, this walk down the corridor.

True, separating the hundreds of placid followers – the bulk of the student body – from their teachers and the outlawed student leaders had further isolated, discouraged, and disempowered them as they were seated in the auditorium, ensuring their continued compliance.

But what about then trooping these twenty-seven teachers and non-compliant students together down the corridor? Did the culling itself transform them into even more of a force to be reckoned with? Perhaps create an urgency and sense of mutual support?

The Dregs had initially discussed and debated the issue in their tree house, and finally decided that focused vigilance during the two minutes of transfer time would surely afford the Power Brokers no chance for planning an escape.

But the cause of the resulting tragedy was twofold – the Dregs were momentarily distracted, and the subsequent escape bid was impulsive and improvised.

67

Minutes, hours, days, and months can roll by in life with little change and nothing exceptional to report when, suddenly, years of routine are shattered by moments of sheer panic.

Dixon had been dreading his nine-minute deadline with little to report back to Rod Stanwych, and his time was nearly up when suddenly, within just a few minutes, he was contacted first by the detectives accompanying Marty MacDonald in the ambulance and then by Ronnie MacDonald in the principal's office – Marty reporting the two students killed, and Ronnie the two staff. Up-to-date, eyewitness testimony.

And after quickly debriefing Ronnie and the ambulance detectives for details, Dixon suddenly *sounded* much more knowledgeable than he *felt* when Stanwych picked up the phone at 12:12, exactly nine minutes after their last call, as agreed.

"Five student gunmen confirmed and identified. Most of them armed with .22 calibre semi-automatic rifles, and at least one larger calibre rifle –

probably an M1. They're carrying lots of ammunition. Possibly thousands of rounds, already loaded in extra magazines and ready to go. Two staff and two students confirmed dead. Approximately three hundred and fifty hostages escaped and now safe, one student hostage released with minor injuries and right now being questioned by detectives, another three hundred and fifty still inside. The shooters have a hit list of some kind, they're monitoring police radios, and appear to be very well organised."

Stanwych was silent for ten long seconds as he digested the bleak report. "Any *good* news?"

"We've got a police officer inside – hiding in the admin office, as yet undetected, and monitoring all corridors via live hidden video cameras."

"That's fantastic, Gary! The police commissioner is arguing for wait-and-see, but I've still got some leverage within the Ministry of Justice for launching your Swat team."

"What are the chances?"

"With me as a scapegoat – retiring in seventeen days – and you on-site, the IARD commander? We've got a good case, but I'll have to get back to you."

"Every moment lost is critical, Rod. Five semi-automatic rifles can fire fifteen shots per second easily – even more."

"I realise that, Gary, and I'll pass it on, but the premier's got a million bucks invested in Buster."

"So what's that – three thousand dollars per hostage?"

68

For just one moment, Wade and Slave focused their attention to the rear of the herd as the last students rounded the junction of the right wing and stepped into the main corridor.

Slave removed the empty TI-25 magazine and surrendered cellular phones that Wade had used to wedge open the fire door, thus closing off the right wing as a route of escape, or a hiding place, just as they had with the left.

At the same time, towards the front of the herd, Mr. Ed Zwick the economics teacher calculated the odds. He was a numbers man – risk, return, probability – and he had figured out early on in the piece that Weed was the weak link in the formidable chain of the Dregs.

Ed's wife Jannette had always chided him for being overly timid and cautious – with his glasses and moustache only accentuating the stereotype of the cerebral economics professor.

He would read the financial reports in the newspaper, study business best-sellers, and scour the internet.

And then he would predict the financial future.

To his wife, over dinner, in meticulous detail, time and time again, Ed predicted the stockmarket's future and how he would invest if only he were a risk-taker. Time and time again, with amazing accuracy, he was right. And so Jannette chided, but Ed thought of himself as only a high school teacher, and you can't make a silk purse out of a sow's ear.

He had the brains and the master's degree to become a university lecturer, but he knew the numbers. Redirected government funding and shifting economic tides could decimate a university at any time, and even long-term faculty members were only being offered annual contracts these days. Ed Zwick knew, statistically, that a high school position was more secure over the long run.

In many ways, at only thirty-four years of age, Ed had already retired. He wore cardigans with leather patches on the elbows, continued to chart and forecast financial trends in the security of his study, and even inspired students to act on his financial insights, though he himself would not.

Had the siege occurred two years earlier, Ed would have remained compliant in the herd. But, five months earlier, Jannette had given birth to their twin boys, and, seven minutes earlier, Ed had heard Druid dragging his own brother over the broken glass. Risk, return, probability.

Wade and Slave were near the rear of the Power Brokers. Ed Zwick was right at the front. As he approached Weed, Zwick grabbed her Ruger with his cuffed hands and planted the muzzle at the base of her neck, just above her collarbone. So little time did he have, and so close were Slave and Wade, that he didn't dare rip the rifle from her hands, he just redirected the barrel.

His snatching movement had caught Weed totally by surprise, her finger pulling the trigger and firing a bullet into the ceiling. She reacted to the gunshot by letting go the weapon, and Zwick instantly slipped his own index finger inside the trigger guard.

The group of twenty-six hostages froze in line behind the economics teacher. Slave and Wade rushed forward and aimed their red lasers at Ed Zwick's head, several inches above Weed's.

Ed and Weed looked like they were about to dance. The rifle strap was still around her shoulder and under her black coat, his hands were cuffed together, his right now welded to the trigger, his left squeezing the stock and barrel. Weed's hands rested lightly on the Ruger, not to wrestle for it or to contest his authority, but to hold it steady in compliant cooperation.

Ed Zwick raised his normally subdued voice, "There's twenty-seven of us in this corridor, and we're going to walk straight out the front door – with Miss Stankowski here at the lead."

He lowered his voice from Superman, back down to his usual Clark Kent tone and volume, "It *is* 'Wendy Stankowski', isn't it? I've never actually had you in my class."

Weed nodded in response to his bizarre bureaucratic query, but only slightly, so as not to jar the gun at her throat.

"OR WHAT, EXACTLY?"

When overpowered, Weed had been standing just a few paces from the auditorium doors, with everyone's attention instantly focusing on her and the two Dregs encircling Zwick – that is, until that voice and an unexpected red laser beam shot forth from the inner recesses of the auditorium.

Zwick turned to his challenger, then averted his eyes from the blinding brightness of Leon's laser sight as the captain of the Dregs emerged.

Leon, who had been overseeing the seating of the students within the auditorium, now shouldered his M1 and was ready to fire – his laser dot fixed mainly on Zwick's head, but occasionally on Weed's, as he stepped nearer and as the two dancers moved slightly.

The economics teacher and his student hostage were forced to stay close, restricted as they were by the length of her rifle strap. Leon repeated, in a much lowered whisper, "Or what exactly?"

Zwick raised his voice again, and hoped that no one noticed how the Ruger was shaking in Superman's hands. "If you try to stop us, I have no choice but to pull this trigger and kill Wendy here."

"Call her 'Weed', please. If she's going to spend the last few moments of her life all cuddled up with you like that, the least you can do is call her by her chosen name."

"I'm not joking," said Zwick through gritted teeth, refusing to accommodate Leon's banter.

"I know you're not, Mr. Zwick, and I commend your courage."

There were a few moments of silence. A Mexican standoff.

"So you're threatening to kill one of my dearest Dregs?"

"You've left me with no other option."

"Oh, there's *always* another option, Mr. Zwick. You taught me that yourself – last year in economics. There's always another way of looking at things."

"I'm listening."

"You've made a serious miscalculation in your proposal, professor. All your neat little equations have been upset – they're based on wrong assumptions. Your ordered little world has been invaded by the kingdom of the Dregs ...."

Druid, standing just beyond the auditorium doors, a few paces from Leon and behind his phalanx of ten newly selected hostages, grinned and laughed at the economics teacher in his sights.

".... and that requires a currency conversion, a values exchange. We've commandeered all your teaching authority – you're now powerless. And hostage negotiations won't work with us, because ours is a suicide mission.

You can't threaten us, you can't barter with the life of a Dreg. We love our sister Weed dearly, we really do, but she knew when she walked into this building today that she'd never walk out.

The Dregs are in a covenant with each other. Do you know what that is, Mr. Zwick? A *covenant*?"

"A business contract."

"Oh, *so* much more than that, Mr. Zwick. So much more than a contract or even a promise. 'Blood brothers and sisters' – that's a covenant. 'Cross my heart and hope to die' – that's a covenant. 'I give my word, that I'll give my life' – that's a covenant. And Weed knew all that when she signed in blood as a Dreg."

Leon's discourse, his explanation, his clinical lecture, was over. But now that he had defused, denigrated, and dismissed Mr. Zwick's threat, the young Spitzer's whole tone, his demeanour, even his countenance, changed as he issued his own.

"The other side of the coin, Mr. Zwick, the flip side of the covenant, is that when you cut my brother, I bleed too and I feel the pain. When you hold a gun to my sister's head, you're threatening me.

And that's why you're not to be feared like a Dreg – you threaten, but I promise. I *promise*, Mr. Zwick, that the moment you squeeze that trigger, the four of us will shoot you dead. I *promise* that if you take another step, we will shoot you dead. And I *promise* that I'm going to start counting to ten. Each time I speak a number, Druid here will shoot one of his ten hostages, and it will be your fault entirely. Get your hands off that rifle, and I'll stop the count."

Druid silently redirected the muzzle of his Ruger away from Zwick, and towards the hostages directly in front of him. Weed closed her eyes, and even leaned into Ed's shoulder, horrified by the ultimatum.

The full realisation of the nightmare surrounding him scrolled across Zwick's face – and across the faces of Druid's ten shields.

"You are an economist, Mr. Zwick, numbers rule your life. In fact, to you, numbers *are* life. I, on the other hand, am a terrorist. To me, numbers are death. *One*."

Druid shot Ishna Mahrmoud in the back of the head.

"*Two*."

This was not a slow count. Leon was allowing Zwick no time for reflection. Druid shot Natalie Abrahim at the base of the neck. Weed jumped at the sound of each gunshot, eyes still closed.

"*Three*."

Druid shot Victor Eng in the back of the head.

"Stop! Stop! Here!" Ed Zwick removed Weed's muzzle from the base of her throat, pointed it towards the ceiling, and pushed the Ruger gently into Weed's hands, lifting his own cuffed hands in surrender.

Wade quickly moved in, ready to exact revenge, and shoved Zwick onto his hands and knees.

"Don't shoot him! Let him live with this memory for the rest of his natural life," ordered Leon, saving and condemning Zwick simultaneously.

Victor Eng was immobile on the floor and not even visibly bleeding. He would not regain consciousness for over seventy-two hours, and subsequently faced eighteen months of rehabilitation before returning to school. Even then, he continued to suffer slurred speech, chronic headaches, and bouts of depression. Natalie Abrahim was dead, her spinal cord completely severed with the one shot. Ishna Mahrmoud began a series of seizures shortly after falling to the floor. Druid, disgusted when she vomited on his boots, kicked her unconscious body, fracturing two of her ribs.

Slave moved forward to defend the fallen girl, but Druid raised his rifle to the seven remaining human shields, and Slave stood fast.

Ishna left hospital three weeks later, the .22 calibre bullet still embedded in her brain. She subsequently suffered an attack of encephalitis, as a result of infection, and faced a lifetime of powerful medication to control her trauma-induced epileptic seizures. Risk, return, probability.

Wade gave Weed a hug and commended her for staying cool. But she didn't look cool, she looked frozen – and numb.

Ed Zwick couldn't take his eyes off the three fallen bodies, and he slowly crawled over to them on his hands and knees, like a little puppy dog.

"What about me giving them first aid?" asked Zwick meekly, now fearing the horrendous human cost of making another move without permission.

"You mean '*second* aid', don't you?" corrected Leon, "'*First* aid' would have been your cooperating as requested."

Leon and his M1 remobilised the twenty-six behind Zwick. "All teachers into the staff lounge with me – all students into the gym with Wade and Slave."

Robyn Turner, the mother hen in the green tracksuit, sought to elaborate, "But I thought all the students were staying together in the auditorium?"

"Do you see those three students lying there on the floor, Ms. Turner? That's what happens when people question my instructions."

Turner remained silent.

Leon led his hostage teachers away to the staff lounge, and Wade went to make sure that the 330 hostages were settled into the auditorium, while Slave and Druid remained in the corridor watching their fifteen student troublemakers and seven shields, respectively.

Mr. Zwick had only enough time to cover Natalie Abrahim's head with his cardigan, and turn Ishna and Victor onto their sides to prevent choking should there be any further vomiting. In such times of trauma, onlookers frequently voice their regret that they had not sought better training in first aid, and report their feelings of incompetence to even read vital signs – yet many of those who witnessed the shooting of Druid's three shields at the door to the auditorium later referred to the lifeless look in Natalie's eyes, as though a spark, or flame, or spirit had left her. No one doubted that she had died instantly.

Zwick hurried off to join the eleven other teachers following Leon, while Weed took off her black Driza-Bone riding coat and covered Ishna, wounded and in shock as she was. Slave followed her lead, removed his own long black coat, and covered Victor.

And there Weed remained, squatting beside the three bodies, her chin on her knees, her arms embracing her shins. Slave took out his pocket knife and freed the wrists of the three fallen hostages.

"It was you or them, Leon had no choice," Slave assured her.

Weed responded without taking her eyes off the bodies, "It wasn't worth it, *I'm* not worth it. I'm throwing my life away in twenty minutes – these three had their whole lives ahead of them."

"We're not throwing our lives away," insisted the young Slavic idealist.

"You sure of that? Then give me the right words, Slave, to describe this mission, because 'honour' and 'justice' just don't do it – won't do it."

It was 12:10, and the body count for the day, so far, was now seven dead (Vernon Linder, Beryl Wade, Eva Forman, Earl Kennedy, Andy Stewart, David Sheridan, Natalie Abrahim), five wounded (Drew MacDonald, Fireman Jordan Reece, Marty MacDonald, Victor Eng, Ishna Mahrmoud), one blinded (Tessa Briggs), and fourteen students with various degrees of glass laceration.

69

Gary Dixon was anxious to get back on the line with Ronnie MacDonald – his eyes and ears in Hunter High.

It had been over five minutes since their last call and Dixon's mobile had been running hot with calls to Linda Minnetti, Wally Martin, and Rod Stanwych. In addition, the Swat commander had to take the time to brief his four commandos on each update and development – they all had to be on the same page in their thinking at every moment. Their survival and success depended on it – one mind, one heart, one mission.

And now the Scotsman was slow to answer his mobile. Had he been captured? Did his battery die?

Ronnie finally answered on the eighth ring.

"I need an update, Ronnie, what's been going on?"

The voice that came back from the principal's office was more subdued than before – almost raspy. "The left wing looks deserted."

"It is, forget it. Half the students and teachers managed to escape."

"The European and the short guy emptied all the classrooms in the right wing," Ronnie summarised.

"You're sure?"

"Positive. Most students – ninety-five per cent – were taken into the auditorium. All teachers and maybe fifteen students were held back – I don't know why.

Drew and the Dreg girl were near the door to the auditorium. Drew had gathered a second group of eight or ten students around him and held *them* back from entering the auditorium as well.

I don't know what they were saying – I have no audio, Sergeant."

"I realise that, Ronnie. Just tell me what you saw."

"They were quite far from the camera and I don't know what was said," Ronnie started crying. "My view was obstructed …. but I think maybe one of the teachers grabbed the girl's rifle near the auditorium and tried taking her hostage. It was a standoff, they had guns in each other's faces."

Ronnie's voice broke, and then *he* did. He moaned a deep, guttural moan.

Dixon spoke softly this time, "Tell me, Ronnie."

Silence.

Then, finally, "Drew shot three of the students standing right in front of him – point blank. I think he shot them each in the head." The heartbroken father just groaned.

"You're my eyes, Ronnie," whispered Dixon with a gentleness that was surprising from such a powerful man in such violent circumstances.

"Then the teacher surrendered the rifle and let the girl go."

"And then?"

"And then *my son* kicked one of the girls that he shot while she lay on the floor – he kicked her twice."

Then Ronnie's voice changed and he began to rationalise, "There's no way of telling – he's only got a .22, so the three could easily survive."

"There's no way of telling," Dixon countered.

"There's no way of telling with bullet wounds – you know what it's like."

"Are they moving at all – the three students who were shot?"

"I can't be sure – we can't be sure, Sergeant."

"What's happening now?"

"They moved everyone on – most into the auditorium, teachers into the staff lounge I think it is, and the last group of twenty or so students are still waiting by the auditorium doors."

Silence. Pause. Dixon just listened.

"And I think that maybe one of the teachers may have covered the head of one of the three wounded students with a coat – a Muslim girl, I think."

"She's dead, Ronnie."

"Maybe not – maybe they missed a weak pulse."

Dixon decided to end Ronnie's denial before he became useless to the operation, "Drew murdered Marty's two friends."

"What?!"

"In Marty's classroom, just before you saw him dragging his brother down the hallway. We got all the details from Marty himself."

Ronnie just stared at the split-screen monitor before him – surrounded by the police electronics and nightmare of his own creation.

Maybe if they had had a daughter things would have been different, girls are softer. Drew had kicked her in the ribs while she lay unconscious, dragged his own brother over broken glass. If only they'd had a daughter – they would have never lost a son, who'd stolen other sons and daughters. How was Ronnie ever going to tell Drew's mother? And what would the relatives say *now* about Drew being such a quiet boy?

Ronnie was giving up hope and letting himself slide. Sitting on the floor, he wrapped his arms around his shoulders, closed his eyes, rocked himself back and forth, felt himself retreating into a cave of darkness, slipping back into the pool of despair.

When he heard Dixon's voice, calling out from the phone in his hand, it seemed tiny and distant – a still, small voice. Ronnie put the mobile phone back to his ear.

"Stick with me, Ronnie. It's not about you as a father, or him as a son, or the relationship between you – I know this is your darkest hour – but it's about your duty and your oath as a police officer to enforce the law and protect the public. There's over three hundred souls in that building that still need to be saved."

"What do you want me to do?" MacDonald asked, desperate for any guidance or direction.

"Get off the phone, conserve your battery. I've got a lot to coordinate out here – you just keep your eyes on those monitors. God knows we need a break – we've lost touch with all the students in the auditorium, we have no eyes and no ears in there.

Maybe you'll get a chance to contact those teachers in the staff lounge with that intercom of yours.

Keep your eyes open, Ronnie, and expect an opportunity – a door. There's always a way in, and there's always a way out – look for it."

70

Eight doors away in the chemistry lab, Wally Martin and his twenty-six trembling students had heard every word and gunshot of Ed Zwick's failed escape bid, reverberating down the deserted corridor.

Wally whispered to his fellow hostages, "Now that we know for sure that students are being executed like that, we need to vote whether or not we will allow ourselves to be taken prisoner without a fight."

The students were horrified by the options, and cowered from making a decision.

Wally continued, "I have a plan for how we might get their guns if they come after us."

Student Mark Devito raised his hand, "I'm with Mr. Martin – there's no sign of the cops, and I'm not going down without a fight."

Devito's confidence inspired the other students' support of Wally's suggestion. The vote wasn't unanimous, but close enough, given the limited time frame.

Wally Martin silently closed the lab door and began instructing his students.

Subsequent police investigations confirmed Mark Devito as having been a participant in Slave's toilet stall attack, and the principal instigator of the flagpole assault.

In the weeks just prior to the siege, Devito had twice heard reports of the self-exiled Slave Latska being seen around town – *with* Leon Spitzer, and wearing the Dregs' black coat.

When he went to school on Black Friday, Mark Devito knew nothing of the Dreg blacklist, but as soon as he heard the name "Leon!" shouted by Wade, and the M1 gunshots outside the chemistry lab door, he knew immediately that he was being hunted and he leapt at Wally Martin's plan – cornered prey that he was.

71

Once Wade was assured that Weed could carry on, he led her from beside the fallen students and into the rear of the auditorium.

He then dimmed the house lights, considerably, and yelled out his instructions to the 330 seated hostages, all silenced and deeply shaken by the shooting of the three students out in the corridor behind them.

"Do not turn around. Keep your eyes to the front and listen carefully. We have no plans to hurt anyone in this auditorium. All you have to do is sit here quietly for about ten minutes, then take part in a short assembly. Nothing more. After that, every one of you will be free to go by 12:30. But if you turn around or get out of your seat *before* 12:30, you will be shot without any further warning. If you have to go to the toilet – go in your seat."

Wade turned to Weed in the darkened rear of the auditorium and whispered, "They shouldn't give you any trouble now – they don't know how many of us are watching them from behind. Slave's waiting for me to back him up in the gym. I gotta go. Call me on the walkie-talkie if you need me."

Wade ducked back out into the main corridor, quietly closing the auditorium's heavy, soundproof doors behind him.

72

With Barb, Kieran, and me still in tow, Leon herded the twelve new teachers from the right wing ahead of him into the staff lounge, and called out to those already under house arrest inside. "I hope you guys don't mind, but I invited twelve more of my very closest teacher friends to join us here in the lounge.

My throat is *parched* from barking orders for the last half hour. I don't know how you teachers do it, honestly, I don't. Day in and day out – bark, bark, bark. I just need to sit down and relax, who wants to hold my gun?"

The teachers glanced back and forth at each other.

"Just kidding! I saw you reaching for it there, Dr. Khoury, you little rascal."

But Dr. Khoury was too nervous to appreciate the humour, "I did nothing of the kind, sir."

"You're a mathematician, Dr. Khoury, what do you think are the statistical chances of me shooting you for getting on my nerves?"

Khoury thought for a moment and composed himself. He was, after all, a department head and being watched by all his colleagues.

"Too many variables – mood, emotion, more than seven hundred people in the building – anything could happen."

"Three-fifty, give or take," corrected Leon, "half of them escaped."

"Three hundred and fifty, then. Algebra, geometry, physics – they are my fields of study. Not statistics or psychology."

"And if you die this afternoon, Dr. Khoury, was it a life well spent, in this mathematical world of yours?"

Khoury seemed more confident now as he was forced to think.

For he was, at heart, a thinking man, and he conveyed a certain assuredness as he quickly reflected upon his life, taking stock.

Focusing on his past life, rather than his potentially imminent death, he replied, "I taught all my students that there is an amazing, beautiful, mathematical order to the universe."

"Doesn't appear to be a lot of order in this school this afternoon, though, does there?"

"*Apparently* not, but I come from India, a country with over one billion inhabitants, Mr. Spitzer. Chaos is everywhere. And I've come to learn that the chaos of man does not negate the order in the universe."

Druid stuck his head into the room. "Is it okay with you, Leon, if I grab three more from the auditorium to rebuild my wall?"

When Leon paused to ponder, Ed Zwick spoke up. "Don't take any more students – let *me* replace the three."

Leon looked him over.

"Please," said Zwick.

"Give me a moment, Dr. Khoury and I are doing the math – are you *really* worth three, Mr. Zwick?"

"I'm not even worth one. They're each so young – they haven't even started living yet, haven't made any real choices, haven't yet made any mistakes that will haunt them for the rest of their lives.

I won't give you any more trouble. I know, now, the terrible cost. I'll cooperate – pick three more students from the auditorium, and they may not."

"You present a very persuasive argument, Mr. Zwick. You should be a teacher when you grow up."

Leon turned to Druid, "Take *him*. That makes eight, that'll do."

As Zwick was led away, Leon called after him. "This grand sacrifice of yours won't lighten your burden of guilt for the other three, you know."

Ed Zwick stopped and looked back. "Nor yours."

"Touché," said Leon with a grin, "but I only have to carry *mine* for a few more minutes, don't I?"

Zwick headed off, and then Leon called after Druid, "May as well take Dr. Khoury here with you while you're at it – and get him to show you the beautiful mathematical order of the universe."

73

"There's an elephant in the room that we've all been ignoring."

Gary Dixon was respected (almost revered) by his commandos as a leader on all levels – not merely as the commander of their Swat team, but more like their mentor or father – and they listened intently to him now, inside the construction shed.

"I trained you to kill armed men – not kids. I know that you never signed on with me expecting you'd have to shoot a fifteen-year-old member of a student gang.

If this doesn't sit right with you – with any one of you, or even all of you – then I want you to step down right now. I *order* you to step down right now.

There's no dishonour in it. You will not lose your place on this team, nor one ounce of my respect – you have my word.

All I know is that, by my reckoning, the Dregs are now confirmed murderers. I will offer them the same measure of mercy that they offered their victims – and any man who backs me up has to feel the same way.

There can be no hesitation on the trigger, this day, and you'll have to live with your actions from this afternoon for the rest of your lives."

74

Druid signalled his seven remaining student hostages to head into the lobby, fifteen paces away from the staff lounge. They obeyed, dragging their shocked and exhausted bodies in compliance, haunted by the memory of their three fallen comrades – draped with coats and still lying by the auditorium doors.

Druid herded them from behind, while escorting the new conscripts Zwick and Khoury by his side.

"What mathematical order, Dr. Khoury?"

"I just told young Mr. Spitzer that I believe there is a mathematical precision, even amid the apparent chaos of life."

"Like a universal order?"

"Precisely."

Druid stopped. "Have you ever heard of Russian roulette, Dr. Khoury?"

Khoury was about to answer when Druid suddenly silenced him with a finger to his lips, and began staring at something down towards the left wing.

Druid snapped his fingers, then silently signalled all nine shields to be still as he stuck his head back into the staff lounge.

"Leon, did you close the door to the chemistry lab after I checked it?"

"No."

"Did Slave?"

"I don't think so. Why?"

"Because I definitely left it open, and now it's shut."

75

As Ronnie MacDonald watched the main corridor on his monitor, he thought he saw Druid staring at the closed chemistry lab door.

Dixon had already apprised the Scotsman of the situation in the lab – how Wally Martin and the students were preparing to defend themselves – and as soon as Druid paused to look at the door, Ronnie MacDonald was on to him.

Ronnie dialled Dixon – with only one bar flashing on his mobile phone.

On the monitor, Druid now silenced Dr. Khoury with a finger to his lips.

"Drew is suspicious of the chemistry lab."

"Where is he now?"

"Gone back to the staff lounge."

Dixon borrowed a mobile phone from one of his commandos and started dialling Wally, while maintaining an open line with Ronnie.

76

Crowds trying to be silent, rarely are – people invariably whisper in libraries, tap pencils during exams, and cough in waiting rooms. But the Hunter High auditorium was as quiet as a morgue.

Many of the 330 students and staff detained in the auditorium later told me that, after all the violence of the preceding twenty-five minutes, they felt like they were in the cattle pen of a slaughterhouse awaiting their turn.

I have since been informed, by a farmer friend, that such condemned cattle and sheep are actually quite oblivious of their fate, but that horses and pigs are usually the noisy ones – emitting fearful, panicked, cries as they smell the blood from the abattoir.

I don't know about livestock, but the herding of the Hunter High hostages, and their smelling of blood, had most certainly silenced *them*.

Wade's promises of freedom by 12:30, though offering a tantalising hope, provided no real assurance whatsoever. What assurance from a liar and thief who promises not to steal again, or from gunmen who promise safety while the smoke still curls from the barrels of their rifles after their last murder?

These 330 had heard Zwick's last stand, Leon's ultimatum, his counting to three, and Druid's cold-blooded gunfire.

Under ordinary circumstances, good luck trying to elicit silence in a high school auditorium – but, under the extraordinary circumstances of that Black Friday, you could have heard a pin drop.

But no one dared to drop a pin – or lift a voice.

Except for Ricky Russell.

Ricky was sitting in the back row, only steps away from the rear entrance, alongside the seven Christians who had fled Leon's death threats in my office, and just behind Pam and Mrs. Argyle the librarian. The nine of them had simply grabbed seats around Pam, in wordless support, after the traumatised secretary had slumped into her own.

Because of the sepulchral silence, Ricky only had to whisper in order to be heard, only had to speak out in order for his words to surf the great acoustic waves of the auditorium into every inner ear in the place.

"Wade? Hello, Wade – or whoever's guarding us. It's Ricky Russell. I'm not moving out of my seat, and I'm not turning around. I just want to let everybody in the auditorium know that I'm praying for every one of us here in the school today, and all the police outside, and everyone who's worried about us."

Ricky stopped speaking and the blanket of silence rolled back over the room.

It was about thirty seconds later that one lone girl, somewhere in the auditorium, started crying. Two things were obvious from her wordless sobs – she was trying to be quiet, and she couldn't contain her emotions.

All this time, Weed, on sentry duty in the dark at the back, remained silent.

Then the weeping spread.

The sobbing became contagious.

One became two. Four. Six and ten. All muffled, muted, and heartfelt. From different seats, different rows, and different sections, the floodgates opened.

Some cried alone, others in twos and threes. And no longer exclusively female, either.

Finally, a second male voice dared to speak. "See what you've done, Ricky?"

And then a third, "Weren't they upset enough already?"

Next came a faceless female voice from a hard-to-determine location, "Shut up and leave him alone – don't listen to them, Ricky."

And then one of the Scripture Union boys beside Ricky spoke up, "Don't listen to them, Ricky, listen to God – what is God telling you?"

The auditorium hushed. The sobbing faded. Everyone craned to hear. The silence of dread became the hush of anticipation.

Ricky continued. "I think God wants us to know that no one is here today by accident. God wants everyone in this building today to learn how to live and learn how to die – always trusting Him, God our Father in heaven. Just like Jesus lived and died.

God is calling out to us today in the halls of Hunter High School. He walks the halls of Hunter High every day, but we're usually too distracted to hear Him.

If any one of you wants Jesus to teach you, today, how to shelter in His Father's arms, put up your hand. I know I do."

Ricky raised his hand into the air and held it there. The seven Scripture Union members who fled my office immediately did the same.

Then, throughout the dimly lit auditorium, here and there and everywhere – first dozens, then hundreds of hands went up and stayed up.

Certainly not all, but definitely the majority.

While Dregs plotted and murdered throughout the building. While police officers, patrol cars, command posts, and walkie-talkies squawked, and communicated, and coordinated. While the local media broadcasted to a global audience. Amidst all of that noise and static, in the darkened and hushed auditorium of Hunter High School hundreds of desperate students sought a silent communication of their own – a communication that was never referred to subsequently in any police statement, or inquest's testimony, or media report. A communication that was forgotten, or denied, by most in the auditorium after their release.

But, months later, before testifying at state and federal inquests, I watched again the video footage, still amazed at the hundreds of hands raised in their hour of need.

And it was only *years* later, that I noticed, on Weed's Dregcam footage, a blur in the corner of the screen. It was only in freeze frame that I finally saw it – Weed's own hand, with her black nail polish, in the dark, at the back of the auditorium, being raised along with all the others. The hand of Wendy Stankowski, raised where no human eye could see it.

77

Wally Martin's phone vibrated silently in his pocket. Not recognising the caller's number, he answered warily and in a whisper, "Hello?"

"They're seconds away from entering your lab," Dixon warned the chemistry teacher – who promptly hung up on him, without a word.

Wally was standing behind the lab door with a fire extinguisher at the ready. He had discussed an array of possible weapons with his students – blinding strobe lights, eye sprays or magnesium flares, electrical current wired to the doorknob, boiling water, acid, smoke bombs, explosives, scalpels, garrotting wire, butane torches, and molotov cocktails.

The students were amazed at the potential arsenal at their disposal – and even more amazed that their usually mild-mannered chemistry teacher could be so devious, even sadistic, when cornered.

Wally only suggested options for which he had the materials immediately at hand, or which could be prepared in minutes. Like dinner guests overwhelmed by a huge menu, his students seemed unable to decide – forcing Wally, once again, to grab hold of the reins and present his proposal.

"I think we need to focus more on seizing the intruder's rifle than on incapacitating or really hurting him. That way, if things go wrong he'll be less angry – simple as that. I'm no hero."

The students agreed with Wally's logic and k.i.s.s. philosophy ("keep it simple, stupid"), so Wally now stood poised behind the classroom door with a red fire extinguisher in his hand, its safety pin pulled, and ready to release a blast of white, powdery fire retardant.

Wally urged all students to remain in hiding behind their storage cupboards so that they might be protected from both flying bullets and potential retribution – Wally would attack alone, and the students could deny any participation in the conspiracy, should it fail.

But Mark Devito insisted upon acting as Wally's accomplice and grabbing the Dreg's rifle. Wally argued against the risk, but Devito wouldn't listen.

It was one of those situations in life where winning the argument was actually the worst thing that could happen to you, because there was no way that Wally could both assault and disarm the Dreg on his own. And, even worse, should multiple Dregs enter, the rifle would need to be utilised immediately – but Wally would still have both hands wrapped around the fire extinguisher.

Wally and all the students were greatly appreciative of Devito's apparently courageous volunteering of defensive support – though it was, in fact, neither courageous, nor voluntary, nor defensive. But, rather, because of his past cowardly acts of harassment, Devito was now being forced onto the offensive. He knew that if he could take out the Dregs with one of their own rifles he could become master of their vendetta, rather than victim.

Ronnie watched the monitor as his son motioned his nine shields to stand still and be quiet. Drew MacDonald tiptoed over and put his ear against the lab door.

"Gary, that's my son with his ear to the door," Ronnie was half pleading, half pouring out his anguish, to the Swat team commander.

"And someone else's son on the other side, Ronnie," countered Dixon.

Wally's phone again vibrated silently and he put it to his ear, this time without saying a word.

"One of the Dregs is at your door right this second – don't hang up."

Druid stepped back from the door, walked over to his shields, and said, "Mr. Zwick, you're obviously an action hero kind of a guy. I want you to walk over to that door and, when I give you the nod, I want you to burst into the lab growling like a commando."

"And then what?" Zwick was not trying to be smart in any way, he was just trying to be cooperative so that casualties were kept to a minimum from now on.

"Then we find out who's inside, and whether there's any other action heroes among them."

Once Ronnie saw Zwick making for the classroom door, he whispered into his phone, "Gary, looks like one of the teachers is being made to enter the lab first." There was no need for Ronnie to whisper in the principal's office, of course, he was just unconsciously empathising with those hiding in the lab.

Dixon immediately recognised the potential danger and relayed Ronnie's message as a warning. "Wally, it's a trap – they're sending in a hostage first – one of the staff is heading for your door right now."

There was no response from the chemistry teacher.

"I hope you haven't hung up on me again, Wally!"

78

Leon sent Druid off to check out the chemistry lab, closed the door of the staff lounge behind him, and returned to his eighteen captive teachers and Carol Spargo with a sigh, "The mantle of leadership grows heavy sometimes, doesn't it? You can be honest with me, don't you ever get tired of it?"

Barb, Kieran, and I stood silently in the corner, not daring to interrupt the coming tirade that we sensed was about to spew forth from Leon's lips.

The teachers looked at each other. Should they reply? Dare they reply? Did Leon prefer a monologue or a conversation? How best to appease the gunman? They agreed wordlessly, wisely, to remain silent and let him continue uninterrupted.

"All that responsibility and authority has gone to your heads! Power corrupts, and absolute power corrupts absolutely.

Demanding more respect than you really deserve – certainly more respect than you show your students.

Using that impatient, sarcastic tone of voice on students, that you'd never use with a fellow teacher – or *any* adult for that matter.

And what about choosing your pets and your prey? Do you choose just by looks who you're going to favour and who you're going to pick on? There's just *something* about that kid you never liked – isn't there?

Grading students' homework with a higher standard than you judge your own, content with that sloppy class preparation of yours.

Expecting students to discern and accommodate your moods.

Taking out your marital problems on your pupils.

Treating students in ways you never would if their parents were watching, or the principal, or a news camera. Well, the camera is on you now, but I'm not hearing that 'condescending teacher' tone of voice *now*, though, am I?

Any one of you want to assign me extra homework with a sneer, as you abuse your power and take your life's frustrations out on me because I'm the only one lower than you on the totem pole?

Or how about assigning mathematics homework just beyond what you taught today in class, so that I get frustrated tonight at home and you look like a genius tomorrow explaining it in class?"

Suddenly Leon shot his hand into the air like a five-year-old, "Miss, Miss!! Sir, Sir!!! May I ask a question, please? Miss, Miss?

Can someone in the room please tell me *why* I was made to sit on my bum on the floor of the classroom and the ground of the schoolyard all though primary school? If it was so comfortable, why didn't *you* join the students and sit there? Or maybe it was just something to do with power or control – forcing the students to look up to you, the way you can't force your spouse or your own kids.

Sit on the floor now, and see how *you* like it. EVERYONE SIT!"

The nineteen staff members all began, hesitantly, to comply. No one daring to be first, no one wanting to be last and aggravate the gunman. "Go on, sit down. Don't be so pompous and fragile – at least you've got a carpet to sit on. No fighting, and no talking to your neighbour! Back straight, eyes front!

Sorry, not you, Mr. Newton. *You* may stand. You, sir, shall sit on the sofa. I have never heard a bad word spoken about *you*."

Kevin Newton, the baby-faced thirty-three-year-old English teacher with kinky blonde collar-length hair, smiled – actually smiled at gunpoint – as he rose back to his feet. "You've never met my wife."

"Are you not happily married?" asked Leon with sincere concern.

Newton responded as he made his way over to the old leather sofa, "Very – but my wife knows me infinitely better than my students do. You can't really judge a person by six hours a day at school."

"Why can't I?" interrupted Leon, "Teachers do it all the time: labelling, libelling, grading, failing, scarring students for life."

"Everyone's story is much bigger than that. Take you, for example, Leon – don't tell me that this attack today is just because of your dissatisfaction with the school system. There are surely other issues in your life that created all that anger."

"Counsellor," Leon called out to me, "I think Mr. Newton here is after your job."

Then he turned back to Newton, "If you really want me to open up, Kev, I would have to lie on that sofa – but for now the sofa is all yours, and you deserve it. You love literature, you have inspired many a student, and I have never heard a bad word against you."

Newton spoke softly now, "There is greatness and failure in every man, Leon."

Leon ignored Newton's last comment. "Please stand when I call your name: Carol Spargo, Bill Arkapaw, Les Mantiss, and Mrs. Timms."

The four rose cautiously back to their feet. Precious few were their options, and they knew it.

"You've probably heard of the dean's list? Well, congratulations, you four have just made the Dregs' list. It's teachers like you who inspire students like me to take revenge."

"But I'm not even a teacher," protested Carol Spargo, secretary in the admin office.

"Then why are you always lecturing the students, judging them, wounding them for life with your gossip?" attacked Leon.

"I'm not," her protest was weak, quavering, not far from tears.

"Are you going to tell me that this staff room is not a breeding ground for gossip and a cesspool of student labelling that scars young lives forever?"

"If I've got anything to say, I tell people to their faces."

"Do you or do you not always refer to me as 'The Golden Boy' behind my back?"

"Mrs. Forman made up that name, not me," Carol was getting a bit testy, there was some fight left in her yet.

"And you embraced it and gleefully passed it on, and on, and on."

"Perhaps you should talk to Mrs. Forman."

"Oh, but I *did* talk to Mrs. Forman. She was number one on our blacklist. And now that she's dead, I'm talking to you."

Leon, always master of the dramatic flair, hesitated so that Ms. Spargo could fully appreciate the threat.

"But I can't talk *now*, Carol, I've just got to pop into the gym for a minute. You don't mind if I call you 'Carol'? I know that you usually prefer cruel nicknames."

Then Leon addressed the room, "Apologies, everyone, I've just got to check on my Dregs next door in the gymnasium – they're about to stage a dramatic recreation of the Roman gladiators. Yes, I *know* you told us all about it, Mr. Horvath …."

Tibor Horvath, history teacher and the oldest member of the faculty, sat cross-legged on the floor, in the far corner of the staff lounge. He was a fanatical devotee of the ancient Roman empire, ad nauseam, and he actually broke into a broad smile when Leon mentioned the gladiators.

"…. and we're all sick to death of it, to be honest – was ancient Rome really that great, or have you just exaggerated your childhood memories? That's what I want to know."

Leon reached for the door, "While I'm gone, I want all of you sitting down there on the floor to use your time brainstorming testimony to share when I return – either incriminating or defending the four colleagues standing here before you. But you must work quickly – insufficient evidence, and I'll be forced to call a mistrial and execute everyone in the room.

It's like group grading, giving the same mark to everyone even if it's unfair, even if you work best alone. Like forcing everyone to study Japanese even though some kids have no foreign language capability. Some boy just wants to build houses, and you force him to study history and memorise dates. Hammering square pegs into round holes. Where is the justice in that?"

Leon headed out the door, herding me, Kieran, and Barb before him once again.

79

Druid held his Ruger at the ready, with twenty-five bullets in his magazine, less the three now embedded in the heads of the students lying outside the auditorium.

The young MacDonald was hiding off to the side of the chemistry lab door, his back to the corridor wall. Ed Zwick already had his hand on the doorknob. Druid nodded the go-ahead, and Ed shot a quick glance past the other eight human shields to his left – who Druid had quickly flexi-cuffed to lockers spread out along the corridor – one last glance at the three distant bodies lying outside the auditorium, for whose wounds he was responsible.

Zwick burst into the lab with the same kind of attacking-monster growl that he used when tickling his five-month-old twins. He hadn't planned it, it was just instinctive. But now, as he recognised the love growl, he felt no embarrassment, only a sudden pang to be home with Jannette – with the boys chewing and drooling on his fingers again, as they had earlier that very morning.

The door burst open, Ed's monster growl ended, and Druid stepped cautiously through the doorway after his decoy. No sign of life – the lab seemed empty. Druid looked behind the door – nothing, except the red fire extinguisher hanging on its wall bracket as usual.

Wally Martin was huddling back among his students on the floor, when something caught his eye. It was Druid's blood-covered hand, with its amputated fingertips, waving at him over the desktop counter.

Slowly rising into view above the counter came Druid's flaming red hair, then his wild, red-rimmed blue eyes and, finally, his delighted grin.

"Mr. Martin, please don't disappoint me by saying that your students here were just doing a floor-based experiment. You're a nonconformist, Wally – always smirking at the system – and I would much prefer to think of you as the only teacher to ignore the fire alarm, and defy the round-up of the Dregs."

"If I admit it, Druid, will you give the class an early mark and let us all go home now?"

"*You* are in no danger here, Mr. Martin, although I can't say the same for Vesna D'Ambrosi there, Sharon Tilden, and young Mark Devito. We've been looking for you three. If only you'd left the lab door open," Druid mused, cruelly.

The two girls were terror-stricken and squeezed each other's hands. Devito had been forced to quickly grab a place on the floor next to his teacher as they hurriedly aborted their fire-extinguisher ambush.

Devito had then tried to avoid Druid's gaze as the Dreg focused initially on Wally. But now that his attempts at strategic ambush and camouflage had both failed him, Devito was left with only reflex action and survival instinct. Waiting, passivity, and cooperation were all suicidal options because he knew that somewhere just outside the lab door Slave, like an enraged bull, was waiting for him – and that meant certain death.

Devito shot to his feet and plunged a razor-sharp scalpel dead centre into the back of Druid's already wounded left hand, impaling it to the top of the desk.

Druid, who had been hunched over the desk while talking to Wally, now stood upright as he howled.

Devito's right hand let go the imbedded scalpel and grabbed the muzzle of Druid's Ruger.

Devito's left hand wrestled Druid's right for control of the trigger.

Wally fell upon, scooped, shovelled, and pushed his students across the floor and away from the bullets about to fly from Druid's barrel.

Devito and Wally had both responded instinctively, but Mark Devito's instinct was to attack, while Wally Martin's was to defend.

If only Wally's reaction had been to support Devito's attack, the siege might have ended quite differently.

As it was, Druid's right-handed control of the trigger was only ineffectivly challenged by Devito's left, while Devito's solid grip on the muzzle (and, therefore, control of the aim) was easily contested – Druid simply pulled the trigger.

The first bullet slammed harmlessly into the ceiling, but its muzzle flash burned Devito's right hand. Devito quickly repositioned his hand, enclosing the muzzle in a tighter grip.

Druid fired again as he yanked the stock of the rifle, shooting Devito through the palm. Devito, fighting for his life, refused to let go.

Druid's wild blue eyes, crazed now in anger and pain, squinted as he pressed the trigger three more times, shooting and burning Devito's palm over and over.

Then Druid's mouth contorted into a psychopathic smile as he ripped his impaled left hand from the desk, the scalpel slicing cleanly between the bones of his index and middle fingers until he was free.

Blood now *spurting* from his left hand, Druid wrapped it around the Ruger's stock – securing his total control of the weapon.

Devito let go the muzzle, the trigger guard, and all hope of victory.

"You wrecked my left hand – but I wrecked your right," gloated Druid like a little boy, adding with psychotic glee, "and now you've gotta face Slave – without a right hand."

Druid stomped his feet in hysterics, Devito fell to his knees in pain, and Wally began ripping bandage strips off his lab coat for both their wounded hands.

Druid's walkie-talkie crackled to life with Leon's voice, "What's up in the lab, there, Druid?"

"You can tell Slave that his friend Mark Devito and I have just been engaged in a little hand-to-hand combat. I'll bring him out to you right now – along with a couple of Weed's nearest and dearest friends. I also have a teacher to deliver to the staff lounge, and some students to the auditorium."

Ed Zwick was leaning against the wall near the classroom door – pale, shocked, and shaking, after his second shoot-out of the day.

Mark Devito was "known to police", as they say. When the police investigation into the siege began that very afternoon of Black Friday, when it was all over, after all the shooting and all the rain had stopped, the investigators were not at all surprised to find out that Mark Devito had been involved.

Months before, when Earl Kennedy called in the police to investigate Slave's flagpole assault, Devito was the first person they questioned. But when no one was willing to talk – least of all the victim – there was little the police could do but issue Devito with a warning, a warning that they themselves knew carried no weight in a grossly ineffective juvenile justice system.

The true nature of police work bears little or no resemblance to its popular portrayal in books and movies – and it is *very* popular, with crime fiction titles consistently topping the best-seller lists, and the genre's appeal only growing.

Perhaps this reflects mankind's appetite for the thrill of the hunt or the triumph of good over evil – both of which seem so seldom satisfied in the ever-increasing urbanisation of a world daily rocked by exposés of scandal and corruption.

Or perhaps it's because such stories of crime and murder somehow allow readers and audiences to maintain the veneer and respectability of law-abiding citizens while vicariously quenching some thirst, scratching some itch, satisfying some craving from their dark side – where the anti-hero is respected, or even envied, and his lawless ways admired. The loveable rogue, without conscience and without accountability, answerable to no one. Broken promises, broken hearts, broken laws, broken bodies, broken lives. Such are the media role models, the heroes, the anti-heroes, of today's society.

The ever-exalted rights of the offender, the quagmire of the courts, and the ineffectiveness of the penal system to rehabilitate – all of them fuel police frustration.

But they are only fuel. The spark was ignited, the flame was fanned, in the nineteenth and twentieth centuries when humanism, relativism, and modernism were all welded together by science and technology. Man was on the ascent and answerable to no one. God was declared dead and irrelevant, while the absolutes of right and wrong, of crime and punishment, were rejected.

If, after all, human life is not created in the image of God but, instead, evolved from a primordial swamp, then the standard is lowered, each life devalued, and the severity of murder diminished. If murder warrants a jail sentence of only three years, how much less for drunk driving, and even less for the irresponsibilities of youth?

Only a few decades ago, the local cop could take the local teenage troublemaker out behind the police station and kick him in the bum – thereby putting an early end to his criminal career. Linear. Beginning and end. Point A – disrespect and disobedience. Point B – firm discipline by parent or police.

But today in Australia linear thinking has given way, yielded, surrendered, bowed to the circular – and most police work involves the recycling of chronic offenders through the criminal justice system over and over again. Then much of this circular behaviour becomes cyclical as it is modelled and passed on from generation to generation.

Irresponsibility inherited, disrespect bequeathed. Circular and cyclical

– society spiralling in vortex and accelerating down the drain, with thirty per cent of Australian police officers suffering burnout and fifty per cent of new teachers quitting within their first five years.

And while such selfish, destructive, and inherited anti-social behaviour may seem most prevalent, most repugnant, most loudly condemned, and most often associated with criminal behaviour in the lower classes – it is simultaneously lauded, applauded, rewarded, and envied as "ambition" and "achievement" when manifested in its more polished forms amidst the addictive materialism and human consumerism of the upper classes.

And thus the young men of Australia inherited the sins of their fathers.

Alphonse Devito, Mark's father, was well known as a licensed builder in Newcastle. But he was actually an *unlicensed* builder. He had been trained and ticketed only as a bricklayer, but he belonged to a tight-knit fraternity of relatives and peers in a building industry where one tradesman often "signed off" on another's work.

This fraternity extended beyond the law, beyond the building site, beyond working hours, and even beyond one's own family. Alphonse certainly provided for the *material* needs of his wife and children, but the pub was the true centre of his life and all the time, money, fellowship, smiles, and laughter that he had to spare were invested there – and not at home.

It was a fraternity in the truest and ugliest sense. Women were not respected, not trusted, not allowed to enter. There was no place for them except in dirty jokes, or as illicit girlfriends on the side. There was to be nothing feminine in this fraternity, for this was Australian mateship in the dysfunctional extreme – a fraternity of shared loneliness, a brotherhood of wounded men, a clubhouse for little boys ill-equipped for intimacy and sworn to secrecy.

And in their shared conspiracy of macho silence, both the ability and opportunity to express weakness, pain, or mercy – whether physical or emotional – was denied them.

Such was the world awaiting Mark Devito after high school, the inheritance handed down to him by his father Alphonse, and his grandfather before him.

And as Mark endured his final Year Ten obligation at Hunter High before beginning his trade-schooling and apprenticeship, he chafed at the bit. He was forced to attend classes ill-fitted to his personality, which offered no relevance whatsoever to the building trade for which he was destined.

Too young for the pub, Mark built his own high school fraternity, and cemented his mateship with underage alcohol binges and the harassment of misfits like Slave.

It was now mid-October, and all Devito, his blue-collar schoolmates, and their victims had to do was survive just two more months. Then the school year would be over and they'd all be free, as simple as that.

Except that now the victims themselves had upped the ante, hijacked the schedule, turned the tables, and reduced the chances of survival.

80

Everyone was deeply upset, trembling, numbed, and in shock – those seated in the auditorium because they didn't see the execution-style shooting of the three, those standing in the corridor because they did.

Not seeing left the mind free to wander, wonder, and imagine atrocities without limit. At least the corridor witnesses were restricted to their recollections – although there was no telling how long, or how vividly, those horrific memories would flash back, echo, and haunt.

Survivors reported chattering teeth, and wobbly legs that would not stop shaking. Two students puked in the corridor at the sight of the three shootings – the sour odour of their vomit as repulsive to the nose as the sight of the shattered bodies was to the eye.

Wade and Slave led their captives into the gym, situated next door to the auditorium and back towards the admin office. Black-soled shoes like those worn by the fifteen students and their two guards were normally prohibited on the varnished gymnasium floor but, then again, so was the hunting and killing of students and staff – so in they all went.

Spread out around the perimeter of the gym were trampolines, pommel horse, vaulting box, balance beam, and a half-dozen other gymnastic stations with their safety mats.

Wade stopped beside the trampolines. "Feel free to stand in the peer group of your choice – Jocks to my left, Bullies to my right."

Wade's camera recorded their effortless and almost comical self-sorting into groups – no discussion, no hesitation, no doubt. Everyone knew their gang, their identity, their role, and their place – the food chain, the pecking order, their ranking in the pack.

The "Jocks", proud school sports heroes, were Doug Mallick, Hans Widmer, Dean Mosdell, and Trevor Cooper. They were joined by Trish Corby, Bethany Stanwood, and Jamilla Grey – the three founding members of the fledgling Hunter High School cheerleading squad.

The students, who immediately clustered together as "Bullies" on Wade's right, were Sammy Sawd, Joe Andarry, Stan Sawchaszyn, Mitch Soldat, Treena Carr, Zoe Moustakis, Sadie Pickersgill, and Crystal Banasik. They always referred to themselves proudly as "Thugs" and, under normal circumstances, would have never tolerated the more common title of "Bully". But, under normal circumstances, they were never the ones being threatened.

Their individual identities had long ago dissolved into the gang, yet each of the eight boys and seven girls had their own story, their own set of life circumstances, their own unique context, that led them into my story and into that gymnasium at 12:14.

I know, now, many more of their personal details than I knew on the day, and have since been amazed to learn the twists and turns of fate that brought them together on that Black Friday, but I have not the time or space to document even a fraction of that here.

Each of the eight boys (and Mark Devito) had physically attacked Slave Latska in the past, alone or in groups, at least once that Slave knew of for certain. They were also all suspects in the masked toilet stall and flagpole assaults – and they were only *half* of the twenty that Slave had written on his blacklist, the other eleven having vaulted out the left wing at 11:50 and made good their escape.

Because they had all proven themselves old enough to attack and fight, Slave considered them young men, held them fully accountable, and afforded them no more mercy than they had him.

The seven girls were their accomplices, molls, girlfriends, female counterparts – considered guilty by Slave, but not targets of his revenge.

Wade began addressing them all without formality or introduction. "You all know that the federal government of Australia and the state government of New South Wales have taken a hard line against verbal and physical bullying in our schools, don't you? They spent millions on a totally ineffective media campaign, warning everyone that such behaviour was unacceptable."

The assembled students knew exactly where all this was heading.

"In contrast to the government, we, the Dregs, are taking a very, *very* hard line against bullying. We have a very *small* budget that we have decided to invest entirely in discipline and punishment, and so far today it's been *very* effective.

I am standing here, representing Miss Wendy Stankowski – defending her because she never defended herself. Did she?

Defenceless she *was* – but not anymore. *I* am her defender, now. And my associate, there behind you ….", the fifteen turned around to face Slave, who had slipped on a rubber Mickey Mouse mask while Wade had focused their attention frontward, "…. is representing Mickey Mouse, who had always enjoyed a good reputation until a certain flagpole incident."

Never before had a cartoon character struck such fear into the hearts of a young audience.

Slave pulled off his mask to address the fifteen captives.

"I remove my mask now because a true man shows his face. My father taught me that only a coward or a thief wears a mask. Today I am here to restore honour to three names: Wendy Stankowski, Mickey Mouse, and Slave Latska."

Wade interrupted, "Slave is now going to deal with you boys. He will not avenge himself on girls no matter what their guilt, or their association with the guilty. But I subscribe to no such standards – I'll deal with you girls myself, later in the auditorium, where Weed can finally see justice done. We've just invited you along into the gym now because we know that these boys, here, perform best when surrounded by a gang, and supported by their cheerleaders."

Then Slave stepped to the front of the crowd and ominously handed his Ruger to Wade, before speaking.

"I have removed my mask. Does anyone now, perhaps, wish to remove my clothing? No masks, no guns, face to face, one against one, with bare hands?"

The eight boys were silent, pale, sweating – some even averting their eyes from Slave's piercing stare.

"Please, I invite you. But this time, I insist, one at a time. Now I am ready – you may begin."

Doug Mallick, blonde and handsome sports star, built as solid as a brick wall, spoke up. "Slave, there were some terrible things done to you."

"This is true," answered Slave quietly, his voice totally devoid of inflection – no sarcasm, no anger in it. He seemed strangely at peace, as though confronting his enemies was now his natural element, bred into his family over many generations.

"And we're sorry."

"So am I. But today is not about apologies or regret – which have no value in my country. Today is about restoring honour to a name, and this is priceless – in my country, if not in yours. Australia perhaps has different ideas of time, and value, and cost. But in my country, in my valley, a family name – Latska – is precious, and written in blood throughout history. Now, who will begin the attack?"

Silence. Thirty long seconds of silence.

"Perhaps you would feel more comfortable to attack me in the toilet stall? I can escort you, perhaps, two at a time – but I think, myself, that it was too tight last time with four of you, was it not?"

More silence.

"I have never before known any of you to be shy with me. Perhaps when alone, but never shy when in a gang – always so bold in a gang."

"What do you expect when Wade's holding a gun on them?" blurted Trish Corby, head cheerleader and still supporting her team.

It was then that Leon entered the gym with me, Barb, Kieran, the bleeding Mark Devito, Vesna D'Ambrosi, and Sharon Tilden.

81

Carol Spargo only managed to maintain silence for twenty seconds after Leon had left the staff lounge.

"I strongly suggest that everyone finds themselves a piece of paper and begins writing defence and praise points about each of the four of us on trial here. You heard Leon – no good arguments in our defence and we'll all die."

"He also said that we could offer incriminating testimony," Kevin Newton smiled from the sofa.

"Anyone speaks a word against me and I'll counter-attack two to one – I've got dirt on everyone in this room."

Carol's venomous reply silenced the lounge.

"I was kidding," Newton clarified quietly, without apology, fear, or rancour.

"Well, I wasn't." Carol grabbed her purse from the bottom shelf of the tea-and-coffee trolley.

"What are you doing?" asked Robyn Turner, mother hen.

"Calling the police to let them know where we are."

"But Leon said he'd kill anyone caught using a phone!"

"Let's just hope he's a liar as well as a murderer," replied Carol as she rooted through her bag.

"The school is surrounded by police, Carol, they know we're in here," reasoned the always-reasonable Mr. Sartor.

"I mean specifically *us*, under threat *in this particular room*," Carol said, finally retrieving her mobile phone.

"They targeted fifteen students in the right wing, and only four teachers – I think the students are in more danger than we are," argued Sartor.

Carol dialled Triple Zero. "That's because you're not one of the four on trial here."

"PUT THE PHONE AWAY!"

Carol dropped her phone in terror as all the staff members looked around the lounge for the source of the voice.

"Who said that?" asked Robyn Turner.

"I *am* the police, and we know *exactly* where you are. Now put that phone away before you get more people killed," came the Scottish voice from the speaker on the wall.

Kevin Newton looked to the intercom and saw its red light glowing.

"You're in the admin office?" Newton tried to grasp the implication.

"Yes."

"How'd you get in?"

"We have no time for details – can you cover the intercom's red transmission light with some paper or tape so that none of the gunmen can see that I'm listening?"

"No problem."

The intercom was mounted on the wall beside a cork notice board. Newton simply moved over a couple of the pinned notices and the light was completely hidden.

"You're covered," said Newton, directly into the wall speaker.

Ronnie continued, "First question – how many of you are there in the staff lounge, total?"

"Eighteen teachers and one admin office staff."

Carol Spargo was always the uneducated, the unqualified, the uncertified one – she *had* been all her life.

Ronnie continued, "Okay, listen carefully. I am the eyes and ears of the police in this building. The problem is that I have only eyes in the corridors and only ears in the classrooms. I've *seen* everything that's gone on for the last ten minutes but I haven't *heard* anything. Do they have a plan?"

"It's a suicide mission," said Mr. Newton succinctly.

There was a pause – a long, silent pause – from the Scottish cop.

"Are you sure?" asked MacDonald.

"Positive."

"They actually said that? They used the word 'suicide'?"

"One of the teachers tried to take Wendy Stankowski, one of the Dregs, hostage and their leader said threats and deals didn't apply, that theirs was a suicide mission, and they knew when they walked into the school today that they'd never walk out."

"Anything else?" asked Ronnie.

Robyn Turner approached the intercom. "I purposely lagged behind when they started shifting us towards the staff lounge, and I heard what Wade shouted out to the students in the auditorium. He said 'Wait here for about ten minutes, then there'll be a short assembly, and then you can all leave at 12:30, unharmed.'"

"12:30? Is that all?" asked Ronnie through the speaker.

"And they're targeting people on some hit list of theirs – four staff members here in the lounge, and another fifteen students in the gym," said Kevin Newton, concluding the summary.

"My thanks to all of you – that information is vital to the police, *vital*. I've got to go now, we've got a lot to coordinate in different areas of the building."

"What's your name?" Carol Spargo asked the intercom.

"Ronnie."

"Ronnie who?"

"'Ronnie' will do for now – let's not complicate it."

Sons were supposed to honour and advance the family name and reputation. But now Ronnie dared not even utter his surname because of his son's atrocities.

Oh, the seasons of life – when Drew was born he was referred to as "Ronnie's little boy". Only a few years later, and Ronnie found himself being constantly addressed by Drew's teachers and the parents of his little mates as "Drew's father". Then, during his adolescence, Drew seemed somehow embarrassed by his own parents and didn't even want to be seen with his father, often ignoring him in front of his peers. Now, apparently, Ronnie had entered a fourth stage of parenthood – denying his own son.

"Well, Ronnie, my name is Carol. After you switch me off, please remember that I'm on trial for my life in here."

"I won't forget you, Carol."

"You'd better not – because I won't forget you, Ronnie. And the last thing I'll tell these lunatics before they kill me is where you're hiding."

Silence hung heavily in the staff lounge.

"She doesn't mean that, officer," Mr. Sartor assured Ronnie.

"Oh yes she does," warned Kevin Newton, "every word."

"Carol, I assure you, the police out there are trying to save as many lives as they can, as quickly and efficiently as they can."

"That's all good, Ronnie, but what if these lunatics in here suddenly try to kill as many people as *they* can, as fast as *they* can?"

"Don't panic, Carol. So far the Dregs have been following a plan, they have a timetable – and the information you've given us is vital – but now we need a few minutes to form a counterplan of our own, so I've got to sign off." The intercom fell silent.

Kevin Newton lifted up the notices covering the red light – it was off.

82

After dropping off Wally Martin at the staff lounge, and handing Vesna D'Ambrosi, Sharon Tilden, and Mark Devito to Leon at the gym entrance, Druid led the twenty-three remaining chemistry students and Ed Zwick back down the corridor towards the seven surviving student shields and Dr. Khoury.

All eight of them had been left cuffed to the combination locks of lockers between the gym and the staff lounge, spread out far enough so that they could not help each other loose while Druid was storming the chemistry lab.

"Any of you students own a locker right around here in the corridor" – he checked the locker numbers beside him – "between 150 and 250?"

Two of the chemistry lab students raised their freshly cuffed hands and Monica McLean – student council vice-president and one of the original shields – waved her hand tentatively, unable to lift it any higher than the combination lock near her waist, but keen to cooperate.

"Which ones?"

"162."

"170."

Monica pointed to a locker very close by. When Druid stepped toward her, carrying the bloodstained scalpel that had sliced his hand open in the chemistry lab, Monica quickly added "211!"

But she had panicked for nothing – Druid was just cutting the cable tie that bound her to the locker, while leaving the one around her wrists still intact.

"Unlock them and empty them out – throw all your stuff on the floor as if it were worthless, which it is. Textbooks have no answers for you now."

The three students complied silently, while their idols smiled down at them from the glossy photos and posters taped inside their lockers. Sporting champions, musical divas, and movie stars – young, beautiful, airbrushed, blind to see, deaf to hear, mute to advise, and powerless to save.

"No one else has a locker within ten paces?"

All the other student hostages in Druid's charge again shook their heads, so he herded the twenty-three now-useless chemistry students into the auditorium while Weed held open the door. Druid then stepped into the rear of the auditorium and called out, "Anyone who has a locker between the staff lounge and the gym – between numbers 150 and 250, that area – raise your hand NOW."

Twenty hands were cautiously raised. And twenty of one hundred locker owners was just about right, considering that half of all students had bailed out of the school in the initial great escape up the left wing, and half of the remaining captives were just too fearful to respond. As previously instructed and threatened by Wade, all hostages in the auditorium kept their eyes front forward, even those with now-raised hands.

Druid quickly walked up to the seven raised hands nearest the rear entrance, pointed them out and said "Go stand by your locker."

When these seven were in position by their lockers, Druid repeated the instructions he had issued to Monica and the two chemistry students earlier, and the seven obeyed, hastily clearing out their books and belongings.

Except for Jeff Noonan.

Jeff was a tall and thin basketball player in Year Eleven who was now experiencing the same frustration shared at some time by all owners of combination locks, worldwide.

The right numbers in the right sequence, following the mandatory clockwise and counterclockwise turns as usual – but it just wouldn't open.

There was, of course, the same universal Murphy's Law in operation here that applied to all mechanical and technological devices. Sometimes the cellular phone, or computer, or combination lock, or widget just didn't work. No telling why, no telling when, but often at the most critical moment.

And, then, when it finally *did* work on the fourth attempt, or when someone else had a go – there was no explanation.

At first it just didn't, and then it just did.

To the cruel frustration of that law, add the trauma Jeff had already experienced as a hostage. Then multiply that by the humiliation of the other six locks opening easily all around him, and factor in the stress caused by Druid drawing ever nearer – with his Ruger poised and his blood-soaked bandage now dripping onto the student's shoulder.

Even after the other six lockers had been emptied of their contents, Jeff still struggled, rifle muzzle to his temple.

"Most people work best under stress, don't you find?" mocked Druid.

Jeff was encircled by the six other locker owners, who all felt powerless to intervene, relieved that their own locks had opened, and guilty for their sense of relief.

"Let *me* give it a try." Ed Zwick had been standing off to the side, watching Jeff's plight, before offering his assistance.

Druid invited Zwick's support with a sweep of his hand, while maintaining the placement of the Ruger to the side of Jeff's head.

Druid whispered close to Zwick's ear, "If you don't get it on the first try, I'm pulling this trigger."

Zwick spinned the dial several times to clear it, then looked to Jeff for the combination. "Right to 17, left past 0 to 25, right to 48."

Never was a lock handled more tenderly.

After the third number, Jeff's eyes widened like saucers, while Zwick closed his eyes and pulled.

The lock opened with a click.

Zwick's eyes opened, while Jeff's closed.

"Your talents are wasted teaching economics, Mr. Zwick. You should definitely apply for the job of super hero," then Druid turned to Jeff, "you're looking pale. Return to your seats in the auditorium – all of you, except 211."

Monica McLean stayed behind with the other six student shields, as ordered.

"Mr. Zwick here can empty the last locker – *other duties as assigned, super hero*."

Zwick began piling Noonan's belongings neatly beside the locker, while Dr. Khoury curiously examined the two cable ties that held him fast.

"I'll be back in a second, guys." Druid cut the other six student shields free from their lockers, and herded all seven towards the lobby.

83

When they were originally printed, the high school building plans and the AR-15 instruction manuals were pristine and unwrinkled – the former with their neat, tidy lines, the latter with their glossy photos.

But the rooms and corridors of Hunter High were now jammed with hostages, scarred with bullet holes, and splashed with blood, while the once shiny-new carbines had fired thousands of practice rounds and were now scraped, scratched, and stuffed with double magazines held together by ugly grey duct tape.

It was an old infantry trick – two loaded magazines taped together, "jungle style", side by side and head-to-toe. When the first was emptied, the thirty-shot magazines were simply flipped, the second inserted, and the bolt pulled back – sixty shots from an AR-15 in less than twenty seconds. Devastating power.

"Listen up," Dixon barked as he tore his four commandos' attention from the building plans – none having accepted his earlier offer of withdrawing from the mission. "Focus is everything, agreed?"

"Yes, sir," they replied, as one.

"There's wall-to-wall hostages in that school, and we can't afford any raging gun battles. Think of it as five gunmen, each surrounded by seventy hostages.

Every time you squeeze the trigger, in a crowd like that, you'll kill someone – that's a promise. So make sure it's someone you want dead – that's an order. Am I understood?"

"Yes, sir," they replied, as one.

"I trained you. I know you. I trust you with my own life. Do you trust me?"

"Yes, sir."

"Then *trust me* when I say that any one of you, on his own, could terminate this mission with ten shots – ten well-placed shots.

There's only five targets, they're not professionals, and we know where they are in the building at all times.

Now unload your weapons."

Dixon followed his own orders as ten magazines were pulled from five carbines.

"Separate your magazines."

Five razor-sharp blades sliced through the duct tape.

"Now reload your weapon with only ten bullets."

Each commando removed twenty shiny, copper-and-brass bullets from one of his magazines, and then reinserted it.

"Better *you* should die, than one of the hostages you've come to save. Have I got your attention now – are you focused?"

"Yes, sir."

Each one of them, of course, realised that there was an extra fifteen shots in the Glock strapped to his thigh, but that wasn't the point.

Gary Dixon, a commander who led from the front and was ready to die for the downtrodden, had unloaded his own magazines – *that* was the point.

84

The seven student shields stood shoulder to shoulder and clumped together somewhat like bowling pins, staring through the rain-lashed double glass doors of the lobby and out into the storm.

The encircling ring of police cars around the parking lot was discernable through the downpour – their flashing lights even more so, the officers crouched behind them even less.

"Don't turn around," the seven heard Druid's rasping, whispered threat from behind them, as he fell to his knees.

They heard him pulling cable ties from his ammo pouch, felt him fastening them to their ankles, recognised the little plastic zipping sound as they were tightened, winced as their ankles were pinched, panicked silently as the plastic dug into their flesh, the blood flow was cut off, and the pins and needles began prickling their toes.

The earlier fastening of their wrists in the right wing had been uncomfortably snug, but this was cruel.

It took the seven a few moments to realise that Druid was also cross-binding them with multiple cable ties – my feet together, then your left to my right, my left to the student in front of me and so on, the criss-cross pattern varying – to ensure that any escape attempt down the slippery front stairs and into the downpour would be difficult, impossible, or fatal.

Then Druid rose to his feet and whispered in their ears as he paced behind his phalanx of hostages, "I must leave you now to play a little game with Dr. Khoury, and I might be gone for several minutes at a time – perhaps enough time for all of you to waddle down the front steps, into those waiting police cars, and off to freedom. Perhaps not.

Three questions to ponder: Do you have the guts? Am I really gone? Or am I standing here, silently, behind you still?

You never know when the eyes of the Druid are upon you – like a red laser sight.

All you can know for certain is that if I see any one of you turning around, I'll shoot you dead."

85

Druid was back with Zwick and Khoury in less than two minutes.

"Dr. Khoury, Leon wanted you to demonstrate for me the mathematical order of the universe. You need to convince me, Doctor, because we Dregs believe only in chaos."

Druid illustrated such chaos by kicking Jeff Noonan's locker contents across the floor and destroying Zwick's nice, neat pile.

"Are you familiar with Russian roulette, Dr. Khoury?" Druid asked as he cut the cable tie that held the mathematician fast to the locker.

"In theory," answered Khoury.

"In *theory* it should be one bullet hiding somewhere in the six dark chambers of a revolver. But, for the purpose of today's demonstration, let's try one doctor hiding somewhere in the ten dark lockers of a high school. I'll just duck around the corner while you choose your lucky coffin.

My parents were always so worried about all the shooting I did on my video games and how I neglected my studies, but they'd be proud of me now, don't you think, Doctor? This is a scientific experiment."

"Please," Zwick pleaded, "you don't have to do this. I just can't see the logic …."

"WELL THEN MAYBE YOU NEED NEW GLASSES!" Druid spat out the words as his left hand, covered with its bloody oozing bandage, ripped Zwick's glasses off his face and threw them onto the floor to be crushed under the heel of his Doc Marten boot.

"Or maybe there *is* no logic in the universe for you to see. No logic, no order, no reason, no justice, no hope after all – just chaos. That's the whole point of this little demonstration. You have ninety seconds to choose a locker, Dr. Khoury."

Even before Druid had disappeared back into the lobby, the ever-cautious Ed Zwick began retrieving the emergency set of contact lenses that he always kept in a small plastic case in his left hip pocket. A sign, perhaps – for the first time since the fire alarm had sounded – that the Dregs could be outsmarted, after all.

86

Ronnie picked up his mobile phone and pressed 'Recall'.

"Sergeant?"

"Go, Ronnie."

"I just contacted the staff lounge via the intercom. Teachers have been told by the Dregs that it's a suicide mission that will end at 12:30. Three-hundred-plus students in the auditorium have been promised they will be released unhurt. Four teachers in the staff lounge and fifteen students in the gym have been targeted on a hit list and segregated. There's some kind of assembly scheduled to start in the auditorium at around 12:20."

"12:30 deadline," replied Dixon, as though he had heard nothing else, "the Sydney tactical squad won't even be here by 12:30."

"The Dregs were probably counting on that."

"And then we confirmed it for them on the radio."

87

Donnie Fairholme, student council president, noticed his vice-president Monica McLean suddenly looking down at her feet.

The red laser dot was back, flitting over their shoes and the carpet.

> "Firefly, firefly, shot from my hand.
> Firefly, firefly, where will you land?
> Firefly, firefly, who can outrun?
> Firefly, firefly, we'll have some fun.
> Hunter High, Hunter High, freedom awaits.
> Hunter High, Hunter High, just through those gates.
> Hunter High, Hunter High, out there fresh breath.
> Hunter High, Hunter High, in here just death."

Druid's dirge over, the red dot disappeared.

But was he gone – or still watching?

88

At 12:15, Rod Stanwych's phone rang, displaying Gary Dixon's mobile number.

"12:30 deadline, suicide mission, but first they'll execute another twenty students and teachers on their hit list – this is confirmed by a police officer in conversation with teachers locked in the staff lounge. And Buster probably won't get here until 1:30."

Dixon expected more questions or a longer wait, but Stanwych responded quickly.

"You've got a green light for a Swat response. Go ahead."

Dixon had prepared himself for a debate or an argument, but not an immediate green light.

"Did the premier already authorise it, did he?"

"Don't question my authority, Sergeant, you have your orders."

"Yes, sir. Thank you, sir."

"Any idea how long?" Stanwych's tone was different now. Decision made, responsibility passed on to Dixon. With his mantle laid at the feet of a specialist in a different field, he was now asking anxiously, even humbly.

The conversation slowed. They both knew they would not talk again until after the assault, assuming Dixon survived.

"Difficult to say. Timing is everything – finding the right moment. Less than fifteen minutes, obviously. It's got to be soon, and it's going to be fast."

"What's your gut feeling on this, Gary? What do you reckon?"

"I reckon I've been training for this day all my life."

Stanwych hesitated before replying. "God speed, Sergeant."

His four commandos were ready to grill Dixon as soon as he got off his phone. "We've got a green light to go?"

"No," replied their commander, quietly. Dixon had heard the tone in Stanwych's voice – had recognised the lie.

"We're not going?"

"*You're* not, I am."

89

The student lockers at Hunter High were not very big. But, then again, neither was Dr. Khoury.

Height was no problem because Khoury was short, but any man of average height would have found himself vertically challenged by the bookshelf that cut horizontally across the top quarter of the lockers – challenged, stressed, compressed, perhaps even suffering claustrophobic panic.

But Khoury's head was only just snug up against the bottom of the shelf, and the locker door closed quite easily without crushing his body – although a coat hook did gouge him between the shoulder blades, and his two feet were somewhat squashed within the floor space.

No, physically folding and fitting himself into the confined space was not so difficult. It was the psychological folding and fitting into Druid's nightmare that proved torturous – bullets ripping through metal and flesh, not knowing where they would impact or when.

Waiting. Just waiting.

Surely it's not the physical confines of the prison cell that breaks a convict's spirit as much as the mental curse of his sentence and his constant calculation of time served, time lost, and time remaining. A pointless, fruitless, endless mental reckoning of imaginary moments past and future that no longer exist, or may never yet.

The cell itself would be infinitely more bearable if its occupant was there for only a short term and knew it, or had only a short-term memory and never felt himself confined for more than a few minutes.

How much of our brief lives do we spend, and waste, elsewhere and otherwise? Emotionally tortured by regret, remorse, resentment, and blame directed against ourselves, and others, and God, for offences and disappointments long since passed? Mentally imprisoned by longing, expectation, and future fears that are never even realised? In many ways, our lives are no more shaped and bound by the physical and material than they are by thought, attitude, and expectation.

And so it was with Dr. Khoury. No sooner had he closed the locker door before him, than he began to replay the memories.

Khoury and Zwick had begun consulting with each other as soon as Druid headed off, circumstances demanding that their conversation be brief, practical, and brutally honest.

"I think the odds of me surviving his locker game, without being killed or wounded, are very slim. I would take my chances and run out that right wing, right now, had they not locked the fire doors."

"So what are you going to do, Suman?" Zwick's voice was filled with compassion, and a determination to support the decisions that only Khoury had the right to make.

Whether due to Khoury's years of mathematical study, or an innate ability to think quickly under pressure, or simply the crystallising influence of impending death – whatever the inspiration – Dr. Khoury's plan was crisp, clear, and solid.

"I see no other alternative, and I have no time, so I'll choose a locker. But you must shut your eyes and block your ears, Ed, as I close the nine other lockers and enter the tenth. I do not want you to know which locker I'm in, because we cannot afford your giving away my location with a telltale glance.

Once inside, I will cover my head and chest with my hands and arms to deflect or slow down any potentially lethal shot. To my advantage, he is only using .22 calibre bullets, and the metal of the locker itself should slow down the velocity considerably – even more so, I should imagine, if hitting a reinforced edge or hinge upon entry.

I was also thinking of shielding myself with one or two of these textbooks on the floor – they might even stop a .22 completely – but he knows that the lockers were emptied, and it might enrage him if I do."

That was it. Options considered, decisions made.

Here was Suman Khoury, at fifty-seven years of age, strategising his game of hide-and-seek with little Eddy Zwick – asking him to close his eyes and count to ten. Khoury remembered organising such street games in India, many years ago, with his little brother Ramesh.

Suman last saw Ramesh, a merchant banker in London, three years earlier, when he came out to Australia for a visit. It was now just 2:00 a.m. in England. In five hours, Ramesh would wake to hear the news of Hunter High. Khoury wondered if he himself would be listed among the dead and, if so, how his brother would react. Would Ramesh fly out for his funeral?

Not only was Zwick unable to contribute any strategic suggestions to Khoury's plan, he also felt ill-equipped and unqualified to offer any emotional support or spiritual advice – feeling as battered, defeated, and guilty as he did after his own experiences in the last ten minutes.

And then, to add to his overall sense of powerlessness and despair, here Ed Zwick – adult, husband, father, and teacher – had to close his eyes and cover his ears like a child, while Dr. Khoury faced death like a man.

And as Zwick awaited Druid's return, confident that he had done nothing right, Dr. Suman Khoury sweated inside locker 189 fearing that he had done everything wrong. Perhaps he should have just refused to play Drew MacDonald's version of Russian roulette and been killed on the spot, rather than entertaining the young psychopath by suffering terror and pain for the last remaining minutes of his life.

Maybe he should have shielded himself with those textbooks after all and, then, when Druid opened locker 189, Khoury could have hidden them underfoot – perhaps even assaulted the boy with them, and escaped with the eight other human shields.

Or what if he had chosen to hide in a locker further down the corridor?

And so the greatest source of Dr. Khoury's discomfort was not the cramped locker itself but, rather, the companions with whom he shared it: Should Have, Would Have and Could Have – the terrible and tormenting Triplets of Regret.

Then he started to shake. He had already been trembling, ever since initially facing the armed Leon at the door to the staff lounge. But now the tremors escalated into severe shaking, and threatened to expose his hiding place.

He had read somewhere that gunshot wounds were accompanied by searing pain – yet shock usually causes cold and chills.

Was it true, he wondered, that you never hear the shot that kills you, because most bullets travel faster than the speed of sound? "Not hearing the fatal bullet" must refer only to *instant* death. If you died three seconds after impact, then surely you *would* hear it.

How many bullets would Druid shoot into each locker, and would crying out in pain cause the student to cease firing so that he could open the locker door to view his cornered prey – or would he just pump in more bullets until the locker fell silent?

Light from the corridor leaked into the coffin through three horizontal slits in the door. When he peered through these slits, Khoury could see only the floor outside, because they were angled downwards. But they let the air in, and might allow a glimpse of his stalker's boots, or the sound of his approach.

Khoury tried to visualise his wife Saffira and their two university-aged sons – not in any way to attempt a spiritual communication with them, but just to comfort himself with the thought that his personal life had been fruitful, that there had been *some* return on his investment. Because right there, in the near-dark high school locker, with a coat hook poking into his back, his professional and academic life seemed headed for a rather sudden and ignominious end.

And then the well-educated mathematician Dr. Suman Khoury became suddenly perplexed by a logistical problem. Who would walk the dog if he was killed? Einstein, his Bassett hound, and Saffira shared a long-standing contempt for each other; his sons were seldom home and often unreliable.

Would a Bassett hound be the last thought on his mind before a bullet smashed into his brain? How depressing.

Suman suddenly felt like calling out to a God for deliverance, or comfort, or mutual acknowledgement, or something. But Suman had aged into an apathetic Hindu.

More frustrated than apathetic, really. He had tried to emulate his mother's piety, he really had. But, as a mathematician, he could never reconcile the myriad of Hindu gods and godesses – possibly over three hundred million – with her choice of seven particular deities to worship as their household gods. Why those seven and not seven others? The statistical improbability of satisfying the right gods, without angering the rest, was high – and variable under constantly changing circumstances.

So he and Saffira nodded respectfully to the gods on holy days, while actually capitalising on the festivals more as occasions for family gathering. And now he stood, cramped and quaking alone in the dark, with no incense, or offering, and nothing to pray, as Druid's footsteps grew louder.

All this, and more, passed through the mind of Suman Khoury as he waited in his tiny metal coffin for sixty seconds – ninety at the most.

90

"What do you expect when Wade's holding a gun on them?" blurted Trish Corby, head cheerleader and still supporting her team.

It was then that Leon entered the gym with me, Barb, Kieran, the bleeding Mark Devito, Vesna D'Ambrosi, and Sharon Tilden.

"Please go on, Mr. Latska," said Leon to Slave, just as a principal would to a primary school teacher, when slipping into the rear of his classroom to observe.

Slave took Trish's criticism on board, but without any immediate acknowledgement or response. He just held his empty hand out to Wade and received back his Ruger. Latska then walked ten paces over to the pommel horse, placed his rifle upon it, and walked away a further ten paces. "Your cheerleader is right, you obviously do not like to be outnumbered the way I was always outnumbered.

This will be our new game. Mr. Wade will not interfere or fire his weapon at anyone who follows the rules. Agreed, Mr. Wade?"

Wade nodded.

"There sits my rifle on this pummelling horse – ten paces from me, ten paces from you. Anyone of you who can get to it before me is free to shoot me, or kill me – then walk out of this gymnasium and out of this high school as a free man, and leading all the rest of you in here with him. But you must only use the weapon on me, and then drop it immediately – otherwise Mr. Wade there will kill you. Understood?"

"And what about the girls?" asked Trish Corby.

"I am only dealing here with the young men – the girls, this is Wade's business."

"And what if *I* ran for the gun right now? Could *I* not play your little game?" Zoe demanded to know.

"No Latska would ever shoot a woman."

"But I have no such standards," Wade interjected, "I would shoot you down, Zoe, like I would anyone who doesn't play by our rules – *I* am an equal-opportunity umpire."

Leon offered his advice as he led his six hostages, including me, over towards Wade's fifteen, "If I were you, Zoe, I'd try the competition we have planned for you next in the auditorium. It'll be even more ruthless than in here – I'm sure you'll do well.

And look who we found hiding out in the chemistry lab," Leon continued without waiting for Zoe's reply, "Mark Devito – I hope he's not too late to join in your game."

"We were just about to start," said Wade.

"I could tell that he was getting bored in class, and I knew he was headed for mischief – you all know the signs: couldn't sit still, fidgety, tried to cut off Druid's hand. I wouldn't keep him waiting if I were you – I think *he* should be your first contestant."

"You heard the man, Mr. Devito, step right up," said Wade.

Kieran thrust himself forward to Devito's side. "Look, he's already hurt. Even if he got his hands on that gun he probably couldn't ...."

Wade cut Kieran's protest short with the butt of his rifle.

Kieran was a towering basketball player and Wade was the shortest boy in Year Ten, so it was quite an upward arc for the Ruger to reach his nose, but it did with the loud crack of breaking bone and cartilage. There was an immediate gush of blood from Kieran's nostrils, as though a plastic bag of red dye had been broken, which slowed quickly to a trickle.

Everyone was shocked by Wade's seeming overreaction to Kieran's protest. Everyone but me.

For Wade had always been one of a half-dozen high school students in the Hunter Valley whose daily struggles and home lives – or lack of them – had tugged especially on my heart strings as a counsellor, and I had watched him closely.

At first, Wade was drawn to my office by the subdued lamplight and comfortable furnishings, and then, later, by its quiet, safety, and acceptance.

But, ultimately, the lonely Aron Wade was drawn to my office in the hopes of seeing Barbra Burser, one of my most faithful visitors. Day by day, bit by bit, and comment by comment, it slowly dawned on me that Wade was in love with Barb.

Most adults, teachers, and counsellors would dismiss it as just a teenage crush or infatuation, but I always felt quite the reverse. First love, and young love, is often the deepest and most unforgettable.

And how, exactly, can young love be dismissed as selfish fantasy any more than its more "mature" adult version?

What the modern media glamourise as "falling in love" is often, in essence, the worshipping of romance itself, or idolising the end of one's loneliness – while the breakdown of relationship is usually the incremental dawning of the true identity (the flaws and shortcomings) of the beloved upon the initial fantasy of the lover.

Perhaps all human love begins as selfish, childish love, and few there are who ever mature to be truly selfless lovers – regardless of their age.

So, I watched as the shortest boy in Year Ten fell in love with the shortest girl.

Wade, of course, upheld his non-caring façade like a shield, always dismissing girls in general and romance in particular. But I noticed him brighten up whenever Barb was in the room, I saw him showing off to her – not by embellishing his skills or accomplishments but, rather, more loudly vocalising his apathy.

He didn't care about anything, didn't feel any emotional or physical pain, didn't need anyone – but, coincidentally, always showed up in my office when Barb was there, and seemed to have little reason to stay after she'd gone.

It was bittersweet to watch such a stoic little warrior as Aron Wade, unconquered by the greatest of bullies – whether student or stepfather – so utterly smitten by the smallest of girls.

And only in light of that secret red ember of love did Wade's overreaction to Kieran's intervention truly make sense. Here was Barb's boyfriend, her tall and handsome boyfriend, stepping forward to challenge Wade's authority right in front of everyone – in front of the hostages, in front of the Dregs, and in front of Barb herself.

Stoic, tough, little fighter – that was Wade's whole identity, his area of expertise, his only source of pride and respect – and here Kieran had threatened it all.

First Kieran's head reeled back from the blow, then he doubled over with the gush of blood. He covered his whole face with his hands and dropped to his knees.

Leon and Slave seemed stunned. Barb bent over to her boyfriend, overwhelmed with empathic pain. Then she turned on Wade and yelled point-blank in his face, "He was cooperating! He was just trying to talk some sense into all this madness!"

Her beautiful green eyes were wide in rage, Wade's eyes dropped in shame. Kieran was on his knees and bleeding, but he had won. Kieran had driven a wedge between Wade and his young love, forever destroying the fantasy and the hope – the only hope Wade had ever really embraced, even if he had never embraced her.

Wade placed his hand on Barb's shoulder and pushed her away. Playing back the video later, it almost seemed like the touch electrified him, sending waves of alternating current through his heart and mind. Positive and negative, love and hate, attraction and repulsion. His ideal love defiled, his loneliness sealed, the long-dreamed-of touch turned now into a nightmare.

Then his open hand closed into a fist upon her shoulder. Gripping her white school blouse, he shook, and ripped, and tore open the innocent uniform – the buttons sent flying, then rolling across the varnished gymnasium floor.

Beneath the uniform blouse she wore a red, sheer, lacy brassiere with scalloped edges.

Everyone stared at Barbie, the innocent Barbie doll, suddenly and publicly exposed as the beautiful young woman that she was. There was nothing indecent about the bra, but it was meant to be discreet, personal, and private.

The indecency was all in Wade. In exposing the young woman that he loved, Wade had exposed himself – the selfishness of his love, and the fantasy of his infatuation.

Barb never took her eyes off Wade's face as she slowly tied the ripped blouse closed again with a knot above her exposed navel.

And then I realised.

She never mentioned anything to me, but Barb had known all along that Wade had loved her. Her eyes now tried to reach out to him in compassion, and grace, and acceptance. She had never flirted, had always been like a sister to him, had always reached out to him as the lost and confused brother that he was, and she had always known how he felt. She knew even now.

"Leave her, Wade." Leon spoke softly, but it was obviously a command as the M1's red laser dot swung lazily towards Wade's position – not to threaten a hostage this time, but rather to warn a Dreg.

The command, however, was unnecessary, because Wade had already let go his grip of her. He had already left her, or his gaze had left her, or the spark in his eye had left him, or something.

You just knew by his eyes that something had died inside him, in the same way that Natalie Abrahim's eyes had immediately registered death.

Some people might dismiss the thing that died in him as just a fantasy, or romantic illusion. And it *was* all that, to be sure, but it was also more. I know, for him, that it was hope itself.

I realise that Wade still had a strong relationship with Weed – but that represented more a rectifying of the *past*, with Wade offering himself to her as the defender that he himself had never known. Barb, in contrast, represented to him a whole new fantasy *future*, inspired by the character and integrity he saw in her, and had never known in anyone else.

And so Wade fell into the primal human self-deception that, though the past is strewn with the pain of my wrong decisions and actions, somehow my ideally imagined fantasy future circumstances will inspire and enlighten my responses and decisions. The Triplets of Regret – Should Have, Would Have, and Could Have – now replaced by the Foursome of Fantasy: If Only, Someday, Elsewhere, and Otherwise.

And as he returned to the gladiatorial exhibition at hand, I knew that I would never again see Wade look at Barb in the same way.

Wade's relationship with Barb opens up the topics of romance and sex at Hunter High. Although sex is used daily to sell music, clothes, toothpaste, soft drink, fast food, and movie tickets to students, it was really a non-issue within the life-and-death atmosphere of the siege. Sure, students clustered with friends and clung to intimates whenever possible under the Dregs' death threats and in the face of their gunfire, but sex falls well down the list of human needs and priorities when compared to survival, safety, and security.

And though the influence of Hollywood Boulevard and Madison Avenue was firmly entrenched in Hunter High School, and at the very heart of the siege – with much to answer for in the bullying of Weed and Slave, the obsessive ambition of Anton Spitzer, the fantasy world of Druid, and the alcoholic abuse of Wade – as the bullets flew, and the glass shattered, and the bodies fell, the halls of Hunter High seemed far removed from the Hollywood dream factory and the Madison Avenue marketing campaign.

As in an intensive care unit, a morgue, or a funeral parlour, much of the triviality and joviality of everyday life – in fact, even the very *daily-ness* of life itself – seemed somehow ashamed to enter Hunter High on Black Friday, and waited silently outside while, inside, each life soon came to be appreciated as sacred, and each moment as precious – whether for the first time, once again, or finally.

91

"Come out, come out, wherever you are."

Dr. Khoury was about to obey and placate the gunman – until he recognised the sarcasm in Druid's voice.

"I love shooting games," Druid mumbled to himself as he scanned the ten lockless lockers around about him, and considered the odds.

"You don't have to do this – there's been enough killing today already." Through the three slits, Khoury listened to Ed Zwick arguing in his defence. "That video camera on your head can provide proof of your mercy – legal evidence that you spared Dr. Khoury."

"You teach economics, Mr. Zwick, you're just a little nerd. For you, everything is about business. Lighten up, you take it all much too seriously. Life's not a business, *Mr. Edward Zwick* – it's a game.

For me it's all about pleasure, recreation, fun, entertainment. I don't kill because I'm driven or crazy – I kill because I like it.

The people watching this video are only spectators. I'm a player, and I'm playing to win. You've played video games, Mr. Zwick? Nintendo, Xbox, PlayStation?"

"Yes, of course."

"Then you know about the game cheats, don't you? The gold coins, or keys, or weapons, or ammunition, that you can pick up along the way, down the corridor, through the maze, in the dungeon, or the castle? Pick them up and you gain points, or power, or strength, or extra lives, right?"

"Yes, I know."

"Well, along these corridors in Hunter High I gain power when I kill. I pull this trigger and I get bigger, and stronger, and I possess more life force – I can feel it coursing through my veins as they die. I'm out to win this game, Mr. Zwick. I've been a loser long enough."

Druid turned away from Zwick, discussion over, focused fully on the lockers before him, and raised his voice so that his prey could hear. "Let the games begin. Dr. Khoury, let me explain to you the mathematical principles that govern *my* universe.

I have ten lockers scattered around me with their locks removed, and a twenty-five-bullet magazine in my rifle. I call this game 'teacher tag'.

My chances of winning and your chances of surviving are inversely proportional the longer we play – again, let me explain: I will choose from the ten lockers at random – I say they're random, you say it's the mathematical order of the universe, or the hand of some God – and I fire *one* bullet into locker number one. My lovely assistant, Mr. Zwick here, then opens locker number one and, if Dr. Khoury's inside, he's now a free man with one bullet wound. (The producers of the show bear no responsibility for the survival of the contestants, by the way.)

If, however, there's no Doctor in number one, then locker number two receives *two* gunshots. My lovely assistant then opens door number two and, if Dr. Khoury's inside, he walks – or limps – away a free man with two bullet wounds. And on it goes.

By my calculations, I'll run out of bullets by the seventh locker. When I run out of bullets, the game is over, and the good doctor lives or dies as a free man – depending on his wounds. If he's in lockers eight to ten, he walks away without a scratch – that's the grand prize.

If, at any time, Dr. Khoury decides that there really *is* no beautiful mathematical order to the universe after all, then all he has to do is yell out 'I guess I've been an idiot all my life' at which time the game will continue with two changes.

Number One: I will feel much better, knowing that my theory of universal chaos has been proven correct yet again, and *Number Two:* Dr. Khoury will have seriously decreased his chances of survival by giving away his location. No mathematical order, and no mercy, in *my* universe – let us begin."

Without a moment's hesitation, Druid fired a bullet dead centre into a locker three paces away to his left.

92

Kieran had sunk to his knees, tears poured from his eyes, his face now a bloody mask of throbbing pain.

Barb placed her arm around his shoulder and ran her fingers through his hair.

I don't know if any of the others in the gym, besides me, even noted the two anomalies: Barb's public display of affection towards the basketball player, and her actually having to reach *down* to touch his shoulder.

"He needs to sit down. Can I take him to the auditorium?" Barb asked Leon.

"He can make it there on his own. I want you here with me."

Kieran shook his head, refusing to go, but Barb tugged him to his wobbly feet and gently shoved him on his way, saying "I'll join you there in a few minutes." Kieran squeezed her hand good-bye and stumbled off, leaving a bloody trail behind him.

"I am still yet waiting for you, Mr. Devito," the familiar Slavic voice called out from twenty paces away.

Devito nursed his bandaged hand and winced in pain – whether from his multiple gunshot wounds or his dread of Slave's challenge, it was impossible to know.

"I'll take his place – let me go first," a very deep but very gentle voice, reluctant but determined, broke the tension.

All eyes looked back to Doug Mallick.

Slave didn't hesitate, "As you wish. But then Devito is next."

Latska was clearly confident of dispatching all contestants, one after another.

Leon produced Pam's scissors from his coat pocket and cut Mallick's cable ties.

Doug Mallick was one of those rare "all-rounders" who managed to score soundly in all four quadrants of a high school student's life: academics, athletics, social skills, and dating. As such, Doug had long been respected by both peers and teachers, but had only recently begun to respect himself.

In the previous ten months he had come to acknowledge and detest the fact that his appetite for popularity and acceptance had led him to disregard his parents' advice, his common sense, his ethical standards, and his health, with regard to smoking, alcohol, drugs, sex, and bullying.

In the past, Doug had been quite content with his standards lowered to meet the crowd's and he had a lot of fun. That is, at least, until he came under the influence of Kieran, his basketball teammate, and his Uncle Allen.

Doug held any Christian commitment at arm's length and decided instead to watch Kieran closely while simultaneously taking up karate at his Uncle Allen's martial arts academy where he quickly became committed to the fitness, discipline, and code of honour.

Three years ago, Doug had begun mocking and trying to intimidate Slave. After all, it was considered a school sport, and Doug was an athlete.

Last year, they both ended up bruised and bleeding when Doug's assault ended in a draw. Then Doug came up with the idea of the toilet stall attack, but he pulled out of the planning because of his uncle.

Doug had turned over a new leaf – bullying was out and accountability was in – but, because of his past transgressions, he had now been included on the Dregs' blacklist and swept up in their dragnet.

So it seemed that Barb and Kieran were right, after all, when they warned him that there was no way in the world of escaping the sins of the past – and this was judgement day.

Less than two minutes earlier, Doug had tried sincerely but unsuccessfully to apologise to Slave and right the wrong, but it was too late. Then he watched as Kieran – his mentor, and an innocent man – had sacrificed his face defending the guilty Mark Devito. And, finally, Barb had been attacked for defending Kieran – even little Barb.

So now Doug found himself picking up Kieran's fallen torch – and risking his life for a young man that everyone knew Doug didn't even like or respect. But Doug's intervention was because of who he was becoming, and not because of who Devito had been.

Everyone, who had been gathered together there in the gym, naturally assumed it was the *old* Doug Mallick facing off against Slave one last time. Only Kieran and Barb knew different.

Barb squeezed Doug's hand and Doug squeezed back, but he didn't look at her. He was focusing now on Slave.

Then he looked down at the shiny, varnished floor and seemed to be calculating the distance. Mallick pursed his lips and regulated his breathing. I noticed movement on the floor and saw that he was balancing on his toes.

Finally, Doug turned his head to see if Kieran was still in the gym, and he was. Kieran had stopped by the exit doors after he heard Mallick volunteering to stand in for Devito. The two young men nodded to each other, and everyone else in the gymnasium wondered why.

Doug turned and sprinted across the room, his long legs pumping, his feet devouring the ten paces.

Doug's gentle voice and laid-back demeanour had effectively caught Slave off guard, causing him to underestimate his opponent. Now Slave, too, rushed for the waiting Ruger.

Mallick's legs were longer, but he carried more weight. Slave may have been surprised at the burst of speed, but he was more familiar and confident with the weapon waiting at the finishing line, whereas Doug had never even touched it. Both were equally disadvantaged in their footwear – neither school shoes nor Doc Marten boots designed for running.

Slave's focus was on the weapon – as it had been all his life. He was raised a soldier. Weapons, feuds, revenge. Anger boiling over in the brain, flooding and overflowing the heart, running down the arms to the weapon in the hand and the finger on the trigger.

Doug's focus was on his opponent – as it had been all his life. He was raised an athlete. Naturally gifted at any sport he ever played, he had grown accustomed to defeating all the opponents he had ever faced on these varnished floorboards – and so he expected to win again today.

Slave knew the weapon, but Doug knew the arena and the power of the home crowd to drive his legs and extend his reach. Today's audience of student hostages was much smaller than Mallick was used to, but a crowd one thousand times the size never willed an athlete more passionately towards victory than did these seventeen.

And these seventeen peers, who had grown up as spectators in a media-glutted world, now watched yet another star, yet another hero, do their running for them, and they ran vicariously through him – because if Doug beat Slave to that Ruger, then they all walked away free.

Slave got there first.

You get what you focus on. His hands gripped the Ruger, and his finger instinctively found the trigger but his all-consuming focus left him no time, energy, or attention for self-defence – a fatal mistake when pitted against a martial arts devotee.

Slave swivelled the barrel towards Mallick – not yet aimed, just towards him. Doug deflected it with his left arm (his focus was not on the weapon) and channelled all the core strength of his body into the heel of his right hand which he rammed upwards into Slave's nose.

This was no street fight, and Mallick was not untrained like Wade. The blow was not an angry outburst or a lucky shot. It is only a myth that such a blow can drive nasal bone into the brain and prove fatal – the lower nose is softer cartilage, the upper nasal bone too short, and the brain too well protected by the skull at that point. Mallick knew all that, and was simply protecting his knuckles from fracture, while selecting the softest target that would produce the greatest shock wave when backed with the momentum of his run-up.

Everyone in the room heard a loud, sickening crack and assumed it was Slave's nose breaking – it was, in fact, his neck.

As Slave's legs buckled, Mallick grabbed the Ruger while simultaneously driving his left fist into Latska's throat. Martial arts, applied in a true combat situation, bears no resemblance to a Hollywood fight sequence which has been choreographed for days or weeks, and lasts for several minutes on the screen. The goal of Hollywood: extended entertainment, the goal of combat: pre-emptive killing.

Mallick's survival required speed – now, more than ever. He grabbed Slave's crumpling body from behind, clutching on to his black hoodie, so that by the time Wade and Leon's red laser dots zeroed in, their only available target would be Slave's chest, Mallick now propping him up as a human shield.

Analysts later asked why Mallick shielded himself with Slave's body when Mallick himself, only a few minutes earlier, had seen that the technique had proven so fruitless for Ed Zwick with Weed. Hindsight is 20/20, while foresight is often impaired by time pressure and limited options.

And, besides, Mallick's strategy was the polar opposite to Zwick's. Ed, thinking economically as always, sought to use Weed as equity or collateral in a bloodless escape bid – a kind of bartering, a win-win situation where no one was hurt.

Mallick, in contrast, was a fierce competitor, a warrior, an athlete out to win at any cost – trying to gain a momentary advantage by shielding himself with a defeated opponent who was only the first of the Dregs he was prepared to kill.

Zwick was a businessman-in-theory, an armchair analyst, who still naively believed in the promise of a handshake, while Mallick had seen too many tournaments won by foul play, or lost through biased refereeing.

Perhaps the depths of one's character are only ever truly revealed at the extremes of time – either slowly over the decades, or in a momentary flash of crisis and panic. Perhaps not.

All I know is that, in that split second of reaction time, once Mallick had grabbed Slave's Ruger, Leon instinctively shielded himself behind my body, while Wade stepped in front of Barb – and then both Dregs held us there in place.

"What kind of a sports hero are you, Mr. Mallick?" Leon shouted. "You're not playing by the rules."

Mallick yelled back, invisible behind Slave's slumped and unconscious body, "This is no *game*, I'm not *playing*, and there *are* no rules."

"Agreed," Leon replied calmly as he opened fire.

Ten .30 calibre bullets from the M1 slammed into Slave's chest in three seconds. Of the ten, seven passed right through his body. Of those seven, five struck Doug Mallick – one in the shoulder and four in the chest. Of those four in the chest, two penetrated his heart.

The two sixteen-year-olds fell to the floor, dead – boys, young men, veterans.

Post-mortem reports concluded that the fractures to Slave's nose and cheekbones were not fatal nor, in fact, was his crushed windpipe. His broken neck and four of his bullet wounds were each considered potentially mortal but the coroner could not determine, with any certainty, the *exact* moment or cause of death.

Leon, however, had no such difficulty – he considered Slave dead the moment he became more valuable as a target than as an accomplice.

Doug Mallick's death was clinically described as instantaneous but, more colourfully, "dead before he hit the floor" in later courtroom testimony.

93

"Mr. Zwick, would you please reveal the contents of locker number one for our home audience."

Ed anxiously opened the locker – empty except for an exit wound in its rear wall.

"May the gods be praised, Mr. Zwick, that's amazing!"

And so it continued, with absolutely no predictable pattern to Druid's targeting – sometimes neighbouring lockers, sometimes alternating from one side of the corridor to the other. Random shooting in Khoury's ordered universe.

Druid shot twice into the second locker at approximately Khoury's head and heart level. Zwick opened the door – empty again.

Druid tried his best to maintain his parody of the smiley game show host, but there was now a slight edge to his voice as he raised his volume and called out, "I suppose I should have mentioned earlier, Dr. K, that if I don't find you in one of these lockers, I will have to assume that Mr. Zwick here was part of the conspiracy, and kill him. Then I will hunt you down in your little hidey-hole – wherever that may be – and kill you like the coward that you are."

Druid's camera recorded a fleeting expression of doubt flashing across Zwick's face. What if Khoury *had* ducked into the admin office, or the toilets, after all? Zwick had closed his eyes and covered his ears as Khoury requested – and would know nothing of such an escape plan.

Like alternating current running through his mind, Zwick again vacillated between courage and compliance, hope and despair, order and chaos.

But Zwick wasn't really given any time to rein in his emotions, because Druid suddenly accelerated the pace – perhaps wanting to confirm Khoury's location, for himself, as quickly as possible.

The third, fourth, and fifth lockers were each shot in different patterns – vertical, horizontal, and diagonal, in that order.

Yet Zwick noted the common denominator in all three – it would have been impossible *not* to hit Khoury with any of these semi-automatic barrages, as Druid placed and spaced his shots with cruel precision.

And, each time, it almost seemed as though the red laser dot itself was *actually* burning through the metal of the lockers – an optical illusion as the trigger was squeezed, the red dot became a .22 calibre hole, and then momentarily remained, ringing each new bullet hole and creating a hot molten effect before moving on.

In each case the lockers proved empty but, by the fifth opening, Zwick's hands were shaking and he could clearly see the ten bullet holes – five entry and five exit.

Druid placed the index finger of his butchered left hand to his lips and indicated, with a flick of his head, that he wanted Zwick to follow him quietly towards the lobby.

Zwick obeyed, wondering what would be worse for Dr. Khoury in the darkness of his locker – if, indeed, that's where he was – the blast of gunshots or the sudden, mysterious silence.

Druid avoided treading on the worst of the broken glass as he pilfered seven school sports medals from their shattered trophy cases.

He then yelled a greeting so as to startle his phalanx of seven student shields, "Good for you! You haven't moved a muscle. I'm so very proud that I'm going to hang a medal around each of your necks – but don't turn around, remember?"

In mock-Olympic fashion, Druid placed the ribbons bearing the blue-and-gold school colours over the heads and around the necks of the seven students, with the medals left dangling behind their backs.

"I'm sorry I can't congratulate you face to face, but I need to keep you between me and the snipers out there – you know how it is. I've also hung the medals between your shoulder blades to give myself a nice shiny target to aim at should you decide to pull a runner on me. Carry on."

And then, with his taunting and threats concluded, Druid led Zwick back to the lockers.

94

Everyone in the gym seemed to be frozen in a stare.

Many stared at the floor to avoid eye contact, or at the two crumpled teenage bodies, or at each other as they chose to focus on the living rather than the dead, or at Leon, the executioner, still shielding himself behind his female hostage – which Slave never would have done – or at the smoke still swirling from the muzzle of Leon's M1.

The first one to move was Kieran. I heard the gym door open behind us and turned in time to see him leaving with his hands covering his face – whether nursing his broken nose, or crying, or shielding his eyes from further horror, I could not tell. Perhaps all three.

Leon was next. He walked over to the two fallen gladiators, confirmed for himself that Doug Mallick was dead, retrieved Slave's Ruger from under the bodies, and placed it back on the pommel horse.

The most haunting image of Leon's approach was recorded on Slave's Dregcam, lying now at floor level. The GoPro first captures Leon, full-length in a long shot, twelve paces away. But as he approaches the fallen camera, Leon's lower body, legs, and feet loom larger and larger until, finally, only his boots fill the frame.

And just as his Doc Martens arrive at the camera, a pool of blood flows out to meet them. Whose blood I could not tell, perhaps a blending of both – a communion, finally, in death, that had eluded them in life.

Wade's boots then approach the puddle. When he finally speaks to Leon, only his disembodied voice is heard off-camera. Though Wade's face remains unseen, he is obviously speaking through angry, clenched teeth.

"Didn't you think that guy standing in front looked a lot like Slave?"

"He was dead, Wade."

"We know that *now*, but you didn't know that for certain when you opened fire."

"Mallick was trained in martial arts – *obviously* – he hit Slave with two lethal blows."

"So it was all Mallick's fault, somehow *he* pulled your trigger?"

"If there's anyone else to blame, it's Slave himself."

"So it's suicide now?"

"The man was blinded by revenge."

"And we're not?" Then Wade's boots returned to Barb.

With the Ruger repositioned on the pommel horse, Leon began addressing the captive audience once again. "Our initial offer remains unchanged."

Zoe Moustakis erupted like a volcano, pent-up fear and tension spewing from her mouth and drowning her feeble attempts at self-control. "But Slave *said* that if Mallick beat him, we would all go free!"

"No, Slave said Mallick could *lead* you to freedom – but he's in no condition to lead anyone anywhere now, is he? If Mr. Mallick had dropped the gun as instructed, he would now be free – as would you all. You've just seen that it can be done – you *can* beat a Dreg at this game. Who wants to be next?"

Silence. Averted eyes. No takers.

Leon stepped back ten paces from the gun on the pommel horse, and then three more.

"There. I'll even give myself a handicap."

More silence.

He placed his M1 on the shiny, varnished floor and slid it away with his foot – scratching it more than any black-soled shoe ever had. "Zoe! Now's your chance. I'm not Slave – I'll compete against a girl."

"What's my option in the auditorium?" Zoe asked, negotiating.

"Here in the gym it's one-on-one against a Dreg. In the auditorium you'll face a much crueller opponent – the gang, the pack, each other. Back-stabbing. Feeding frenzy. I can hardly wait."

"I prefer team sports," replied Zoe, decision made.

Leon retrieved his M1, with a sigh, and headed towards the exit.

"To the auditorium, everyone, or should I say the colosseum? It wasn't the gladiators – or even Caesar himself – who held the real power of life and death in the colosseum, you know. It was the spectators."

95

Druid whirled so quickly to sight a locker, across the corridor, that Zwick was forced to jump aside in order to avoid being shot himself.

Without a word, and wearing only a blank expression, Druid had pumped two bullets into his sixth locker, just below the horizontal shelf and both around head level.

And then Druid's Ruger made a little click.

The explosion from the last bullet had blown back the bolt and recocked the weapon, working perfectly as designed. But the click of the firing pin, when Druid pulled the trigger for the third time, indicated that no live bullet had been fed into the chamber as the bolt slid back into its firing position.

Druid was clearly surprised. The Rugers themselves were so dependable that there seemed only three probable causes, all related to ammunition: dud bullet, spent shell casing caught and jammed by returning bolt, or –

"I'm empty," blurted a shocked Druid to himself, "I can't believe it." The beautiful, mathematical order of the universe had struck again.

Druid had pulled the bolt halfway back, and immediately realised three things – no spent shell casing had gotten jammed, there was no bullet in the chamber, and there was no more ammunition in his precisely tooled and machined TI-25 magazine.

His cold-blooded game of Russian roulette was experiencing technical difficulties and, absurdly, he now stood in the corridor doing mental mathematics while pointing to the lockers that he'd already shot up.

One, plus two, plus three, plus four, plus five, equals fifteen bullets, plus two bullets into his sixth locker equals seventeen. But that was eight shots less than the twenty-five bullets held by his magazine.

Amidst all the panic, and horror, and brutal bloodshed of the day, he had lost count – not surprising, it was certainly easy enough to lose your composure, your bearings, and your sanity.

Druid had forgotten about the three, earlier, execution-style shots into the student shields before him – Victor Eng, Ishna Mahrmoud, and Natalie Abrahim – as well as the five bullets discharged in the chemistry lab tussle with Mark Devito. That accounted for all twenty-five.

Ronnie MacDonald watched, on his monitor, as Zwick missed a golden opportunity – an opportunity for them all, Drew included.

Even though Ronnie was watching the events unfold on a silent monitor, he could instantly tell by Drew's reaction, body language, and inspection of the chamber, that he had a weapon malfunction.

"MOVE, NOW!" Ronnie yelled at the deaf and dumb monitor before him. Zwick had seconds – an eternity in this type of situation – in which Drew was distracted and virtually unarmed.

If only Zwick would grab the rifle – before it could be reloaded – perhaps strike Drew with it (just hard enough to immobilise him), hopefully pull that other teacher from the locker, and run out the front door with the seven students in the lobby.

"Come on, do it, mate!" Ronnie pleaded.

But real life is very different from its portrayal on a television screen and Ronnie, unlike Zwick, was not mentally weighed down and paralysed by the bodies of three high school students lying at the entrance to the auditorium.

Ronnie was, in fact, incapable of truly empathising with *anyone else* at that point, so overwhelmed was he with paternal anguish. His sole agenda was now to contain his deranged son's violent rampage, and minimise his offence.

In Ronnie's tortured mind, Zwick, Khoury, and the seven lobby students were not victims to be saved as much as potential targets to be removed from his son's line of fire.

Powerless and isolated in the dead principal's office, Ronnie MacDonald could only watch the escape opportunity dissolve on the screen before him, and the nightmare continue, as his son loaded a fresh magazine.

96

Wade, Barb, and I had been directed by Leon to escort the seventeen surviving student hostages out of the gym and into the auditorium. They were now being herded like cattle to the slaughterhouse and they knew it.

Some of them looked back over their shoulders as we led them down the corridor – peered longingly back towards the lobby and the exit that they knew lay just beyond, mentally weighed the odds against a successful breakout, and immediately gave up hope. Between them and any possible escape from the insanity stood Druid, in all his madness, shooting up the lockers.

We knocked on the auditorium door, and Weed opened it up – ironically and absurdly greeting us with a welcoming smile while she did so. Weed opened it, and I held it open. It was the least I could do, I felt so useless.

Within the last half hour I had witnessed Barb, Kieran, Ricky, Ed Zwick, and Doug Mallick all risk their lives, lay their bodies on the line, and sacrifice themselves for others (either human, or divine, or both) while I – Danielle Bennetton, Student Counsellor, Little Miss Peacemaker – had only hidden under my desk, listened and watched mutely, followed along submissively, asked a couple of questions, and offered some spineless advice.

Peace at all costs – as always – while those five others had deemed passive submission to the kingdom of darkness as too high a price for peace with the Dregs. They refused to just go along quietly.

I was theoretically, academically, professionally – and now experientially – "qualified" to counsel about the fear, stress, and trauma of being a hostage. But all I would ever be able to do was envy those who had actually taken a stand at gunpoint.

So, yes, I held the door open, while Barb and I touched, patted, or rubbed the backs of all seventeen trembling students on the blacklist filing past us, and reminded them each to take a seat in the front row as per Dreg directive.

On his way back to the staff lounge, just after passing Druid and Zwick at the lockers, and as he approached the lobby, Leon tersely called back to his comrade-in-arms, almost as an afterthought, "Slave's dead, stay alert."

Perhaps Druid didn't hear – he certainly displayed no reaction – but all seven student shields in the lobby certainly did, terrified by the killers' lack of emotion.

And while we entered the cocooned confines of the auditorium, and the Dregs closed the soundproof doors behind us, Donnie Fairholme risked his covert communication with the outside world.

97

Druid shouldered the Ruger and placed his red laser sighting dot just below the two head-level bullet holes already drilled into the sixth locker.

"You're breaking your own rule, you know," Ed Zwick interrupted.

"What?" asked Druid, lowering his rifle.

The red-haired gunman seemed as surprised by Zwick's audacity to interrupt as he was by his comment.

"You said that when you run out of bullets, the game is over, and Dr. Khoury lives or dies as a free man – depending on his wounds."

"No, I said the game is over after I've shot twenty-five bullets into seven lockers."

"You've got that camera on your forehead – why don't you play back the video and prove it to me?"

Druid's total focus now shifted to Zwick.

Ed's eyes momentarily flicked to the lockers.

If Khoury was in the sixth or seventh locker this debate was critical. But if he was in eight, nine, ten, or had hidden himself elsewhere, then Zwick was risking his life for nothing.

Druid smiled as he decided on his next, cruel response. "We'll look at the video and, if you're wrong, I'll kill you on the spot."

"Okay."

Druid was shaken by Zwick's quick and confident reply.

For the first time since the fire alarm started ringing, Ed Zwick was really thinking clearly.

He was not, by nature, a violent (or even a particularly physical) man. He was a thinker.

He had tried to beat the Dregs at their own violent game and lost – tragically. But he now knew enough about Druid to challenge him in a mental chess match, so he continued.

"The only problem is that Leon wants constant video coverage – and there can be no recording while we look back at what you said."

Druid was angry. He raised his Ruger and pointed it in Zwick's face. "I don't need to look at the video – I know what I said, and I've got *eight shots* left in this game."

Druid slowly swivelled his weapon back and was about to burn his third laser bullet into the sixth locker.

"And what about the Lord of Mathematical Order?" Zwick asked, over the gunman's shoulder.

"What do you mean?" Druid eased off the trigger slightly, and only for a moment.

"You know much more than I do about such things – you're a druid, are you not?"

"A druid, and a wizard, and a seer," Druid elaborated on his psychotic credentials.

"A magician?"

"Yes."

"You know all about other worlds, ruling lords, and their kingdoms?"

"I am destined for other kingdoms."

"Well, Dr. Khoury is a mathematical wizard and he serves the Lord of Mathematical Order – it was *that* lord who made sure Khoury won this game of lockers. It was *that* lord who cast a spell upon you and made you forget about those eight other bullets."

Druid smiled slightly – feeling suddenly at home within Zwick's mythical world.

"You know that last click of your rifle? That was the Lord of the Beautiful Mathematical Order of the Universe declaring this game over," Zwick ended his fantasy tale.

"He beat me!" A pawn of Zwick's logic, Druid was being a good sport about it all, lowering his rifle and shaking his head. "I would have won if he hadn't cast that spell."

"And it was while under his spell that you vowed 'when I run out of bullets the game is over.'"

Druid nodded unconsciously. It all made perfect sense now.

Zwick nudged him into the final, logical ambush, "Break your vow, and offend the Lord."

Checkmate.

"Release your friend Khoury," said Druid, submitting respectfully to his magical defeat. What else could he do?

98

Leon burst into the staff lounge, "Mr. Horvath, you would have been very disappointed. Gladiatorial combat has obviously lost its appeal over the centuries – today's youth evidently preferring video game violence.

Not to worry, though – they refused to fight *us* in the gym, so we'll make them fight *each other* in the auditorium."

Leon then turned from Horvath to the four still-standing staff members, "They're actually waiting for us in there right now – so instead of you being tried in here by a jury of your peers, we might just relocate ourselves into the auditorium, where we can have *the students judging you* for a change. How does that sound?"

"What right have you to judge anyone?" demanded Newton of the Dreg king.

All eyes turned to Leon.

"You are feisty, Mr. Newton, in a gutless world – so I will answer your question. You've heard of the Golden Rule?"

"Do unto others as you would have them do unto you."

"No, that's the fairy-tale version. The marketplace, workaday, real-time, real-world version of the Golden Rule is 'He who owns the gold, makes the rules'. That's the essence of business, and government, and education.

And the currency of the Golden Rule is power – he who owns the gold, buys the guns, and pays the gunmen, that rule the world. Civilisation is a charade. Take away the law, the police, and the army, and one of those civilised neighbours on your street would kill you tomorrow for your food.

So the answer to your question, Mr. Newton, 'by what right do we judge?' – by the right of might.

And my question to you, Mr. Newton: how is *my* judging any different from teachers judging students, and expecting respect they don't deserve, simply because they wield the Pass or Fail power of the report card? Take Mr. Les Mantiss, here ...."

Leon turned to one of his four standing defendants. Because he was tall, and thin, and loved biting the heads off students and devouring them, he had been nicknamed "Preying Mantiss" by his victims.

".... he's supposed to teach social studies and politics – but he actually teaches sarcasm, humiliation, and the abuse of power. Don't you, Les?

You never told us the truth about society – that a diploma is like the emperor's new clothes, that degrees offer no real-world qualification whatsoever. Exams only test short-term memory, and regurgitation skills. Employers *never* ask to see academic transcripts – rarely even proof of a diploma, or degree.

You never told us, Les, about your mid-life crisis, your gnawing sense of unfulfilment, and your sadistic compulsion to take it all out on your students. You envy our youth – you even resent it. Misery loves company, so you're out to ruin our adolescence.

A little man, wielding what little power he has, on the powerless students beneath him on the food chain – thanks, Les, I guess you really did teach us about social studies and politics after all."

Leon moved on to the next defendant. "Bill Arkapaw. *Coach* Arkapaw. Did you *really* dream of becoming a high school gym teacher when you grew up? And if you did, then what are all those old framed photos in your office of you playing rugby and soccer as a teenager? The shrine to past glories and fleeting youth? Did you never, once, dream of being a professional? Please correct me if I'm wrong, Coach, it's just that I'm looking for the reason why you're always so obsessed with your students winning.

If only you knew how much pressure you add to the lives of already-stressed-out teenagers – living vicariously through them, trying to drive them to become the champion you never were. Those who can't do, teach.

You're teaching idol worship, Mr. Arkapaw. Everyone loves to worship a winner, because everyone's day-to-day life falls so far short of the gold-medal fantasy – even the lives of the medal winners themselves.

And you, Mrs. Timms, are charged with murder. You kill what are perhaps the last remaining embers of life and creativity in a dead and soul-destroying academic institution – music and art.

Under your instruction, Mrs. Timms – your stern, sour, cranky instruction – hundreds and thousands of students graduated from Hunter High School, over the decades, convinced that they hated the arts. But it was actually *you* they hated, Mrs. Timms, you old sourpuss.

Mr. Newton here somehow managed to inspire a love for literature amid all the mind-numbing essays and pedantic little exams demanded by the curriculum. But you killed the love of art, for art's sake. You twisted and tarnished it into consumerism like every other subject in the place.

You insulted all forms of contemporary music, and forced your students to study set pieces that you played decades ago when you had a love for art, that has long since died."

"Are you quite finished, Mr. Spitzer? May *I* respond now?" asked the short, and slightly hunchbacked, teacher who looked like she was long past retirement age.

Leon gave her leave to speak with a sweep of his hand.

"You think you are the only one to have suffered in life, but there are always others worse off than ourselves. I was abused and betrayed many times in my life – and I'm not about to tell you the details, or ask your forgivenes, or beg for my life – but it filled me with bitterness, and consumed me with hate.

Now I hate my life and I hate myself, so your gun doesn't scare me, and your death threats have no power over me because I've had my fill of this world. But even though *I* would consider it mercy killing if you shoot me – *you* will still be tried for murder."

"Ahh, but *I'm* not on trial here today, Mrs. Timms, *you* are," said Leon, "*my* trial will have to wait for another day."

"But I thought you said this was a suicide mission?" Kevin Newton challenged him.

"I was just referring to judgement day at the end of the world – in deference to little Barbie's Christian beliefs."

But Leon's Dregcam recorded the expression of suspicion on Newton's face, then realisation, then shock – Leon was plotting and planning to survive the siege after all. But did the other Dregs know? And what were Leon's plans for *them*?

99

Dixon's focus on the school building plans was interrupted by a sudden hammering on the roof of the construction shed.

It was Popeye with an urgent message. It had taken the sniper sixty seconds to notice Donnie Fairholme's hand signal, and a further thirty to understand.

Straight index finger, index finger pulling an imaginary trigger, thumbs down symbol, four fingers, index finger pulling trigger. And then the sequence repeated itself, over and over again.

"The student at the front door is making hand signals," shouted Popeye over the howling storm, and without taking his eye away from the scope.

"What's he saying?" asked Dixon, his eyes squinting almost shut against the downpour as he peered up to the roof.

"Looks like 'one shooter down, four shooters'."

Darren Hayes confirmed the report through a pair of binoculars. "He's right, Sergeant. One shooter down, four shooters – one shooter down, four shooters. Over and over again."

Dixon rang Ronnie immediately. "Ronnie, we think one of the Dregs is down – wounded or killed – is that possible?"

"I was just about to call you. Three Dregs, one staff, and twenty students went into the gym – but only two Dregs, one staff, and nineteen students came back out. I was just going to wait one more minute before calling to tell you."

"Who didn't come out?" asked Dixon.

"I don't know which student, but the missing Dreg is that East European who cleared the right wing with the short guy."

"Slave," said Dixon. A great believer in knowing and respecting your enemy, the sergeant had memorised every shred of information that Luke had passed on to him about the Dregs. "Okay, we'll assume Slave's down – but if you see him coming out of that gym, Ronnie, you let me know immediately."

100

Donnie Fairholme didn't *hear* Druid sneaking up on him as much as he *felt* him, and then the feeling was confirmed when Monica McLean began feigning a coughing fit as a warning of impending danger.

Donnie stopped the hand signals in front of his belly and began to scratch around his navel, just as Druid poked his head to the front of the phalanx. Donnie avoided eye contact, looked at the floor, and kept scratching.

When Fairholme looked back up, Druid was gone. But the student council president decided to cool it with the signalling for a while anyway. Just in case.

Donnie peered out into the storm and saw a distant police car, blurred in the downpour, flashing its headlights. Four times, then stop. Four times, then stop.

101

Ed Zwick flung open the sixth locker and was instantly splashed with blood.

Suman Khoury tumbled out of his metal coffin and into Zwick's arms – falling, fainting, escaping, and embracing his saviour, all at the same time. It seemed to Ed that Suman was wanting to be laid down, but Ed held him up – pinned him, actually – against the lockers until Suman could get hold of himself, and Ed could assess his condition.

A vague and distant memory of advice from a book or movie echoed in Ed's mind, "go to sleep now, and you'll never wake up".

It had something to do with men lying down and freezing to death but, to Ed, it meant that this was not the time for he or Suman to rest. If they wanted to survive the Dregs' assault, they had to stand.

Ed remembered Earl Kennedy's impassioned plea from the lectern at that school assembly a lifetime ago, "all that good men need do, for evil to triumph, is nothing". Do nothing, give up, lie down.

Suman was covered in blood from his cheekbones to his armpits. He had shielded his face and head with his hands and arms, as planned, but each time Druid had targeted a new locker, Suman's instinctive reaction was to turn his face and eyes away from the gunman's voice and duck down – cringing in anticipation of a blow to the head.

Six times Druid had targeted a new locker, six times Khoury had cringed. The good news: only seven lockers were to be shot. The bad news: the sixth locker was slated for six bullets – more than any other – and Khoury was in the sixth locker.

Because Suman turned and ducked, the first bullet was not slowed by his shielding forearms but, rather, entered the left side of his jaw at full speed – slicing through cheek muscles and blood vessels, gouging a deep furrow across the top of his tongue, and destroying hundreds of taste buds and nerve endings that would never regenerate.

The .22 calibre bullet then struck two teeth on the right side of his mouth – knocking one out, and shattering the top half of the other – before exiting Suman's right cheek.

Khoury dropped his hands from their head-shielding position to grab both wounded cheeks, and leaned his right shoulder against the side of the locker to support himself, again exposing his left flank.

After a momentary numbness, blood began spurting from his mouth. He barely had time to spit out his teeth before the second bullet struck him near the base of his neck, creating a hairline fracture of his left collarbone, deflecting internally through his shoulder, and exiting near the childhood vaccination scar on his left arm.

The pain that electrified Khoury's whole shoulder region was similar to that experienced when slamming your elbow, right on the funny bone – a hot flash, then numbness, followed by pins and needles, and a wave of bone ache.

Suman rested his head against the right side of the locker to steady his weakened knees and keep from fainting. He just stood there, cramped in the near-dark, fighting waves of fear, pain, and nausea, while feeling his shirt collar soaking with blood – his efforts to suppress the sound of his panting and moaning, soon aided by the rapid swelling of his wounded tongue.

Suman leaned his forehead against a poster of an Australian cricket superstar – the celebrity's glossy cheek now torn by the same bullet that had wounded the mathematics professor's, the million-dollar face now ironically splashed with blood. But still the idol shed no tears, and showed no signs of pain or empathy.

Through the locker's three slits, Suman heard first the click of Druid's empty Ruger, then his colleague's mythical argument for ending the brutal game.

Khoury could visualise Druid's expression, could almost hear the wheels turning inside the teenager's brain, as Zwick convinced him to stop shooting.

Once again, Ed had entered the right combination and saved another of Druid's victims.

And now that Khoury was safe in his saviour's arms, Ed had to force himself beyond the emotional to the analytical – had to look past Suman's blood and shock, to assess his actual wounds. Mouth, collarbone, and shoulder – they were not life-threatening, and surprisingly superficial for two bullets aimed at his head.

Once Khoury had steadied himself, both physically and emotionally, he embraced Zwick and whispered in his ear. Despite all the carnage, swelling, and blood in his mouth, his slurred message was clear enough. "That's two of us you've saved today, Ed – me and that boy with the lock."

But numbers now provided little comfort to Ed Zwick. "My little sons are priceless – the laws of economics don't apply to people. I can never make up for the three outside the auditorium – I can never balance the equation."

Suman just nodded and patted him on the back.

Druid, back again from the lobby, had stood by silently for a few seconds as he watched his hostage teachers reunited – cold, curious, and observant, pausing for a moment just like he had as a young boy while torturing a fly or a frog.

"Follow me," commanded Druid as he headed for the lobby.

Zwick reached down and grabbed a gym towel off the floor, discarded earlier from one of the ten emptied lockers. He handed it to Khoury for the bleeding, and led him away by his good arm.

102

While the seventeen condemned students made their way up the long centre aisle of the auditorium, Barb squatted beside the back row aisle seat into which Kieran had flopped himself.

Weed was on her feet behind him, still sheltering herself in the darkness at the rear. I squeezed past Kieran's knees and sat beside him in the back row – Kieran on my left, his swollen face now hidden behind a bundle of blood-soaked tissues, Ricky on my right.

Barb ran her fingers through Kieran's hair. "How are you?" she asked him.

He simply moaned. His eyes were closed, his head was pounding, and he didn't want to talk. But he acknowledged her presence, and her care, by patting her hand atop his head.

"What happened to your blouse, Barb?" asked Weed. It seemed like such an innocent comment between two teenage girlfriends – but all remaining shreds of innocence had now been torn away amidst the fear, and shattered glass, and bullet holes, and blood, and broken bodies, that surrounded them.

"I tried to protect Kieran from Wade."

"That's not like Wade, he's usually the first to offer protection – and he *really* likes you, even loves you."

"He *thinks* he does, Wendy. But there's a lot of wrong thinking and feeling in this school – and that always leads to wrong words, and actions, and people getting hurt."

Weed reached into the aisle, took hold of Barb's hand, lifted her to her feet, and retreated with her back into the darkness.

"I think and I feel, maybe, that I'd like to become a Christian like you, Barb – am I thinking and feeling wrong about that, too? I stopped believing in God the morning my father died."

"Well God still believes in you, Wendy Stankowski. He always has. He believes in the transforming power of His eternal flame inside you – His clay jar – igniting that Spirit-spark deep within you."

Wendy began crying again, the tears streaming down her cheeks, her red laser dot dancing on the carpet as the Ruger bounced on her shuddering belly.

"Isn't it too late? I'll probably be dead in a few minutes, and I've signed a blood covenant with the Dregs."

Barb placed her hand on Wendy's cheek and held it there, Wendy tilted her head and rested it in Barb's palm.

"It's counterfeit, Wendy. The Dregs have all been deceived. Leon's a counterfeit lord of a counterfeit kingdom that's about to end, and you signed a counterfeit covenant.

Jesus is the one true Lord of the one true Kingdom, and He says it's *never* too late to accept Him as your blood brother in His eternal covenant.

There is hope, Wendy, even at the end of this dark corridor that you've chosen to follow – you have not walked into it alone, you *are* not walking it alone, even now.

Leon won't lay down his life for you – Jesus already has.

Leon will lead you to destruction – but Jesus will save you, even now.

All that Leon has to offer is the bitter dregs at the bottom of a cup of revenge – Jesus is offering you a sweet, overflowing cup of forgiveness."

Wendy pulled the silver Dreg covenantal ring from her finger and handed it to Barb – thrust it into Barb's palm with its engraved, spilling chalices, and closed Barb's fingers over it.

103

Dixon turned to his police commandos. "Bodycams are on. This conversation is being recorded, and it *will* be used as evidence."

The four menacing figures were all dressed in black, soaking wet, quiet, tense, aware of the time, worried about the kids, willing to cross the line, trained to kill, and feeling helpless. They all nodded.

"Ronnie MacDonald has good reason to believe that it's all going to be over in less than twelve minutes – final executions, then suicide. No way will the Sydney tactical squad be here in time, and police command will *not* authorise a Swat assault.

I'm going in alone. Once I've finished it, I'll call you on the headsets. I repeat – when I call you, it's all over, and I want you to rush the building not as a Swat team to kill, but as a security team to clear the school. No one goes in or out until I have confirmed that all Dregs are down. Understood?"

The officers began volunteering to back up their commander, but there was nothing else to say and no time left to say it, so Dixon headed for the door of the construction shed with his AR-15 in hand. On the way past the lunch table, he grabbed the architectural plans of the school – now memorised – and wrapped them around his small black carbine.

He covered his trademark bald head with his black woollen watch cap, and stepped out into the rain, wordlessly shaking Hayes' outstretched hand in the downpour.

Dixon then walked surreptitiously towards his unmarked car – uncharacteristically hunched over as though cringing from the rain, and with the nondescript blueprints under his arm.

In the SAS, stealth was everything – they didn't shoot their way in, they were just suddenly there, they completed their mission, and then they were gone.

He started the motor and drove slowly around the perimeter of the parking lot, stopping at the far end to make sure that no media people were following him. The last thing he needed was a cameraman running after him into the school.

Unnoticed and unfollowed, he proceeded to the corner of Alcorn and Loftus, and then on to the chain-link fence as per Ronnie's directions. It was 12:20.

104

For 12:21 it was extraordinarily, almost eerily, dark outside – more like dusk than noon. The skies were black, *literally* black, and the Newcastle storm pelted down its wind and rain unabated.

Dozens of heavily armed police officers wearing bulletproof vests had been huddling ineffectively in the pouring rain for twenty-five minutes, while five untrained adolescents orchestrated hundreds of hostages inside.

The seven student shields stood together at the front door, sharing in their communal nightmare. They were separated and distanced from all the rest of the students, left unguarded for much of the time, and able to hear only muted conversation and gunshots from Druid's gruesome game around the corner, along with all the other sporadic shooting behind closed doors and throughout the school.

Outside they could see all manner of emergency vehicles – their would-be rescuers, fully trained and equipped, yet powerless to assist them. Paramedics waited helplessly in their ambulances while two young students with gunshot wounds to the head lay unattended on the floor just outside the auditorium.

Live, global, multimedia coverage via satellite link had been established in the parking lot, yet the seven shields themselves were unable to communicate with worried relatives gathering only three blocks away at the police safety cordon area outside a shopping mall – in fact, ever vigilant of the blood red fireflies, they dared not turn around, or even whisper to each other.

Surreal, bizarre, and timeless. The passing seconds marked by myriad raindrop splashes in countless parking lot puddles – no help in accurately gauging the minutes, but appreciated instead for their soothing hypnotic effect. Splashes and ripples unaware of, unconcerned with, unaffected by, the chaos of man all around.

None of the seven even noticed the firefly's return. Without warning, the doors before them erupted amid a sensory overload of twenty-five gunshots, exploding glass, screaming students, howling wind, and pelting rain.

From behind them, Druid called out as he loaded his eighth full magazine of the day, "Since you're obviously all too afraid to go out into the weather, I thought I'd open the portal and bring the weather in to you."

The landing at the top of the outside stairs was sheltered by an outcropping of roof, so that the pouring rain only entered the lobby for a metre or two, wetting the students' feet. That was the *pouring* rain.

The *gusting* rain, however, driven and whipped by bursts of wind every fifteen seconds or so, invaded much deeper into the lobby and had the potential to drench the hostages from head to foot.

The students quickly recovered from the shock of the unexpected assault on the school entrance and, to their credit, never lost their heads or turned around – Druid's earlier death threats still ringing in their ears.

The police helplessly looked on, through binoculars and telescopic cross-hairs, at the bizarre sight of Druid addressing his phalanx from the rear.

"As the time of our occupation draws to a close, it is important to bolster our defences. My seven shields will now become nine, with two of your teachers manning the forefront.

Dr. Khoury, your mathematical wizard, will take the point – with Mr. Zwick supporting him from behind – so that the enemy will see that our magic is stronger than theirs.

And I want all of you to step outside onto the landing at the top of the stairs, *right now*, so that their archers can better see the faces of those who will die first if they storm the building."

Several students gasped as Zwick escorted the blood-soaked Khoury through their ranks. Donnie Fairholme patted the two teachers on the back as they stepped ahead of the students to lead them out into the storm. At the top of the stairs outside, the nine shields were soaked to the skin in seconds, their fearful trembling now masked by their chilled shivering.

When I was asked to analyse the Hunter High School siege, as a participant in the coroner's inquest, I initially made the same mistake as other investigators – and studied the siege as an adolescent aberration, or as yet another episode in a violent societal trend. So the narrow and short-sighted context of our analysis was always really urban/suburban Western society in the early twenty-first century.

It took me many months to realise that that line of inquiry was about as worthless as parents seeking to know how their teenagers are *really* doing in school by comparing their report cards to state averages, without ever questioning the curriculum, their teachers' character and methods, the workplace relevance of the subject matter, the unique strengths and weaknesses of their children, their peer influences, and their media intake.

But every time I revisited the evidence from Black Friday, I realised a bit more profoundly how each event was fraught with much deeper meaning than anything revealed at the initial inquests, and could never be fully appreciated without considering the motivation, life context, emotional and spiritual significance for each participant.

A perfect example is found in Druid's erratic behaviour regarding his "portal", and what it reveals about his tortured mental state – his conflicting comments too easily dismissed as yet more of his ice-induced ramblings.

Druid coveted the portal as the Leon-appointed station assigned to him because of his supernatural vision, yet feared it as the enemy's route of attack and, potentially, the doorway to his own death. He challenged his seven shields to escape through it, yet argued that his life depended on their strategic positioning there. Druid shattered the glass façade of Hunter High to hasten the final clash between the outside world and the kingdom of the Dregs, yet positioned two teachers there to bolster his defences.

Despite his apparently passionate participation in Leon's suicide mission, perhaps Druid did not desire escape to a spiritual world as much as he longed to enjoy supernatural power and treasure in this one, to exchange a mundane world of struggle for a fantasy land of constant victory – a supernatural kingdom where every challenge was overcome, every battle won, and every enemy defeated, even if that demanded he was the only one armed as he faced legions of human targets.

For Drew MacDonald was not addicted to video games as many have proposed – he was addicted to winning. A spoiled child imprisoned and tortured by his moods and appetites, brought up by parents who dared not deny him, and brainwashed by media marketeers who fed his fantasy addictions. Consequently, Druid was able to enjoy the shooting gallery of his dreams throughout the halls of Hunter High, while embracing the concept of a suicide mission as the ultimate avoidance of accountability.

Suicide, that is, specifically by his own hand, because he couldn't bear the thought of being killed by any other – no one kills a druid but a druid, or above. For a mere mortal with no supernatural powers – such as the police "archer"/sniper that he so feared – to slay a wizard would be like the great Achilles to be felled by an arrow in the heel.

I tried, for years, to reconcile Druid's apparently contradictory thoughts and actions about that portal. And I finally realised that he was not so different than any of us – constantly wavering between reality and fantasy. Illogical in much of our thinking, or our refusing to think. Rarely beginning with the end in mind, perhaps never truly considering the aerial, bird's-eye view of the maze, the long-term contextual appreciation of life that would inspire truly wise choices and responses, rather than emotional and often erratic reactions.

105

Weed closed the auditorium doors behind Leon, as he escorted his twenty staff lounge hostages to their reserved seats in the front rows. Then he and Wade herded the seventeen student defendants onto the stage of the auditorium, single file, and had them face the audience.

Leon stepped up to the lectern and the microphone, while Wade stepped back to cover the defendants from the unlit shadows of the stage.

"Good afternoon, staff and students of Hunter High School. Thank you for your patience, this year's final full-school assembly will be over in just a few minutes as will the lives of twelve of these students now standing on stage before you.

You will, no doubt, recognise them as members of the gang, or pack, that outnumbered and harassed you without mercy, and without fear of reprisal or justice. But now they must turn on each other in order to survive. Now they will taste the fear of being outnumbered, as the pack devours itself – predators torn apart in their own feeding frenzy."

Leon turned to address the defendants, "Twelve of you will face a firing squad, five will be allowed to live. You have two minutes to complete your voting. Each cast ballot is final. You may begin."

Stunned silence enveloped the room like a suffocating foam. But not for long.

Zoe Moustakis pointed to Vesna D'Ambrosi (Weed's stolen friend) and Sharon Tilden (the thief who stole her), both cowering off to the side of the stage. Though they were never in a gang themselves, they had been the first to call Wendy "Stinkweed", to stab her in the back, make Wendy bleed, and draw the feeding frenzy down upon her life.

"Let's dump those two, agreed?"

Several raised their hands in agreement, one nodded, a couple just grunted. But only about a third of them voted. The majority resisted the pull of the kingdom of darkness which sought to enlist, expose, and betray them. Gossip, slander, rejection, mocking, bullying, persecution, verbal and even physical assault – all done behind their backs, with a whisper, two-faced, on the sly, in the dark, on-line, anonymously, along with a crowd, or wearing a mask – that was one thing. But to condemn to death, to raise a hand and cast a vote on stage, under the spotlight, standing before an assembly, and while being recorded by Dregcams – that was another, and the majority resisted.

"One minute, forty-five seconds remaining, folks. Those not voting will be shot immediately. Now – who agrees with these two nominations?" Leon was the referee, hurrying the game right along.

Vesna and Sharon cowered as fifteen hands were raised against them. No choice really for the fifteen voters, no better options, certainly no time.

"Anyone opposed?" asked Spitzer.

The two condemned girls didn't even bother to cast an opposing vote. Fifteen to zero.

As Wade culled them from the herd and made them step back towards him, Vesna cried out into the darkened audience, "Wendy, I'm sorry – *we're* sorry."

Wendy covered her face with her hands and shook her head near the back doors.

"Next!" Leon urged his combatants.

"The three cheerleaders," Zoe responded without hesitation.

I did the math, as I'm sure did dozens of other spectators in the auditorium.

With Doug Mallick dead, Trevor Cooper now led the remaining Jocks: Dean Mosdell and Hans Widmer. Adding the three cheerleaders – Trish Corby, Bethany Stanwood, and Jamilla Grey – created an athletics gang of six.

And these six quickly realised that they were easily outnumbered and outvoted by the gang of Thugs: Mark Devito, Sammy Sawd, Joe Andarry, Stan Sawchaszyn, Mitch Soldat and their girls Zoe Moustakis, Treena Carr, Sadie Pickersgill and Crystal Banasik.

Nine against six.

"All in favour of terminating the new cheerleading squad?" Zoe asked her crew.

Not only was Zoe in control, she was beginning to enjoy it.

Eight Thugs raised their hands in support of Zoe's proposal.

Trish Corby, head cheerleader, looked to Trevor Cooper. "Trev?"

"We're outnumbered," Trevor mumbled as he shrugged his shoulders and raised his empty and powerless hand. Voting was compulsory under penalty of death, and the result was indisputable.

Dean Mosdell and Hans Widmer then toed the party line, just as they'd toed it all their lives.

Beth and Jamilla instinctively followed their leader, as Trish slid into panic and despair.

"Step over towards Wade please, ladies," directed Leon.

Beth and Jamilla moved over to death row with Vesna and Sharon – shattered, blubbering, and holding on to one another because now, suddenly, there was no one else, or no other thing, to hold onto in their shrinking world.

But Trish took one step towards the front of the stage, shielded her eyes from the blinding overhead spotlights, and cried out to the teachers that she could barely see in the front rows before her. "Can't you do anything to stop them?" But no reply came from the audience.

"Each cast vote is final," reaffirmed the referee.

Trish joined the other condemned cheerleaders. Now broken, helpless, and without team support, all the positive thinking and encouragement in the world was worthless.

"Only eighty seconds remaining." Leon's announcement, Leon's threat.

Trevor Cooper, head Jock, snatched the ball from Zoe's hands.

"Devito, your guys and my guys together equals eight votes – let's eliminate the four girls."

Insiders and outsiders. Us against them. Winning at all costs. Selfish alliances. People as objects. Consumerism.

Suddenly Cooper was offering to shift the whole war – not Jocks versus Thugs, but Men versus Women. Adam and Eve all over again – conspiring together one moment, betraying each other the next.

The audience stared, transfixed, at the mortal combat being played out on stage before them.

Ruthless betrayal – Devito was thinking it over.

Ten long seconds of silence.

Zoe was aptly described as a cobra. Not just because poison was on her lips, but because she spat it out at her victims – she was fast, and her devious venom spewed now into Cooper's ears.

"Cooper, if you vote us four girls out, there will be only your three guys and Devito's five guys left. His five Thugs will then dump you and win. You three Jocks need to join with us four girls *now* and dump Devito's five while you still have the chance."

Now Cooper was thinking. Zoe was calm. Devito panicked and yelled out, "Don't listen to her!" while holding out his hands in a stop gesture.

Cooper stared at Devito's torn and bloody hand – a bloodstained and sweaty hand that could not be trusted, that would stop at nothing, that knew no allegiance, that would not hesitate for a moment to condemn Cooper's jocks just as it had his cheerleaders.

Cooper's arm shot up, "Five Thugs out," he bellowed. His two jocks joined the vote, Zoe and her three girls backed them up.

Seven against five.

Wade called out from the shadowy wings as he aimed his laser dot at the centre of Devito's chest, "Your time's up, Devito. We've been waiting for you. It's just too bad Slave couldn't be here."

Then the cobra struck again, spitting out her next orders as Wade began herding off the five Thugs.

She caught Cooper's eye amidst the commotion and shot her hand in the air, even before she spoke, so as to speed things up, "Treena, me, and you three guys – that's the best we can do."

Just like an auction, like kids picking teams in the playground.

Looking back on the video, it's clear that their four hands were rising even before Zoe had finished speaking, such was their drive, such was the urgency and panic, to be one of the five survivors. One of only five to escape the firing squad, only five to scramble onto the life raft while kicking away the twelve others who floundered in the water.

Mark Devito and his four Thugs were now under armed guard.

Sadie Pickersgill and Crystal Banasik began lodging their protests, "We weren't even ready for that last vote!"

"All cast ballots are final, thank you, girls."

106

Gary Dixon was at it again – standing at the back of his vehicle in the pouring rain, getting dressed in his tactical gear, while hiding from the police officers stationed in the high school parking lot.

After donning his body armour, kevlar half-finger shooting gloves, elbow and kneepads – all black – Dixon swapped his black watch cap for a black balaclava and pulled it down over his head and face.

The balaclava provided the commando an unimpaired field of vision while fostering a sense of laser focus, assuring personal anonymity, and instilling fear into the heart of the enemy.

Finally Dixon strapped his helmet tight under his chin, activated its temple-mounted camera, and adjusted his earpiece/microphone headset before checking his watch.

Only when he was fully ready for action and completely soaked, did Dixon open the back door of his Landcruiser and motion for Luke to get himself off the floor and out into the rain.

The two men shook hands, Dixon handed over a small radio and stood guard as the Maori warrior punched the combination into the electronic keypad, and slipped inside his maintenance workshop.

No one had seen Luke enter, there was no access door between workshop and school interior, the rear entrance would lock behind him, and he would be safe enough inside.

Dixon walked over to Ronnie MacDonald's van with his AR-15 in hand. All doors were locked and the keys in a little magnetic case inside the driver front wheel well, just as Ronnie had said.

In the back of the van Dixon found the Baker Batshield – impossible to miss with its brand name and logo embroidered boldly on its carry case.

Ronnie MacDonald was *always* researching, trialling, and assessing the latest police equipment on the market – everything from electronics to armaments.

He was in constant communication with local, state, and national Australian law enforcement offices, as well as police forces and manufacturers from around the world, regularly attending international police conferences and trade shows – either as delegate or speaker.

Ronnie was well respected Australia-wide and manufacturers were always sending him prototypes, samples, literature, and DVDs – knowing that Ronnie was probably their best conduit for potential law enforcement sales around the country.

He had currently been testing and obtaining Australian feedback on the Baker Batshield sent to him from America. Australian police already owned and utilised portable, bulletproof, ballistics shields both in riot control and tactical squad operations but they were all rigid, some heavy, and some transparent. In contrast, the black Batshield was flexible, lightweight, and opaque – looking essentially like an old-fashioned baseball umpire's chest protector, but shaped somewhat like a bat's wings around the edges.

What piqued Ronnie's interest was its exceptional portability, its resilience in the face of gunfire (Ronnie had seen 9mm, .45 calibre, .44 Magnum and 12-gauge test rounds all deflected with ease), its body coverage, and its efficiency as a platform for returning fire.

The Batshield covered the average-size man from head to mid-thigh, and was wide enough to comfortably shield even a large officer. In the case of direct confrontation, the officer could drop to one knee and shield himself completely or rest his weapon (handgun, shotgun, or rifle) in the centre top notch and return fire while exposing only one hundred square centimetres (sixteen square inches) of his forehead and eye – and that's a very small target, even smaller when the officer is wearing a kevlar helmet.

In a combat situation, even the head is considered too small a target and police are trained to always aim for the centre of the chest – the largest core area of the body. Aiming to wound an opponent in the arm or leg presents too small and mobile a target, and is best limited to Hollywood portrayals. So, out in the field, one hundred square centimetres is considered almost absolute protection.

Ronnie also argued that while the currently issued transparent ballistic shield offered optimal visibility, it also left the officer feeling exposed and prone to flinching when under fire, whereas the larger, black Batshield afforded a greater sense of security or "impenetrability" which inspired confidence and, therefore, improved effectiveness.

MacDonald had been raving about the Batshield, for weeks, to any Newcastle officer who stood still long enough to listen. But, then again, Ronnie was always raving about something – like a kid in a toy store.

As soon as Dixon removed the shield from it's carry case in Ronnie's van he was impressed – amazed – and his confidence soared. Even while wearing his kevlar vest and helmet, his limbs, groin, neck, and face had all remained exposed and vulnerable. But now that he was also armed with the Batshield, he felt *totally* bulletproof.

This reckless, renegade, and career-destroying course of action upon which Dixon was about to embark might well endanger hostage lives, but he himself would probably emerge from behind his Batshield unscathed – physically fit to face all police disciplinary, criminal negligence, and civil lawsuit proceedings that would surely follow.

107

Leon addressed the assembly once again from his lectern. "Twelve students now condemned to die, by peers legally too young to vote. Their eyes scream silently for help from their powerless teachers seated in the audience before them, teachers whose subjects and lessons are now, ultimately, all proving to be irrelevant and worthless.

And why were they elected to die? Because, boys and girls, life in the twenty-first century is a selfish series of strategic alliances – that's why. The food chain, the feeding frenzy, consumerism, cannibalism. Disposable income, disposable people, recyclable relationships, backstabbing, betrayal, the seasons of life, moving on, graduating, marriage and divorce, discarding the unwanted, institutionalising the needy, washing our hands of them all in a selfish series of strategic alliances.

Remember *that* when the media interviews you as survivors of the Hunter High School siege. Readership, viewers, ratings, advertising revenue – to them you are just a momentary human interest story, soon forgotten.

And where do you fit into this whole world order, this indoctrination they call the education system?

This is not a school – this is a science laboratory where lab rats are trained to run a maze by rewarding them now with marks, and one day with money. This world system is a maze, you are all rats, and few there are who ever climb the walls to get their bearings.

And now for my final lesson – Carol Spargo, Bill Arkapaw, Les Mantiss, and Mrs. Timms, please join me up here on stage.

Three hundred of you in this auditorium are just trying to keep your heads down and get out of here alive so you can resume your fantasy lives of safety and security.

You think I speak too harshly, and you like to think that you are made of nobler stuff than I and not, yourself, a cannibal on the food chain. You, and all the television audience watching this video, enjoy small doses of exposure to the kingdom of darkness because it makes you look lighter, and brighter, and whiter, in comparison and contrast – that's why even the most depraved criminals in prison will persecute sex offenders – because each of us is desperate to justify ourselves as 'not that bad' or 'superior to them'.

But now I will prove to all three hundred of you in the audience just how selfish and guilty *you* really are. Two of these four staff members joining me up here on stage will be executed, and two will live. You, the audience, must now decide which two will die – you will all vote twice and cast your votes like this: Spargo? Raise your right hand while seated. Arkapaw? Raise your left hand while seated. Timms? Stand up. Mantiss? Stand up and raise your right hand.

If you refuse to vote, you will be shot. Take a minute now, each of you, to prepare your excuse – your alibi, your lie, your self-deception – so that you can live with yourself after you walk out of this auditorium today as a survivor: 'they made me do it', 'I had no choice', 'it was a case of self-defence, really', 'everyone else voted', 'if I didn't vote they would have killed two anyway', 'why throw away my life for nothing', 'I was irrational due to stress and, therefore, not responsible for my actions', 'I may have voted, but I didn't pull the trigger'.

You may even find that you need to make up more excuses as the years go by, as your initial rationalisations wear thin, and your conscience again rears its ugly little head.

While the vast majority of you gutless spectators and consumers are making up your minds how to judge, how to condemn, and how to excuse it, I might take just a moment to ask if anyone is *refusing* to cast a ballot."

Almost immediately, one of the teachers rose to his feet and lodged his protest vote. "I am."

Even though the faceless teacher was only a couple of rows back from the brightly lit stage, he had taken a seat in the shadow of the wings and would have been difficult to identify in the dim light had it not been for that white lab coat of his.

Up at the lectern Leon smiled, immediately recognised the lone challenger, and began reciting the classroom mission statement that he had always loathed. "At this school, and in society, we expect you to be responsible for whatever you choose to do, Mr. Martin, no matter why you do it."

Leon then raised his M1 and shot Wally in the forehead.

108

Dixon now realised that he and his men had wasted precious minutes in the construction shed debating whether or not to use their transparent ballistics shields and, if so, whether each lone commando would carry one, or only one man of each proposed two-man team.

But their green light never came and, like all men before them, they had squandered much of their limited time planning solutions for problems that never arose.

It was almost one hundred metres from the school's rear garbage bins to the front doors – should he walk, run, or drive? Wait for Ronnie's final call, or head in now – closing the gap and saving some time?

Dixon stood in the pouring rain to think it over. Because no one could see him there, behind the bins, there was no immediate urgency, he had seconds to think it over – and that was a luxury in an assault situation like this, an eternity even. So he just stood there.

The rain pouring off the lip of his helmet was diverted from running straight down his neck, but it did soak his shoulders and he was thankful for it. It kept him uncomfortable – like the hostages – alert, impatient, and cranky.

On-site in the field, the mission for most tactical squad members for most of the time was to encircle, contain, cover, and wait – patience was a virtue. Like all combat situations: long periods of boredom, shattered only occasionally by sudden moments of panic. And Dixon could handle the boredom when need be.

But not now. Now it was action stations. Only seven minutes or so. Count to four hundred slowly and it would all be over. Action stations. It paid to be cranky. Get it over with. No time for patience, no place for mercy.

Immediate action, rapid deployment. Swat before they could sting. Disarm or dispatch – whether with an array of Less-Than-Lethals, or with hollow-point bullets. They even carried commando knives, just in case all their other killing technologies failed them.

Suddenly Dixon saw the green jump light glowing in his memory. SAS parachute run. Amber light – approaching drop zone. Green light – out the aircraft door as fast and efficiently as possible.

Initiative – the ability to make snap decisions under pressure.

Flexibility – the willingness to modify plans on the run.

Mental toughness – the mindset to live with the results of your best efforts, without regret or the torment of hindsight.

He would walk briskly towards the shattered front doors – a refusal to wait, a compromise between walking and running. Count to four hundred – not much time. Decision made, he was off. Action stations indeed, no time to second-guess.

Focus, now – laser focus.

School on his right side, Baker Batshield strapped to his right forearm, AR-15 in his left hand – its barrel resting in the gun notch.

School curtains closed over those few windows facing the parking lot. Walking briskly, but not running – no "go" yet from Ronnie.

Not too slow in case a Dreg sniper was peeking from behind a curtain – following him even now in his sights, about to squeeze the trigger.

The sergeant was exposed and on his own for ninety metres, with no possibility of precision covering-fire from the police sniper, because Popeye had been ordered to keep his scope focused on the student shields during Dixon's approach past the front windows, and shoot only if a hostage was about to be executed. Popeye could *only* cover Dixon during his final run up the front stairs, but never at the risk of endangering any hostages in an effort to save the Swat team commander.

And what about his police colleagues, huddled behind their cars in the parking lot, shooting him by mistake? They had not been notified about his unauthorised lone assault. Nor had Vincent DeGroot, crime scene commander, nor the police commissioner, nor the minister of justice as far as Dixon knew.

But, not to worry, "POLICE" was clearly printed in white reflective letters across the back of his bulletproof vest and the front of the Batshield, each clearly visible even in the Newcastle downpour.

And no general-duty police officer from a patrol car would dare open fire without a confirming order from a commander – most police officers (like most civilians) were followers, not leaders.

If they saw an unrecognised Dixon approaching the school, they would not err on the side of initiative but, rather, on the side of excuse or rationalisation – "no one ever tells me what's going on", "someone else is in charge and responsible".

109

The red .30 calibre entry wound was small, and neat, and located just above Wally Martin's right eyebrow – one third of an inch in diameter, eight millimetres – with only a trickle of blood running out of it.

The exiting bullet, however, had blown a piece of skull the size of a tennis ball off the back of his head.

Subsequent autopsy reports concluded that although Wally did not die instantly, even emergency surgery could not have prevented his dying within minutes.

Immediate, total, and stunned silence once again fell upon the auditorium, except for a dozen suppressed whimpers and sobs.

"Any other conscientious objectors?" asked Leon from the stage.

Wally Martin's head and shoulders had fallen into the lap of Kevin Newton, his long-time friend and neighbour in the next seat.

Newton realised immediately that Wally was mortally and hopelessly wounded. So, in response to Leon's second challenge, Kevin Newton tenderly slid Wally Martin's dying body back over into his original seat and stood up.

"No one else besides Mr. Newton?"

Newton stood alone, covered now in Wally's blood, and Newton alone stood – there were no other dissenters.

"I always liked you, Mr. Newton, so I'm going to include you with the exceptions to compulsory voting – all those that came out of Miss Bennetton's office: the counsellor herself is my official, impartial observer; Barbie, Ken, and their adopted son little Rick-eeee, have already proven that they'd lay down their lives for another, and the seven other young Christians with them already proved that they wouldn't. All exempt.

You, Mr. Newton, may now vote for the two staff members on stage who you'd like spared. Only you, Mr. Newton, can vote for life – everyone else in the auditorium must vote for death."

All eyes were upon Newton.

"These are days of excuse and entitlement. You know that, Leon – we've discussed it many times in my class. We shun all responsibility, yet demand all rights, and assume all authority to judge. But, truly, I have no more power to assign guilt or to proclaim innocence than do you, Leon. Not really."

"Inspiring words, Mr. Newton. You remind me of Winston Churchill – no one ever shot him either, and talk is cheap when you haven't been wounded. Now sit down won't you, Kevin – and shut up."

Once Newton had complied, Leon continued instructing the audience. "Inspiration and self-sacrifice are two very different things. You've been instructed how to vote – now let the voting begin.

Mr. Wade here will be the electoral officer, strolling though the auditorium and enforcing the compulsory voting by-laws."

Wade descended the stairs from stage to audience.

"Carol Spargo? Raise your right hand while remaining seated and keep it up in the air while we count."

Leon watched the polling from the stage. Wade monitored the crowd from the aisle.

No one wanted to be the first to condemn or, at least, to be seen to condemn. This hesitancy was due in part to the angry, threatening glare with which Carol Spargo scanned the auditorium, peering into the darkness, defying her accusers to identify themselves.

Finally, the oldest right hand in the auditorium was raised. Tibor Horvath, of ancient Rome, closed his fist and gave the thumbs down symbol of gladiatorial contests.

Next Mrs. Timms raised her hand – poor dear, unaware that as one of the accused she was not, herself, eligible to vote.

Then, like a growing wave accelerating as it crashes against the shoreline, hands starting rising around the auditorium.

Juniors, seniors, teachers – hundreds of right hands bore silent testimony to past acid attacks by Spargo's tongue. Invisible scars, hurt feelings, damaged reputations, intimidation, fear of her wrath, pandering to her moodiness.

There was no need for a count. It was close enough to unanimous and Spargo knew it. She was surrounded by enemies, cornered, and left with no option but to attack.

Spargo turned to Leon, "Why don't you just kill *all* of us? Why should I die alone – you've got hundreds of bullets left, don't you?"

The evil in her heart vomited out her mouth and filled the auditorium.

When Leon finally broke the silence, he did it in a whisper, "The next word from your lips will be your last."

Almost as one body, the audience craned its neck to see and hear if the woman would finally hold her tongue – *could* finally hold her tongue – and deny herself the last word, for the first time.

Most teachers, who had been present in the staff lounge during Carol's intercom conversation with Ronnie, doubted whether even Leon's death threat would suppress Carol's vow to expose the police officer's hiding place in the admin office. But Carol Spargo just shut her mouth, ground her teeth, and glared into the audience.

The voting continued.

110

Ronnie MacDonald had lost his firstborn son Drew – and all the surveillance know-how in the world, and all the CCTV monitors in the school, couldn't find him.

Ronnie had last seen him escorting Zwick and Khoury into the lobby and out of camera range. Dixon had then confirmed, by mobile phone and with Ronnie's last bar flashing, that Drew had shot out the lobby's glass entrance and exposed his nine hostages to the elements outside, at the top of the front steps. But Popeye, from under his waterproof tarp, could no longer tell if Drew was still standing behind his phalanx.

Ronnie got distracted during that conversation with Dixon, he had looked away from the monitor for a few seconds, and might have even missed Drew ducking back into the admin office or sprinting into the auditorium. And now he wasn't sure.

Dixon was ten running strides away from the school's entrance, lying in the mud under a bush with his back up against the front of the school building, where it was impossible for him to be seen – or shot – from any of the corridor's windows or even the front steps. He had decided on one final contact with Ronnie before storming up the stairs.

Ronnie's mobile phone rang.

"I'm in position ten paces from the front steps. Your son still in the lobby?"

"He must be. I'm pretty sure I would have seen him if he moved away."

"'*Pretty sure*', Ronnie? 'Pretty sure'?! If you're not certain, you're in doubt, and doubt is fatal."

"Certain. I'm certain," Ronnie lied desperately.

Dixon calmed himself and lowered his voice, his tone morphing from commander to brother. "You're *not* certain, Ronnie, you're hoping – I'm coming in now."

And Ronnie knew exactly what that meant, because it was Ronnie MacDonald himself who had originally researched, and costed, and argued in support of the Swat weaponry that Gary Dixon was now carrying.

In round figures: fifteen hundred dollars for each AR-15 A3 Tactical Carbine and Trijicon scope, five hundred for each kevlar vest and ballistic helmet – well over five thousand dollars per commando including Glock, uniform, boots, bodycam, and radio headset.

The two of them had even discussed the reticle sighting pattern options of the ACOG scopes – Ronnie suggesting the traditional black cross-hairs, yellow triangle or red chevron, Dixon choosing instead the red donut, or "circle of death" as he called it.

Now Ronnie could imagine Dixon running up the school's front steps and sighting his son's chest – perhaps even his head – within that deadly red circle at the centre of his scope, knew the exact weight of the 5.56mm ammunition that he had recommended – 64 grains – copper-jacketed hollow-point bullets travelling at a muzzle velocity of 920 metres per second (almost three times the speed of sound) that would shatter his son's body with an impact force of 1296 foot-pounds.

Up until now they had all just been numbers on a page.

"No, *please* give me sixty seconds, Gary – promise me sixty seconds before you storm the lobby."

Dixon brought his micro mouthpiece to his lips and pressed his transmit button, contravening his earlier orders for radio silence. "Popeye, how are your legs?"

The powerful telescopic sight, already adjusted for wind and distance, was now boosted in magnification as it scanned the nine pairs of hostage legs.

Druid's black pants and Doc Marten boots finally stirred in the background and Dixon's earpiece crackled with Popeye's confirmation, "Legs are good."

Over the phone, Ronnie had heard Dixon's question to the sniper, followed by fourteen endless seconds of silence before the confirmation.

"Your boy's still in the lobby, Ronnie. You've got sixty seconds to take him down."

"Thank you, Gary, thank you."

"Don't thank me yet, Ronnie. If he's still on his feet when I come through that front door – *I'll* take him down."

Dixon heard Ronnie shout "agreed" into his phone before the connection was cut.

111

Bill Arkapaw and Mrs. Timms scored about fifty death votes each – Arkapaw for too much drive, Timms too little warmth.

But it was the sour, caustic, sarcastic Les Mantiss who out-scored them both.

His life's mission – to instill bitterness into the lives of high school students – obviously successful, and now corroborated by over two hundred standing voters with raised right hands.

The voting concluded, Wade now made his way back to the stage while Leon directed the production.

"Mr. Arkapaw, Mrs. Timms, you may be seated. Carol Spargo, Les Mantiss, stay right where you are at the front of the stage.

The twelve condemned students can line themselves up right there beside them, shoulder to shoulder and facing the audience.

Zoe and you four other student survivors, find yourselves seats down there in the front row – the blood of these twelve peers that you betrayed is already on your hands, it may as well splash over the rest of you."

Seven teenage girls, five boys – twelve students.

Now – ironically, finally, and too late, as they faced death – all man-made barriers between them dissolved and they stood as equals, convicted and condemned.

Death was their common enemy – an altogether different type of adversary that could be neither bullied nor outnumbered.

Though huddling together, each of them faced death alone and, from each, the fear of death now sucked all strength, pride, bravado, and confidence – leaving only trembling hands and weakened knees.

Many members of the audience, though themselves seated and not condemned, later testified of sapping strength and an overwhelming sense of helplessness.

Empathy had finally struck the heart of Hunter High.

Three or four of the twelve had to be supported by their peers as they approached the edge of the stage, the gaping black maw of the darkened auditorium, and the great unknown beyond.

Though the stage itself was solid and wide, a number of the condemned felt like they were being forced to walk the plank or balance at the end of a diving board, deep and dark waters all around.

The subjective perception of time again.

The fourteen at the end of their precarious plank felt the seconds pushing them, prodding them towards destruction, rushing them into ever-deepening darkness – while those detained in the audience felt time slowing and their breathing stop while the fourteen assumed their appointed positions.

Les Mantiss fell down on his knees – before the whole school, before a potentially global audience – praying.

Throughout the auditorium a yearning – a desperate, hungry longing for deliverance – was almost palpable. And I shared it.

So Barbra Burser's voice, when it called out in the aisle to my left, seemed only a distraction or annoyance interfering with the satisfaction of that yearning.

Barb and her words were surely no match for the Dregs and their kingdom of darkness. She might only aggravate the situation.

I willed her to sit down and shut up, but *her* will was obviously greater than mine.

112

In his panic to beat Dixon's sixty-second deadline, Ronnie MacDonald tripped on Earl Kennedy's feet and landed face to face on top of Eva Forman, breaking his fall with his left hand pressed into her stomach.

Her lifeless eyes stared into his as the stale air, forced from her diaphragm, blew into his face. It smelled of lipstick and coffee.

He clambered over her body and out the double set of admin doors as quietly as possible.

And there he stood – Drew Malcolm MacDonald. Twelve paces away, with his back turned to his father.

Ronnie stepped silently across the corridor and stopped just where the lobby carpet, the broken glass, and his younger son's blood trail, all merged together.

Ronnie had needed to cover that distance to put himself within firing range. He raised his yellow plastic taser stun gun and kept it aimed at the boy.

He then stepped closer, having decided not to run at him, but to walk at a normal pace across the crunching glass.

After all, the Dregs themselves had been crunching around on broken glass for over thirty minutes. Running or skulking noises would seem alien to Drew's ear – like a hostage or a cop.

At the sound of the crunching, Druid turned slowly, and immediately recognised the man who had been his father, though obviously surprised at his presence.

"Your son is not here …. I expelled him for being a sook and abandoning his friends."

Ronnie had been advancing while Druid spoke. He fired the yellow plastic gun at his son – just as they had fired many plastic weapons at each other over the years when Drew was a child. "Never at the eyes – you could blind someone," Ronnie MacDonald had always warned his three little boys, "besides, the chest is the biggest target."

Ronnie fired two little hooks towards his son's chest – bristling with fifty thousand volts of electricity and designed to discharge twelve hundred upon contact.

As they flew through the air at fifty-five metres per second, trailing fine copper wires behind them, one veered ever so slightly off course, embedding itself into the black canvas webbing strap of his ammo pouch. The second barb shot true and lodged itself just above Druid's left nipple.

But the circuit was broken by the ammo pouch, and the current therefore impeded from running through his body. Druid tore out the two barbs and flung them contemptuously onto the carpet.

"Don't you know that your weapons are powerless against me? I am a druid and a wizard."

Ronnie dropped the now-useless yellow gun as Druid raised his Ruger.

"You're a lost little boy, Drew," said Ronnie MacDonald to his firstborn son, "and we love you no matter what."

Outside in the storm, Sergeant Gary Dixon was counting down the seconds on his watch and trying to decide exactly when he should sprint for the front stairs, when gunshots reverberated from the lobby and the decision was made for him.

Dixon was up and running even before he heard the last bang of the rapid eight-shot volley.

113

"Leon," Barb called out from the back row.

All heads turned as Barb left the wounded Kieran behind, walking towards the stage and into the light.

"Barbie!" Leon acknowledged her and seemed to brighten. "How's Ken? You realise that he might need plastic surgery on that nose, if you two are going to remain the perfect couple."

"He'll be fine." Barb's voice somehow retained its usual upbeat and respectful tone.

As she drew to the brightness at the foot of the stage, Leon remarked, "Modelling the new-look school blouse, I see. Very sexy."

"I'd like the microphone for a few minutes, if I may, Leon."

Little Barb, on the auditorium floor, had to look up to see Leon's feet at the base of the lectern, and then up again to his face – just over two metres, almost seven feet in total.

It was then that I remembered Leon's earlier comment to Druid about David and Goliath – the biblical imagery now highlighted by the fact that Leon's voice was amplified by a microphone, while Barb's was not.

"Not a good time, Barbie. Our GoPro documentary is nearing its climax."

"But you said you wanted me to represent God's point of view – and I think I've got something that He wants me to say, and He wants your audience to hear."

"So you're a prophet?"

"Just a witness."

"But the trial's over."

"I don't expect to change your verdict, or your sentence."

"Then what possible difference can your testimony make?"

"All the difference in the world – in *this* world and in the *next*."

"So you want to tell them a fairy tale before they go off to sleep, is that it?" asked Leon as he gestured towards the fourteen condemned.

"You've been expounding the kingdom of darkness for thirty minutes now, Leon – I just want five minutes for the kingdom of light."

Leon's cold-blooded countenance momentarily melted into a smile. "Barbie, you're a doll! I just *can't* resist your charm or your naive optimism – and you've got more guts than all the people in this room put together.

Tell you what, because this assembly was supposed to be *your* show today, and I hijacked it – I'll give you three minutes."

Barb sprinted up the stairs and towards the mike as Leon stepped back and surrendered the lectern.

Very determined, very informal, no airs about her, yet confident that her four years at Hunter High – indeed, all her sixteen years of living thus far – were preparation and qualification for these three minutes at the mike. Perhaps her final three minutes of living, if her comments displeased Leon or ruined his documentary.

Leon called out from the darkened wings, "Once upon a time …."

Barb simply ignored Leon's sarcasm as she looked out into the crowd.

"I've seen supernatural things in Africa that you could never imagine. Things divine and things demonic. And so I recognise Satan's cold and evil presence all around us in this school today, even as I feel God's closeness and comfort.

The Dregs bound themselves together in a blood covenant of unforgiveness, despair, and death. And today you have been forced to suffer the curse of that covenant.

Jesus Christ, as both Son of God and son of man, bound together God and man in a blood covenant of forgiveness, hope, and life. And today you can freely choose to rest assured in all the blessings of that covenant.

Trust this covenant-keeping God. Even now. Especially now.

I'm not urging you to *believe* in God – because the Bible says that you already do. Paul's epistle to the Romans – chapter one, verse twenty – says that every one of us has witnessed God's character and power through creation and is without excuse in denying Him. We each have the seeds of eternity in our heart. We were created to be the immortal children of God and we know, in our hearts, that death is an enemy.

And I'm not urging you to be *faithful* to God – because we humans, each and every one of us, are inherently unfaithful. John's gospel – chapter two, verse twenty-four – says that Jesus knew what was in the hearts of men, and couldn't trust them.

Jesus said that only God is good – and by entrusting His life, and death, and resurrection, into the hands of His heavenly Father, Jesus fulfilled a blood covenant that man never could.

We can never trust, or rest, in our own human love, or faithfulness, or forgiveness – we'll only ever disappoint ourselves and one another – we can only ever trust and rest in God's, can only ever truly love because He first loved us.

Religion, in all its many forms around the world, is man's proud and futile attempt to satisfy God – all self-effort and striving.

In contrast, true salvation through Jesus Christ is a free gift – an end to all striving, an eternal peace, a covenant relationship, an adoption. An adoption offered to us by our heavenly Father, paid for with the eternal blood of Jesus His Son, and empowered by the Holy Spirit living within us – the Spirit of sonship that calls God "Daddy" and supernaturally develops in us the family resemblance, the heart, and mind of God Himself.

Jesus promised salvation to the dying thief on the cross next to Him – simply because the thief asked Jesus for it, not because the thief was a good person, or had any hope of ever becoming one.

To those of us about to die, and that might include me: our only hope in this world is to trust the covenant-keeping God of love to Whom we are all precious children – trust Him even now, *especially* now.

And to those of you who survive this awful day, even if I don't: we've all got a lot to learn, and we all know that great teachers are hard to find. The greatest Bible teacher I've ever known is Joseph Prince – do your own research, check out his web site at josephprince.com, sign up for his free daily email, watch him teaching on YouTube, read one of his books – each sermon, every page, overflows with the love of God and offers more wisdom than any theological degree ever did. It's all good news, there is no bad news.

And it's not too late for *any* of us to receive God's gift of forgiveness for all sins – past, present, and future – and to pass it on. Forgive your teachers – like us, they have much to learn. Forgive your parents – they

are only kids themselves, just a few years older. And forgive the Dregs –
hurting people hurt people, and we are all Dregs to some degree.

We were, all of us, taken captive by Satan, and only Jesus can set each
of us free."

Leon's solitary applause officially ended the speech as he stepped
back into the spotlight and resumed possession of the lectern and the
microphone, "…. and they all lived happily ever after."

Barb reached out her hand, "God bless you, Leon."

"All the best, Barbra." Leon's tone was uncharacteristically sincere, all
smirk now gone from his face and his voice, his respectful use of her proper
name rather poignant. But he offered her no hand to shake – as if any real
bridging of the chasm between them was too great, or too late, to even
attempt. Barb walked out of the spotlight and off the stage without saying
another word. Her three minutes were well and truly up – and she knew it.

The auditorium had almost seemed to brighten as Barb was speaking,
but now, as she headed down the centre aisle and back towards Kieran, the
darkness again seemed to close in – if possible, even darker than before.
Almost as if Barb had been the embodiment of hope itself, and now all
hope was gone.

Leon called everyone's attention from the departing Barb and back
onto the stage. "Anyone else want to join these fourteen up here for the
altar call? Last chance – express lane to heaven."

The audience cringed in silence.

"Everyone wants to go to heaven, but no one wants to die – how does
that work, Barb?"

114

"Never at the eyes – the chest is the biggest target."

No one knows if Druid was following his father's boyhood advice
when he fired eight bullets into Ronnie MacDonald's chest.

Druid's Dregcam captured the look on Ronnie's face as he fell
backwards – it was not fear nor surprise, but more of a resignation and
sadness that his son was now confirmed as a wanton murderer, fully and
almost gleefully capable of homicide, fratricide, and patricide.

The Dregcam stared down at the fallen Scotsman for a few seconds, then turned back to the ten bowling pins standing on the top step.

No longer nine, but ten.

From Druid's point of view, Gary Dixon – the tenth – stood *behind* his phalanx of human shields, and further out in the rain.

Druid's shell-shocked hostages had heard the words and shots exchanged between father and son behind them in the lobby, then suddenly saw the police figure in black running up to them from their left, carrying a rifle and a black shield.

Dixon had no time to account for the gunfire – not its target, its victims, or its damage – his focus was solely on the student gunman.

The nine hostage heads were in his way as he bobbed left and right to get a clear view of Druid turning towards him.

"GET DOWN NOW!" Dixon screamed – literally screamed.

Zwick pulled the wounded Khoury down with him, and the seven students dropped where they stood.

Dixon had finalised his plan while lying in the mud. If only the hostages would squat down, as ordered, then he could face Druid unimpeded – if Ronnie hadn't already eliminated him as a threat.

If Druid shot at him, Dixon had double bulletproof protection. If Druid turned his gun on the hostages, Dixon would just have to be quicker on the trigger – and, statistically, police officers usually were.

Dixon didn't know if it was their training, their authority, or some anointing from God, but that badge represented an awesome force to be reckoned with.

Dixon had prayed that they would squat immediately as ordered and not freeze, and now all hostages quickly followed Ed Zwick's lead – the day's tally for Mr. Zwick thereby rising to ten lives saved (if you counted Khoury twice) – while Druid had hesitated, surprised as he was by the black-clad intruder.

But Druid faltered for only two seconds before raising his Ruger, while Dixon's line of fire was obstructed for several as he waited for the last two students to duck down.

Dixon raised his Batshield and held his fire for the moment because he also saw that, even as Druid was shouldering the Ruger, his father was rising to his feet unnoticed behind him, somehow resurrected from the dead.

Eight bullets slapped into the Batshield exactly where Dixon's face had just been, only a moment before, leaving eight little pockmarks as the rounds were swallowed up by the polyethylene thermoplastic composite panels, designed and developed to eliminate any deflection or ricochet injury to officers or hostages.

Ronnie MacDonald jerked Drew's Ruger up towards the ceiling as he jumped in front of his son and wrapped him in a face-to-face bear hug – encircling the boy's arms and swivelling him one hundred and eighty degrees to face the admin office.

Dixon lowered the Batshield and slid his AR-15 back into the shooting notch just as Ronnie completed the one-eighty. The Scotsman knew that Dixon would immediately recognise the fluorescent red paint of the concussion grenade in his hand as he pulled the pin behind Druid's back.

"Close your eyes and cover your ears!" shouted Dixon to the nine squatting hostages as he stepped over them and huddled down behind them, protecting their backs from the imminent blast as best he could with his Batshield poised.

Dixon did not see Ronnie MacDonald stuffing the activated flash-bang grenade somewhere between his own heart and the heart of his struggling son just before it exploded.

115

As Barb headed silently back to her seat, Vesna D'Ambrosi, still clinging to the arm of Sharon Tilden, cried out into the darkened cavern beyond the stage, "Wendy! Please, where are you?"

"Yes, Wendy, where *are* you?" Leon echoed Vesna's cry into the cavern as he shielded his eyes from the blinding glare of the stage lights and peered into the darkness.

"I'm guarding the back door," came Wendy's reply. But only her voice, disembodied. She chose to remain in the shadows, hidden from Leon's piercing gaze.

Though the king of the Dregs could surely never see her ringless finger from that distance, perhaps he might notice the missing glint off her metallic green magazine and realise that Wendy was now carrying an unloaded Ruger.

The passage of time always seems to accelerate with the approach of a deadline, and time pressure increases exponentially. Leon glanced at his Mickey Mouse watch and his voice shifted into its commanding-officer mode.

He dispatched concise orders to Wendy Stankowski. "Druid and I have already carried out executions. Now it's your turn to get blood on your hands, Weed. Come up here to the front, right now, and execute these seven girls who tormented you."

"I've already *got* blood on my hands, just by being part of all this – and it'll never wash off. I don't want any more on my conscience. Let the girls go, Leon, I want to pardon them."

"It's too late for that, you put them on the blacklist."

"No she didn't," corrected Wade, "I did."

Wade walked over to Leon and lowered his voice as he approached, "Let the girls go, Leon."

"The blacklist is written in permanent ink and signed in blood – there are no pardons possible, the Dregs dispense no forgiveness," Leon's voice rang out with authority, his lectern serving also as judgement seat.

"Well then let *me* carry out the sentence." Wade lifted his Ruger as a sign of his willingness to obey, and in no way could the movement have been misconstrued as threatening.

But as Wade drew alongside him, Leon lashed out and clapped his palms together on either side of Wade's head – as though he were applauding – boxing his two ears.

It was a Krav Maga move, a stunning blow requiring only minimal force but causing a loud, disorienting ringing in the ears and a loss of balance as the eardrums are jolted, pressurised – and sometimes even ruptured.

Given the tension level of the captive audience, Leon's sudden attack, on its own, would have been startling enough – but its force and impact were underscored and amplified by Leon's simultaneous, accidental bashing of the lectern microphone with his elbow, followed immediately by the blaring of the 12:25 lunch bell.

The result was a jarring, audio explosion perfectly synchronised with the visual outburst of violence on stage before them.

Leon grabbed the wooden stock of Wade's Ruger with both his hands and rotated it, while jerking it violently downwards.

Not only was the bone in Wade's right index finger snapped by the metal trigger guard, as planned, but the digit was almost totally severed – and now hanging on by only a flap of flesh.

Wade yelled involuntarily and grunted with surprise and pain, but his cries were not of protest, pleading, or panic, for Wade was a seasoned fighter who never offered, nor expected, any mercy.

As Wade let loose the Ruger and grasped his mangled hand, Leon flashed Pam's scissors from the pocket of his black riding coat and cut the guitar strap around Wade's neck.

When Leon bent over to snatch Wade's Ruger as it slid to the floor of the stage, Wade reached up with his good hand, grabbed his towering attacker by the golden-highlighted hair, and pulled his head down in an attempt to even the odds.

On his way down, Leon embedded the scissors into the side of Wade's right leg, just behind his kneecap – a Krav Maga immobilisation point, rich in blood vessels, ligaments, and tendons.

In only seconds, Leon Spitzer had disoriented, disarmed, and disabled his opponent.

116

The Batshield and Dixon's warning protected the ten of them at the top of the stairs from any serious injury, although they were all rattled, knocked over, and left with a ringing in their ears.

Only the two students on each side of Dixon, and slightly beyond the cover of the shield, sustained slight lacerations from glass shards that were launched from the lobby carpet in the blast.

The concussion or "flash-bang" grenade is used by the military and police to temporarily blind, stun, or render unconscious gunmen and their hostages. The main difference between the concussion and the fragmentation grenade is the almost complete lack of shrapnel with the former, but, as with all "non-lethal" devices such as capsicum spray and tasers, there have been isolated cases of fatal injuries reported from around the world.

Dixon sprang to his feet – still a bit wobbly from the blast – drew his razor-sharp commando knife, and began slicing through the plastic cable ties that bound ankle to ankle and neighbour to neighbour. "Run towards the police with your hands on your heads, and follow their instructions."

But Dixon had no idea how close police assistance actually was. For as soon as he began vaulting up the school's front steps, his four Swat teammates had disobeyed his orders to stay put, broken ranks with their surprised police colleagues, and sprinted across the parking lot to support him.

Just as they had agreed amongst themselves immediately after their leader had driven away – they would offer maximum support and backup, without undermining his plans for a lone assault.

His four commandos arrived at the foot of the front steps just after the grenade exploded and took up their positions two by two and back to back – one pair covering the front entrance and their commander, the other covering the parking lot.

Although all the other police, and the army of media, that surrounded the school were initially stunned by Dixon's unexpected storming of the front entrance, one message became immediately clear to them – these Swat officers launching an independent action were committed first and foremost to their mission and to each other, and would tolerate no interference or resistance, whether from inside or outside the high school. The two AR-15's pointing down, but back towards the parking lot, made that abundantly clear.

So clear, in fact, that when Assistant Superintendent Vincent DeGroot – over at the shopping mall, consoling worried parents in front of the media – heard about Dixon's renegade action via police radio, and began barking out orders for his officers ringing the high school parking lot to join in on the storming of the lobby, none of them dared lift a finger or move a muscle.

At the top of the stairs, one of the reasons that Dixon and the hostages had suffered so little concussion was because Ronnie had so effectively contained the blast.

It was ironic that Druid – the self-proclaimed seer and wizard with the premonition of being attacked and defeated from a distance, by a faceless and unknown sniper – was actually overcome by a paternal embrace.

Ronnie had purposely entered the school with only defensive or non-lethal equipment. When his taser attack was unsuccessful, his own life was saved by the bulletproof vest worn under his police jacket, although three of his ribs received hairline fractures from the absorbed impacts of Druid's point-blank barrage.

Once recovered from having the wind knocked out of him by the eight .22 calibre bullets crumpled into his vest, Ronnie had risen to his feet as quickly as possible to keep Dixon from firing. His sole mission was to incapacitate Drew, and thus make it impossible for him to cause or suffer any more injuries.

By stuffing the concussion grenade between his son and himself, and in front of his kevlar vest, Ronnie was trying to contain the blast and limit injury to Dixon and the hostages, while deflecting and maximising its knockdown power against Drew.

But even though wearing his vest, closing his eyes, and turning his head, the explosion still perforated Ronnie's left eardrum, his face and throat suffering first and second-degree flash burns.

The blast broke four of Druid's ribs, his left wrist and ankle. He suffered a ruptured spleen, permanently lost hearing in his right ear, received second and third-degree burns to his chest, and required thirty stitches from being struck by and dragged over broken glass. Both father and son were rendered unconscious for several minutes.

Dixon's natural sense of self-discipline, his military training, and years of perilous front-line experience, all gelled together in high-risk crisis situations making him eminently qualified to lead such operations – while condemning him to a life of boredom as a civilian.

Even after such a potentially disorienting blast, his mind keenly and immediately assessed the situation. The nine hostages were hustled down the stairs by his commandos, while Dixon secured the lobby. Though unaware of the exact extent of the MacDonalds' injuries, Dixon could see that Druid posed no immediate danger, so he dropped to one knee behind the Batshield.

Exposing less than one hundred square centimetres (sixteen square inches) around his sighting eye, he waited, AR-15 at the ready, for the Dregs' armed response to the grenade explosion.

It never came.

117

Wade sank to the floor of the stage, with Pam's scissors protruding from his leg, and it didn't look like he'd be getting up any time soon.

With his torn and splintered right hand now out of commission, removal of the scissors from his right knee with only his left hand would be awkward or impossible. And, besides, Wade was reeling and apparently in no shape to launch a counter-attack.

I don't believe for a moment that Leon had misinterpreted Wade's approach as threatening. I think that Leon had simply taken advantage of Wade's proximity to neutralise him as Weed's defender, and free himself to focus on Weed, the object of his wrath.

It was not just Weed's *intent* to hide in the shadows, it was her very nature, and she had been doing it ever since her parents had first coaxed her out from under their protective wings to play with other children.

Though forced to squint against the glaring stage lights, Leon could still vaguely see Weed silhouetted by the exit sign over her head, and framed by the faintly illuminated outline of the auditorium's double doors behind her.

While Wade writhed on the stage with his scissored knee, Leon raised his M1 and rested it on the lectern.

"Time to honour your covenant, Weed."

"I'm not shooting anyone."

Unamplified in contrast to Leon's, Wendy's voice seemed small, weak, and distant. She was not being defiant or disrespectful in any way, but sounded more like a hiker just too tired to take another step.

Resolute and immoveable for the first time in her life.

"Well, then, *I'll* just have to shoot them – after I've killed you."

"You take responsibility for your actions, Leon, and I'll take responsibility for mine. I should have done that all along.

But you can never force me to hate them, any more than I could ever force them to love me." Then she stepped forward.

And as Wendy Stankowski stepped out of the darkness by the rear exit doors – and into the pool of light right behind the back row seats, closer to where Barb was squatting in the aisle – her voice seemed to grow stronger.

Perhaps the acoustics, perhaps her resolve – maybe a combination of the two. "If I've only got a few seconds left to live, then I want to live them in the light – laying down my own life, rather than stealing someone else's."

And suddenly a high school siege with multiple, uniformed, student gunmen on a rainy Friday afternoon in Newcastle seemed no more far-fetched a scenario than did Wendy Stinkweed Stankowski defying the siege's mastermind with noble rhetoric.

But everyone in the auditorium knew that such reckless heroism could incite only one possible response, and all eyes turned to Leon's M1 as it was raised from its resting position across the lectern – and pointed directly at Aron Wade.

Leon was now convinced that Weed was ready to die, but he was also confident that she held her brother Wade's life in higher esteem than she did her own – his recent months of self-sacrificial devotion surely outweighing her sudden magnanimous decision to spare the condemned girls on stage.

The M1's red laser dot roamed across Wade's chest and head as Leon spoke, "This pardon that you're so quick to offer your condemned girlfriends, Weed, it doesn't come cheap – are you willing to pay for it with your brother's blood?"

The two young men locked eyes, and Wade smiled a crooked smile. Leon was an orphan of greed and ambition, but Wade an orphan of violence. Dogged, determined, and tough, Wade never took his eyes off his opponents and he always won his fights. Leon had lost sight of Weed, and Wade knew it.

Wade yelled out, "Hit the deck, Weed, NOW!"

By the time Leon turned back to the audience and shielded his eyes from the stage lights, Weed's backlit silhouette had disappeared once again into the darkness.

118

For more than twenty-four hours after the siege, police investigators were baffled as to how Ronnie's exploding grenade in the lobby did not alert the Dregs in the auditorium to the Swat incursion.

True, the auditorium doors had always been referred to as "soundproof"

– but not *that* soundproof, surely. Not enough to completely muffle a flash-bang grenade designed to deafen.

It was only when they analysed the timing on the Dregcams, that they finally realised the grenade's explosion came at the *exact moment* that Leon struck the microphone while attacking Wade, and the 12:25 lunch bells rang throughout the school.

The detectives were amazed by the timing, the coroner referred to it as "the single most remarkable incidence of synchronicity that I have encountered in my thirty years as a pathologist", Barb just smiled and nodded.

With no immediate response or lobby attack forthcoming from the other Dregs, Dixon had no choice but to quickly reassess and move on.

Nine hostages freed. One Dreg reported killed in the gym. The second, wounded and unconscious in the lobby, had to be secured.

Dixon sliced the guitar strap around Druid's neck with his knife in order to free the Ruger, ejected the bullet in the chamber, threw its magazine down the front steps, tossed aside the weapon, and pulled out his police double-cuff plastic restraints – much stronger than the Dregs' cable ties.

He quickly bound the unconscious teenager's wrists and ankles, then looked for the heaviest trophy case to which he could cuff Druid's ankles and secure him – he saw it seven metres away. Ronnie, still unconscious himself, was spared the sight of his second son in one day being dragged over broken glass.

Druid's Dregcam was blown from his forehead by the grenade blast, and now lay by his feet. Its red operational LED light and the red laser sight on his Ruger had both been extinguished by the explosion. Fireflies, fireflies – Druid had indeed been wrong when he said that they lived for twenty-four hours.

Next Dixon made his way to the gymnasium – quickly – found Slave dead beside Mallick, and cuffed the two bodies together, wrist to wrist and ankle to ankle.

Most observers would think him insane, but over the years he had lost good friends, more than once, to enemy soldiers who somehow managed to take one last shot long after they were declared dead. Dixon had no one to cover his back, and no time to look over his shoulder. He had to be certain that Slave and Druid were each completely neutralised as a threat.

Two Dregs down, three to go – all ahead of him in the auditorium, and it was almost 12:27.

Ronnie's repeated surveillance reports on Weed had placed her by the entrance doors at the rear of the auditorium, described consistently as a "soft target". She seemed emotional, erratic, half-hearted, ill at ease with her weapon, badly shaken-up when taken as a hostage by Zwick, and never seen on the CCTV monitors to fire, or even aim, her Ruger in a truly threatening manner.

Dixon only glanced at the three student bodies lying by the auditorium's entrance. It was a waste of time for him to even check their vital signs – if he maintained focus on his mission, paramedics could be at their sides in a matter of minutes, if he lost focus, he himself could be dead in a matter of seconds.

Dixon squatted beside the auditorium doors, set aside his AR-15 on the floor, held his Batshield in place with his left hand through the support strap, and made sure Ronnie's taser was fully charged in his right, before activating the transmit button of the mini-mike suspended near his cheek.

"Luke, do you read me?"

"Loud and clear," replied the janitor.

"Power off *now*."

"Got it."

Dixon knew human reflex times, was fully aware that he was dealing with a civilian, and estimated there would be a minimum three-second gap before the school was darkened.

He opened the auditorium door and saw a female Dreg in black clothes – but without her Driza-Bone overcoat – on her hands and knees, crawling away from him behind the last row of seats about three paces to his right, and unaware of Dixon's arrival until he shot her in the back with the taser. Her convulsive lurching confirmed an effective hit.

Dixon let the five-second, twelve-hundred-volt electrical charge race through the copper wires at nineteen pulses per second while he reached for Weed's Ruger. By then the lights throughout the building were out, and he had to feel for it in the dark.

By the time Dixon had slid her rifle into the corridor, picked up his AR-15, and closed the auditorium door behind him, the dim emergency lights had been activated. He dropped the taser and cuffed Weed's ankles together and wrists behind her back – probably overkill as she would be unlikely to recover from her weakened state for several minutes at least.

He then whispered to the two closest students sitting in the back row – two of the Scripture Union Christians who had earlier fled my office with me, and who had both turned around to watch the intruder and the scuffle behind their seats, "Police officer. Jump back here and sit on Wendy if she tries to move, cover her mouth if she tries to speak."

The taser had discharged, and its victim had convulsed, in near-total silence. The sudden and unexpected blackout had masked Dixon's entry into the auditorium almost perfectly – everyone's eyes had to adjust to the disorienting darkness, and the light that would normally have flooded in from the corridor, to brighten the back row area and expose him, had been cut only a moment after the door opened.

Dixon crouched behind his shield and moved left into the centre aisle in order to remove any seated hostages from his line of fire. His ACOG scope turned darkness into light and, through it, he was the only person in the auditorium able to see every detail clearly.

As Dixon crept forward in the aisle, inch by inch, one student after another noticed the reflective "POLICE" label on his back, glowing dimly even in the murk.

Word of a saviour in their midst spread silently throughout the audience, but all the players on stage remained unaware.

Because his pupils had previously been so constricted by the glare of the blinding stage lights, Leon's eyes took longer than most to dilate and adapt to the emergency lighting.

"Get up, Weed, and turn those lights back on!" As soon as Leon spoke, he realised that his microphone was dead and that *all* power had been cut, not just the lights. Without spotlights and microphone – bereft of his media magic – Leon suddenly seemed smaller. An image flashed through my mind of the Wizard of Oz, exposed behind the curtain as a little man.

With Goliath's booming voice now cut down to size, the deflated giant was forced to shout out his threats, which only highlighted his growing desperation. "*I* am in command here, *not Wade*. I thought I saw that back door opening – if you're still in here, Weed, show yourself *now* or Wade dies up here on the stage, and you lose the only friend you ever had. Can you hear me?"

Dixon had already ripped the velcro-backed, reflective "POLICE" label from the front of his Batshield. He now slowly rose to his feet and stepped into one of the dim pools of light that illuminated the centre aisle.

From the lectern, Dixon appeared backlit only (the emergency lighting creating a weak halo effect) and Leon saw only a black-clad figure in silhouette, with no discernable shield, helmet, or rifle – to him it was obviously Weed.

From the centre aisle, and over the gun notch at the top of his Batshield, Dixon saw only the face of the armed student at the microphone, the centre point of the T-zone – just above the tip of his nose – lined up and magnified four times within the illuminated red donut, the circle of death, the killing zone in his ACOG scope. Aim small, miss small – and the rounds group tighter.

One Dreg terminated in the gymnasium, a second Dreg neutralised in the lobby, a third immobilised in the back row of the auditorium.

That appeared to be Wade, the fourth, apparently disarmed and wounded up on the stage at Leon's feet.

Now if only Leon, the final Dreg, would turn his weapon away from the downed Wade and onto that bulletproof "Weed" standing in the aisle before him – even *begin* to turn the M1 towards the Swat officer – then Dixon could launch the 5.56mm hollow points.

Travelling at almost one thousand metres per second, the first supersonic bullet would cover the forty-five metres to the stage before Leon even heard the gunshot and slam into the dead centre of his face, shattering it with an impact of 1296 foot-pounds – drop shot, instant kill, thereby ending the siege and securing the release of 394 students and staff.

Dixon *never* placed his index finger on the trigger until correctly sighted on target and ready to fire. He was now lined-up, his finger resting on the trigger, and prepared to double tap – twice in rapid succession to ensure the kill.

But Leon had his M1 trained on the wounded Dreg before him, and Dixon found himself in the typical police officer's predicament – risking his life to save a young man, in this case Wade, who would probably not hesitate to kill a cop. Criminals, with all their rights, threatening cops and victims with none.

Leon continued to revile the young girl before him, shouting abusively. "The rest of the Dregs didn't even want you. We all thought you were hopeless, and we were right – look how you buckled under pressure today.

Wade was the only friend you ever had, Weed. The only ray of hope that maybe you weren't a loser after all. That one ray of hope extinguished right before your eyes – that's the last thing you're ever going to see – stinks doesn't it, Stinkweed?"

Leon's mistake was keeping only his M1 trained on Wade, while his eyes focused on the contemptible black figure in the aisle before him. And as Leon shouted, Aron Wade somehow managed to extricate Vernon Linder's sawn-off .22 calibre from its hiding place within the internal chest pocket of his black Driza-Bone, while keeping his splintered and shredded right index finger out of the way.

Even as Aron lurched to his feet, he opened fire with his middle finger on the trigger, advancing towards Leon and elevating the little weapon with each shot, aiming first at the chest and then raking the bullets upwards to the head.

In four seconds, twelve rounds slammed into Leon's already aching heart, scarred his beautiful face, and stained his perfectly highlighted hair with blood.

Twelve forty-grain bullets – worth less than twenty cents each – that robbed the earth of Leon's priceless talents and unique personality, robbed Leon of his multimillion-dollar inheritance, the precious memories of his mother, and his very life.

It was only because of Dixon's complete surprise at the source and suddenness of the attack that Wade was even able to squeeze off the first twelve of the fifteen bullets in his magazine before Dixon swiveled his AR-15 to the left and cut down the little warrior with three shots to the back of the neck – a hand's breadth above the collar, at the base of his skull.

Dixon was disgusted with his own lack of control and precision – he only meant to fire twice.

Outside, in the pouring rain, Dixon's four Swat commandos received their orders through mini-earphones, "All Dregs are down. Secure the school – hostages out, paramedics in."

It was 12:29 and the body count was now twelve dead (Vernon Linder, Beryl Wade, Eva Forman, Earl Kennedy, Andy Stewart, David Sheridan, Natalie Abrahim, Slave Latska, Doug Mallick, Wally Martin, Leon Spitzer, Aron Wade), eleven wounded (Drew MacDonald, Tessa Briggs, Fireman Jordan Reece, Marty MacDonald, Ishna Mahrmoud, Victor Eng, Mark Devito, Suman Khoury, Kieran Thredbo, Ronnie MacDonald, Wendy Stankowski), and eighteen students with various degrees of glass laceration.

The Dregs had fired 355 shots in 44 minutes, the police only 3.

The Aftermath

It took me years of research, analysis, reflection, and "sorting out" just to recount those forty-four minutes at Hunter High that you have just read.

How impossible, therefore, to even attempt an appreciation or presentation of all that went on in the hours, months, and years following the siege in the lives of the four hundred people most directly involved in the events of that day? Ripples. Aftershocks. Scars, both physical and emotional. Fears. Nightmares. Exposures. Revelations. Decisions. Resolutions.

Again, I admit to myself, and confess to anyone who will listen, that I am totally unqualified – but if I don't attempt an epilogue, then who will?

I tell myself that the greater the lessons to be gleaned, the less futile were the deaths. But, then again, I could be lying.

Once they received his radio call to secure the school, Dixon's four commandos came charging up the front steps – allowing their AR-15s to dangle from their shoulder straps as they drew their Glocks for potential close-quarter engagement.

No other officers besides Popeye heard Dixon's call, transmitted on the Swat team's secure channel, but as soon as the four men in black stormed into the lobby, everyone knew that it was all over.

Dixon had only just finished cuffing the two dead Dregs on the auditorium stage when Luke rebooted all the school lights, as ordered, and Dixon's commando teammates burst in.

Leon was lying on his back, lifeless eyes open and staring up at the bright, overhead stage lights – no longer squinting.

Wade had fallen forward onto his chest, face downwards in the pool of blood and grey matter that had formed around his head – and Dixon had cuffed his hands behind his back without turning him over.

Only in subsequent autopsy photos would Dixon notice that Vernon Linder and Wade shared almost identical bullet-entry wounds at the base of their skulls – but, while Vernon's exit wounds in the throat were small and neat, Wade's were in the centre of his face and catastrophic.

The 394 hostages were cleared from the building in record time, with Carol Spargo one of the last to leave.

Leon's Dregcam, still strapped to his forehead with its little red light silently flashing, recorded Carol's contemptuous smirk as she stared down at Leon's shattered chest and face for the longest time, then pulled out her mobile phone and began taking pictures of her fallen tormentor.

When she finally made her way off the stage, Dixon – still menacing in his black balaclava – met her at the foot of the stairs, grabbed her phone, and ground it to pieces under the heel of his tactical boot.

"That phone cost me six hundred dollars!"

"And if I arrest you for interfering with a police investigation and tampering with evidence, it'll cost you a whole lot more."

"Can I at least retrieve my SIM card?"

"No. Dregs are dead, phone's dead, SIM card's dead, photo opportunity's dead. Just walk away."

Carol walked out of the auditorium, and into the waiting arms of the glossy magazines with their lucrative interviews – though considerably less lucrative than they would have been if accompanied by gruesome photos. Beryl Wade never got to read those issues.

Dixon sat down on the bottom step near the front row seats and removed his balaclava. He clicked on his safety, ejected the magazine from his AR-15, locked open the bolt, and pocketed the live round that fell from the chamber. He rested the weapon across his thighs, leaned on it with his elbows, and was about to bury his face in his gloved hands when he remembered that they were covered with the blood of the two dead Dregs on stage – from when he had cuffed them, and felt for any signs of carotid pulse in their necks.

Dixon wiped the blood from his hands and onto his sopping wet black uniform.

Seated in the back row, Ricky, Barb, Kieran, and I were exhausted. We just sat there. We had insisted that the seven other Scripture Union students go on ahead without us. We four had risked death beside Leon for the last thirty-five minutes – actually *those three* had risked it, even defied it, while I had just cowered before it.

But we had survived together, and we just wanted to sit together for a few minutes. Together, yet each alone – each of us lost in our own individual thoughts.

Or maybe we just sat there because Leon hadn't yet told us we could leave. His power and influence over us would not quickly be forgotten.

In the lobby, Druid, still unconscious, was loaded onto a stretcher and whisked away in an ambulance with two Newcastle cops on board.

As soon as the shooting was over, Weed began to cry out Wade's name. The police officers – who cut her ankle ties, lifted her to her feet, and dragged her out of the auditorium – ignored her sobbing requests to see Wade or be told of his fate. So Barb called out after her, "Wade's dead, Wendy."

"He died for me!" Wendy called back, as she viewed the universe through her egocentric pain – mourning the loss of her brother and saviour.

"No, Wendy – he *killed* for you."

For days after – maybe even weeks – I pondered that last comment of hers, puzzled as to why Barb seemed so determined to clarify and so cruel to argue with the shell-shocked Wendy, to whom she had always previously shown such compassion. And then I realised that Barb was only being true to herself – always brutally and mercifully honest. There was no contradiction there, just two sides of the same coin. Perhaps it was just that now, in the wake of the siege, she dared no longer risk mercy at the expense of truth.

When the four of us finally left our seats – and while guiding the bloody and swollen Kieran towards the lobby, freedom, and a waiting ambulance – I peeked into the gymnasium and saw Luke standing over the intertwined bodies of Slave Latska and Doug Mallick.

And, as we walked through the wreckage that was once a lobby, I was amazed to look outside and see that the storm was winding down.

The media exaggerated, dramatised, and sensationalised the truth when they reported that the storm suddenly ended at the same moment as did the siege – that's simply not true. But, by the end of the evacuation, the storm had largely spent itself, just like the anger, and loneliness, and confusion of the Dregs.

The crippling fear and anxiety, the media build-up and suspense, the lives of the murdered hostages, the violent police response, the puddles and splashes of blood – all spent – leaving us exhausted, drained, depleted, trembling, and weak.

We emerged just after noon, around 12:36. But it seemed, somehow, like early morning. Like the end of a long, dark night. Like waking from a nightmare.

For the first time ever, I noticed the weatherproof surveillance cameras atop their parking lot light poles.

I was bewildered by the dozens of video and still cameras, the television lights and photographers' flashes, the rooftop satellite dishes protruding from news vans and trucks. And I remember thinking how ineffective the media actually were – despite all their technology, their power to influence, their illusion of immediacy and intimacy – how incapable of truly capturing or communicating the experience.

Television cameras, many with red lights mounted on top of their lenses – one-eyed monsters – intruding, never blinking, trying to read and consume our emotions, to transmit them digitally, to engage viewers vicariously, burning into us much like the Dregs' red laser sights. The media – cannibalistic, consuming now the victims to whom they had just given birth.

The blinding red laser dots, the smell of gunpowder, the small clatter of spent shells bouncing and rolling, the longing for daylight, fresh air, and freedom – how could any viewer snacking before a flat screen TV at home ever truly appreciate the claustrophobia and suspense, while already knowing the outcome and watching the recap?

A camera lens, or television screen – no less a weapon than a laser sight, really – taking viewers hostage for life, captivating and herding large groups of people by their fears, and hopes of escape.

It was a shame – the auditorium or gym at Hunter High would have been the ideal location to begin the massive task of identifying, questioning, and counselling the 403 rescued hostages, now including Druid's nine shields.

But there were three overriding reasons to move the herd, fast:

Security demanded that the school be evacuated while all armed Dregs, detained hostages, and wounded victims were accounted for and properly dealt with, all weapons or possible explosives disarmed and confiscated.

Forensics required a building cleared of all civilians and police officers so that the documenting and analysis of all physical evidence, including corpses, could begin unhindered and untainted.

Human frailty and compassion cried out for immediate removal of all hostages from the killing zone. Nerves were frayed, breakdowns were feared, and lawsuits were looming.

Counsellors, local and interstate, had been dispatched to the scene right at the outset of the siege, but subsequent feedback clearly showed that the greatest immediate support came from family, friends, and anyone willing to hug or listen. Ongoing support needs eventually proved almost impossible to track and record – with over eight hundred students, staff, police, and emergency personnel directly involved, dispersing geographically over time, and often manifesting post-traumatic reactions only months or years later.

Even now, three years later, as I write this book, there is currently a class action lawsuit for three hundred million dollars inching its way through the law courts. Lawyers representing all staff and student hostages are suing the New South Wales Department of Education and Police Force for failing to predict, prevent, or more effectively resolve the siege.

Anton Spitzer is pursuing a lawsuit of his own – the only one filed on behalf of a Dreg, the only one based on constitutional grounds, and being argued through the federal courts. Spitzer's legal team is charging the federal government with the infringement of students' civil rights through compulsory high school attendance, and also contesting the use of excessive force by police when handling violent crimes involving minors.

The human mind in the twenty-first century has no difficulty accepting, conceptualising, processing, and imagining even the most fantastic technological developments, science fiction, or fantasy sagas. But it still has a problem with reality.

Birth, death, crisis, tragedy – we of the twenty-first century are no quicker to process these, to appreciate our mortality, to accept the fragility of our frame and the unexpected twists of our fate, than were our ancestors of two hundred years ago.

Slower even, I think, due to the rise of materialism, the decline of spirituality, and the illusion of control.

And so, when the gunfire ended, Dixon was the only person in the auditorium to respond immediately, knowing it was all over and calling for support. The hundreds of hostages took seconds, long seconds – and many took minutes – to fully appreciate that the two Dregs on stage were now neutralised, and all their threats defused.

After Dixon, the first people to *really* grasp the truth – to embrace and treasure this sudden and unexpected gift of salvation and deliverance – were those condemned to imminent death by firing squad. Remember, Leon and Wade were actually killed while arguing over who would be first to initiate the executions.

It is the man with the greatest perceived debt, who most deeply cherishes his redemption and – while many in the audience were still stunned – relief and gratitude quickly swept over the twelve condemned students, and two teachers, lined up on the lip of the stage.

They smiled, and laughed, and cried, and crumbled. Some dropped to the floor, their trembling knees finally relieved of all burdens. Many hugged each other, only a couple approached Dixon to offer their thanks.

Amidst (and in contrast to) all that gratitude and relief around him, Mark Devito stood alone and seething. Still perched on the edge of the stage, Devito just pointed at his betrayers – Zoe Moustakis and Trevor Cooper, seated in the front row – his bandaged right hand dripping blood, and his head nodding.

Then the four commandos rushed in and, after consulting only momentarily with Dixon, began clearing the auditorium.

Before the first hostages reached the rear exit doors, Dixon shouted to his men, "Free their wrists before they go."

This was totally contrary to standard police procedure following a hostage incident, and very uncharacteristic of the highly disciplined sergeant. All rescued hostages were to be treated as hostile until searched for weapons, positively identified, and eliminated as suspects – that was the protocol for any hostage scenario, and all the Swat commandos knew it. Leaving their wrists bound would have been the strategically wiser option.

But Dixon was just tired, I guess. Bone-tired of being the global policeman. Weary, and spent, and ready to drop.

I looked at him, still sitting at the foot of the stairs, and remembered that Barb always said "we don't break the law – the law breaks us". Dixon now looked to me like a man crushed by the weight of upholding the law for too many years. Protecting the innocent, punishing the guilty.

Without questioning their orders, all four of Dixon's commandos drew their knives and began slicing off the cable ties.

Once through the lobby and into the parking lot, all hostages were ushered into twelve waiting school buses, and ferried to a nearby primary school for processing and family reunions.

The moment the siege was over, the police investigation began, and Newcastle detectives were assigned to contact the parents of the Dregs.

Alison MacDonald returned home from her 11:30 hairdressing

appointment to find an unmarked police sedan waiting in her driveway. After all these years, she could spot a cop car from one hundred metres away. Alison ran up to it – Ronnie always drove the van, and officers sent to her home could only mean trouble.

Even as she ran, she began berating herself for turning off her mobile phone – she knew that Ronnie *always* wanted her contactable in case of emergencies, but she hated it ringing when she was at the hairdresser, and she had forgotten to turn it back on when she'd finished at the salon.

Stunned by the news that her husband and two older sons were in hospital, she silently accepted the offer of a lift, and was driven off to face the carnage of her shattered family.

Wendy's mother, Joyce, heard about the siege from a customer around noon. She ran from the bank, forgetting her mobile phone, and drove the forty blocks to Hunter High. Directed by police to the shopping mall parking lot, there she mingled in the rain with hundreds of other worried relatives until repeated rumours about the Dregs forced her to seek refuge in her car – and to pray for the first time since her husband lay dying on the bathroom floor.

After the Swat team assault, Joyce Stankowski raced back to the school with a horde of other parents, but could not see her daughter among the hundreds of hostages evacuated by bus, and so she just sat there in the car – waiting, and watching, and frozen with fear.

After 1:30 there was little activity in the parking lot – all the other parents having gone over to the primary school to be reunited with their children, and the police vehicles no longer in a hurry as they carried out their assignments, coming and going without flashing lights – but still she sat.

The fear had melted away and left her numb, the rain had almost stopped, but still she stared at the windscreen wipers and found herself somehow comforted – almost hypnotised by their intermittent, rhythmic sweep. She recalled some vague and distant memory of being rocked and comforted by her mother, remembered rocking her own little daughter in pink when she was still called Wendy, and before she wore black.

It was only at 1:50 – when a police officer noticed her windscreen wipers squeaking across the dry glass, and knocked on her window to offer assistance – that she finally identified herself as the mother of a Dreg.

Mrs. Stankowski was returned to her home by police car just before midnight – having answered questions for hours without being allowed to see Wendy, who was in custody and heavily sedated. Police were due back at eight o'clock the next morning to begin searching Wendy's bedroom.

Inside, waiting on Joyce's pillow, was Wendy's seven-page letter. Joyce wept all night – tears of regret and despair and then, around dawn, a resolution, a hope, almost even a joy nestled into her heart as she decided to support her daughter no matter how long, painful, or costly the journey. Death may have separated Joyce from her husband, but she would not allow even murder to steal away her daughter.

Thanks to his highly efficient secretary, police were able to track down Anton Spitzer in Melbourne even before the siege was over. But Anton refused to believe the accusations and did not return the call until after his conference meeting was concluded and his son was dead. Eventually, Anton dispatched both his executive assistant and the head of his legal team to identify the body of the young man killed at the lectern.

Only when he was thus convinced, did Anton Spitzer arrange a midnight visit to the Newcastle morgue, hoping to elude the media.

His lawyers managed to secure a private room where Anton could view the remains. This was nine hours before the scheduled autopsy, and the coroner had stipulated that an orderly must be present throughout the allotted five-minute viewing, with Spitzer required to wear surgical mask and gown to safeguard all forensic evidence, and forbidden to touch the body of his only son.

When the coroner arrived for work the next day, a letter of resignation from the orderly was waiting on his desk – although the letter referred to "retirement", rather than resignation.

After two hours alone with his dead son – it had been years since the two of them had spent that much time together in one sitting – Anton emerged and ordered an immediate investigation of the siege be carried out by a team of private investigators (mainly retired police detectives) and forensic specialists. Eleven months, and (reportedly) two million dollars later, Anton's lawyers began the constitutional challenges in court.

Anton Spitzer never isssued a public statement of any kind – neither allocating blame, nor accepting responsibility – and he only ever spoke of his son, or the circumstances surrounding the siege, when subpoenaed to do so. But, even then, it was on Anton's own terms: due to his deteriorating health, Spitzer was eventually allowed to testify at the inquests via live-video link.

Despite all his money and influence, Anton Spitzer's empire and jurisdiction ended at the grave, and he knew it. But the control had to be pried from his fingers, and he pursued the vendetta against his ex-wife to the bitter end. Although Anton was powerless to separate Leon from his mother in the afterlife, he refused to bury his son's body anywhere near his ex-wife's.

When all their attempts to contact Aron Wade's mother, Beryl, by telephone and door-knocking proved futile, the police began questioning her neighbours – but cooperation with the authorities was frowned upon in that Housing Commission section of town.

Finally, just after two o'clock, police forced entry, found the bodies of Beryl and Vernon, and realised that young Aron had finished his homework before leaving for school that morning.

Though both living interstate, Aron's two brothers were easily tracked down through their parole officers. But neither attended the funerals, and why should they? To commemorate their childhood neglect and abuse? To pay respects to the little runt who died blatantly breaking the two cardinal rules that they had tried so hard to impart to him – "never lose a fight" and "never get caught"?

Beryl's two cousins from Sydney decided that, despite the matricide, Aron should be laid to rest beside his mother. They weren't sure how young Aron would have felt about it, but they knew for certain that Beryl was always afraid to be alone.

With no family to claim his body, Vernon Linder was given a civil burial in a pauper's grave. None of his drinking mates attended, opting instead for a wake held at Vernon's favourite pub. And many of his friends gathered there to raise a glass in his honour – he was obviously a different person when he was younger, or sober, or before he became violent, or when dealing with people bigger than him or, perhaps, before he himself was neglected and abused as a boy. God only knows. The ripples go on forever.

All painful memories die hard, but painful memories of tragic death seem, ironically, to live on forever. So when Slave's mother was approached in her fiancé's horse paddock by two uniformed police officers, she saw only uniforms and expected only pain.

In fact, she had *always* expected to lose her son to violence just as all the women in her valley had lost their fathers, and brothers, and husbands, and sons – for generations. So she wasn't the least bit surprised when told that her son had armed himself to take revenge on his enemies, and been killed in the process.

But what *did* shock Lilliana was her sudden realisation that, with Slave's death, the name, pride, honour, and stubbornness of "Latska" had also ended on these Australian shores and in this valley – the Hunter Valley. Back home, in her ancestral valley, there had always been another generation of men, and another, and another after them, to take up their arms, lay down their lives, and carry on the vendetta.

When she viewed the body, Lilliana was greatly relieved to see that Slave's face was unmarked except for his broken nose – back home the remains of the beloved were often left disfigured and dishonoured.

She asked meekly if she could take Slave's body back to his homeland for burial next to his father, then quickly accepted the discouraging reply. To quarrel with the authorities was to risk drawing attention to yourself, to risk being marked, watched, followed, exiled, never heard from again. But her fiancé took up her case, arguing it loud and long.

Lilliana was just about to sign the request form for international transport, when she laid the pen down and asked her Australian partner to take her home. Slave was dead. He had made his decision with typical hard-headed Latska male pride. His decision, not hers. Her husband had lost his life over a chicken. She would not risk losing her new life over a gravesite. "Take me home, Peter, now please."

"To your valley? Right now?" he asked, stunned.

"No, to *our* home, here, with the horses."

She would raise her daughter to find a good Australian husband wise enough to listen to his wife's advice. She would not return to the ancestral valley with Katiyanka – even for an intended few days – and risk, somehow, having her marry into a feuding family.

It was a valley of unforgiveness and revenge, of darkness and death. She had only realised its spiritual pull on her after she had left it, and she now refused to return.

Lilliana turned her back on the last dead Latska, and walked out of the morgue.

And what of the politics of Black Friday? The other blood sport? The gladiators in suits?

Immediately after issuing the Swat green light to Sergeant Dixon, Superintendent Rod Stanwych phoned his superior in Sydney, the New South Wales Police Commissioner, to inform him. The commissioner advised him to revoke the order and await Buster's arrival sometime after one o'clock. Stanwych refused, saying that it was too late, the commando operation was now unstoppable, the 12:30 execution and suicide deadline had left him no choice, and he would assume full responsibility.

The commissioner assured Rod that the blood would, *indeed*, be on his own hands and that, although his retirement was only seventeen days away, Stanwych was not beyond the disciplinary reach of the police commission – that a botched operation would result in the loss of his pension. And, after forty-two years of police service and retiring as a Superintendent, Stanwych stood to lose over one hundred thousand dollars per year, tax-free, for the rest of his life under the older, more generous, and now-abolished public service superannuation scheme of New South Wales.

Stanwych replied, "And exactly how much is that for the life of each hostage I'm willing to risk, in order to promote your armoured car?" Yet still Stanwych refused to call off the commandos.

Again, phone records, accessed through freedom of information injunction, clearly show the commissioner's mobile phone immediately calling the minister of justice and the premier to warn them of the impending commando action. But all three men later insisted that *they* made the joint decision to launch the assault, and then had the commissioner ring Stanwych to issue him the command – entirely the reverse of the phone records.

Years later, Stanwych privately shared with me that the police commissioner rang him back one final time, as soon as Dixon's assault had been confirmed as an outstanding success – with only three police bullets fired and no further hostages harmed. The commissioner then guaranteed Stanwych's full pension as long as the superintendent accredited his superiors with making the decision to green light the commando assault. Stanwych agreed at the time, but has regretted it ever since.

The New South Wales Premier, Justice Minister, and Police Commissioner all lost their power and positions at the next election. Time has moved on, some official records have been "lost" and "accidentally deleted", none of these phone conversations were recorded, and high-powered solicitors have warned me about the cost of slandering their clients.

So the politicians, now retired on generous and tax-free government pensions, shall remain nameless – and, if I were ever asked under oath whether initial phone records revealed that the commissioner placed that disputed final call to Rod Stanwych at 12:35, I would, of course, refuse to testify, although 12:34 would probably be more accurate.

In stark contrast to the political leaders, Sergeant Gary Dixon – ever the faithful, consummate soldier – never elaborated publicly about his orders or the chain of command, never threatened or blamed the men under his authority, bore sole responsibility for his actions, and claimed no personal glory for "only doing his duty".

The funerals of all murdered hostages were delayed because of autopsies and forensic study by the coroner. The premier's office took advantage of the postponements and tried to persuade all bereaved families to participate in a joint commemorative ceremony and funeral service to be televised live with the premier front and centre. Enticements included: honour for the fallen, a sense of shared loss and grieving within the community that would strengthen Australia's resolve to never again allow such a tragedy – and all expenses paid for by the state.

One such televised, sixty-minute ceremony would effectively provide the premier a blank cheque for budgeting law enforcement. Voters were moved by emotion – and politicians by logic, as they plotted the emotional manipulation of voters.

Four families readily agreed to the state funeral (those of Doug Mallick, Andy Stewart, David Sheridan, and Wally Martin).

Natalie Abrahim's declined on religious grounds, thereby costing the premier a big slice of the ever-increasing Muslim vote.

Eva Forman's husband was in no physical or financial state to decline, and died alone without any further visitors twelve weeks later.

Earl Kennedy's wife and daughters refused – loudly and repeatedly, in the media spotlight – as a protest against the education system that they felt had ignored Earl's mounting concerns about school violence. The words of Kennedy's daughter screamed out from the headlines: "Dad gave his life – literally – for his students. His funeral we will keep as a private family affair."

One of the celebrity gossip magazines offered Earl's widow one hundred thousand dollars for exclusive funeral photos and interviews. When the offer was declined, the magazine resorted to publishing grainy telephoto shots and a patchwork of quotes from "close family and friends" who were never identified.

I managed to personally attend every funeral of victim and perpetrator, every hostage and Dreg – except for Leon's. It was shrouded in secrecy, and ringed by an army of private security guards. Two network cameramen who tried to cover the event ended up filing lawsuits for assault and broken equipment, while several freelance photographers settled out of court.

But I attended all the others because I felt it was my responsibility – both personally, and as a representative of the school staff.

I was sadly wanting for any words of wisdom as I listened to the families' anguished whys. And then I remembered that Barb had once shared one of her favourite proverbs with me – Proverbs 17:28 "even a fool, when he holds his peace, is considered wise." Barb used to joke, "better to be silent and thought a fool, than to open your mouth and remove all doubt". So I did what I do best, and just listened.

Perhaps some relatives felt better for my having attended, I don't know. I certainly felt worse – unqualified, incompetent, and powerless. No sense of closure for me, just a yawning, gaping, chasm of unnamed and unnameable aches and longings. Emptiness, despair, and anguish – should have, would have, could have, if only, what if, what now, what next?

Doug Mallick's mother told me that he had felt the flu coming on, early on the morning of the siege, but she pushed him out the door – it was Friday and he had the weekend ahead to get over it, if need be.

Andy Stewart was an only child, an IVF baby who was finally conceived after ten years of failure and frustration. The pregnancy was difficult – his mother, sure she would miscarry time and time again, spent the whole of the last trimester in bed. Andy was a sickly child, always nervous and clinging, with his parents having to constantly reassure him that things would all work out for the best. But they were not there to reassure him on Black Friday, and he died alone.

Wally Martin's ten-year-old daughter came over from New Zealand with her mother, and was given a new gleaming-white lab coat as a present from the student council. The council had initially debated whether they should give her Wally's *actual* coat, laundered of blood yet still torn to make bandages as it had been. But the coroner's office retained it as evidence, so the council presented her with a new one. The little girl clutched it to her heart throughout the funeral as though it were a police or military uniform of honour and, in many ways, it was. The premier posed with her for photos.

The Hunter High School building had to be closed initially for two weeks to allow police to gather all the evidence and fly in their international experts. The Department of Education then required another two to repair damages and interview replacements for Earl Kennedy and Eva Forman. And all throughout those four weeks, the debate raged in homes and in the media – what would best heal the wounded Newcastle community? Should the school be closed as a memorial to the dead, or reopened as a tribute to the survivors?

But there was no allowance in the state budget for a new high school in the Hunter Valley, so an ingenious political compromise was devised and (for only the cost of a plaque, new website, and stationery) Hunter High was renamed Earl Kennedy Memorial High School and reopened in mid-November for the last four weeks of the academic year.

The premier gave an inspiring speech about the indomitable Aussie spirit, and the honour bestowed on the fallen by picking up their torch and moving on. Time had passed, media fervour would die down due to the low boredom threshold of their readers and viewers, and government inquests were underway with their findings not expected for more than a year. Another year, another election, short memories, sleight of hand.

The New South Wales Department of Education bent over backwards to support and accommodate those wounded and traumatised students unable to return to class for weeks or months. Make-up classes were offered in the December-to-January summer break and, again, early in February after school resumed – with fully subsidised, ongoing tutorial support available if required. The Department even awarded diplomas to those Year Ten students who never returned to high school, but needed such certification for admission to apprenticeships and trade school courses. A small investment, after all, as the placated parents of such well-supported students would surely be less likely to pursue their lawsuits.

Leon's prophecy did come true. A couple of freelance journalists somehow managed to copy the original Dregcam videos, edited them together with their own documentary footage and interviews, and sold the program to a European cable network. The Australian government succeeded in legally quashing the telecast, at the last minute, on the grounds that inquests were ongoing and testimony would be compromised.

Vincent DeGroot replaced the retiring Rod Stanwych as Newcastle Police Superintendent, but held the position for only five months, announcing his own retirement just forty-eight hours before signing a half-million-dollar deal for the book and movie rights to the inside story of the siege. DeGroot probably seemed like the second-best choice as police technical adviser after Gary Dixon had refused all requests to cooperate.

The book was a best-seller and the movie an international success, with twenty-something-year-old actors playing the parts of the teenage students – students and soldiers almost always much younger in real life than the actors who portray them on-screen.

The "true story", when filmed, was also embellished with a love triangle between Wade, Weed, and Barb.

The problem-plagued, breakdown-prone, and totally ineffective Siege Buster armoured vehicle was quietly mothballed twenty-two months after its unveiling, when the state parliament was on its summer break and the premier away on overseas vacation.

The actual Dregcam footage was never televised due to fears by the police and parents' groups that it would inspire copycat violence – I wrestled with those same fears as I began writing this account. I appreciate the risk, and realise that the media will skin me alive if copycats strike out. But I also know that the media will never hear of, nor publicise, nor credit me with the dozens, or hundreds, or thousands of teenagers and young adults around the world alerted, by this book, to the dangers and evil of peer pressure and gang violence – their eyes opened, maybe even their lives saved.

Now, years later – long after the shattered glass was replaced, the bullet holes plastered, and the wounded bodies healed – I still worry that we never took the time to truly appreciate or address the psychological devastation and spiritual carnage of the siege. In a culture so easily and so often fooled by façade and appeased by appearance, were we not more concerned about the surface scar than the inner healing? And as it has proven such a daunting task to keep track of even the geographical location of the hundreds of survivors as they dispersed over the years, how much more so their mental, emotional, and spiritual health?

And just as I could never truly know how deeply they were all wounded or how well they will recover, I will never fully appreciate the pain and bitterness that fuelled the leader of the Dreg assault and inspired such hatred and evil in his heart.

When the police found Leon's secret diary hidden in his tree house headquarters, they were shocked to learn that, right from the start, he had planned and plotted to emerge as the sole survivor of the siege.

Investigators discovered records proving that Leon had inquired, several times, about ordering a bulletproof vest – just one – but had never followed through. He outgunned each of his accomplices and was prepared to kill them himself if their suicide pact was never realised: he shot Slave, turned his M1 on Wade, hunted Weed, and left Druid alone to defend an indefensible position at the school entrance.

Leon was recorded, on Dregcam, referring to his father Anton's suffering "for the rest of his natural life", and he used the same phrase repeatedly in his diary when gleefully anticipating the shame and embarrassment that his own life sentence in jail would bring down upon the head of "The Great Anton Spitzer".

Anton Spitzer might well have "paid off" and dismissed Leon's Mum, driven her to an early grave, and then buried her – but her son Leon, mastermind and sole survivor of a high school shooting, would remain in his cell, a living ghost, to haunt Anton for the rest of his life.

But, for Leon Spitzer, even executing his enemies, murdering his accomplices, and torturing his father was not enough. He made sure it was all recorded, so that the imagination of the whole world could be defiled and haunted by the grisly images.

And, finally, he forced every hostage to share the blame for sentencing people to death. Everyone was made to vote, at gunpoint, in the auditorium. Forced to betray other hostages to save themselves, wishing the red laser light upon someone else – anyone else but me. And thereby condemning, even the survivors, to a life sentence of guilt.

But the authorities were quick, and effective, in suppressing that information. The police media unit implored all television, radio, and newspaper journalists not to file reports about hostages, mostly teenagers, being forced to vote on who should face the firing squad. They threatened defiant journalists with imprisonment and pressed charges against several reporters preparing to leak the story, a raft of charges – "hampering a police investigation", "endangering the welfare of a minor", "child abuse", "contempt of court", and "improper disclosure of restricted police information".

So the media were hushed and the true depth of the evil – the extent of the physical, psychological, and spiritual torture inflicted in those forty-four minutes – was never fully appreciated by the public.

But the more immediate problem caused by the compulsory voting of the hostage "jury" was not the guilt of the voters – it was the anger of those they condemned to death. The sentences were never carried out, of course, but the votes had been cast all the same.

The teaching staff was splintered. Some teachers refused to ever again set their foot in a classroom – *any* classroom. Others, like Bill Arkapaw, demanded immediate transfer to another school – *any* other school. Les Mantiss, after being condemned to death by a majority of both staff and students, was never seen again by anyone at Hunter High. Mrs. Timms, however, continued teaching her music classes "without missing a beat", as she said, seeming no more bitter or apathetic than before – some suggested even more gracious, after her brush with judgement and death.

Mark Devito's father, Alphonse, refused to ever let his son return to Hunter High, and was the first parent to demand full Year Ten accreditation so that his son could begin his building apprenticeship unhindered. But Zoe Moustakis, and her co-conspirator Trevor Cooper, had clearly seen the look in Mark Devito's eye as he pointed them out with his bloody finger from the stage, and they fled not only the school, but the state. They had tried to have Devito killed, and they never doubted for a second that he would respond in kind if given half a chance. Zoe reportedly moved to Melbourne and Trevor to Western Australia, but I was never able to confirm this.

Drew MacDonald, though partially deafened for life, recovered from all his other injuries after multiple surgeries and extensive skin grafts. But his drug addictions required further treatment, and his psychiatric therapy is ongoing. His mind became a battlefield of warring images from the media, the occult, drugs, and the violence of Black Friday – that had all scarred his soul.

The newspapers took a particular dislike to him – the multiple-murderer who tortured his own brother and shot his own father – constantly referring to his flaming red hair, and his wild blue eyes.

His psychotic courtroom outbursts did little to ingratiate him to the voters, who let their political representatives know that they didn't want to see Druid MacDreg walking the streets of New South Wales again – ever.

When Drew turned eighteen, nine months after the siege, the juvenile justice system quickly turned him over to the adult courts for resentencing – not routinely done in the case of underage murderers but inevitable, really, when insanity was implied, the media watching, and the public outraged.

Currently his sentence is open-ended and slated for re-evaluation every three years. Drew is held in the Supermax wing of the Goulburn Correctional Centre, with its 141 surveillance cameras – 141 little red lights, unblinking, twenty-four hours a day, perhaps for life.

For his own protection, Drew is isolated from the other fifty or so prisoners in the super security wing of the nation's toughest prison – convicted killers, terrorists, and ultra-violent offenders, each and every one, who yet consider the murderers of children beneath them. Someone, anyone, lower on the food chain, over whom they can exercise judgement and power.

Marty MacDonald recovered quickly from his back wounds – but much more slowly from his emotional trauma. He never returned to a high school classroom after Black Friday, but attempted home schooling for a few years, on and off, eventually quitting altogether after Year Ten to work as a kitchen hand.

Ronnie MacDonald quit the New South Wales Police Force before he was fired. The police commissioner then spent the first two days that Ronnie was hospitalised in consultation with the crown prosecutor as to what criminal charges could, and should, be laid against the former inspector.

The commissioner hated renegades – his critics often saying that he was more interested in order than in law. The media, on the other hand, loved them because most of their audience spent most of their lives toeing the line, and always enjoyed stepping out of the pack vicariously by barracking for a hero or a rogue.

The premier, however, motivated by neither love nor hate, was just a pollster. And so, by the time Ronnie was discharged from Newcastle's John Hunter Hospital on day three, the commissioner had dropped all charges, and was there to wish him well in his retirement, in front of the gathered media.

"Ronnie was a man torn between his responsibilities as a father and as a police officer, torn between two battling sons, and willing to face a barrage of bullets – literally – in order to fulfil both his duties." In the commissioner's mouth the words were soppy, insincere, opportunistic – and scripted by the state premier. But, in the MacDonald family, they were simply true. Ronnie retired and devoted himself to rebuilding his shattered family – bitterly ironic, it seemed, after his own son had shattered so many others'.

And, from all around Australia, untold thousands of frustrated parents – disappointed in their children and in themselves, whose idyllic hopes and dreams for their babies had been eroded by time, reality, and disappointment – empathised with Ronnie, the failing father, who arrested his son with an embrace.

Ronnie's media exposure created a huge demand for his services as a freelance security and surveillance consultant. But, to his credit, Ronnie kept a low profile, turning down all "celebrity" invitations or offers – and only rarely granting interviews to promote either drug awareness or police-sponsored teen support programs.

When "Dregs" (the feature film) was being cast, its producers wavered between portraying Ronnie as a buff hero or a middle-aged, overweight father. Six-pack or paunch? They went with the latest and hottest American star, a box-office drawcard who attempted an appalling Scottish accent – I can't remember his name right now, but I do know that he's no longer the hottest.

Ronnie and Alison make the trip from Newcastle to Goulburn every other week to see their eldest son. Supermax visits are limited to sixty minutes and only on weekends, they must speak to Drew only through security perspex, and always with a guard present. They have not physically touched their son since his last court appearance eleven months ago.

The drive takes about four hours each way, depending on traffic. Drew regularly refuses to see them when they get there, but they sit in the visiting room for their allotted hour anyway, in case he changes his mind. He rarely does.

Whether he sees them or not, they always leave him one of his favourite snacks before driving back home – the treats x-rayed before being passed on to their son.

Ronnie and Alison often considered moving closer to Goulburn, but have opted instead to maintain the extended family and peer support network that Newcastle affords to their two younger boys. They strive to always put their children first and, as a result, seem to have little or no lives of their own – Ronnie referring to his parental responsibilities now as "penance".

He shared with me recently that although they are still haunted by all the senseless deaths in the past, at least they are at peace in the present knowing they are now doing their best to support Drew, and always will. During his descent into darkness, they just didn't know what to do – and love must be active.

When I told Ronnie that I was planning to write this book about Hunter High, he said he wanted everyone to know that although he and Alison are ashamed of his crimes, they have never been ashamed to call Drew their son. And he asked me to remind any teenagers reading the book that imperfect parents can love their kids with all their hearts, even while loving them imperfectly.

Wendy Stankowski received a totally different reception from the media than did Drew MacDonald – eventually, that is, but certainly not initially. Initially the media tore into her – orange and purple hair, studs in eyebrow, nose, and lip, torn black mesh tights, Doc Marten boots. Two surviving Dregs – fair game for crucifixion.

But then one journalist, seeking that unique, exclusive angle – not necessarily "the truth", but "the angle" – began reporting on the Wendy Stankowski who lost her father at twelve years of age, her single mum toiling in a bank, tormented at school until finding a foster family among the Dregs, covering the bodies of wounded students outside the auditorium with her own black Dreg coat, and refusing to join the firing squad under penalty of death.

As I write, and as Wendy approaches her twentieth birthday, it looks as though she will escape severe punishment in the adult legal system – perhaps another five to seven years in a rural, minimum security, women's training and rehabilitation facility.

I was never very successful at getting close to Wendy – not before the siege, and not after. Wendy and her mum, Joyce, certainly drew closer after the attack, but the only other person really allowed in was Barbra Burser. Wendy was like a parched and wilted flower – seeking sunlight and water – and she soaked in all that Barbra had to offer.

While the government system threatened to drown Wendy in a tidal wave of lawyers, judges, psychologists, psychiatrists, and social workers, Barb was a desert island – quiet, attentive, demanding nothing, non-judgemental.

They came at Wendy armed with degrees, courtroom wigs, robes, criminal codes, indictments, legal arguments, verdicts, diagnoses, and prescription drugs. *Barb* came empty-handed save for two children's Bibles by Sally Lloyd-Jones – hard-cover comic books, really, with beautiful illustrations and simple words of resting in the assurance of God's love.

Drew MacDonald's .22 calibre bullet missed fireman Jordan Reece's carotid artery by only a hair's breadth. Reece returned to active duty six weeks later, and his baby daughter overcame her medical problems several months after that.

Probationary Constable Debbie Wassler completed her three-month training stint with Sergeant Darren Hayes and then, while awaiting her permanent posting, resigned from the New South Wales Police Force. She told Hayes that although she truly loved the work, and would always cherish the memories of his support and life-saving guidance, she was returning to property management, where even the crankiest of clients stopped short of shooting.

Ten months after the siege, Sergeant Darren Hayes, who had survived three shootings in his twenty-eight-year career as a police officer without a scratch, and 123 bullet holes in his paddy wagon on Black Friday, was struck and killed by a passing motorist while he was writing a speeding ticket on a main road just outside Newcastle.

Long after the spotlight had faded on Black Friday, the silent and anonymous police sniper, Detective Sergeant Derek "Popeye" Pope, continued to train most Saturdays at the Newcastle outdoor rifle range – the indoor police shooting range simply not long enough for his sniper's rifle. In stormy weather, he would lie under his tarp, sometimes for hours, and often leave without firing a single shot. Whenever questioned about his training regimen, he simply repeated his mantra "ready and waiting".

About a year ago, Popeye first noticed the tremors in his cross-hairs, then his shooting mates started kidding him about the twitches. Derek feared the neurologist's initial diagnosis of Parkinson's disease, but soon longed for Parkinson's in light of the ALS confirmation – Amyotrophic Lateral Sclerosis, motor neuron disease. "Average life expectancy two to three years, fifty per cent survive more than three years, twenty per cent five years or more" – the sniper who once considered ballistic tables as merely tools of the trade, now terrified by the cold and cruel medical statistics.

Derek retired immediately, and comfortably, on his navy pension and police superannuation. He and his wife finally went on their three-month, bed-and-breakfast fantasy road trip around Great Britain, and they now spend every possible moment with their five grandchildren.

One of Popeye's police colleagues recently told me that he is declining rapidly, is plagued with great difficulty breathing, fears going to sleep at night, and has modified his mantra to "not ready, and waiting".

Luke, still the janitor and maintenance man at Hunter High, is now almost halfway through his six years of part-time study to become a high school phys ed teacher. Even though Barb has encouraged him greatly – both as a young Christian, and as a mature-age student – Luke still finds himself struggling with the academic workload and the essay-writing skills required for his Bachelor of Arts in Education. And that's a shame, because Luke has a lot to offer a lot of high school students who need a lot of support.

School secretary Pam Blain, suffering a total nervous collapse after the siege, was medically exempted from ever testifying – and it was never needed, because all events were recorded on Dregcam. Pam only ever once returned to Hunter High, to attend the memorial service on the first anniversary of Black Friday – where she even gave a short speech about her great respect for Earl Kennedy, and her love for all the students.

Dr. Suman Khoury was granted eighteen months of sick leave on full pay to recover from the torture suffered at the hands of Drew MacDonald. During that time he travelled to India to visit with family and study at a Hindu ashram. When he returned to Australia, he transferred to a teaching position at a Sydney high school and, the last I heard, he was also studying advanced statistics and mathematical probability at one of the Sydney universities.

Ed Zwick continues to teach the same courses, in the same cardigan, at the same high school. He refuses all interviews.

Kevin Newton is now head of the English department at Earl Kennedy Memorial High, having twice refused the position of principal. It was Kevin who first inspired, then challenged, and eventually *bribed* me into writing this book – vowing to buy the first hundred copies, and promising to never criticise my grammar or punctuation.

It was Kevin who convinced me that I was the only person in the world truly qualified to tell the whole story – that my first book was far too clinical, and DeGroot's, in many ways, a work of fiction.

Sergeant Gary Dixon was one of the first police officers to view all the Dregcam footage, from all five cameras. He then shocked his superiors within the New South Wales Police by meekly accepting his reassignment to admin duties, pending initial inquiries into the siege – all the fight just seemed to have left him.

After three months behind a desk, he quite happily retired from the police force and received the highest state and national commendations for heroism and bravery under fire.

A few months later, he moved interstate to Victoria, just outside Melbourne, to become an instructor at an Outward Bound wilderness survival school for troubled urban teens.

I last saw Gary, about eighteen months ago, at the closing of a federal inquest in Canberra. He called me and Barb aside, in the lobby of Parliament House, and began raving to us about his youth work and the satisfaction it gave him. But he looked tired, and I couldn't decide whether he was striving to convince us or himself.

When he finally ran out of updates, we all grew quiet – and uncomfortable. Barb and I started to excuse ourselves, but Dixon obviously had something else to say and didn't want to let us go.

He pulled the two of us into a tiny, quiet little alcove off the main lobby. "Do you know what this is?" he asked, showing us a bullet dangling on a gold chain around his neck. "It's the bullet I ejected from the chamber, as I sat at the foot of the stage on Black Friday. I've removed the gunpowder and popped the primer – it's harmless now. I wear it as a reminder. It's the *next* bullet, the one I'll never fire."

And then he began to cry – the battle-scarred and war-weary SAS commando instructor, racked by sobs and shudders, speaking when he could.

"I've killed a lot of men in my life, all around the world. A lot of men.

And I've no doubt that each one of them thought he was too young to die. But Aron Wade was the youngest, the one I most regret, and – after seeing the video of him killing his stepfather, and finally hearing his life story at the inquests – I swore he'd be the last. I realise, now, that I had no right to act as Wade's judge and executioner, and I wonder about all those other men, over all those years."

Should have, would have, could have.

And, as Dixon wept, I too was stabbed with guilt, remembering the conversation I had overheard in my office one time, between Wade and Barb. He told her that he couldn't believe in her God because she said He was like a Father. "And if you had known the fathers I had, you might not believe in God either." Yet I never probed or questioned Wade's many bruises and absences, or even reported my suspicions to Community Services.

What more should I have done? How many might I have saved? And I wasn't the only one.

After all the publicity surrounding Black Friday, I was contacted by Wade's principal from primary school who was still haunted by her memories of him in his filthy school uniforms. In Year Three, Wade suddenly began coming to school in relatively clean, but still wrinkled, clothes – and one day he explained to the principal that he had learnt to do his own washing, but his mother didn't own an iron.

Dixon now turned to Barb for consolation, his eyes pleading for some words of comfort.

"Sergeant, the Bible says – Paul's letter to the Romans, chapter thirteen – that policemen and soldiers are armed and authorised by God to enforce the law. You can walk from this inquest in peace, knowing that you were doing your duty to the best of your ability."

I gave him a hug because I didn't know what to say. But Barb continued speaking to him gently, because she knew a hug wasn't enough. "I've been praying for you since the day of the siege, Sergeant Dixon, and I think I have a word from God for you. I've wanted to tell you for weeks now. Would you like to hear it?"

His sobbing abated. He kept his head down and nodded silently.

"I'll leave you two alone," I said as I pulled away.

He held me closer. "Stay."

Gary Dixon and I listened nervously to Barbra Burser, like children called into the principal's office, both disarmed and painfully aware that his social work and my psychology were insufficient – ultimately powerless. I recorded her on my phone.

"You're a great soldier, Sergeant – but a terrible God. You are trying to work off your guilt now by saving the lost youth of society – but you are no more qualified as saviour than you were as judge or executioner.

You are carrying a burden that you were never created to bear. Jesus said, 'Come to Me, all you who are weary and carry heavy burdens and I will give you rest'. (Drop your regret, your guilt, and all your striving.) Instead, 'take My yoke upon you'. (Enlist with Me, become My covenant partner, My blood brother, trust Me, depend on Me, and you'll never walk alone again) – 'learn of Me as you walk and work daily with Me, for I am gentle and humble of heart and you will find rest for your soul – for *My* yoke is easy to bear, and the burden *I* give you is light'. Trust Him always, depend on Him forever.

Your war can end today, Sergeant, if you want it to. Jesus *has* won, and *will* win all your battles for you. All you need to do now is surrender to Him. That chain around your neck, and that burden on your shoulders – you need to bury them both at the foot of the cross of Jesus Christ.

Your enemies are not flesh and blood after all, Sergeant, they're spiritual powers of darkness – so you need to exchange the world's armour for the armour of God.

Protect your mind and your thoughts with the assurance of God's eternal forgiveness, and peace, and blessing – wear that assurance like a kevlar helmet.

Guard your heart with the bulletproof vest of God's love, His free gifts of reconciliation and righteousness.

Hold up the ballistic shield of confidence and trust in the goodness and faithfulness of the one true God – to deflect the fiery darts of Satan, who has always been a liar and an accuser, while the Holy Spirit is the witness of all truth and your advocate for the defence.

Take off your combat boots, Sergeant, once and for all. Receive peace with God as a gift (fought and paid for with the blood of Jesus, God's Son) – and know that wherever you walk from now on, you'll walk with God as an ambassador of peace, armed with new weapons: the sword of the Spirit, the Word of God, the power of prayer, communion, and communication with God.

Fight no longer as Sergeant Dixon the man of war, but, from now on, surrender as Gary Dixon the son of God – the recipient and messenger of peace."

Her words slew the mighty warrior before her, and he sobbed uncontrollably for several minutes. When he finally spoke, he said, "My father used to read to us at bedtime out of a children's Bible, and our favourite story was always that one about the armour of God – Ephesians, chapter six. After he was killed, my little brothers and sisters always asked *me* to read it to them – but I always refused, and said God's armour didn't save Dad. I never opened the Bible again."

Barb took a long time, before answering quietly. "Sounds like you've been blaming and condemning God for years, and now you think He's blaming and condemning you. But there is no more guilt or condemnation in Christ Jesus. He took the blame and punishment for all men's sins for all times – past, present, and future, once and for all. His divine blood is eternal blood, so precious and powerful that it's sufficient to pardon all men for all time – but efficient only for those who accept it with thanks.

Gary, you've been a prisoner of war for all these years. Today you've been liberated, and you're finally going home. Psalm 23 begins 'the Lord is my shepherd', it ends – literal translation – 'surely God's goodness, mercy, and unfailing love shall hunt me down for the rest of my life, and I will dwell in the house of the Lord forever'. Come home, today, to your Father's open arms, Gary. He's been waiting, patiently, for years."

As soon as the auditorium had been vacated on Black Friday, Carol Spargo demanded time off with full pay and an immediate transfer. She filed her lawsuit three days later – but that was only because law offices were closed on the weekend. She gave no news interviews until after she had been paid for exclusives with a glossy magazine, and a top-rated current affairs television show.

Her proposed book was delayed because of disputes with five different ghostwriters from three different publishers – she threatened to sue them all. She has yet to find another publisher, though she has tried through a half-dozen literary agents.

I have heard that, after more than two years, her lawsuit against the Department of Education was settled with a confidential payout and a gag order attached. No one knows the amount.

If Ricky Russell's becoming a Christian and nestling under Barb

Burser's wing was, for him, a rebirth – then the siege at Hunter High was his coming of age.

Word spread quickly about his death-defying declaration of faith in my office, and half the school witnessed his pastoral care as he offered his prayers in the auditorium. And then, in the weeks and months following, he was *there* – just there, always there, faithfully there. Whether being interviewed on television, or just listening by the lockers, he was unchanging – always simple, always humble. Not proud, usually without advice, always with a smile, a pat on the back, and a quick prayer.

He knew that he was just Ricky, confident that he was special, and that God was trustworthy. Peace, humility, and trust in a trustworthy God.

Ricky's parents loved him and, though often tired, never once thought of him as a disappointment or a burden. But they feared for him in the hardness of the outside world, at some time in the future, when they would not be around to protect him.

Ricky was just finishing Year Ten when he was caught up in the siege. Year Ten in name only. He was one of nine "special needs" students in Hunter High who *appeared* to advance from year to year but who were, actually, each following their own personally adapted and scaled-down curriculum. There was nothing more that high school could teach him – or, rather, there was nothing more that Ricky could learn in a classroom.

Ricky, his parents, and the school, had all agreed that he might be best "graduating" after Year Ten, and then getting a job in a sheltered workshop for the physically and mentally handicapped, operated within a local nursery and gardening centre.

But, as soon as Ricky was reunited with his parents after the storming of the auditorium, he began raving about all that he could do in the next two years to support the school and the students in their recovery from the siege.

In less than an hour – forty-four violent yet merciful minutes, to be exact – Ricky's parents had received a two-year reprieve from the perils of the outside world, and Ricky had graduated into the role of a valued and respected member of the student body.

Four months after Black Friday, Ricky Russell was elected vice-president of the student council and he now works at the nursery, specialising in customer service, and saving his money for a trip to Israel. His parents still don't know what to make of it all.

Kieran's nose recovered so well from its fracture that no plastic surgery was needed, and he preferred to keep the small bump as a lifelong reminder of the day. Along with Barb and Ricky, Kieran embraced the last eight weeks of the term, and all the next year, as an opportunity to support the healing and recovery of the school. No plans, no agenda, just being there.

About six months after the siege, Kieran and Barb split up. Barbra initiated it. Kieran appreciated her wisdom as always, respected her decision, and never wavered in his support – but only God knows the depth of his heartache.

I've always found teenage girls to be about two years more mature than boys – but Barb was even more mature than I was, or might ever be.

They remained friends and partners in Scripture Union, but lots of things had changed for Barb. She seemed restless, and no one was surprised when she decided to leave high school at the end of Year Eleven – fourteen months after Black Friday.

Kieran stayed on to complete Year Twelve at Earl Kennedy Memorial High, and then moved to Brisbane to pursue theological studies.

By the middle of Year Eleven, just about eight months after the siege, Barb was feeling smothered by the materialism and consumerism all around her. And although she was pretty toughened by some of the things she'd seen in her life, she confided in me that she was truly stunned by the forgetfulness, denial, and renunciation (by the vast majority of student hostages) of the demonic and the divine that they had experienced throughout Hunter High during those forty-four minutes on Black Friday.

Meanwhile, across Australia, Scripture Union (and Christian religious education generally) now faced growing criticism and opposition for being "exclusive" and "offensive". Though the need for high school pastoral care had been repeatedly acknowledged in parliament over the years, and chaplaincy allocated millions of dollars in annual support by previous federal governments from both parties, Australian society was now increasingly and ironically being shackled and held hostage by its own dedication to liberty and democracy. So, when fast-growing, but very media-savvy, minorities raised their voices against Christian absolutes, the silent majority cowered.

And so Scripture Union – founded and strongly endorsed in 1867, respected in the recent past, and now often only tolerated – was being restricted in its outreach within more and more high schools, with nothing left to fill the spiritual void in students' lives except a groundless and godless optimism and encouragement.

That's not to say that Barb did not see growth in the number and maturity of Scripture Union students at Hunter High, in the months following the siege – indeed, quite significant growth. The Scripture Union group quadrupled in size after Black Friday, and many of her earlier charges – including the seven who had all abandoned her to face death in my office – had subsequently grown in faith, responsibilty, service, and leadership. Her lambs had themselves become shepherds. The problem now was not that they grew too little – but she too much. Barb chafed at the bit for new challenges.

So, after completing Year Eleven, Barb returned to Mozambique with her parents. Her motive was threefold: to resume the medical missionary work there, to escape the media-addicted high school students and celebrity spotlight still following her as the heroine of Hunter High, and to allow herself time to complete the book she had begun writing – *"Still in the Eye of the Storm"*. It is a quote from *her* book that I have used on the first page of mine.

As for me, for more than a year I juggled my duties as school counsellor with the demands placed on me by the state and federal inquests. I dropped the two other Newcastle schools under my care, and focused solely on Hunter High.

But, then, studying for my master's degree, my ongoing inquest-related duties, and commitments to speak at seminars and in the media, all kept me working overtime and I just couldn't continue as school counsellor. And so, coincidentally, when Barb left Hunter High – so did I.

After graduating with my master's, I was recruited as a university lecturer to undergraduate psychology students, which confirmed not only my shortcomings as a teacher, but also my growing distaste for the whole academic food chain – you need a master's to teach bachelor degree students, you need a doctorate to teach master's.

Those forty-four minutes at Hunter High had undermined my whole life – and it was never all that stable to begin with. High school counsellors really aren't supposed to criticise higher education, or challenge the self-centred students of the Western world. Teaching the basic theories of psychology at university made me feel dirty, an accomplice to the whole con game of selling diplomas to truly unqualified psychologists – like me.

So I set up a private practice and learnt far more from my clients than they ever learnt from me – most people don't really want to learn how to think, don't really want to pay the price to be wise. It's all too slow, too painful, and too costly.

And then it dawned on me – my clients were all bred to be consumers! Bred, brought up, indoctrinated, and educated, to consume as advertised. Customers willing to pay for packaged solutions. But if the solutions they seek are all spiritual, and can only be found by their own painful seeking – then I, their psychologist, am just stealing their money.

That's how I was feeling about four months ago. Then, about ten weeks ago, my father died. In the middle of the night, of a heart attack. And I *actually* wondered if I could have saved him if I'd been in the next room on guard duty with my alarm clock. Still Daddy's Girl, The Nurse, after all these years.

Despite all the relatives and long-time family friends gathered at the funeral, I felt lonelier than ever before in my life. Everyone generously offered comfort, consolation, and their best attempts at spiritual wisdom, but all I wanted to do was hug my Dad and cry on the shoulder of Barbra Burser – and they were both beyond my reach.

After the funeral I went home, feeling empty, and stared at the teak wood and gold leaf lettering of my custom-made desktop nameplate for the longest time. Daddy was so proud of me – the internationally-acclaimed psychologist.

Fake. Unqualified charlatan.

After the siege, I had sheltered under the wings of the *false prophets* – education and the media. I ate from their trough of propaganda – I was the celebrity counsellor from the Hunter High School siege, rewarded with a master's degree for its analysis.

I got too busy and too self-important, and distanced myself from the only *true* prophet that I had ever known – Barbra Burser – who told me that the cause and the solution of all problems is always, first and foremost, spiritual.

She once explained to me the difference between an educator and a teacher. An educator takes simple things and makes them complicated, whereas a teacher takes complicated things and makes them simple. She had been the greatest teacher in my life – the sister I never had, the mentor I had always sought.

So I emailed Barb in the rugged western highlands of Mozambique, told her that my father had died, and asked if she thought I should write this book or maybe go see her for a while. She replied, "You must do both – and in that order. My book is only now about to be published, finish yours and then we can swap."

So I excused myself from all commitments, sublet my apartment, put everything in storage, and came here to my rental cabin by the beach. No television, no music, no internet, no phone. None of the constant, white, electronic noise that keeps each of us distracted every moment of every day. And I surrounded myself instead with the sounds of creation – wind, surf, raindrops, seabirds …. and silence.

I couldn't write a word for the first four days – not one word – and then, when I finally started, it took closer to six weeks than four.

And now it's finished – after writing for forty days (and nights), stopping only to replay the audio and video evidence on my laptop, read the court transcripts, walk by the surf, think, eat, sleep, and cry. Many days not stopping at all, just reliving and re-evaluating the events and writing for eighteen hours at a time.

Tomorrow a courier is picking up the USB flashdrive of this manuscript for delivery to my publisher, and I fly out to Mozambique the day after that.

Barb's dad is building a new school and hospital there. Maybe I can return to the classroom, simplify my life – teach basic literacy and numeracy perhaps.

Or maybe just listen and learn.

I don't know where Barb's advice might guide me from there. All I really know is *who* she was and *how* she was during those forty-four minutes. While the rest of us hoped for nothing more than deliverance, escape, and release from our fear – a happy ending – Barb was trying to make the most of it, looking to see the hand of God in it all, wanting to appreciate the eternal significance.

My brothers are worried that I've become involved in some kind of co-dependent relationship with her. All I know is that my heart feels like parched earth after a long drought, and whenever Barb spoke, her words always felt like raindrops.

Her faith gave me peace and hope – or, at least, the hope of peace and sometimes even a bubble of joy in the pit of my stomach.

After Daddy's funeral service, I stood alone outside the crematorium for the longest time, watching the smoke from his mortal remains floating up into the sky. And then I realised that he had left me no inheritance of faith whatsoever – because he had none to leave. I always loved my father and I always will, but though he may have solved *his* problems by talking them over with me, he never solved *mine*. I feel like a spiritual orphan, and I can't wait to finally meet Barb's father, and talk with him face to face.

In the course of remembering, rethinking, and recounting Black Friday, I've now become convinced that there is sense and order in the universe after all, and a plan for my life – even if I don't yet know what it is. I feel like I'm coming home to a place I've never been. Sounds like I'm just stealing a lyric from John Denver, but I'm not. And I'm not referring to a geographical location either, but a place in my heart – or God's .... hopefully both.

I remember, the last time Barb and I met together for coffee, how I hounded her for an outline of her book-in-progress. She shared *eight significant spiritual truths* that she saw illustrated in the bullet-riddled, bloody, glass-strewn corridors of Hunter High while I saw only chaos.

Most of what she said went straight over my head at the time and, when she emailed the eight truths to me later, they were subsequently lost somewhere in the nether regions of my computer and the great Niagara of the Forgotten.

Then, this morning of all mornings, after writing what I thought would be the last paragraph of this book (about coming home to a place I've never been), I *just happened* to find Barb's long-lost email in a long-forgotten folder on my laptop – a "most remarkable incidence of synchronicity".

I wept when I read it, for the longest time – those tears the culmination, perhaps, of my long-sought "katharsis" (from the Greek for "purification, cleansing, clarification") – and it just seems fitting that I include the eight points here:

<u>One</u>: we're all hunters. Not just the Dregs and not just on that day, but all of us, and all the time. Hungering, thirsting, and hunting for peace. Lost, wandering, and wondering on a modern media superhighway. Information overload, like trying to drink from a fire hose. Constant, live coverage of depressing events from around the globe – but never any wisdom, and only fleeting hope.

Relentless marketing, rampant consumerism, using other people, justifying ourselves and overcoming our insecurities by labelling, excluding, and condemning others. Teachers hunting their second youth, power, or success. Teenagers desperately hunting an identity so they can better face a scary world. And evil – the Evil One – stalking whom he may devour or, better still, whom he may inspire to devour others. Anyone who dismisses evil has never walked a battlefield, or seen innocent children slaughtered.

And above us all, with our self-seeking hearts, there reigns the Lord of Love, the one true Father God, the Hunter High who stalks the hallways of our empty, aching hearts that He might fill them with Himself. Unseen and unknown, He oversees our lives and sends His Son, a lone commando, to be devoured by the lost and ravenous pack below so that Jesus, and Jesus alone, might ultimately satisfy us and lead us home. We often only meet Him in the dark – seeking and seeing Him best when times and deeds are darkest.

Two: the strategy of containment never works. Evil cannot be contained. You cannot manage, bargain, or negotiate with evil. Evil is not a philosophical concept, but an aggressive enemy – and compromise is not an option. The only way to destroy Darkness is to step into the Light and live there – to rest there, forever.

Three: commando tactics are called for. Immediate action, rapid deployment. There is an urgency. Lives are at stake – mine and others' – and none of us knows how much time we have left. *Today* is the day of salvation. All faith is *now* faith in the ever-present God of the present, active tense.

Four: in an age of shirking and shrinking responsibilities, in these days of excusing ourselves and blaming others, in an increasingly litigious society seeking constantly to sue for compensation – Jesus is our only legitimate, and ultimate, scapegoat. But we must take responsibility for inviting Him to take the blame.

Five: we live our lives in chapters. Initially as infants, then children, students, adolescents, newlyweds, parents, retirees and, finally, the elderly. And no *one* human being travels with us through *all* the changing seasons and chapters – our only constant companion throughout them all is God. We ourselves can't even remember, and usually fail to appreciate, our formative years and formative fears as infants and children – but God knows, only God knows – and He never forgets.

Black Friday was only one brief chapter in the lives of all those involved, a point of convergence for only a short time. The players will never again – *can* never again – all be brought together, each day is only lived once. And, then, only God travels on with each of us as our paths diverge.

It is a simple and terrible thing to judge or condemn another without appreciating his whole story – or the context of her life. And I myself can only ever fully appreciate my own story – my own life only ever truly finding its meaning – within the context of God Himself. The context of history is His-story. My story within His.

Six: just like the phalanx of lobby hostages bound to each other by the ankles, or the student-gladiators in the gymnasium desperately longing for a champion to rise up from within their midst – any effort expended seeking deliverance within ourselves, or through our fellow captives, is futile. All such hope is doomed.

We are all prisoners of our own self-centredness, sentenced to solitary confinement, and the key to our escape is found only in the selfless love of God. We are only ever free, at rest, at peace, and at home, in God's love – the same love that radiates eternally between Father, Son, and Holy Spirit.

Seven: life's greatest battles are fought in the mind and the heart. Right believing leads to right thinking and right living.

How will I view a crisis – as opportunity or disaster? With hope or despair? What have I learnt from my journey thus far? What does it all mean? Where am I heading?

Is pain only to be avoided, or will I grow wise from it – knowing that, behind the scenes, there watches over us a loving Saviour who embraced suffering and laid down His own life for my sake, Who knows my name and my every thought, Who has loved me from eternity past, and always will?

Eight: "What's past is prologue" (from *The Tempest* by William Shakespeare). And the end of my story is yet to be written.

Those are Barb's words, not mine (I'm not sure I even understand them all), and you can do with them what you will. But *my* decision has been made and I'm overdue to act upon it. Because I've finally, truly, deeply come to believe – and to know that I know in my own heart – that even in our darkest hour, when feeling like a helpless captive audience forced to watch pain and suffering played out before us on the stage of our lives: *we are not forgotten*, we are under God's constant surveillance. *We are not alone*, God's special agents are planted here among us. *And we are not without hope*, there is a plan of salvation and deliverance being outworked. Even now. Even for me ....